The Warrior

Alterealm Series

Book 6

By J. Risk

Family tree at the end of The Chronos

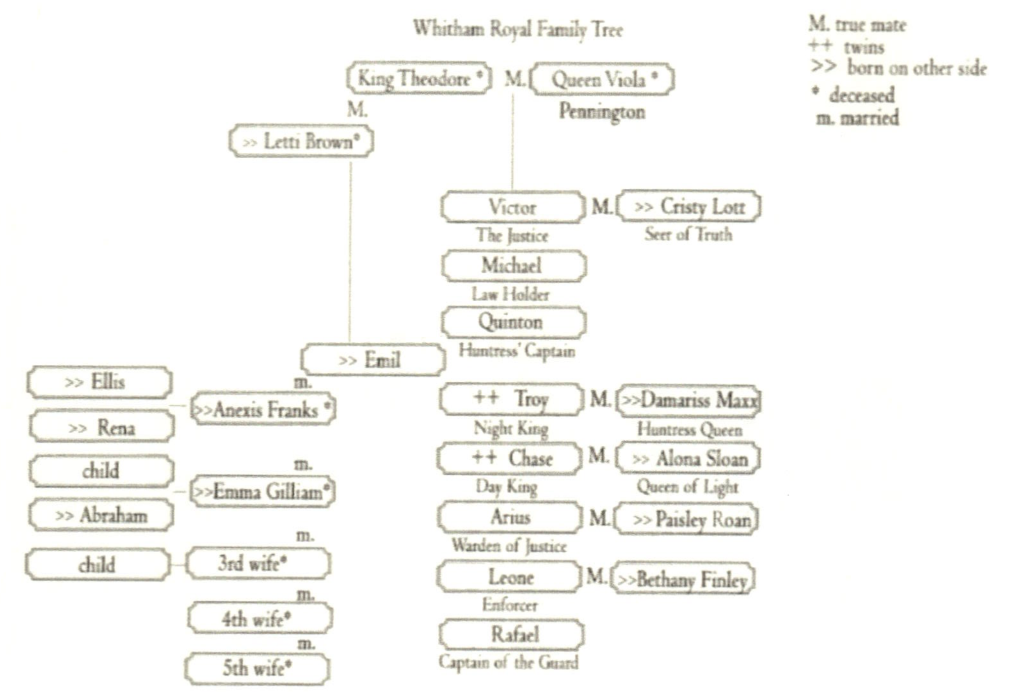

Published by FRP
Copyright © 2019 Roxane Kerr
Edited by Gaele L. Hince
Cover art by: Off the Wall Creations

Updated 2020

Excerpts from *The Telepath* by J. Risk and *Scent* by Jacqueline Paige copyright ©2018, 2019 by Roxane Kerr

ISBN (paperback): 978-1-7774387-7-7
ISBN (digital): 978-1-7774387-6-0

Prologue

I stepped out the back door of the gym, rolled my shoulders, and took a moment to appreciate the quiet of the neighborhood. I liked this time of day. It was silent, calm, no noise from traffic or the bustle of people. Times like that in this city were rare.

Stretching from side to side a few times, I zipped up my sweatshirt, then pulled up the hood and started a slow, steady jog.

This is how I started every day. Just as the sun was appearing in the sky, I ran through the alley's and reminded myself that although I came from the streets, I'd fought hard enough to stay off them. Each day seeing this was my reality check.

I rounded the corner at the old restaurant and slowed my pace to watch the old woman, I think she called herself Betsy, roll up her blankets. I waited until she spotted me before I spoke. "The kitchen will have breakfast started soon, if you go now and ask for Albert, he'll give you some hot coffee."

The only acknowledgement I got was a slight nod, before she looked back to the pavement. Betsy never made eye contact for long. I would have liked to know her story, but that was for her to share, not for me to ask.

I picked up the pace again, making short jabs with my hands as I went. I felt good today. No aches, or gripes from my muscles. It had been a week since my last fight, and this may have been the longest in my life that I wasn't injured on some level.

Someone stepped out of the shadowed doorway in front of me. He lifted a hand as hello, and then became invisible in the low light before I went by him. Living in the shadows was a hard life, not knowing who to trust and who not to. I had a roof over my head now, but those feelings that tell you to run would never go away, I thought, not that I'd want them to.

The only sound I could hear were my shoes hitting the pavement in a steady rhythm. It was just loud enough to warn any hiding their existence that I was present, and to scare off any rodents or lost pets living in the area.

A clatter to my left had me turning fast, ready, just in case. Relief washed over me when I saw it was only the old guy with the cane. He was struggling to get his wagon out from under the fire escape ladder. He'd probably slept there last night. I stopped and went over to duck under the metal ladder and pulled his wagon to clear the bar that was hanging down. He grinned, his toothless smile and patted the red hat on his head. I'd given him it a few months ago when we had cooler weather. "Kitchen will be open soon. Make sure you fill your water bottles with clean water." He nodded and turned to pull his creaking wagon down the alleyway.

Rolling my shoulders, I started with a slower pace, in no hurry to finish my run today. I hadn't been to the south park lately, I should probably drop by later today and see if anyone was around. I'd been so caught up helping the guys in the gym, I hadn't taken the time, and the guilt rode me hard for that.

The stench of the dumpster I went past had me wrinkling up my nose until I was clear of it. That was one thing I would never miss, the odors that went with living on the streets.

Turning right into the next alley, I grinned to see the light from the rising sun shine down. If there was any way to see this deserted space as beautiful, this brief moment each day was it. It made you forget that rats and homeless lived here in this dirty space that others used to toss unwanted things in. For a brief moment each day, it glowed with the chance to be something better, something more than it appeared to be.

Walking toward me quickly was a woman that lived in this alley, I didn't know her name, but everyone knew her as the lady that sings. She was always singing. I frowned, she wasn't singing today. Her expression was one of fear. I slowed as she reached me.

"No, no. Go back." She said quickly and ran past me.

I jogged on the spot and watched her move away. That was unusual. I looked around, there was no one that I could see. She turned down the dark alley I'd come from and was gone. Odd. I'd have to swing by the kitchen later, after I opened the gym, and see if the guys there could shed some light on what was bothering her.

I grimaced when a sharp pain traveled down my left calf. That would teach me for skipping my stretching this morning. Muscle strains were a tricky thing. Feeling a bit breathless, I turned to keep moving. Getting tired and dizzy before I was half way through my route had me mentally scolding myself. One chocolate bar the night before messed up a carefully maintained metabolism.

I wasn't one to quit. I'd keep going through the light-headedness until I burned that artificial garbage from my system. I glanced up, blinking to try and focus, gone was the bright sunlight as blackness closed in.

Chapter One

The blood trailed down his face, dripping from his nose as he came at me again. As he widened his stance, I knew there was no chance I'd be sweeping his legs out from under him a second time. My movement was restricted by these bagging clothes they made me wear, otherwise my roundhouse kick would knock him flying. I'd learned the hard way yesterday, the clothes constrained my movement and I couldn't follow through. The bruises on my arms were proof of that.

"Told you it wasn't going to be easy." Blondie said to him from the doorway. His face was sporting a black eye from the day before. He rattled the chain in his hand. "Just grab her and I'll get these on her legs."

The other guard wiped the blood across his face and gave an abrupt nod, then stupidly started to come toward me again.

When they'd dragged me in the day before and tossed the jumpsuit at me, I thought I'd been wrongfully busted for something. After a few moments of trying to justify their error, I'd realized this was not a jail, they were not cops, and I was in a different kind of trouble. The kind of trouble that wasn't on any books, had no rules, and was a matter of life and death.

People usually react three ways in situations like this. Fear, that causes them to comply. Shutting down and doing nothing. Or freaking out, I wasn't big on screaming and crying. Fight or flight. In my case I had to do the fight the part first to get to where I could run. Fighting. That lead to a much larger problem with the size of these guys. I'd fought big men before, but these two were taking that to the extreme. I couldn't execute a good elbow-knee combo if I couldn't reach anything vital to hit.

I could taste the blood in my mouth and it made me want to break his nose again. He knew it too and was shielding his face better now. If I could just get past him and drop blondie at the door, I might be able to find a way out of here.

"There's nowhere to go." He growled, hunkering down further, his arms outstretched.

It was a perfect position for me to inflict damage. I sneered at him. "What are you waiting for? Come and get me." He charged at me, I ducked his arm and jumped up to land an elbow on his temple. He grunted and swung, catching me in the side of the face. The pain radiated up through my eye. I hated face shots, they hurt more than a blow to the kidneys.

"What is going on?"

The guard stumbled back and turned toward the door. Blondie was now standing erect and looking straight ahead.

I wiped the blood off my mouth and stared at the tall woman in the doorway. She had long red hair and her aura and expression both spelled out the same thing: b.i.t.c.h.

"You're supposed to be transporting her over, not fighting with her." She looked from one guard to the other. "No one is going to want a pulverized woman. It's going to take a week for those to heal."

I backed up, trying to decide if I could make it through the three of them. The words were echoing through my mind. My heart started thrumming out of control. I'd been abducted by human traffickers.

"Sorry, ma'am. We can't get near her long enough to transport her." Blondie said, still looking straight ahead.

She turned and looked at the man dripping blood all over the floor. "Go get that dealt with."

Holding his nose, he moved by her quickly.

Turning, she looked at the chains in the other man's hands and then to his face. I wasn't sure, but it looked like she smirked when she saw my handywork.

I didn't feel bad about his black eye. He'd walked up to me the day before and grabbed my arm. No one grabbed me. No one touched me if I didn't want them to.

With cold eyes, she looked at me. "Look, Autumn—"

I scowled, she knew my name.

"While I admire your fighting spirit, I simply can't have you beating up the guards and giving the others any ideas." She gave me a tight smile that looked more like she was in pain.

I glared at her, if she was waiting for me to throw my hands up, apologize and comply, she was in for a big surprise.

With a slow nod, she sighed and looked at the guard. "Sedate her, get those on her," she looked back to me, "you may want a pair for her hands as well. Then transport her." She snickered. "After the walk, she'll be too tired to fight." She walked away without another word.

The guard slammed the door. I heard the lock click into place.

Exhaling, I slumped my shoulders forward. My face was throbbing. I'd baby my injuries later. I had to come up with a plan. If they thought they were sticking some needle in me to knock me out, they were in for a world of hurt.

The door opened.

I spun toward it, ready.

Blondie smirked and raised a gun and pulled the trigger, then closed the door again.

The sting of it registered in my leg. I looked down to see a dart sticking out of it. Grabbing it, I pulled it out and tossed it across the room. My head felt weird. I blew out a breath and hopped up and down trying to shake it off. The room tilted, and I stumbled and hit the wall. Sliding down, I glared at the door.

The door started to blur, I shook my head and it felt like I was moving in slow motion. My body was slipping sideways—I think, everything was too fuzzy to be sure. I couldn't command my arm to stop the fall. I blinked, trying to focus, it was like someone was playing with the light switch and dimming the light in the room. I tried to fight the darkness. My last thought was that I was going to have to teach blondie a lesson.

Chapter Two

"She's coming around."

I rolled, my stomach clenching violently. I breathed through it, wondering what they'd given me to make me feel this ill. Beaten and bruised was bad, but apparently making me throw up was allowed. The guards were standing a few feet away looking around. It was starting to get dark. I'd either lost track of how long I'd been in that room, or I'd been knocked out a long time.

"Remind me again why we have to walk up." Blondie asked the one with his nose bandaged up.

"Something about wards and only royals can port in.." His voice was so nasal, I almost laughed.

My face was throbbing, reminding me of the blows I'd taken in the last few days. Neither man bothered to look at me, so I took that opportunity to look around. I didn't see a car, so that left out that option of escape. All I could see were trees and grass. Run long enough in any direction and eventually you'd find a road. It could be worse, I could still be in a room with no windows.

When I went to move my arm to push me up, the clank of a chain reminded me why they'd been trying to get hold of me in that room. I was shackled. So much for running. Getting away from them was going to be a challenge. I flexed my foot to confirm there was a cuff around my ankle too. This was going to be a workout without being able to kick. I owed blondie for the dart, and I always paid people what they were due.

Pushing myself up, I sat there and waited for the light headedness to subside. "Can I get a drink? What the hell did you shoot me with?"

Blondie turned and smirked at me. "Just enough to get those on without you getting another shot in." He motioned to the cuffs on my arms.

I held up my hands. "Take them off and I'll let you get the first shot in."

He snorted, "I have nothing against sparring with women, but you take it to the extreme."

I glared at him. "Gee, I don't know why."

"Give her a drink so we can get going." He turned and looked around again.

The one with the busted nose came over and set a bottle of water a few feet away from me, then backed up.

It was hard not to smirk, but I knew I needed to play it cool and try not to offend their delicate feelings until I figured out where we were. Getting to my knees, I picked up the bottle and checked the seal before opening it. Thirsty or not I wasn't going to drink something they'd tampered with. Taking a few sips, I looked around. I still couldn't see anything different. "So, is this like recess? Just out for some air?" That's when I noticed they were wearing swords on their hips. What. The. Hell. I couldn't even process why they'd need those. The weapons didn't scare me, I'd been around enough of them that the fear of them wasn't for that reason. The why they had them concerned me though.

Blondie grinned, "Lots of exercise."

I touched my lip, feeling how swollen it was. "I'm good there, the last few days with you guys have taken care of that."

"We need to get started." Nasal mumbled.

I looked the direction he pointed, then down to my feet. "Don't suppose you stopped to consider how hard it's going to be to walk in long grass with chains dragging."

They both looked at my feet.

I shrugged, "it's going to be slow going."

"Twenty minutes until we reach the road." Blondie said. "You'll just have to deal with it." He motioned for me to start moving.

I had to take short steps, so the chain didn't trip me up. Every few feet I had to stop and pull the grass out of the chain. "So where are we going?" I asked tossing the handful of grass to the side.

"Up there."

I turned to see where he was pointing. In the low light all I could make out was a mountain and what may have been a road winding up it. "Seriously? On foot?"

He smirked. "Unless you can fly."

I scowled at him and looked back at the mountain. I had to get away from them before we reached that. Running down a mountain, chained, wasn't something I wanted to do. Blowing out a breath, I started walking again.

"Stop." He touched my shoulder.

I froze, debating on using my elbow on his face, but doubted he was going to squat down so I could reach it. They were both looking away from me, swords drawn. I listened, and squinted, trying to see what had them so spooked.

Crouching down, blondie pointed and the other one nodded and started to move in that direction quietly.

I looked again and could make out two people on horses. Where the hell were we? I didn't know who they were, but if these guys didn't want to be seen by them, that meant I wanted to be. Reaching down slowly, I grabbed the chain between my feet, so I could turn without getting hung up. This might be my only chance. Adjusting my footing, I paused when blondie glanced at me over his shoulder.

"Stand there quietly and I'll take those off," he motioned to my feet, "after we deal with these two. They'll drop you in the cells and forget about you." He whispered.

That made me pause. So far, I'd been abducted, locked in a room, drugged and shackled and the two on the horses were worse? Something my mentor said popped into my head, the enemy of my enemy is my friend. I hope he was right.

I nodded, so blondie would look away from me again.

He gave me a brief look before turning to watch the other guard moving slowly through the grass.

Shuffling closer to him, like I was scared by his words, I waited for him to turn his attention back the two men. When he did, I dropped the chain and straightened up, raising my hands together. I'd never done a double elbow move before, but I couldn't get enough momentum with my arms attached. He turned the second I was dropping them. "Hey! Over here." I screamed at the same moment my elbows connected with his face.

"Son of…" He growled and lunged for me.

I backed up and tripped when the chains got hung up. Keeping an eye on the sword in his hand, I waited until he bent over to grab me and kicked up with both my feet into his face. I heard the sword hit the ground beside me as he dropped to his knees. Scrambling to my feet I got up and picked up the weapon. It took both of my hands to lift it. I pointed it at him. He was too busy holding his face to move.

I glanced in the direction the other one had gone and heard the clang of metal on metal before I saw him. He was fighting one of the men from the horses, and the other one was running toward me. I looked back to blondie, he was still hunched over holding his face.

The man slowed when he was a few feet away, he also had a sword half the size of my body. He held out his other hand, showing it was empty, the sword pointed at the man on the ground and not me.

"It's okay." He said softly. "I'm here for him." He sheathed the sword on his back without hesitation and held his other hand out.

My arms were starting to shake with the weight of the sword.

"Leone." The other man barked. "He's over here." The man in front of me said without taking his eyes off me.

The second man came running toward us, then slowed a few feet away. I glanced from the first one to him to see him put his weapon away. He held his hands out from his body. "You're safe now." He said softly.

I jerked the sword toward blondie. "He said you'd toss me in the cells."

Blondie moaned and then coughed.

The second man shook his head slowly, a sneer on his face. "That's his fate, not yours." He moved another step in my direction.

I had to turn my whole upper body to aim the sword toward him. I wasn't going to be able to hold it up much longer.

"Leone, grab him." He said calmly, still moving in my direction.

Leone nodded and stepped away from me and grabbed blondie by the back of his jacket. "Oh shit, Michael, she messed up his face good."

Michael nodded, his eyes not leaving me. "Other one was recently patched up too." He jerked his head in the direction they'd come from. "Get him out of here. Call Arius and tell him the doc is needed at the intake cells."

Leone dragged blondie away.

I tried to widen my stance to support the weight of the sword, but the chain ran out. "I just want to go home." I told him.

He nodded. "We'll get you there."

I looked at him, trying to see in the low light. "Are you a cop?"

"Yeah. You're safe now." His tone was calm, soothing.

I jerked my chin toward the swords sticking up on his back. "Since when do cops carry hardware like that?"

He smirked, "fight fire with fire." He looked at the sword I held. "I can stand here all night until you decide to trust me, but I can see how fatigued your arms are getting and how your body is shaking from the shock and cool air." He held out his hand slowly, palm up. "Let me help you. We'll get those chains off you and patch you up."

I went to bite my lip and weigh his words, then winced when my teeth connected with the swollen flesh. "Don't touch me." I warned him.

Michael nodded slowly. "I won't." He stepped closer, his hand nearer to the weapon. "Let me take that."

I looked at my hands and the way my arms were shaking and let the weight of the sword drop my hands toward the ground.

He grabbed the handle and tugged it from my grasp.

Leone came back toward us slowly. "Arius says he's looking forward to meeting the woman that laid a beat-down on those two." He stopped and looked from Michael to me. "You're safe." He pointed to Michael. "My brother and I will take you back and get those chains off you."

I straightened up, but wasn't about to relax and let my guard down. I tasted blood and realized my lip was busted open, probably from my fall. Raising my chained hands together I wiped at it.

"Go get the horses." Michael told him. "Porting her right now isn't going to help her trust us." He held out the sword to him.

Grabbing it, Leone nodded and spun on his heel.

"Porting?" I frowned, then glanced around. "Where the hell are we?"

He stood, his eyes moving slowly over my face. "That's hard to explain."

I looked around again and it hit me, there were no lights from the city and the air was the freshest I'd ever smelled. "But I get to go home?"

He nodded. "If you want to." He pulled out his phone. "Are you injured anywhere else?" He motioned to my face.

I shook my head. "Few bruises. They got a couple bumbling shots in yesterday."

His brows creased, then he looked to his phone. Tapping it, he raised it to his ear. "Yeah. Not yet. We're going to need keys or someone that can get shackles off." His eyes never left my face. "No. Just one." His mouth quirked like he wanted to smile. "Wasn't from us." He shook his head. "We'll take the horses back to the guard house, I'm not sure she'll cope well with transporting. Bring Paisley or Bethany, I think we're going to need the female touch." He nodded, "see you shortly." Tucking his phone in, he motioned to my feet. "You're going to have to ride with us, unless you can sit side-saddle."

"Side what?" I gave him a wide-eyed look. "On a horse?"

He nodded. "Can you ride?"

I turned to see Leone leading two horses back. I didn't see blondie and his friend. There must have been more men out here then and I had seen. "I've never even seen a horse up close."

Michael held up his hand and Leone came over and put a strap in his hand.

I gawked at the beast on the other end of the thin strap. It was massive and beautiful at the same time.

"He won't hurt you." Michael said in that soft tone again. Motioning with his head for me to come closer, he reached up and grabbed the harness on the horse's head. "This is Hachi." He rubbed his hand along the animal's large jaw. "Hachiman."

I bent down and picked up the chain, so I could move. "Like the Japanese god of war."

Michael gave me a surprised look. "Yes, well, god of warriors."

I nodded, "my mentor used to tell me stories." I stepped closer, not sure if I wanted to be close to the man or the beast. Dropping the chain, I raised my hands up toward the animal's nose. It sniffed at me, then its large lips nuzzled my hands.

"He likes you—what is your name?" Michael made no move toward me.

I smiled up at the horse. I was touching a horse. "Autumn." I said quietly not wanting to spook the animal that could crush me without effort.

"Autumn, you're going to have to ride in front of Leone or I. With those chains on you'll bounce off the back."

I looked from the horse to him. I didn't have a lot of options. I wouldn't get far with the chains on, and with the length of legs on the horse, I couldn't outrun it. I turned and looked at Leone, he watched us, patience his only expression. Shifty people, I'd learned a long time ago, always looked impatient. I looked back up at Michael and nodded. "Okay. Just don't drop me." I looked back up at Hachi and rubbed my hand on his nose. "I don't want to get stepped on."

Michael smirked, "I've never dropped someone before."

Leone snorted. "Not true, you dropped me on my face that time."

Michael looked over at him. "You deserved it."

Leone shrugged. "Maybe."

Moving cautiously, Michael backed the horse away from me, then swung up into the saddle.

I stepped back. He looked even bigger sitting up there.

"Give her a hand up." Michael told him.

With a nod, Leone dropped the strap for his own horse and came toward me. "I'll just pick you up and set you up there." He stopped and looked at me.

I looked nervously up to where he'd be setting me. "You guys ever hear of cars? Safe metal things you ride in not on?"

He grinned. "Little hard to drive them out here."

I looked around at the grass and sighed. "Valid point." Nodding, I held up my hands. "No wandering hands, just lift me up there."

Leone lifted his hands. "Beth would blast them off if they even thought to wander."

I nodded. "Okay." I was more nervous of being on the horse then being touched. He stepped in front of me and it suddenly dawned on me how big he was. When he grasped my waist, I tensed and held my breath until I was sitting in front of Michael, a lot closer then I would have liked. I looked down at the ground. Okay, maybe close was good so he could stop me from falling off.

Hachi moved around a bit and I grabbed Michael's arm like a sissy.

"He's just adjusting to the extra weight." He rested his hand on my waist, holding me where I was.

I nodded. "Tell him there's a novice up here and to dance smoothly."

Michael's mouth twitched. "He knows. I'm going to have to pull you closer, so you don't bounce off." He held his hand away from me, watching my face until I acknowledged what he said. Moving his hand slowly, he reached behind him and pulled something out. Holding his arm out away from us, he motioned to it with his head. "You can hold this knife and if I do anything out of line, you have my permission to stick me with it."

Leone snorted and got on his horse. "I didn't get a knife."

Michael didn't look away from me. "That's because you would have stabbed me just for fun."

I reached and took the knife from his hand and looked at it. "Okay."

Michael looked at it. "Point it away from me so I don't get stabbed if we gallop."

I looked down then turned it away from us.

He slowly circled my waist, pulling me tight against his chest. "Lean into me and swing your legs over mine, so I don't have to squeeze to keep you here."

I took a shaky breath and leaned against his hard chest. "How far are we going?"

He jerked his other arm and Hachi turned. "Fifteen minutes."

Hachi started walking. It was the weirdest feeling, sitting on a creature as it moved.

"Let me know when you're ready to try something faster." Michael said, his voice rumbling through his chest as he spoke.

Leone was beside us, looking around.

All I could think was that if I fell and Hachi didn't step on me, Leone's horse would.

Leone pulled out his phone then answered it with a smile. "Hey, love." He looked at me. "Bit taller then Paisley." He grinned. "Everyone is bigger than you." He nodded. "See you soon." Tucking it back in a pocket, he looked at Michael. "I told Arius to get Victor to send a patrol out here. If this is where they're landing it will make our lives easier."

Michael sighed. "If Autumn hadn't called out, we would have ridden on by."

"I can't believe they're dumb enough to bring them here on our land." Leone mused quietly.

"It's the last place we'd look." Michael answered. He leaned back and looked at me. "Ready to try a bit faster?"

I inhaled and blew out a breath trying to summon some courage. I nodded. "Sure, give him the gas."

He gave me an abrupt nod. "Hold on."

Gripping the knife in one hand, I made sure it wasn't aimed at any body parts before I turned my head into his chest and squeezed my eyes shut. I was thankful it was dark enough so no one would be able to see my face and know I was being a wimp. Hachi's stride increased and the first few bumps were alarming, then as I relaxed as I picked up the rhythm. Michael's arm held me firmly against him, even though this was far closer then I was usually comfortable with, I was glad he held me in place.

"You can see the lights up ahead." He said quietly, leaning down by my ear.

I turned and looked where we were going. There were a lot of buildings lit up. It was the best thing I'd ever seen after never having been out of the city, I was way out of my comfort zone without lights and buildings.

I almost forgot I was on a horse until we rode into a yard and Hachi stopped. The lack of movement took me by surprise. Michael turned him and then released my waist. I looked to see about a dozen men standing there looking at me. Even from atop the horse, I knew they were as big as Leone and Michael. Where the hell was I that men were this big? I moved my legs and kicked, jumping down. I landed in a crouch for a second, then straightened up.

A man with long black hair started toward me, then spotted the knife I held. He glanced up to Michael, questions in his eyes.

"Don't crowd her." He told him.

The man stopped and moved his hands out from his body, showing me they were empty.

Hachi nudged my shoulder. "Thanks for the lift, boy." I told him.

The men moved, and a tiny redheaded woman appeared. "Give her some room guys, it's bad enough when it looks like land of the giants when first seeing you guys." They backed away. She turned and looked at Leone, giving him a quick once over.

Releasing the reins, he went over and kissed the top of her head. "Stay out of her reach, Beth, she beat the holy hell out of two guys."

Beth smiled at me. "Good." She glanced briefly to the knife in my hand, then motioned to a door. "I'm Bethany. Come in and let's get those chains off you."

I looked at Michael quickly then to the door.

"How did she get the knife?" The one with the long hair asked Leone.

He smirked. "Michael gave it to her, so she could stab him if he got touchy-feely."

The dark haired one looked at Michael. "I don't see any blood."

"Guess he didn't get touchy-feely with her." One of the others said.

Bethany glared at them, "you guys aren't…"

"Hey, I heard—"

A tall blond came out of another door to my left, I spun and crouched, flipping the knife into a defensive position.

He threw his hands up. "Whoa, take it easy. I just came to talk to my brother, Michael."

Moving only my eyes, I glanced to Michael, he was side-stepping, moving in my field of vision. His hands were open and empty.

"As much as Rafael deserves to have some woman stab him, I'd prefer it not be with my blade." He held his hand out. "No one here is going to touch you." He nodded slowly. "And you don't need a knife to do damage."

I looked back to Rafael, he returned my look with a steady gaze. He was tense and ready, but there was no sign of impatience in his expression. Straightening slowly, I held the knife toward Michael.

He extended his arm, his palm up and let me set it on his hand. "Let's get those off you and get your injuries looked at, Autumn."

I touched my mouth, then shrugged. "Just a busted lip and bruised cheekbone. I've had much worse."

In the light I noticed how blue his eyes were, right now they were assessing my face with a look of anguish in them. He motioned to the door again, then snarled at the men standing near it. "Back up and give her space."

I looked to see all of them comply, leaving Bethany standing there alone. She gave me a soft smile and nodded.

Chapter Three

Bethany tried another key. She gave me a brief glance. "We'll find it." Turning she looked at Leone on the other side of the room. "I don't suppose the men you found her with had the key?"

Leone shook his head. "It wouldn't have ported with him, and I'm not going to try to find that spot in the field."

Bethany sighed, "I'll just keep trying."

The one with the long black hair came back in and stood beside Michael. His eyes were on me when he spoke. "The one with the busted nose is doing okay. The other one," he turned to look at Michael, "his nose is broken, or should I say broken again, and the bones around his eye are cracked in three places."

Both men turned and looked at me. I shrugged. "He grabbed me." Beth glanced up at me, a smirk on her face. "It's not my fault they don't know how to keep their weight balanced and hold a proper stance when they fight."

There were a few quiet chuckles from the men.

I looked down to see Bethany going through the keys. "Anyone here pick locks?" I looked around. "Its not in my skill set."

Rafael nodded. "I think I know someone who probably has every lock mechanism on memory." He pulled out his phone and started typing on it.

"Victor won't be happy bringing her here when we're not sure about…"

Rafael looked at Leone. "I'm messaging him to bring her." He grinned. "I know how big brother works."

I looked from him to Rafael then to Michael, "another brother?"

Bethany laughed, "*so* many brothers." She turned and motioned to the one with the dark hair. "Arius," then she waved her hand, "you met Leone and Michael," she smirked, "and Rafael." She pointed to the one leaning in the corner. "That's Quinton and I'm sure you'll meet Victor, Troy and Chase shortly. Probably Emil if you stick around."

I looked at her then back to the men. "There's nine of them?"

She nodded. "Do you have family we can call to let them know you're safe?"

I dragged my eyes from the men and shook my head. "No." Looking back at the *brothers* I tried to find a family resemblance. I didn't see it. Rafael was blond with a player vibe and blue eyes. Not the same blue as Michael's, but the shape was similar. He had black hair like Arius, but his eyes were grey. I'd never seen grey eyes before. Leone had red hair, but his eyes were the same brown as Quinton—who was still looking at me with more of a scowl on his face then anything else. The one thing I did notice was all of these men were very good looking, with that sculpted, Greek god-like iron jaw. Michael was the only one that had any imperfection on his face. There was a large scar on the right side of his face. To me it made him the most appealing out of the good-looking males, scars held stories and more importantly, survival. I had my share of battle wounds…

The door opened, and a large redheaded man stepped in. The vibe coming off him made me tense.

Bethany jumped up and spun around her hands up.

I was on my feet.

She huffed out a breath, her posture relaxed. "Victor."

He looked nowhere but at me. "Cristy will be here momentarily." He didn't move anything but his head. "I was just at the cells."

Arius nodded, "she messed them up good."

He looked back to me again. "Using what?"

I looked from Beth, who was chill with him being here, to the scariest man I'd ever seen. "Feet, hands, elbows, knees," I shrugged, "my face. Whatever they were dumb enough to get closest to."

His eyebrow went up. "Kickboxing?"

I shrugged, "more Muay Thai than straight kickboxing."

He inclined his head to me in a formal way. Stepping back, he opened the door and a small brunette came in.

"I don't know why I had to stand out there, Victor." She looked up at him.

His entire demeanor changed as he looked down at her. "I wanted to be certain you'd be safe."

She nodded. "Okay."

"Hey, little sis, can you pick locks?" Rafael asked.

Turning, she looked at him and smiled. "It depends on the style of locking mechanism, some of them are really complicated and I don't know how to see inside them to move the tumblers to get them to open."

He motioned to me.

She turned, and I held up my hands. With a serious expression on her face she came over and looked at the cuff locked around my wrist, then stared off into space. "I think I can do those." Dropping her back pack to the floor, she squatted down and opened it and started digging around in it.

I sat down, keeping my eye on Victor, yet his eyes never left her.

She pulled something out of the pack, it looked like wire with a paperclip. Moving closer to my foot, she looked up at me. "I was told not to touch you, but I can't do this and not touch you."

I turned my foot and motioned to it. "Go for it." There was something familiar about her. "You ever hang on the southside?"

She glanced up and me and nodded. "They have lots of trees there." She nodded.

I didn't know what that had to do with anything. "I go there once a week and teach the kids how to defend themselves and deal with bullying."

She was quiet for a moment, then I felt the cuff fall off my leg. Smiling she looked up at me. "I used to watch you. It's very nice what you do to help kids." She reached down to my other foot.

"You two know each other?" Rafael asked.

I shrugged. "Not really. I just remember faces." The cuff came off my other leg. "You're awesome."

She grinned and took my wrist when I held it out to her. "You asked me if I wanted to learn how to get away from a bully once…"

"And you said you'd just climb high, so they couldn't reach you. Strangest answer I've ever gotten." I grinned, then winced when my mouth stung. "I remember you. What's your name?"

She didn't look up from my wrist. "Crissy."

"You teach defense classes?" Michael asked, his blue eyes going from my swollen mouth to my eyes and back again.

"Not formal classes. I just help the kids on the street hold their own." I looked down when the cuff came off my wrist. "Glad to see you're doing all right, Crissy."

She paused before moving to my other hand. "I am very happy here. I have a home and a tower."

I didn't know what that was about. Before I could reply, the door opened and two tall twins with blond hair walked in. The only way to tell them apart was one had a goatee. "Let me guess, you must be Troy and Chase."

The one with the goatee grinned, "I love it when our reputation precedes us." Then he frowned and really looked at me.

I glanced at the other one, he was scowling.

With long strides he went over to a fridge on the other side of the room and opened it. Pulling something out of the freezer, he turned and came back toward me. He stopped far enough away not to crowd me and held out an ice pack.

Michael had done a good job relaying that I didn't like to be touched. I took it. "Awesome, thank you. My face feels like a tribal drum right now." I held it against my cheek and hissed out a breath when it burned.

"You should drink some blood." Crissy said, her head still down getting the last cuff off.

I looked at her briefly, shocked, Not even knowing where she could be going with that. "Thanks, but I've drank enough of my own the last few days." I touched my tongue against my lip. "I'm going to have one of those permanent pouty mouths if this opens again."

One of the men made a sound that was almost a growl.

Another one cleared his throat. "Did either of you go to the cells and check out Autumn's handywork?" Arius asked the twins.

The one that had handed me the pack stood back, crossing his arms over his chest. "We just came from there. One has been transferred to the medical wing."

"He won't be winning any beauty pageants for a while." The other twin said while smiling at me.

Crissy got up and went back over to stand with Victor. He put his arm around her. It was an odd match, but she wasn't on the streets and seemed healthy and happy. Compared to the hollowed-out cheeks she used to have, she looked great.

Bethany turned and picked up something, then came toward me. "I wasn't sure about your size, so it's just a track suit." She motioned to a door. "You can change in there."

I looked down at the grey coveralls I had on as I took the clothes. "Thanks. These are a little too prison-like for my taste."

Leone straightened up. "I'll get the doctor…"

I shook my head, "I don't need a doctor. I've had worse injuries." I touched my ribs from when blondie tried to check me through the wall. "I've had busted ribs before, this is just bruising."

He frowned and looked at Michael, who gave a quick shake of his head.

Leone gave him an odd look and motioned to the door. "Get changed and we'll be outside."

Stepping into the room, I looked around. It was a bathroom with not a window in sight. Sighing, I went over and looked in the mirror. It had been a few years since my face had looked like this. My entire bottom lip was inflamed and red, my jaw, up to my cheekbone, was a dark purple and twice the size as normal. Across my forehead was another bruise. No wonder they all looked at me that way. I looked like a badly abused punching bag. Usually I kept people from hitting my face, then again, the guys I was used to fighting weren't the size of those guards with arms that were longer than my legs.

Flipping on the water, I leaned down and splashed water on my face. It stung but felt good at the same time. Standing up, I leaned over the sink, just dripping. These people seemed decent, maybe I could get bus fare out of them and catch a lift back to the city.

Unzipping the coveralls, I pulled them off my shoulders and looked down. Was it bad when you didn't feel the bruises on your own body? I looked in the mirror, from my collar bone to shoulder was dark purple. I lifted my arm slowly, yeah, I was a little tender. Looking down, I checked my ribs, they were about the same along my right side. I knew my legs would be beat up a bit too, that was normal with my style of fighting, I used the lower femur and side of the tibia to block shots.

Kicking off the cheap canvas shoes, I climbed out of the ugly jumpsuit, kicked it across the floor and picked up the clothes Beth had handed me. The pants were loose at the bottom, good for easy movement. I pulled them on before I started cataloguing the marks on my legs. My right hip was a bit roughed up, and I couldn't remember how that happened. Picking up the top, I turned it around, then pulled it over my head. Pulling the shoes back on, I grabbed the coveralls and opened the door.

Michael stood a few feet away, but the rest had all cleared out.

I held up the coveralls, then spotted the cuffs sitting on the desk. Going over I put them on top of the pile of chains, then remembered the watch thing on my arm. Taking it off quickly, I tossed it on top. I didn't know what it was, but I'd woke up with it on and I wanted nothing that reminded me of being shot with a dart.

When I turned, Michael's eyes were huge.

I looked behind me, "What?"

He blinked, his brows furrowing. "How do you feel?"

I shrugged. "Like I went ten rounds with an ogre or two."

Straightening, he looked at the watch and then to me. With slow and obvious movements, his gaze traveled the length of me. Then he scowled and started to step toward me and stopped. "That's a bit high to be called ribs." He motioned to my neck.

I looked down and realized the neckline on the top hung low enough to see the bruising. "Yeah, I think that was when blondie tackled me, I hit the wall." He just stood there giving me an odd look. "He deserved what I did to his face, he shot me with a dart."

His lips quirked, then he sobered. "We were going to go get something to eat. I'd like to ask you some questions and get some information about how they managed to get you here."

I really wanted to go home, but if I could help them stop this from happening to others, then I had an obligation to the other women to help. "I could eat." I picked up the ice pack and held it against my face.

He motioned to the door. "Please don't beat anyone if they accidentally come up to you. No one here intends you harm."

I licked over my swollen lip for a second and then nodded. "I'll try. It's a gut reflex." Going out the door, I stopped to see just one twin was left. I looked around.

"They'll meet us at the dining room." He looked me over, then motioned to my face. "Are you sure you're all right?"

I nodded. "I'll be fine."

He inclined his head. "I'm Troy." He glanced to Michael. "We just have to stop and get the girls from the practice room."

Michael nodded and motioned to a door on the other side of the yard.

I watched a small group of men sparring with each other as we went toward it. "The one with the shaggy hair is over-extending to reach his opponent. He'd be so easy to take that way." I said quietly.

Both men with me turned to look.

"Yes, he would." Troy stated.

"I'll talk to Ira about having them go over the basics." Michael said dryly.

Chapter Four

We walked for what felt like miles through tunnels. There was no conversation, just walking. I was okay without chatter. How a person handled silence said a lot about them. Some couldn't handle quiet. The restless ones never made good fighters, their focus was all over the place.

We stopped by two doors, I followed them in. It was a huge dojo-style gym. The wall of practice gear was outstanding. I turned to see the other twin and a blonde woman watching a woman on the mat. She was doing some very well practiced Tai Chi moves. She performed them with an elegant grace, it was amazing to see.

It took me a minute to see she was almost to the end of the standard twenty-four moves. Kicking my shoes off, I stepped over to the side of the door out of the way and picked up the move she was on, then followed through the push and stepped in time to her move. It had been a long time since I'd had the time to concentrate on the gracefully disciplined moves. I did the last three poses until we ended on the final position. I bowed to her after she finished, and she returned it.

"That was perfect. Your form is very well disciplined." I went back over to my shoes.

She paused a moment looking at me, probably because of my banged-up face. "Thank you. It's been a long time since I've had someone to hold me in check with those."

I started to smile, then my lip stopped me. "Your form needs no corrections."

She smiled. "You instruct?"

I shook my head. "Not tai chi. I've used it to help students learn focus or defense moves, but my style is more—" I glanced at the wall of practice tools, "violent."

Slipping her boots on, she came over. "I'm Alona." She gave me a small smile. "I'd love to see the moves at a faster pace." She shrugged. "I could never quite manage it."

I touched my ribs. "I'm Autumn. I'd show you now, but I'm a little banged up and wouldn't be able to do it justice."

Alona glanced to the twin with the goatee. "You should have called me."

"Beloved, I don't like to interrupt your peaceful moments." He motioned to me. "There was nothing to tell as of yet. Aside from the fact that she messed up some of Hubert's guards."

The smaller blonde spoke up. "I ran down to the cells to check it out." She grinned. "Nice work."

I shrugged, "they started it." I glanced to Michael and motioned to the wall. "May I?"

He nodded, still standing beside the door with an odd look on his face.

I went over and walked along the wall, then turned around. "This place is like a slice of heaven."

Troy looked at Daxx and raised an eyebrow.

"All you need is a few bags and padded poles to make this room perfect."

Michael motioned to the door. "We should go, the others will be waiting."

One twin gave the other a quick look, then started for the door.

Alona went to the bearded one, he wrapped his arm around her shoulders and hugged her into his side, a look of concern on his face.

"I'm fine," she smiled up at him. "That's my bleeding compassion, not from her."

He kissed the top of her head. "There will be no bleeding anything on you. Emotions or otherwise."

I turned and followed them out the door.

I stayed at the back and listened to the obvious couples talking as we walked. It took a moment to notice the tattoos they had on their left arms, if I wasn't mistaken, they matched. It was different, but not the strangest thing I'd seen couples do. At least it was just a pattern and not each other's name. I'd seen that often enough, then when they broke up trying to cover the name of their ex always proved to be a challenge.

Michael was a few feet ahead of me, but his posture told me he was completely aware of how many steps behind I was the entire time.

They turned and went in a door, I followed then stopped to see a huge table with chairs lining both sides. Large portraits hung on the walls, all of couples. They all looked happy and regal, like they could have been royalty. I waited until everyone sat down then took the chair closest to the door. It was a habit that I would probably never break. You never knew when you'd need a fast exit.

A petite redheaded lady came in carrying a tray. She set it on the table, paused for a moment and looked at me, then turned and went back into the kitchen. A few glanced at me as they began heaping their plates up. I was bit taken back by the amount of food they were going to eat. The lady came in again with more trays.

Michael glanced down the table at me and motioned to the food.

I nodded. "I'll wait until everyone has theirs."

Bethany smiled down at me. "You met Alona and Daxx on the way here," She motioned to a dark-haired woman beside Arius. "This is Paisley."

She turned and smiled at me. "Sorry, I completely forgot to introduce myself." Glancing around the table, she shook her head. "I'm still getting used to this family thing."

I nodded. "Autumn."

The lady came out of the kitchen again, this time she only carried a plate and was coming toward me. I looked to see if anyone else was watching, they all were.

"Here you are, love." She gave me a sweet smile. "That's broiled, no oil." She pulled a bottle of water out of her apron and set it in front of me.

I looked down to see a huge chicken breast and vegetables on the plate. "Oh, you are a dream." I told her, trying hard to smile without splitting my lip again. Using my foot, I shoved the chair out at the corner of the table. "Grab a seat."

She turned and looked to the faces watching us from the other end of the table.

I looked at Michael, then Troy. "It's all right if she sits?" No one moved. I shrugged and motioned to the chair. "Yeah, go for it."

She sat down. "I'm Mitz, dear."

I nodded and picked up my fork. "That's going to be hard to say until my lip goes down, without spitting."

Mitz gave me a compassionate look. "That's fine, love."

I motioned down the table. "Do you want some coffee or tea?" I started to get up.

She touched my hand, "No, I'm fine. But thank you."

I sat down again and looked at the others, they were watching, but didn't seem upset. "You should grab a plate and take a break." I pointed to the door. "You've set a few speed records flying in and out of there." I held my hand over the plate she brought me. "Do you want some of the chicken? It smells amazing."

She shook her head and stood up. Leaning down she kissed the top of my head. "Thank you, but I'm fine. Enjoy your food. Let me know if you need anything else." Her eyes briefly looked at my face again, "You're a refreshing heart." Then she hurried from the room.

She'd kissed me. I looked around at the others, then had to look at my plate. Emotions I didn't deal with much started to bubble to the surface. "She's sweet." I nodded, hoping they were looking at their own plates again.

It was silent for a few minutes, the clank of forks hitting plates, not much else.

"Okay—I can't sit here for a minute longer in this quiet."

I looked up to see Daxx was talking.

"I saw what you did to those guys. Where did you learn to fight like that?"

I held up my hand, so I could chew and swallow. "Sorry. Mouth is a bit tender. Chewing is a work out." I rolled my eyes. "Well, when I was young—" I shrugged, "like nine or ten, around there, I'd hide up in the—" I frowned. "I don't know what they're called. The old buildings have them near the top, they're like a ledge with an overhang." I looked to see Crissy nodding. "New shiny sky scrapers don't have them…"

"They're great in bad weather." She nodded.

I pointed to her. "Right? You have to share it with the birds, but…"

She smiled. "It keeps the rats away."

"Exactly." I glanced to the others to see them looking from Crissy to me. From the expressions, the women seemed to get it, the men didn't look impressed. "Any way, I found this one, it was perfect. The wind from the bay never hit it."

Crissy nodded again, she knew.

I grabbed the bottle of water and opened it. "This isn't going to be pretty." I joked and carefully took a sip slowly, so I wouldn't drool it all out with my lip. Swallowing, I put the cap back on and set it down. "So, I found this sweet spot across from a martial arts school—I'd dive for dinner…"

"Fish?" Rafael asked.

I smirked, then held my lip for a second.

Beth and Crissy both turned to look at him. Alona and Daxx both grinned.

"Oh, you're cute." I told him. "I meant dumpster diving."

"You ate other people's garbage?" Michael looked horrified.

I shrugged. "I was ten."

Crissy looked at him. "You can find tasty food sometimes."

I nodded. "Right. Restaurants are the best locations.

She grinned. "Those banquet halls."

"Oh, the best desserts there." I nodded, then looked to see everyone watching me. "So, I'd hole up and watch classes for all these different fighting styles." I shrugged. "Then I'd practice—it's a great way to stay warm." The expressions around the table ranged from startled to understanding, so I continued. "When I was twelve or thirteen, I went to the teacher in that school and asked him if I could beat his best fighter, would he train me? He agreed." I shrugged again. "So, I did." I noticed no one was eating. "Sorry, I talk too much when I'm nervous or around a lot of new people—" I motioned around the table. "The size of you guys equals a lot of people."

Victor leaned back, his hands on the table. "That's fine, please continue."

I let my gaze touch on a few of the others, they seemed interested. "Okay, ah, when I was seventeen, I became one of his instructors. When I didn't have a class, I'd hit the streets and show young kids how to defend themselves," I sighed, remembering some of those kids. "Teach them how to have a chance out there." I paused, needing another sip of water.

While I was wrestling with trying to drink and not embarrass myself, Michael shoved back from the table and went out into the kitchen. I was capping the bottle when he came back out and down the table. He stopped a few feet away and held out a straw. I took it. "Oh, thanks." I nodded and opened the bottle again and put the straw in, taking a bigger drink. When I was done, I pulled the straw out and set it beside my plate and capped the bottle once more. "Thanks, that's much better." I cleared my throat. "I was an instructor for five years, then the sensei died—the school shut down."

"That's incredible." Alona said quietly. "That you help the kids on the street."

I opened my hands and held them up. "When you live it, you know what it takes to survive it."

She nodded and sighed. "I don't miss that."

"Neither do I." Beth said quietly.

Crissy shook her head. "It's nice knowing I get to eat every day and be warm and dry."

I nodded. To look as these women, you'd never know they'd been on the streets. "It is. I can't find them homes, but I can give them chance."

Michael had been watching me without looking away. He pushed his plate away and leaned his arms on the table. "What have you been doing since the school closed?"

I licked at my lip, trying to keep it from drying out too much. "I bounced around for a bit, trying to find my footing elsewhere. No other schools want a street rat teaching their privileged students. Then I found old Joe at the gym…"

"At Joe's Bronze Ring?" Crissy asked.

I nodded. "Yeah."

"He's nice, he let me sit inside when the weather was really cold." She nodded looking excited.

"Yeah, he's a peach. I give him a hand with light training for his guys and he sets up fights on the down low for me, you know? I split the winnings with him and he lets me crash in the old storage room."

Michael frowned. "Wait. You fight for a living?"

I nodded. "Girls gotta eat." I shrugged, "I don't have any other life skills and I get my choice of showers after it closes."

Michael turned to look at Troy, then to Chase.

Both twins turned to look at me.

"I think until we figure out how you were taken, you should stay here." Alona said softly.

I looked at Michael. "I totally forgot, you wanted to ask me about that." I waved my hand to the plate in front of me. "The food distracted me."

He shook his head. "That's fine. If you'd like to eat, go ahead, we can talk when you're finished."

I looked at the food on my plate, then back to him. "Are you sure?"

"I insist." He looked back to the twins, then around to some of his brothers.

I waited to see if the others started eating again, before picking up the fork.

Chapter Five

I got up and picked up my plate.

"Autumn." I looked to Alona.

She shook her head. "You don't have to clear the table."

"Are you sure? I don't mind." I looked to the others, then back to her.

She motioned to the table. "Please. You must be hurting."

I put the plate on the table and sat down. "I'm a little sore, but it's nothing I'm not used to."

The expression on her face was concern. "If you'd like to rest, we can discuss this later." She gave a few of the men a hard look, daring them to say otherwise.

"She's right." Paisley said. "If you'd like to go soak and then lie down we can talk later."

I shook my head. "I'm good." I shrugged. "I'm afraid to stop, you know? It's going to hurt worse later, always does." I glanced to Michael, his look told me he wasn't impressed that I admitted to that. Looking from him, I motioned to the plate. "I am so stuffed after that. I refused to eat or drink anything they gave me."

"I think we should discuss this, soon, so Autumn can go begin her recovery." Victor said with a tone of authority. He didn't wait for responses. "Can you tell us how they got you?" He lifted his hand, "with your combat knowledge, it has eluded me how it would be possible."

I looked at him for a moment. He spoke so stiffly. Shaking my head, I inhaled slowly. "I don't know how." I sat back and set my hands on the table. "I was out for my run, like every other day and then I woke up in a room. I thought I'd been busted for the fights," I rolled my eyes, "they're not exactly legal." I made eye contact with Michael, hoping he would let me off with that confession. I'd forgotten he was a cop. "Then," I said slowly, turning to look at Alona instead, "when blondie—the guy with the busted face, came in I knew there was something wrong about the whole thing."

Paisley looked at Arius. "It's like me. I was on the pier then woke up on an island."

"You woke up on an island?" I tried to smirk and failed. "Sounds better then my little windowless room."

"Was there anything familiar in the room, or something that might tell you where it was located?" Michael asked.

Now he sounded like a cop. I shook my head. "No, just a plain white room with a toilet and sink." I sighed. "I couldn't hear anything, smell anything. It was white silence." I glanced to Paisley. "It was very unnerving."

She gave me a huge eyed look. "That kind of silence is the worst."

I nodded. "So how did you get away?"

Smirking, she glanced to Arius then back to me. "I jumped off a cliff into the water."

I would have done the whole mouth drop, shocked thing but my jaw was having none of that. "Never been much for water myself, but you do what you have to."

With a smile, she nodded. "Yes. You do." Her smile faded to concern. "I know we are supposed to be talking about details, but I have to ask—how did you end up on the streets so young?" She glanced at the other women. "Most of us were in our teens before we landed there. The foster system wasn't for us."

I'd asked myself this a thousand times. "I didn't do the foster route. I've seen the damage that system does. I don't know how I ended up there."

"You don't know your parents?" Michael asked me quietly.

I shook my head. "As far back as I can remember, I've been on my own. I mean, sure at some point I had to have parents, right? I didn't just magically appear—a six-year-old on the streets."

"You were only six?" Bethany asked, her hand over her mouth.

I tried not to let her reaction get to me. I'd had my share of sympathy about my life. "Yeah. I stayed hidden until I was old enough to get around." I sighed, remembering and trying not to let the feelings flood me. "There was this lady, on the street, she called herself Melody, she kind of took me under her wing and kept me alive through the bad years."

Daxx sat there, a blank look on her face. "Is Autumn your real name?"

I shrugged. "It's the only one I got. Melody gave it to me. So, Autumn I am, this many years later. I think it was her favorite season. She gave me the last name Mercer, I think it may have been her own at some point." I looked around and didn't like the sadness in their eyes. "She taught me to read, and how to survive." I nodded then glanced at Alona, she looked like she was close to tears. "Hey. Don't. I'm here. I have no regrets. I've helped many live through it, and if I hadn't gone through that I couldn't have helped."

She closed her eyes for a moment. Chase leaning close to her talking softly in her ear. Shaking her head, she gave him a soft look. "I'm sorry, I'm very emotional at times."

Michael stood up and walked into the other room, I could only assume was the kitchen. Everyone watched him leave, then looked back to me.

"I'll be right back." Troy said and got up, following Michael.

I'd definitely crushed the mood with my sad tale. "I didn't mean to bring everyone down." I connected with as many looks as I could handle around the table. "I'm okay with all of it. I stopped the woe is me party a long time ago." I opened the bottle and put the straw in, needing a minute to figure out how to get the topic away from my past and onto other things.

Troy came out, he glanced briefly to his twin and then sat back down. "He just needs a moment." He said quietly.

Everyone looked at me, then to the kitchen.

Sighing, I stood up and picked up my plate. No one tried to stop me this time. I walked into the kitchen, then paused it was huge and shiny clean. Michael stood on the far side, his hands on the wall and head hanging down. Even though his back was to me, I knew by the way he tensed he was aware I had come in. I took my plate and set it beside the sink. Resting my hands on the countertop, I watched as he lifted his head and looked at the wall. "Hey, hero, I'm sorry, I didn't mean to…"

"Do *not*—apologize." He all but growled at me. Straightening, he turned and looked at me. "You have nothing to apologize for." His blue eyes locked on my own.

I was a bit taken back by his mood. The vibe coming off him right now could rival his scary brother, Victor.

He waved a large hand around. "I am not a hero." His voice was softer now.

I couldn't look away from his eyes. They say the eyes are a window to your soul, and I was seeing his was haunted and full of regret. "Sometimes the ones that say they aren't heroes are the ones that do more than those that claim to be."

He huffed out a breath. "You are the definition of the word." He motioned around the room. "I was raised with privilege and hide in it each day. You raised yourself with no home, living off garbage and have done more to help others than I have in my lifetime."

I could see he was getting worked up again and didn't want to go back there. "I get it. Your pissed off. If you want to turn that into something useful, be mad at that redheaded amazon that's running this abduction ring."

His brows furrowed. Reaching into his pocket, he pulled out his phone and tapped the screen a few times. "This redhead?" He came over and held his phone out to me.

I looked at the screen. She looked a bit different, her hair was shorter, but it was the same woman. "That's her."

"You saw her?" he didn't lower the phone.

I nodded. "Yeah, she came in and told blondie to stop damaging the merchandise—me."

Lowering the phone, his jaw clenched a few times. He inhaled through his nose deeply, then blew it out quietly. Motioning to the door, "Please, I'd like to finish this discussion."

I turned and went back into the dining room. Several pairs of concerned eyes moved to me as I walked in.

"Autumn saw Eunice." Michael stated as he walked in behind me.

"She was there when she was taken?" Troy turned to watch me sit back down.

Quinton looked from me to Michael. "Is she sure?"

"The picture is a bit different, but she has the same R.B.F., so yeah, it's her." I said.

"R.B.F?" Quinton looked at me.

I looked to see Paisley smirk, then back to him. "Resting bitch face." I gave him a wide-eyed look, "hers is so hard, I'm pretty sure it will be stuck like that for life."

Victor rubbed a hand across his forehead. "It makes sense," he glanced up to Quinton, "in a morbid way—she always wanted children to rebuild the Hubert line."

I watched to see if he was going to continue, but he didn't say more. "What does that have to do with human trafficking?"

Paisley frowned. "They didn't take you to sell you." She looked quickly to Arius. He leaned closer and picked up her hand, holding it in his lap. She turned back to me, a scared look on her face.

I glanced around. "She told the guard no one would want a pulverized woman. I just—" I turned back to Paisley, "what else could that mean?"

"They're breeding women." She said quietly.

I stood up and looked at her. "They're making a human farm?"

Paisley nodded slowly, her eyes were tearing up.

I paced away and stared at the wall. My pain forgotten. "You hear about this sort of thing on the streets all the time—we all know it's happening everywhere—" I turned and glanced back to Paisley, then to the other women, one at a time. "But when it's right on your doorstep…"

"We got away." Paisley said then nodded.

I shook my head. "I'm not upset for me—the other women may not—"

"We've found many women and taken them to safe houses." Bethany told me.

I nodded. "Good." I looked at Michael. "I hope you beat any males in the vicinity to a pulp." I shrugged, "off the record of course."

He met my look with a hard one. "Our cells are their new homes."

"Good." I took a deep breath and paced a few more feet. This room was plenty big enough, I'd never run out of space. "Makes me so—pissed," I looked to Alona, "pardon the language."

She shrugged, "no offense taken." She waved a hand.

"Just knowing they're taking women that can't defend themselves." I snorted. "Joke is on them for taking me for their breeding—"

"What do you mean?" Daxx looked at me. "Because you kicked their asses?"

I shrugged. "That too, but no, I can't have kids." I waved my hand in front of my stomach. "One of my first underground fights—the guy hid a shiv in his arm wrap." I touched my lower stomach. "Stuck it right here. I pulled it out, then broke his face." I rolled my eyes. "I was out of the game for a few months." I shook my head, "but when the doctors said they'd try to save those parts—I told them not to bother. I mean what could I offer a kid? A bedroom in the back of a gym?" I nodded, still knowing that I'd made the right choice.

The expressions had changed again. I really needed to stop talking. Michael sat there with his eyes closed, taking deep breaths. I could see his chest rising and falling. Most of the men watched him carefully.

"Okay, I have a plan." I waited until they looked at me. "Pop me on a bus, I'll take a few days and heal up—then I'll go see if I can find that redheaded bitch again." I shrugged. "Or her find me. She seemed almost impressed that I'd beat on her guards."

Michael stood up suddenly. He leaned on the table and gave me a hard look. "You are *not* using yourself as bait."

I licked over my fat lip, trying not to bark back at him and open it again. "Now you're taking the hero thing a bit far." I lifted my hand then dropped it. "I appreciate the sentiment, really, but," I motioned up and down my body, "my body, my choice, sort of thing."

He made a sound that actually sounded like a growl.

I frowned and glanced at the others, the only one that didn't look shocked was Chase. He was smirking.

"I don't mean to interrupt."

I spun to the door to see a woman with short dark hair and a friendly expression on her face.

"Clairee?" Rafael stood up.

She gave him a quick smile. "Mitz messaged asking for some salve."

Rafael motioned to me.

She turned, then her expression changed to shock. "Oh my stars." She rushed toward me.

I back up a few steps.

"What happened?" She gave Rafael a look then glanced down the table to the others.

"Salve?" I asked.

Clairee turned, nodding and held out a jar to me. "It-it won't do much for the lip, but the other injuries…"

I took the jar and opened it then sniffed the contents. Blowing out a breath, I nodded. "Yeah, that stinks enough, it must work." I put the lid back on. "I have this balm at home I use, but thanks, I'll give this a try." I pulled the neck of my top aside. "It will work on this, too?"

A look of pain appeared on her face. "Yes. Yes, it should." She turned and looked at Daxx.

Daxx stood up and came down the table, her brows creased. She gave me a steady look and walked right up to me. "How far down is that?" She pulled the shirt a bit more and looked at my shoulder.

"Kind of blends into the bruising on my ribs." I pulled the side of my shirt up a bit. "So, it's hard to tell where that one ends."

"How are you still moving?" She shook her head. "I've had almost every part of me banged up, but not all at once."

"Occupational hazard." I joked.

"Thank you, Clairee." Michael said in a tone that dismissed her.

I tried to smile at her. "Yeah, thanks. I'll give it a try."

She smiled, then covered her mouth and hurried out the door.

I looked at the jar in my hand and set it on the table.

Daxx turned on her heel and went over to Michael. "Do something." She flipped her hand against his arm. "You've called dibs or whatever you Neanderthal's call it—then own it. If you're not going to then Quinton or Rafael can."

Michael looked down at her without so much as blinking. I could see the muscle in his jaw tensing.

She turned and glared at Quinton. "You do it."

He opened his mouth and then looked up to Michael. "I I-if-he—" He lifted his hands and then lowered them.

Daxx made a loud noise of frustration then stomped back to her seat and sat down.

Troy gave her a wary look, then turned to Michael with his brows drawn together.

I had no idea what they were talking about.

"I'm with Daxx on this." Alona said. "I'll even volunteer my mate. I can't just sit here and—" she put her hands over her face and took a deep breath.

The other women nodded.

Chase moved only his eyes and looked at his twin. I didn't know him at all, but his 'help me' look was universal.

"You think I enjoy seeing her like this?" Michael said through clenched teeth. He motioned to me.

I huffed out a breath. "I hope not, or I'm revoking your hero status." I was aching all over now. "Look, I'm running out of steam. Thank you again, really. If you could spot me a bus ticket, I have some money stashed at the gym. I'll mail it back to you."

"I'm afraid—" Chase glanced at Michael for a moment, "a bus would not be able to get you home."

I looked at him for a moment, then closed my eyes and sighed. "Shit. Don't tell me they flew me here." I opened my eyes. "Explains the field with no cars." I looked at Chase. "I'll have to win a fight or two, but I'm good for the money. I'll pay you back."

"Money is not the issue," he said glancing to his twin, "the plane is—"

"Take a seat, Autumn, this is gong to take a few minutes to explain." Daxx said in a hushed tone.

I frowned and watched Michael drop back down into his chair. Nothing good ever happened when someone told you to sit down so they could talk to you. I sat on the edge of mine, not sure what was going on. Were they about to tell me I couldn't get home again? I wasn't sure, but the tense looks going back and forth among them didn't encourage me.

"The reason you can't take a bus or plane home—" Daxx looked at Troy briefly, "is because you are in another realm."

The silence in the room became heavy. Moving just my eyes, I looked from one face to the next, to the next, all the way around the table. No one was cracking a smile. I looked back at Daxx. "I don't get it."

She looked at me then to Troy.

"Told you it's not easy to explain." He said quietly.

Crissy knelt on her chair and leaned on the table to look at me. "They ported you here." She nodded. "Transported." She frowned, "I don't think you can bring a car." Turning to Victor, she tilted her head to the side. "Can you? You do bring weapons made of metal—so a car might…"

"Cristy." He said softly.

She nodded and looked back at me. "You were ported here. Did you feel funny?"

"Like your stomach was trying to climb out of your throat?" Bethany asked.

"Or filled with butterflies." Paisley looked at me.

"Light headed?" Alona added.

"I just thought it was from the drugs in the dart—"

"They shot you with a dart?" Daxx looked at Troy. "They shot her with a dart."

Michael glanced at her. "That's why she broke his face."

"You broke his face?" Daxx glared at Troy. "How come I didn't get to break his face? I was shot in the ass with a dart." She frowned.

"Should we scan her for trackers?" Leone looked at Victor.

"They can't trace her in these chambers and they're the ones that brought her to Alterealm, so I don't see why a tracker would be necessary…"

I held up my hand, so he'd stop talking. "Okay, I was transported to another realm—but you can *port* me back, right?"

Crissy nodded. "We go back and forth all the time." She held up her arm and showed me a watch similar to the one I'd taken off.

I looked at my wrist. "That was to go back? I took it off with the coveralls." I looked at Michael.

He shook his head. "That one was a stabilizer, not a transporter."

I sighed. "Can I get a transporter?" My head was really pounding now. I touched the ice pack to see if it was still cold. It wasn't.

"I'll get you a new pack." Bethany got up and went to the kitchen.

I touched the side of my face. The swelling was moving toward my eye. I didn't know what to make of this realm stuff, or porting.

Bethany came back out and hurried along the table. She handed me the ice pack.

"Thanks." I put it against my face, hoping if I could numb it, I'd be able to understand what they were telling me. "So, you can take me home?" I clarified, looking around at them.

"Yes," Alona answered, "but—"

I held up my hand. "No. No buts right now. You are able to get me home by some means?"

She nodded.

"Okay." I pushed the pack so it was half over my eye. "This other realm—why would they bring me here?" Maybe it was the knocks I'd taken on my head, but for whatever reason waking up in the field seemed to fit what they were saying.

"We've found most of their locations on your side." Troy said, then looked to Michael. "Except this white room they had you in."

"Could it be in the files and we missed it?" Leone asked.

"We can double check, but I feel like it's a new location so they could avoid us." Arius said and then looked at Michael.

"I agree." Michael answered, then turned to me. "Did it feel like it was underground?"

I shook my head slightly. "No. I didn't have that pressure feeling you get when you are in a tunnel or underground." I motioned around the room. "So, there's a whole population in this—realm?"

Troy glanced to Daxx. "Are you planning to explain more to her?"

Daxx shrugged. "Thought a bit at a time would be better." She gave him an odd look. "I can't do the flashy eye thing to scare the hell out of her."

The more they said, the less I understood. "Flashy eye thing?"

Daxx nodded and looked at Troy, she motioned to me.

He turned his head to look at me, his eyes were glowing red.

I moved the pack to my forehead. "I think I whacked my head harder then I thought."

"That may be." Chase said quietly.

Lowering the pack, I glanced at him. His eyes were yellow. I blinked then looked again. Still glowing yellow. Another realm. Glowing eyes. I'd seen a movie once like this. It didn't end well for the person in my seat. The room was silent. All eyes were on me. I lowered the pack to the table. Fight or flight my brain screamed at me. I wasn't in any condition for fight just yet. I inhaled slowly through my nose and blew it out gradually. Hoping I remember the way out I bolted for the door.

Chapter Six

I ran as fast as I could, passing halls and hoped I was still in the one we'd walked.

"Autumn." One of the girls called after me.

I didn't pause to see who. I could hear several feet hitting the carpeting hard behind me. Turning down a hallway, I spotted the double doors from the dojo and poured on a burst of speed. I raced by them when Michael appeared in front of me.

I skid to a stop, almost falling forward onto my face. He just appeared. He wasn't near any doors, so he hadn't taken a short cut. Just appeared.

"Cheater."

I turned to see Quinton leaning one hand against the wall behind me trying to catch his breath.

"Don't crowd her." Michael warned the rest coming up on us.

I turned and looked up at him. "How did you do that?" I backed against the wall, so I could see him and the others out of the corner of my eye.

"I ported." He said quietly, then glanced to the others. "We'll be in the girl's room."

I was about to ask where that was when he grasped my shoulder.

Then I was standing somewhere else. In a room, not the hall.

He let go of me and stepped back.

My stomach cramped hard enough I had to lean forward. It was the same feeling I'd had when I woke up in the field. "Shit," I whispered, "they did do that to me."

"Take deep breaths, it will pass."

I looked up at him as I waited for my guts to relax again. "This is really another realm, isn't it?"

He nodded, his eyes not moving from me.

"Yeah." I nodded and huffed out a breath as I straightened. "The eye thing—" I checked to make sure they were still blue. "Are you guys aliens?"

His lips twitched. "No."

"Human?"

"Of sorts." He said quietly. "No one will harm you here, Autumn, you *are* safe."

I cocked my head to the side. "Isn't that what sickos tell their victims?"

"I wouldn't know." His tone monotone, like he was working to stay calm.

The door flew open.

I jolted and spun around, ready.

Daxx held up her hands. "Sorry." She lowered them, then shook her head while looking at Michael. "That's one way of telling her."

He jerked his shoulders in a quick shrug. "She can't deny it if she's done it."

I could hear the others in the hallway, but no one came in.

Daxx motioned to a door on the other side of the room. "Grab a robe out of the closet and," She pointed to the door behind Michael, "go soak. We can talk more after you've cleaned up."

I licked over my lip.

"Don't say you're fine." She motioned up and down my body, "because you are obviously not." Taking a deep breath, she gave me an exasperated look. "All of us girls are from the same place as you. The fact that you don't need to wear a device to not drop dead on this side means fate wants you here." She looked to Michael, "even if some aren't happy about it."

I looked at Michael, he raised an eyebrow at Daxx.

"I could have died when I took that off?" I remembered the look on his face when I had tossed it on the desk. The details fit.

He nodded, "I would have gotten it back on before it came to that."

I touched the side of my face, wishing it would stop throbbing.

Daxx gave me a wide-eyed look then glared at Michael. She looked over her shoulder. "Arius."

Arius walked up behind her.

"Can you help?"

He looked at her for a second and then over her head to Michael. "Which one?"

She lifted a hand, "Both?"

"I could try but overwriting something that is as ingrained in his memory for this long—" he glanced down to Paisley beside him, "takes a lot. It may not work." With a quick look to me, he shrugged, "not to mention putting a hand on Autumn might prove to be bad for my health."

Daxx threw her hands up, then shook her head and stomped over to the closet. She flipped on the light and went in.

I tried to open my mouth further, but the muscles in my jaw objected. This wasn't good. "What day is it?"

Daxx came out carrying something over her arm. "Tuesday, why?"

"I need to call Joe, before he bets everything. I have a fight tomorrow and there's no way I'm going to be ready for it."

Michael snorted, "let him lose it…"

I turned to him. "The fights are my idea. He gives his half to the soup kitchen."

His hard expression deflated, he turned to Daxx.

She nodded. "I'll find the number.'

"Ask for Bert—" I shrugged, "that's his real name. Tell him I got jumped and I'm laying low for a few days recovering." I touched my lip, checking it wasn't bleeding again. "They'll be pissed it's postponed, which means I have to win."

"Do you always win?" Troy stood in the doorway now.

I nodded. "I've had a few bad ones, but not in a long time. For the past two years, everyone wants to try and beat the crazy blonde chick." I pointed to myself. "Joe and I have done some great things for the community with the money."

"I'll call Joe." Daxx said then pointed to the other door. "Come on. We'll have a chat as you soak, or you won't be fighting anything but a bed for days."

I sighed. My legs were already threatening to give out. No sleep for two days, plus the exertion from the sprint were adding up. "A tub huh? Can't say no to that. The idea of a shower and water pelting off me right now makes me okay with being dirty."

"Is it okay if the girls join us?" She motioned to where Bethany and two of the others stood inside the door.

"Why not. When I pass out, you can stop me from drowning." I wasn't used to a lot of female company, but right now they were the only thing that made sense with everything that was happening around me.

Michael and Troy exchanged a look as I followed Daxx in. I stopped inside the door. This was a bathroom? Half of Joe's gym would fit in here. The tub was the size of a small pool. I looked around. "I guess we'll all fit." I mumbled.

Daxx snorted. "I know, it's probably the biggest tub you've ever seen."

"We had a wine tasting party in one when Bethany was hurt." Crissy said coming in behind me. She sat beside the door.

I looked a Bethany as she closed the door behind herself.

"I fell off the fire escape from the second story in one of those abandoned dives behind the old Chinese market."

I knew where she was talking about. "They need to tear those down, or fix them for shelters."

I watched Paisley turn the tub on as I kicked off the shoes.

Bethany picked them up. "We'll toss these and get you some real shoes." She dropped them into a small garbage can.

Daxx motioned to my top. "Do you need a hand?"

I rotated my shoulder slowly, it wasn't too seized up yet. "No, I think I got it." Reaching down with my good arm, I pulled the other side of my top up and slipped my arm through it.

"Had a lot of practice with that?" She smirked.

I nodded. "Yeah. You could say that." Once the shirt cleared my head, I went over to the mirror. I looked at Daxx in the reflection. "Think they'd let me go break more than his face? He slammed his whole weight into me and the wall stopped me from getting out of his way."

The pain on her face matched how I felt. I looked back in the mirror. The bruising was going to take a few days to come out. "Yeah, better tell Joe I'm down for a few days. Tell him I'll do a double to keep the organizers happy."

She nodded and walked out.

I turned to see the other women look at me, compassion oozing from them. "Its been worse." I told them. "I got cocky and didn't consider their size until it was too late."

"You should drink some blood." Crissy said quietly. She pointed to Bethany. "It healed her after she fell."

I struggled out of the track pants, then glanced to Beth.

"I should have died." She gave me a pained look. "Shattered my leg, hip, shoulder and cracked my head." She lifted her hands, "a week later I was walking."

I stood there staring at her. "From drinking blood?"

Paisley smirked. "I know. You're wondering if you've got brain damage right now, or think you're having some kind of epic dream."

I nodded slowly. "Close enough."

"Its true though." She leaned over and checked the temperature of the water. "The brother's blood, there's something special about them."

I just continued to stand there and stare at here.

Grinning, she held up her hand, then grabbed the robe and held it out. "Put this on for a second. Unless you want Arius to see you in your underwear."

I took the robe.

She waited until I put it on then went to the door and opened it a few inches. "Arius, can you come here for a second?"

Bethany got up and turned the water off.

A skeptical Arius opened the door a few inches and looked down at Paisley.

She smiled. "I need you for a demonstration please."

He glanced over his shoulder then back to her. "For?"

She laughed. "To show Autumn how you heal."

"Oh." He looked relieved and stepped in further, leaving the door open halfway behind him. Reaching behind himself, he pulled out a small blade and held it out to her.

She took it then held his hand open on hers.

I moved closer, a bit concerned she was going to cut her man.

He didn't take his eyes off her as she sliced across his palm.

She looked over at me. "Watch."

I looked down to see his hand bleeding.

With his eyes glowing red, he looked at her, then raised his hand and licked over his palm. Still looking at her, he turned his hand and held it so I could see.

The cut was gone. No mark was there at all.

"Behave," she said softly to him.

"How did you do that?" I looked at his hand again.

"My blood, my brothers' blood—it heals others, and us, rapidly."

I pulled the robe tighter around me. "I've never heard of anything like that."

He turned and looked at me. "Good thing for us, or we'd be hunted more than we already are."

He had a point there. I couldn't argue with that logic.

"Their saliva works too—those who are essence feeders with red eyes." Crissy said quietly.

I looked back to Paisley.

She frowned. "It's very hard to put into words."

"No doubt." I whispered and backed away.

Daxx pushed the door open and came in. "Joe—Bert, says to rest up, he'll handle the arrangements and set it up in two days."

I blew out a breath. Relieved he hadn't placed bets yet. "Great. Thanks. I should be okay by then."

"And if you're not?" She asked, tucking the phone into the back pocket of her jeans.

"Don't let them hit me and find any tender spots." I shrugged.

Paisley patted Arius on the chest. "Thank you."

He grinned down at her. "Anytime, babe."

She blushed, "behave." Then she pushed him back toward the door.

Alona brushed past him, then glanced over her shoulder. "I'm fine, Chase. It's my own emotions I'm struggling with this time." She closed the door and leaned against it. "I love him, but sometimes…"

"It's a little smothering?" Daxx offered.

"Yes, a little." Alona turned to look at me and motioned to the tub. "Please. I know it's a bit awkward, but it's us explaining or—" she motioned to the door, "them."

I took off the robe and then looked at the tub. "No offense, but I'm leaving these on," I motioned to my underwear.

"None taken." Alona said. She stood there and looked at me, her emotions plain on her face. Scowling, she turned to Daxx. "And *why* aren't they helping her?"

Daxx sat on the counter beside the sink. "I'm not even sure I know what the issue is."

I went over and slowly stepped into the large tub. Lowering carefully into the water, I sat back. "I'm sleeping here." I said to no one in particular. "My muscles are very happy right now."

"I can understand that." Daxx said with a smirk.

Bethany sat on the tiled area by the foot of the tub. "Leone told me that Michael," she touched her cheek, "and his scar have something to do with Willis Hubert, Nelson and his sister Eunice and a girl—" she looked at me then to Daxx, "*years* ago."

"Vengeance and heartache. Great this could get messy." Daxx said, then put her head back and sighed.

Alona stood beside the tub, still looking down at me. "If I could give you blood to heal, I would without hesitation." She frowned. "I have the healing saliva. I've been working my way up to deciding if I could lick another woman's mouth—" she sighed, "it's not going well."

I leaned my head to the side and looked at her. "You're like them?" I looked to Daxx. "You said all of you were from my—our side, realm."

Daxx nodded. "We are."

Alona knelt beside the tub. "My father was from here, my mother was not, she was just human." She glanced to the other women. "We're fairly certain all of our fathers, or mothers possibly, were from here."

"Really? And we were all just left behind?"

"No." She shook her head. "We're not sure what happened in all of our stories, but I was with my mother until she died when I was a child." She pointed to Paisley. "Her grandmother raised her."

I looked around at them. "So, you're saying we're all half-breeds from here?"

Bethany shrugged. "We don't know for sure." She smiled. "I don't care what label goes with my background. I'm happy here with Leone." She sighed, "Okay, I'd be happier if we could put a stop to this Hubert guy, so he'll stop abducting and hurting people."

"How bad is it?" The looks on their faces told me more was going on.

'It's bad." Paisley said quietly. "I won't go into the *whole* story right now, because it's a lot to deal with while learning that another realm exists and—all that goes with it, but I've seen pictures of women whose faces look like yours, and they didn't get that way fighting the guards." She sighed. "It's bad for both realms right now."

"So, I've landed in a war is what you're saying."

She glanced to Bethany then nodded.

Putting my head back, I closed my eyes. My entire life I'd been fighting to help people in one way or another. I always knew deep down in my soul this was what I was meant to do. Now here I was in another realm, in a time when women, and people in general, were in a war. Whatever fate's reason was for landing me here didn't matter. I opened my eyes and looked at each of these women I felt a kinship with. "I'll help." I nodded. "I wasn't kidding about going back and seeing if I can find that redheaded bitch. She told them to drug me and chain me up. We have unfinished business, her and I."

"The guys aren't going to like it." Daxx said.

"I'm not really asking." I told her softly.

"The guys—" Crissy whispered, "are out there arguing."

All of us turned and looked at the door.

"That's bullshit, Michael." One of the men growled.

I wasn't sure which one it was.

"Look at what I went through to help Bethany."

I glanced at Bethany, it must be Leone barking on the other side of the door, judging by the gentle smile on her face.

"Its been over three hundred years, get over it." Leone spat out.

I looked back to Beth, she nodded.

"Perk of this realm, you live *a lot* longer."

"Shh." Daxx held up her hand.

"Let Arius help you."

That voice I knew, it was Troy. He had a tone that commanded, and you couldn't mistake it for one of the others.

I glanced to Paisley for clarification about what her man could do.

"Arius can place suggestions inside your head." She whispered.

My eyebrows went up, despite the pain from my face. Lived hundreds of years, can get inside peoples' minds—what had I been dropped into?

"Stop looking at me like that."

Michael said it loud enough to understand clearly through the door.

"You think I want it to be this way? Right now, I'm fighting my impulse to go to the cells and crush their throats in my hands." He sounded like he was in as much pain as I was.

The women were all looking at the door. The next voice was too hushed to hear.

Someone tapped on the door. "Daxx."

It was Troy.

She jumped off the counter and went over and opened it a crack. "Yeah." She looked up.

"Please ask Autumn to cover up. I'd like to come in for a moment."

She turned to look at me. I started to get up when Alona waved her hand for me to stay and went over and grabbed a towel. She brought it over and put it in the water, then pulled it up, making sure it covered me from thighs to armpits.

Glancing over her shoulder, she nodded to Daxx.

Daxx opened the door further and Troy came in.

"I'll go find something for you to put on after." Bethany rushed to the door and went out before Daxx closed it.

Troy stood there for a moment, his jaw tense, then he looked at Alona. "Chase and Arius had to go to the apartment to stop Emil from doing something he'd regret."

She frowned. "What's going on?"

The nerve in his jaw pulsed. "Rena is pregnant."

The women's gasps had me sitting up, clutching the towel against my chest.

Alona covered her mouth and then nodded. "I'll go over for Rena."

He nodded.

She turned and looked at me. "I'll be back shortly."

I shrugged, not knowing what was going on. "Do what you have to."

Nodding abruptly, she closed her eyes, then was gone. Vanished. Disappeared., Just gone.

"Shit," I whispered.

Paisley let out a shaky breath. "We didn't get there in time."

I gave her a look, once again not understanding what was going on.

"Emil's daughter, Rena was taken to the island—" she shook her head not saying anything further.

I looked to Daxx, then to Crissy, both were fighting to keep their emotions at bay. I grabbed the side of the tub and got up, not caring if the towel covered everything or not. "Okay, chief," I nodded to Troy, "give me blood or whatever it takes. I don't have time to be down."

Paisley got up and quickly held out her hand, so I could balance better.

Troy's gaze moved down over my body slowly. "Sit back down." He said in a low tone. "Please."

Daxx came over and helped hold the towel while I lowered my stiff body back into the water. Once I was seated, she looked over her shoulder to her man. "We could use her skills, Troy."

He nodded. "I'm aware." His expression showed pain for a brief moment as he looked at me, then he turned to Daxx. "Even if I could overcome the bonds of fate binding us together for a brief moment—" he motioned to me, without looking at me, "with her mouth that way she couldn't take it unless you stabbed me in the heart with a straw." He rubbed the back of his neck. "I can not even—" he straightened and looked down at her, "contemplate healing her mouth, the very image of it makes…"

Daxx went over to him and rubbed her hand on his chest. "It's okay. I'm not going to hold fidelity against you."

He huffed out a breath. "I'm one step short of strangling my own brother right now."

She nodded. "Get in line."

I looked from them to Paisley. "What am I missing? I know my face isn't pretty right now…"

She shook her head and smirked. "It has nothing to do with you." She lifted her arm and touched the inked design on it. "This is a mating mark. No two couples have the same. Once completed, neither can even contemplate cheating on each other."

I looked at her arm, then to Troy watching me carefully. "There's nothing wrong with that. If that could work in my realm, there would be fewer kids from broken homes."

He inclined his head in a regal way. "Your understanding is humbling." Taking a deep breath, he glanced to his wife, mate, whatever she was. "I don't know if it will work, but if we move quickly it may aid her a bit."

Daxx frowned. "What are you thinking?"

Troy looked over to the sink. "Grab that glass." He came over and stood beside the tub.

I felt like a tiny child looking up at him looming over me.

"The blood needs to be fresh, pulsing—" he glanced to me, then pulled a knife from his boot. "If we move quickly it may benefit you." He looked to Daxx. "I don't know if it will work."

She looked at me, then held up the glass. "Brownie points for trying."

My brain caught up. I tilted my head back and tried to open my mouth further. It wasn't wide open, but it would work. "Just pour it in." I said then struggled to keep my mouth open. Later, I was going to have some serious creeped out moments when I thought about this. I was letting them pour warm blood in my mouth from a strange man in another realm. How hard *had* I cracked my head?

Daxx sat on the edge of the tub and held the glass up. "Better make a double cut." She said softly.

He nodded. "My thought as well." Holding his hand over the glass, he scored it twice with the blade. He didn't even wince.

We all watched the blood drip in the silence. Then Daxx nodded and turned to me. "Bottoms up." She whispered, then emptied the contents into my mouth.

I swallowed it and then looked at her. "That's one for the memories."

She snorted. "Oh, I know, it's a never-ending adventure here." She stared at my mouth then looked up at Troy and shook her head.

"Fuck." He clamped his jaw shut.

Bethany came in, her eyes were red like she'd been crying. "I just sent Leone over to help with Emil and his sons."

Troy nodded. "Quinton and Rafael still here?"

She nodded. "Leone told both of them to stay with Michael."

"Good."

She looked from him to the glass, then to me. "It didn't work?"

Daxx shook her head and stood up. "No."

Going over to the counter, Bethany set the clothes down. "I found a cami set." She motioned up and down her body. "So, it doesn't press against any injuries."

I didn't know what a cami set was but nodded. "Thanks."

Troy huffed out a breath. "Help her get dressed." He went to the door. "Give me a moment." He said under his breath. He opened the door and went out. It didn't close completely behind him.

"Oh shit." Daxx whispered, then hurried and grabbed a towel. "My king is about to speak."

Paisley and Beth came to the tub and held out their hands to me. I didn't know what was going on, but I took them and let them help me up. Daxx held out the towel and then wrapped it around me.

I bent down and pulled off the wet underwear.

"I just tried." Troy's voice came through the door. "Raf, go bring Abraham and Ellis back to the guard compound. They're to not go anywhere without an escort."

"On it." Rafael said quickly.

"Quinton you stay."

I pulled my arms free of the bra as Paisley undid it for me. Bethany knelt and patted my legs dry.

There was a loud thud in the other room. The sound you'd hear when someone was smacked up against a wall.

"You *will* help her. If you can not bring yourself to do it— step down and Quinton will." Troy said in a tone that sent a shiver up my spine.

I took the silkie shorts from Bethany and pulled them on.

"I am *not* asking, Michael." Troy growled.

Taking the top from Bethany, I pulled it on, then slipped my arms into the robe Paisley held out.

"Ladies," Troy said in a rough voice through the door, "let's give Michael and Autumn a few moments of privacy."

Daxx looked at me and gave me a questioning look.

I nodded. I didn't know what to expect, only knew if they could help me, I'd take it. I had retribution to dish out, and right now I couldn't win a fight against a mannequin if I tried.

Paisley and Beth both gave me a quick look, then went out the door. Daxx followed.

Michael's large body filled the doorway. His expression was hard. No emotions. He was completely closed off right now.

I could respect someone that was able to shut off their emotion that way. Only the best fighters were able to do that.

His gaze moved down over me slowly. The blank look on his face turned to anger.

I looked down and realized the robe was hanging open, the silky underwear Bethany had brought wasn't hiding much. I moved to close it and he came toward me quickly and stopped my hands. Normally I'd break them if someone touched me like that, but the hard expression on his face stopped me.

"I didn't know it was this bad." He said quietly and moved the robe aside to look again.

"Nothing is broken." I said and pulled the robe closed.

His blue eyes moved to hold my own in a gaze filled with torment. "I'd—" he inhaled sharply. "Let me help you."

It was more of a statement than a request.

It was on the tip of my tongue to tell him thanks, but no when he motioned to the counter.

"Please." He said softly.

I licked over my swollen lip and went over and hopped up on the counter, then immediately regretted doing it. The sudden movement made all my injuries remind me of their locations.

Michael made a soft noise in the back of his throat and came over. He stopped before he reached me. "To do that I will have to be close to you."

I could hear the hesitation in his voice. "Look, I know you don't want to—donate blood, or whatever…"

"It isn't that I don't want to, please don't misunderstand." He motioned to my face. "I could not in good conscience allow anyone, any innocent to suffer."

"I wouldn't say innocent, that—"

"You did not ask to be pulled into a battle that was not your choosing, to become a pawn in another's sick plan, so you are the innocent here."

I couldn't argue with that reasoning. "If you don't want to, your brother…"

"Will *not*. It is who you are that I struggle with."

I frowned. "No idea what your saying."

He took a deep breath. "Explanations will have to be another time, when I've reconciled with it." He reached toward my face, then paused, his gaze flicking to mine. "I apologize if the intimacy of this offends you, just know it is the only way to hasten your recovery."

I looked at his mouth, then back to his eyes. "You're going to lick my mouth, aren't you?"

He gave me a blank look.

"Alona debated doing that, but couldn't bring herself to do it."

"I see." He took another deep breath and touched my jaw, gently tipping my chin up. His hand was shaking.

I looked up to see his eyes closed and wondered what kind of demons he was fighting.

When he opened them, red eyes looked down at me.

"A bit freaky," I whispered but didn't look away.

His gaze looked at my mouth as he leaned closer.

I could feel his breath on my mouth, reflexively I licked my lips a second before his tongue stroked over my throbbing lip. It stung and was awkward, but exciting at the same time. I decided I'd better keep the last part to myself. When he lifted his head, I licked my lip and went wide-eyed when the area that had been split open was healed. I looked from his eyes to his magic mouth, ready to joke about how he could make a fortune when I noticed fangs. "Uh…"

"They are not what you think." His voice was shaking.

"I think they're freaking fangs for biting."

"They are not to harm."

I leaned back and looked up at him. "Yeah, you just need them for chewing steak?" My heart was racing now. Stupid, stupid brain. Should have listened to my flight alarms.

"Autumn," he said quietly. "I am not going to bite you."

I looked at his mouth to see no fangs, then quickly to his blue eyes. "Freaking out here. Not a good thing." I told him.

"I know. If it helps, I'm freaking out too."

I raised an eyebrow and looked at him. "Yeah, you look like it, standing there like a statue, no emotions at all."

"I've just had more time to learn to control my emotions."

I nodded. "Yeah, caught that earlier. Three hundred years, huh?" I looked him up and down. "You'll have to give me a list of supplements you take to look that good."

His mouth quirked. "I'll be sure to do that." His eyes searched mine. Then with a shaking hand he reached up and touched the swollen area surrounding my eye. "I'm trying to work up the courage to help take this away."

"You don't strike me as a man that is lacking courage." I was lying to myself through this, I wanted to see this magic blood in action, but after the whole fang thing, my own nerves were prodding me to bail.

"I hadn't thought I did—but I've never found something I fear this much." He said quietly, dropping his hand away.

I licked my lip that was now just swollen. "You swing swords—two of them that outweigh me, I can't possibly scare you."

He reached and started to undo the leather vest he wore. "You I don't fear, but it is what you represent that I do."

I watched as he undid his vest, trying to figure out what exactly that meant. No sleep was catching up fast, I couldn't put it together. Then I was a little distracted when he bared his chest and abdomen. Not only was he over three hundred years old, he had muscle tone the guys at the gym would kill for. When he pulled a blade from behind him, I leaned away.

"It's not for you." He said, his voice uneven.

I looked up to see the battle taking place behind his eyes. "You're cutting your chest." I looked at the perfectly toned muscle. "*That* chest—is a work of art."

He shook his head. "I heal fast."

"Right." I licked my lips nervously, this time, not just to feel the lack of injury to them. "I thought you'd just cut your hand like Troy did."

"Closest to the heart works best." He cleared his throat. "My brother was only trying to save me battling demons."

I dragged my eyes from his bared flesh back to his face. "Demons?"

Something sad went through his eyes briefly. "It's been a long time since I've—" he looked at the swelling in my face. "We'll have a slight bond after this."

"Bond?" I was starting to feel like my intelligence was lacking when all my brain could come up was one word at a time.

"I wasn't sure if the women had explained." He said softly, looking back to my eyes. "We'll have a connection—" he frowned, "I'm not sure how to put this into words. A temporary emotional connection after this."

I searched his eyes. "Seriously?"

Michael inclined his head. "Yes. It's not intrusive. I am able to control my emotions, meaning that you won't even know it's there."

"So, you're what, inside my head or something?" I frowned, not even able to know how that was possible with drinking blood. Yeah, I'd just thought that. *Drinking blood.* "I'm—I'd like to wake up now. This is all just a dream—I must have a concussion, right?"

He glanced at my forehead. "You may, in fact, have one."

I blew out a nervous breath. "Okay, before I wig out, lets recap." I nodded. "Your blood will heal my injuries—but we'll have some temporary emotional bond that will be void anyway because you can be iceman, right?"

His blue eyes locked on mine. "Close enough."

Inhaling deep, I exhaled, then nodded. "Let's do it before I wimp out. I have some retribution to dish out and a fight to win in two days, and I need to be at one hundred percent."

The muscle in his jaw pulsed for a moment, then he lifted the blade. "It will heal closed within a minute, so…"

"Move fast. Got it." I huffed out another nervous breath. This was really happening. Not that it was going to be a hardship to put my mouth on *that* chest, but still—blood. I winced as he dragged the blade across his own chest. I didn't wait to see if he bled like normal people, just leaned forward and put my mouth over it before I could change my mind. It didn't have the metallic taste that Troy's had, which I'd think about later. Michael inhaled deeply and rested his jaw against my head. When it sealed closed, I moved back and looked at where the cut had been. There was no evidence of it at all. If this was an illusion, I wasn't sure I wanted to wake up from it, because honestly that was the coolest thing I'd ever seen. I looked up to see glowing red eyes looking down at me. He searched my face.

"Get some rest." He spun on his heels and stomped from the bathroom.

I sat there for a second.

Quinton leaned around the door and looked in. He smiled at me, then winked. "Get some rest." He left as well.

I sighed and dropped my head into my hands. I was… I turned and looked in the mirror. There was no swelling on my face, anywhere. Slipping from the counter, I turned a looked again. It was still slightly discolored in a few spots, but that was nothing compared to what it had been. I opened the robe and yanked it off my shoulder, then looked in the mirror again. Other than a few faded marks, it was like none of the blows had happened.

"Shit." I whispered and the bit my lip lightly, just checking to see if it was all a hallucination. It wasn't.

Chapter Seven

I was going through the positions for the third time when Troy walked into the large dojo. I stopped and gave him a nod. "Hope you don't mind. I woke up and ran out of things to do in the room. You can only jog in one spot so long before you need a change of scenery. Thought about jogging the halls, but—" I shrugged. "Way too many. I was afraid I'd get lost."

He grinned and touched the side of his head. "Found her in the practice room."

I frowned and then realized he was talking to someone.

Pulling the piece out of his ear he shook his head and put his hands on his hips. "We've been looking for you for over half an hour now."

"Oh." I leaned on the bo and offered my best 'I'm sorry' look. "I didn't know where anyone was to tell them." I motioned around the room. "I found my way here and it was too hard to walk out and go look for people."

Troy tucked his hands in his pockets. "That's fine. We'll get you a phone, so you can find someone."

"Ah, thanks." I shrugged. "Never really needed a phone before."

Daxx came racing in the door. She stopped and shook her head. "Next time leave bread crumbs." She grinned. "We don't do well when we misplace people."

Arius and Paisley came in behind her. "Don't remind me." He said, then looked me up and down. "You look much better then the last time I saw you."

I waved a hand down my body. "Little magic blood goes a long way." I bounced up and down. "I feel like I could run a hundred miles today."

"Please don't." Quinton said walking in.

"Yeah he's old." Rafael said with a grin coming in behind him.

"Are we skipping food and doing practice first?" Chase asked walking in with his arm around Alona.

She smiled at me. "I think she started without us."

I smiled. "Just warming up."

Crissy came in, dropped her bag on by the door and ran to the ropes.

Leone and Bethany came in from another door behind the room. "Doesn't count if you start without me, Crissy." He shook his head and went toward the ropes.

Victor walked in, looked up and shook his head as he came over. "Michael is getting Autumn a phone."

"How's his mood?" Daxx asked.

"Brooding." Victor said quietly then inclined his head to me. "You look a great deal better then you did."

I nodded. "I feel it too. I slept like a rock."

"Rocks don't actually sleep," Crissy called down from the beam she was sitting on, "they have no identified consciousness."

I opened my mouth, closed it and looked at Daxx, she gave a quick shake of her head.

Rafael motioned to the bo in my hand. "That your weapon of choice?"

I looked at it and shook my head. "No, I was just working on the positions to warm up." I titled my chin toward Alona, "she reminded me yesterday how beneficial they can be to form."

"Well I don't know about that, but they put my mind in the right place when it's needed." Alona said.

"I can do that for you too, beloved," Chase said winking at her.

She laughed. "I'm sure we aren't thinking of the same place." Smirking at his dramatic pout, she turned to me. "What weapon do you prefer?"

"I'm not big on weapons." I held up the bo, "this is good for focusing and using as an extension." I looked at the wall of weapons. "Sharp and pointy is not my style, I'm more comfortable with the dan bong, or a pair of them."

"The what?" Paisley looked at the wall.

I nodded to Rafael and tossed him the bo. He caught it without pause. I walked over to the wall and stretched up to get two short batons, without handles, down from their pegs. I turned and held them up. "These. One is great for defensive fighting. Two is good for sparring."

Daxx gave me a curious look. "How are two of those good for sparring?" She pointed to a few of the men. "The guys prefer swords or bos. Add a bo to their arm length and it's like fighting an octopus."

"Then they're just being lazy by using a longer weapon, it just increases their reach instead of improving skills."

Daxx smirked and looked at them.

A few looked offended.

I shrugged. "But what do I know, compared to men with *years* of experience?"

"Oh." Rafael backed onto the mat. "It's on now."

I grinned. "If you insist." I looked around. "Rules of sparring?"

Rafael shrugged, "I heal."

"Ah," I glanced to Troy. "I do not. So, I'll ask that head shots be taken off the table."

He shrugged. "Fair enough."

"And do not stop or back off if you do hit me." I rolled my shoulders, making sure the muscles were loose.

Rafael frowned, "I don't want to…"

"If you do, then I've done something wrong."

He glanced at Troy, who looked at me then inclined his head to his brother.

I stepped onto the mat and gave him a slight bow.

He bowed his head to me.

"Come at me, I'll do defensive first." I tossed the one baton to the side.

He raised an eyebrow, then advanced on me. For a large man, he was very light on his feet.

He swung the bo, I ducked and came up and blocked his elbow using the baton, then twisted and he dropped the bo.

Daxx clapped. "Do more." She shouted, jumping up and down like a cheerleader.

Rafael gave her a blank look and picked up the bo again.

He wasted no time turning and aiming for my feet.

I jumped as he swung and followed through with a side kick against the arm holding the bo, then ducked in to block his elbow and twist, making him drop the bo again.

With a grin he picked it up. "You could go easy on me, it would be less embarrassing."

I laughed. "I'm moving in slow motion. Any slower and I'll have time for tea between moves."

He stood there, leaning on the bo. "No more slow motion then."

I shrugged. "Okay." Going over I picked up the other baton and smacked them together. "Now. Come at me like you would your brothers and stop treating me like a girl."

"You got this, Raf." Leone called down from the beam he sat on.

"I believe in you, Autumn." Daxx said. "Kick his ass."

Rafael widened his stance this time, his body language giving me plenty of warning that he was going to try harder this time. He held my look, instead of looking in the direction he was heading before stepping into his swing.

I used both batons to block and deflect, then spun and used a crescent kick to knock his arm away.

His recovery was fast, I ducked his next swing, then sweeping my leg out, I tried to break his balance. As he stumbled back, he used the bo to right himself. I was up and turned his own weapon into my leverage, grabbing it to land a double kick on his chest.

I landed on my knees and rolled to see him flat on the mat.

He dropped the bo. "I'm out." He looked up at me. "You're in ten places at once."

Daxx clapped again, then looked around. "Who's next."

Victor came walking toward me carrying two batons like the ones I held.

I backed up a few feet and looked at him. I grinned. "I feel like you know how to use those."

"I used to." He said and smacked them together. "My mentor used to have me use them to practice speed and reflex."

"How long ago was that?"

He smirked, "Best not ask questions you won't like the answers to."

I nodded my head slowly. "Warning received." Putting the weapons together in my hands, I formally bowed to him.

He did a full bow back.

The next few minutes were invigorating. All that could be heard were the batons connecting in rapid succession. I had to push myself to keep up with his hits. He changed the direction and sweep often. I changed when I advanced on him. We didn't stop until both of us were out of breath.

I bowed again. "That was great."

He returned the bow. "It was a challenge. You were hard to keep up with."

I smiled. "I was thinking the same thing."

"I don't know about the rest of you, but I'm starving after that workout." Quinton said from where he sat on the mat.

Troy looked down at him. "Watching was hard work?"

Quinton nodded.

"I'm sorry." I wiped the sweat off my brow. "Did I hog the mat?"

Arius shook his head. "No. We've been getting more than enough practice lately with chasing down Hubert's army and their locations."

"Have any to hit today?" The idea of getting back at the people that took me sounded like something I needed to do. I looked at the others, then back to Arius.

"We have a few places to check." He crossed his arms over his chest.

"Need any help?" I wiped my brow again.

"Not until she's had practice dodging real weapons."

We turned to see Michael leaning against the wall by the door.

I looked back at Arius.

"He out-ranks me," he offered with an apologetic look.

Looking down at the batons in my hands, I went over to put them back on the wall. When I turned Michael was walking toward me.

"We're heading to the dinning room." Troy called out. "Michael, bring Autumn so she doesn't get lost."

Michael paused and turned around to watch everyone leaving. Looking back to me, he motioned to the door.

I put my hand over my stomach. "I'm so hungry. Woke up hungry. I slept like a rock…" I pointed to him, "don't tell me rocks don't sleep."

He gave me an odd look. "Crissy?"

I nodded. "She says the strangest things, knows the strangest things."

He opened the door for me. "She has visions, hundreds a day, so her focus is always scattered—or she'll blurt something out without realizing it."

I paused. "Visions? That actually explains a lot. She'd come to my self-defense training, but never participated. Just mumbled to herself."

"She's helped us on many fronts. With locations," he motioned for me to turn, "if she hadn't seen Paisley jump off that island inside her head, she may have drowned."

"Don't suppose she can see what my next opponent looks like? Big, small?"

Michael gave me a brief look. "No, she can't summon what she wants to see."

"Too bad."

He reached into his pocket and held out a phone. "This is yours, so we don't have a repeat of this morning."

I took it.

He held out an ear piece.

I put in in my pocket and looked at the phone. "I've never had a phone." I pushed one of the buttons on the side and the screen lit up. "Never had anyone to call."

He stopped and held out his hand. "This brand is relatively simple. Makes it easier for us to use it while we're on the move." He pushed the button, then tapped the screen. It opened with four symbols on the screen. "Messages, calling, camera and our group." He held it out to me again. "Anything else is accessed by pushing the middle button and scrolling through the list that pops up."

I nodded. "Thanks. I can leave it here when I go back."

His blue eyes darkened slightly as he looked at me. "Keep it. It's yours."

"Are you sure? These can't be cheap." I kept it in my hand, afraid it might fall out of the pocket in the workout pants I was wearing.

"I'm quite sure. My family can afford it."

We started walking again. "I guess so. You've had several hundred years to get good at managing money."

Michael turned and looked at me, a look that seemed like doubt on his face. "The girls didn't tell you?"

I blew out a breath. "I was really out of it during our bathroom chat. I'm still remembering things they said."

"That's understandable after your day and state of your health. In case they didn't tell you, my family and I are the royal family here. Troy and Chase are both kings."

"Wow. I thought *my king* was a pet name Daxx used to call her man."

He shook his head. "Not a pet name."

"You're a prince?"

He gave me a brief look. "I am."

I smiled. "I've never met a prince before, or kings and queens. That's one for the memories. I got to fight with royalty."

He motioned to a door. "We're here."

I touched his arm, so he'd stop, then dropped my hand away. "Thanks for the assist last night." I motioned to my face. "I know you didn't want to, but I appreciate it." Stretching up, I kissed his cheek quickly then went into the dining room.

When I walked in Mitz was setting down a tray. I put my phone on the table carefully then hurried to help her.

Walking into the kitchen, I saw two more trays on the counter. "I'll give you a hand."

She turned and looked at me. "You look much better."

I grinned. "I feel much better." Picking up the dish, I turned and followed her out.

Setting it on the table, I went back and sat down at the end of the table. Mitz smiled at me and went back into the kitchen.

Daxx looked at Michael. "Did you catch Autumn in action?" She grinned. "A beautiful thing."

Michael gave her brief look, then grabbed a bowl. "I did. Saw her knock Raf on his ass."

Rafael waved his fork at him. "You try catching her long enough to stop her."

Michael turned and looked at me. "Another time, perhaps."

I cocked my head, then smiled. "Anytime you want." I looked around to the others. "New sparring partners are great. The guys at the gym are so predictable now, it's hard to stay fresh when you know what they're going to do next."

Mitz came in carrying a plate and cup. She walked down the table and set it in front of me. "Green tea and breakfast. All fresh, no oils."

My mouth dropped open as I looked at the plate then to her. "It's like you read my mind. Thank you."

"It is my pleasure, love." She nodded then turned and went back in the kitchen.

I looked back to the others.

"You don't drink coffee in the morning?" Alona inquired.

I shook my head. "I never drink caffeine. I try only to put natural ingredients in. Too many oils and stimulants can weigh you down and burn you out fast."

She toasted me with her cup. "Good for you. I, however, require the caffeine to motivate."

I shrugged, "each to their own, right? I took a sip of the tea. "How's that girl, Rena?"

Alona sighed. "Trying to come to terms with it all."

I set my cup down. "It's hard. Seen it a lot in my neighborhood. I could go talk to her." I shrugged, "I know this woman that makes rounds with women in that situation, or unexpected pregnancies at least. She helps them fall in love with their baby before it's born." I glanced around to a few of the women. "You know, so they don't end up like me, with no home or family."

"It's that common over there?" Troy asked.

Daxx and Bethany both nodded.

I sat back. "There are a lot of children without homes."

Michael waved his hand around. "How can there be children—young children just wandering around, no homes and no one notices?" He scowled.

"It's not that no one notices, Michael," Alona said quietly, "most are not in a position to do anything about it."

I nodded. "She's right. When you're struggling to keep from starving or trying to keep a roof over your own kids, you have to look the other way and pretend it's not happening." I looked from his glare to Troy. "What about over here?"

Troy glanced to his twin for a moment. "I'll admit not all areas of our realm are perfect, but we strive to help those that are lacking."

Leone nodded. "We go in and set up sites, help them build—find work, even train them if needed."

Rafael glanced up from his plate. "The witches from the temple make rounds and help those that need healing…"

"Witches? Like *witches*, witches?"

He grinned. "Yeah like witches, spells and magic."

"That's real?" I looked to Daxx then back to him.

"Yeah. Very real." He took another bite.

Crissy knelt on her chair and held up a notebook. "I don't know what this symbol means." She waved it around. "Have any of you seen it?"

Daxx took the book and looked at it, shaking her head. "I've never seen it."

She passed it across the table to Alona.

Alona looked at it. "There's something vaguely familiar, but I can't place it." She handed it to Bethany.

"We need to find it." Crissy said then shook her head. "It's got bad all around it."

"Another location, heart?" Victor asked her in a gentle tone.

"I don't know." She looked upset. "Its all pieces, I can't figure them out."

He reached over and clasped her hand. "You'll figure it out."

Bethany shook her head and handed it to Paisley.

Paisley frowned, "I have seen it, but it could be anywhere." She glanced at Arius, "I've done some gigs in some pretty strange places." Turning she held the book down the table to me.

I stood up and reached and took it. Sitting down I looked at the symbol. It was sketched and not in color, but I knew what it was. I looked up at Crissy. "You'll find it at abandoned warehouses, and other places. It's the symbol the organizers use for the underground fights." I shrugged. "I'll be at one of them in two days." I got up and went back and gave her the notebook.

She took and nodded her head quickly, then turned to Victor. "We have to be there."

He frowned and glanced to Troy, then Michael. "For the fight or to go there now?"

I went and sat back down. "You can't be there ahead of the fight. Joe won't even know which location is being used until a few hours beforehand. They send it out at the last minute, so the cops—" I paused and looked at Michael, "don't find out."

"Send it out?" Leone asked.

Daxx nodded. "Probably have a list they text it to."

"What did you see with this symbol, Crissy?" Michael turned to her.

Crissy sat back and looked around. "It was important, urgent," she nodded, "there's no blood. But we need to be there."

Michael glanced to me then turned to Troy.

Troy looked down the table at me. "We had hoped to dissuade you from going to it…"

I leaned forward in my chair. "You can't. I don't show up and they'll come after Joe. It's already set up, they don't like people backing out."

Leone looked at Michael. "It's possible Hubert is behind them."

Michael tapped his hand on the table while looking at him. "In an attempt to raise money?"

Chase gave me a serious look, "How often are they held?"

I shrugged. "I only fight a few a month, but they have them all the time. I could do a few a week if I wanted." I shook my head. "I can't do that many. The last few months the opponents keep getting bigger and bigger. I don't know where they're getting them from, but it's all I can do to walk after the matches."

Michael gave Arius a hard look. "Sounds like she's fighting some of ours."

I snorted. "They're not stacked like you guys are, but they're still big."

"It may be how they found her." Arius mused glancing to Victor.

"Her name isn't in any of the files." Bethany told them. "I checked."

Victor glanced to me briefly, a soft look on his face. "Her birth would have to be registered for them to trace her."

I frowned, "wait, your saying they're tracking down women like that?"

He nodded. "Yes. As far as we can tell they've found a way to track any that may be children from—" he looked at Paisley, "relationships with residents from our realm."

"So, you guys really think I'm part," I waved my hand around, "that one of my parents are from here?"

"Yes." Victor gave Michael a quick glance. "The fact you fight as well as you do, would make you extra appealing."

I snorted. "Well if they're setting up fights to watch me, they're not making any money on their guys," I frowned, "unless they're betting against their own fighters." I nodded. "Let's hope they're looking for me at this next one. I have some serious business to settle with that redheaded…"

"You're planning to fight still?" Michael scowled at me.

Nodding, I picked up my fork. "Oh yeah, and if I see that chick again, the fight will be off the platform."

His jaw clenched shut, I could see the muscle pulsing in the side of it. He turned slowly to look at Troy.

"We'll be there, Michael."

Crissy sighed loudly. "Now if I could just figure out the plants in my head."

"You're still seeing herbs?" Rafael asked her.

She nodded. "I don't know if they're herbs now, I've read all the books we could find and haven't seen them."

I swallowed what I'd been chewing. "Maybe it's a foreign plant, like Chinese or other oriental origin." I picked up my cup. "My mentor used to have some pretty strange looking plants."

"Oh." She looked at Victor then stood up on her chair. "I have to get to the library." She leaned over and kissed him quickly, then grabbed a biscuit off her plate and hopped off the chair. "I need to get Bronx to carry the books." She pulled out her phone and ran out the door.

Chase turned to look at Victor. "You're going to have the whole library in your room soon."

Victor gave him an unamused look. "We just went through all the books and took back those she'd committed to memory."

I put my cup down. "She can do that?"

He nodded.

"She has these visions and a photographic memory," I looked to Paisley, "that's what it's called right?" She nodded.

"Yes." Victor said.

"Troy says inside her head is unlike anything he's ever seen." Daxx said as she reached for the pitcher to fill her glass.

I looked at Troy. "You see inside people's heads?"

He nodded. "I can."

"Wow, stay out of mine, can't have you knowing all my moves."

He smirked.

"Do you have an ability?" Bethany asked.

I gave her a wide-eyed look. "I can fight and talk at the same time, that's about it."

"You don't need anything extra after what I saw earlier." Daxx said with a smile.

"Thanks." I looked at the others. "So, do you guys all have abilities?" I motioned to Arius and then Troy. "Or just these two and Crissy?"

"I don't need one," Chase said, "I have my charming ways."

Alona laughed quietly. "I'm an empath—I'm basically an emotional sponge."

My eyebrows went up. "I don't envy that. It's gotta suck with some of the people out there."

"Oh, yes. It's not always a fun time." She said dryly.

I glanced to Bethany, she held up her hands and bright red colors and sparks moved between her hands. My mouth dropped open.

"It's energy, I can hit things with it—" she lowered her hands and shrugged, "I haven't figured out if I can use it other ways." She smiled. "I'm a witch."

"That is—so cool." I nodded and looked at Leone.

He shook his head. "I'm just me. What you see is what you get."

Bethany leaned against him. "I'm good with that."

He smiled down at her then leaned closer and kissed her.

"I get the odd vision." Rafael said, "nothing compared to Crissy, and mine don't seem to lead anywhere important."

"You saw Daxx before she was here." Troy said. "That's important." He winked at Daxx.

I looked at Paisley.

She grinned. "I manipulate time." She tossed her fork in the air and held her hand out. The fork stopped and stayed there.

"That's—I don't have a wow word to describe that."

She grinned and closed her hand. Arius caught her fork before it hit the table.

Daxx looked down the table at me. "The rest of us are just plain normal people," she glanced at them, "well mostly."

I blew out a breath and sat back. "At some point all of this is going to sink in, and then I may run screaming down the hall."

Everyone turned to look at Chase.

He scowled. "Hey. It was one time."

Alona covered her mouth and laughed.

Michael pulled out his phone and frowned at it. He stood up. "I have to go." He motioned to Leone with a jerk of his chin. "I'm going to need you."

Leone leaned over and kissed Bethany and stood up.

Rafael pushed his chair back. "I'm headed to the temple, to see if Clairee's coven picked up anything off those chains we took off Autumn."

I gave him a startled look. "Like what?"

He shrugged. "Hoping for a direction to start with. See if we can figure out where they took you."

I got up. "Can I do anything to help that?"

He shook his head. "Not unless you know locator spells."

I huffed out a breath. "Not that I know of."

"You can help us in the woman's cave." Daxx got up. "We're going through the files again on the computers, see if we missed anything of use."

I bit my lip. "I'm not good with computers. I can read, but it's not my strength."

Troy stood up. "Autumn can come with me to the guard's training yard. I need to speak to Ira before I have a nap. She can see what it's like with real weapons." He turned and gave Michael a look.

Michael gave him a cold look then turned to look at me. "Just watching, don't try to jump in against swords."

I shrugged. "I know my limits."

He gave an abrupt nod of his head and turned on his heel and walked out through the kitchen.

I picked up my plate. "Just let me take this out." I hurried along the table out to the put the plate in the sink.

Chapter Eight

I tried to remember the turns and halls as we walked to the guards' training yard.

Troy looked down at me. "If you're trying to memorize the halls, good luck. Daxx is still trying."

I frowned. "Did you just read my mind?"

He laughed. "No, It's the intense focus on your face."

"I like going for a run when I wake up." I shrugged. "I guess it's not important. I won't be here long."

He was quiet for a few moments. "I don't think it's a good idea to go back right now." He motioned for me to turn. "You're important to them. They haven't brought any others to this side, at least not yet."

I looked down a hall we went past. "I don't know why. Unless they want a fighter." I waved my hand up and down beside him. "With the size of the males from here—what could I possibly offer that they need?"

Troy opened a door. "Until we find out what it is, you need to stay here."

I stepped through to see we had reached the yard. "As long as I get back for the fight, I guess vacationing in another realm with the royal family will be okay." I smirked.

"When you put it that way, it sounds much better than it actually is." He motioned to the building I'd been in last time.

"I have to speak with Ira—that's Mitz's mate, he runs the guards' house." He smirked. "Try not to break any of my guards."

I held up my hands. "I'll try, but no promises." I watched him walk away, then stood there looking around. It was a giant outdoor gym, with some horses at one end. I turned to see Rafael talking with a few other large-bodied males. Seriously, why were all these guards so big? I went over to him.

He smiled when I reached him.

"How did you get here before us?"

He shrugged. "I don't walk around here or I'd never get anything done."

I realized he'd ported here. I motioned to the door. "We took the long way."

"This is where you'll find me, if I'm not hanging out at the temple."

I looked at him. "Witches all females?"

He smirked. "How did you know?"

I shrugged. "You have a bit of a player vibe about you."

"Uh," he put his hand against his chest, "I'm crushed you think that of me."

I rolled my eyes and then looked around. "So, what do you do here?"

"I'm Captain of the guards." He started walking, keeping his eye on the six men practicing.

"So, I guess you don't want them knowing I disarmed you a few times this morning?"

He gave me a charming smile. "I'd prefer them not to know things like that."

"I'll keep it quiet for now." I stopped and watched one of the men using two of their large swords to warm up. I could barcly lift one, and here he was swinging two around like they were made of plastic. "Does he fight with two or is he just warming up?"

Rafael turned to look. "Just one. There aren't many others not in my family that use two anymore." He grinned. "I can still feel the aches that went with learning to use the two in the beginning."

I snorted. "When your brothers found me, I was trying to be threatening, holding one and not tipping over on my face."

With a smirk he looked me up and down. "You weren't in great condition then—not to mention you couldn't get the right balance with your legs chained."

I bit my lip and frowned. "That's true."

Rafael waved his hand to the man, then held it out. The guard tossed one of the swords to him from ten feet away, and Rafael caught it without so much as a muscle flinching. He looked down at me. "Want to try again?"

I glanced around for Troy, then nodded. "Okay, but if you see Michael let me know. I'm supposed to be spectating."

Rafael shrugged. "He'll get over it." His expression was serious. "I wasn't born for one hundred and thirty years after it happened, so I don't really know all the aspects of the incident that has him so on edge right now."

I gaped at him. "I'm still having trouble with the age thing here."

He laughed. "Yeah, I guess it's hard to grasp." With a nod, he held the sword out to me. "This one is heavier then our actual weapons."

I nodded. "To work the muscles so that the real deal is easier and more fluid"

"Yes." He smiled. "It's cool talking to a woman that understands fighting and training techniques."

I reached for it with one hand, he shook his head. I wrapped both around it, then had to adjust my balance as Raf let the weight he was carrying go. "I'm very impressed with anyone that can swing these around with one hand."

Rafael stepped beside me, "check your form, you're leaning forward—and I can't fight the way you do, so we're even." He nodded as I righted my frame so my shoulders and hips were aligned.

"Daxx uses two katanas like we do the swords, it's much lighter. You may want to give those a test and see." He shrugged. "The way you moved with Victor in practice, you could be as lethal as a tornado with blades."

I moved both hands in one direction checking the weight. My muscles were sure they didn't like swords. "The guy—" I glanced at him, "the one I messed up, he's lucky I didn't drop the sword on him accidentally and do a lot more damage."

Rafael chuckled, then reached out and took the weapon to relieve me of the weight. He turned and whistled. A guard a few feet from us turned around, then Rafael tossed the sword in the air toward him. The guard caught it. Rubbing the back of his neck, Rafael turned back and gave me a serious look. "Ira told me you spotted a few in here yesterday that were sloppy."

"I wouldn't say sloppy, but there was over-reaching, and you guys aren't exactly fighting exhibition matches with wooden weapons."

"Exactly." He motioned to the large group. "Want to come watch and point out any that need correcting?"

I gave him a curious look. "I know you could spot them."

He nodded. "I can, but a new perspective never hurts—" he motioned the men we were walking toward, "these are first-year recruits, so now is the time to fix all those bad habits."

I was having a blast. New bodies, fresh minds, and a totally different style of fighting. Not like the same guys from the gym. A few times Rafael and Ira let me step into the center of the recruits and show them how to correct their stance and reach—minus the heavy sword of course. Rafael tossed me a lightweight wooden one, so I could show the recruits how easy it was to disarm someone with sloppy form.

Troy stood back and watched, not saying much. I realized it was because he was a king. If he spoke it would come across as a command.

I was standing off to the side, talking with Rafael and Ira when two of the men got a little loud. One tossed his sword a few feet away and motioned for the other to come at him. The second straightened up and, without looking, tossed his weapon—it was coming right for us. I tried to step out of the way and bumped into one of the others. It hit my thigh.

I felt the sting a second later and looked down to see blood soaking my pant leg. I sat down and pressed on it. Rafael dropped down beside me and pressed his hand against it.

There was a low growl, as Michael grabbed the man by the throat and glare at him. Ira was there and said something to Michael, who released the man with a shove and rushed over to me.

"How bad is it?" Troy was beside him.

"Pretty deep." Rafael answered without looking away from my leg.

Michael pulled a strap off one of the cases strapped to his leg and dropped down to his knees. Wrapping it around my leg, he made a quick tourniquet. Before I could say a word, he scooped me up into his arms, like I weighed no more than a doll.

Then the cramping filled my stomach. Inhaling, I blinked to see we were in the bedroom. "Don't be mad at him." I said.

His eyes flicked to mine as he carried me into the bathroom and set me on the counter. "Tossing one of those weighted swords without looking could end fatally. It will be months before he touches a weapon again."

I hissed out a breath as he ripped the pant leg open. "What-what will they do to him?"

He straightened and pulled the weapons off his back, setting them on the floor quickly. The straps that held them came next. "He'll go back to the first day of his training and start again."

I grabbed a towel and pressed on my leg. "Everyone deserves a second chance."

Michael unbuttoned his jacket and shrugged out of it. "You are more forgiving then I am."

I looked at the blood seeping through the towel. "Could be from blood loss."

He growled softly as he undid his vest, then pulled a knife from behind his back.

I leaned my head against the mirror. "Have enough weapons on you?"

He stepped closer to rest his thighs against the counter. "Too many at the moment." Without ceremony, he sliced into his chest and grasped the back of my head, pulling me toward the wound.

I remembered how fast he healed and wasted no time closing my mouth over it.

He inhaled sharply, and I figured it had to sting a little.

When it sealed, he leaned back and cut himself again, his red eyes locked on mine as he did.

I licked the trail of blood from his skin, then sucked on it until it closed.

His hand released my head and he stepped back, pulling my hand and the towel off my leg. Then he undid the tourniquet cautiously.

I was going to turn on the water to wash when he bent down and licked over the still tender wound. I touched his thick black hair as his tongue moved carefully over my leg. This was a new feeling, unsettling as his mouth moved on my leg. When he stood up, there was no blood gushing from my leg, it left just a faint red mark.

"It will heal further with the amount of blood I gave you."

I looked up at him. "That's amazing by the way. Thank you."

"It shouldn't have happened." His voice was hoarse.

I studied his red eyes briefly, then looked at his mouth. "The fangs," I looked back to his eyes, "you were going to explain them, later." I could see the indecision on his face. "I go back tomorrow, so now is a good time."

"I don't want you to fight tomorrow."

I opened my mouth to tell him I was when he gave me a look that stopped me.

"I know you have to." He said quietly.

I nodded.

He continued to just stand there, his glowing eyes holding mine.

My heart felt like it was doing its own workout inside my chest. "The fangs?" I said in an unsteady voice.

He looked at my neck.

I held my breath.

"My kind live on more than food and water. We believe it's what sustains our longevity…"

"If you say blood, I'm out of here." I warned him.

His gaze moved back to my face. "Not blood."

The breath I'd been holding whooshed out. "Then what?"

"The different colored eyes mean different feeding requirements—" he tilted his head, "except magic users who seem to be the exception."

"So, red eyes." I searched his as I asked.

"Essence." He whispered.

I nodded briefly. "Which is?"

His gaze went back to my throat. "It's best described as your life force, the invisible energy that flows through your body in your blood."

I swallowed the nervous lump in my throat. "But you said…"

"Not blood. It's a complicated explanation, the anatomy of our fangs—one I don't care to go into right now."

I nodded again. "You bite," I looked at his mouth then back to his eyes, "you bite people to get this essence?"

"Yes." He stood there, his chest rising and falling visibly, but that was the only movement.

"That sounds painful for the one without fangs."

"Not if I don't want it to be." He licked his lips.

I caught a brief glance of his fangs; a shiver went through me.

"We can inject an agent into the person that numbs the bite, so there is no pain." He stepped closer.

I held my breath again. I'd asked and pushed for an answer, so I couldn't freak out about it now that he'd obliged. "So-so everyone smells like a snack to you?"

His gaze shifted to my face again, the black lashes in contrast surrounding them sent another shiver though me.

"Some do."

I licked my lips, my mouth suddenly dry. "Do I?" I couldn't look away from his gaze. "Smell like a snack?"

He reached out, moving so I would see his motions and not react on reflex. With a soft touch he ran the back of his hand down the side of my neck. "And so much more." He whispered.

I looked up at him. "It may be the blood loss, or adrenalin, but I'm finding all of this really sexy right now."

Michael looked at my mouth. "I know."

"Autumn." Daxx screamed from the room.

Michael stepped back.

Daxx came running into the bathroom. "Troy called me." She rushed over. "Oh, shit."

I looked down to see I still held the blood-soaked towel.

"How bad?" She looked at it then to Michael. "Did you heal it?"

Michael waved his hand down his open vest.

She nodded, then leaned down to look at it. "How the hell did this happen?"

"Carelessness of a recruit." Michael bent down and picked up his jacket, then swords.

"Guess he's going to be a recruit a bit longer." She let out a loud breath and looked at me. "You good?"

I looked at Michael, meeting his blue eyes. "A little shaky." I wasn't sure if it was from being close to him or the blood loss.

"Get her some juice and something to eat." Michael said in a quiet voice. "I'll stay with her until you return.

Daxx nodded and went out the door quickly.

Stepping back over, he tucked his swords under his arm with his jacket and held out his hand. "Go slow. The muscles may take a few moments to accept your weight."

I turned, letting my legs hang over the counter, then took his hand. Gradually I stood, checking for any pain or weakness. "I think it's good."

"Don't overdo it until you've replaced the blood loss." He didn't release my hand.

When he tilted his head and looked down at me, his thick hair shifted to hang over his forehead, making his blue eyes seem brighter. With my free hand, I reached up and touched his jaw. "You being my hero is becoming a habit."

His gaze flicked to my mouth a few times. "One I'd like not to repeat too frequently."

Keeping the weight on my leg that hadn't been injured, I stretched up and brushed my mouth over his. He didn't pull away, so I did it again. He closed his eyes for a second, his breath tickling my lips, then opened them and kissed me back with a firm kiss.

Straightening, he stepped back and held our hands up. "I have to get back." He let go of my hand slowly and stepped back again. With an abrupt nod, he spun on his heel and walked out.

Daxx came in right after he left, a bottle of juice in one hand and a plate in the other. "He's trying to outrun his shadows."

I shook my head. "He's hot one second then ice the next."

She snorted. "That's a family trait." She looked me up and down. "First thing, we need to get you new pants, then Crissy needs our help mapping the halls."

I looked down at the blood covered material hanging off my leg. "I remember now why I don't like pointy weapons."

Daxx laughed. "They're better then guns."

I nodded slowly. "That's true, even I can't dodge a bullet."

Chapter Nine

An hour later I stood in a hallway with Bethany. We both looked at our phones looking at the diagram of halls Crissy had sent us.

"If I open this and someone jumps out at us, I'm going to scream." Alona's voice came through the ear piece.

"I'll stab them." Daxx said dryly.

Beth looked at me and grinned.

"Can't be worse than me opening the door on those maids, they bowed to me." Paisley's voice whispered. "Too bad I can't pipe some music through the phones as we look."

"Then I'd want to dance." Crissy answered. "What's behind the door, Alona?"

There was a sigh. "It's a storage closet." She answered sounding relieved.

"Okay." Crissy sounded excited. "What about you and Autumn, Beth? What's behind your doors?"

Beth looked at the two doors on either side of the hall. "Pick one." She told me.

Taking a deep breath, I stepped to the one on my left and then looked at her. "Should I knock?"

She nodded. "I think we should start doing that from now on."

I nodded. "Okay." I raised my hand to knock and the door opened. Michael stood in the doorway.

He looked at me, then to Beth, and raised an eyebrow. "Were you looking for me?"

I shook my head. "No. Just wondered what was behind this door."

"My room." He gave Bethany a curious look.

She held her hand against the ear piece. "Left is Michael's room."

"Well there goes my theory that he lives in a cave." Daxx said.

I grinned.

Bethany pointed to the other door and looked at Michael. "What's this room?"

He frowned, "Rafael's room." Stepping closer he grasped my hand lightly and turned my phone so he could see the screen.

"One to the right is Rafael's" Beth said, still smirking.

"You're mapping the halls?" He looked at me.

I nodded. "Crissy is, we're just doing the legwork."

He glanced at the phone again. "The hotline?"

I looked at the little icon at the top of the screen for the group call thing Daxx had set up and shrugged.

Beth laughed, "you have the connection with your brothers, we had to cheat."

He glanced at her, then back to me, his gaze moving over my face. "The last thing I need are my brothers' voices in my ear non-stop."

There were a few chuckles through the ear piece.

"I hit a dead end, Crissy." Paisley said.

"Okay. Go back to that other hall." Crissy sounded distracted.

Michael just continued to stand there and look at me. He hadn't released my hand yet, either. I watched his blue eyes darken as he looked at my mouth. He leaned closer.

I held my breath when I could feel his breath against my cheek.

"Meeting in Victor's office in a half hour, ladies." He whispered in a rough tone. Straightening, he looked at me again for a second, then let go of my hand and turned on his heel and went down the hallway.

"Jeeze, scare the crap out of me." Daxx said.

"Sent a shiver up my spine," Alona said with a chuckle.

Beth hissed out a breath. "I thought Autumn was going to fry a chip in her ear piece the way they were looking at each other."

I dragged my gaze from the man walking down the hall and looked at her. "He has that being intense thing mastered."

Someone snorted.

"Another family trait." Daxx said in a quiet tone.

"What's the meeting about?" Crissy asked.

"No idea." Paisley answered first, "Arius hasn't been very communicative today."

"That's never good for us." Alona said.

"Yeah. We better get to Victor's." Daxx mumbled. "Good time to try out this map."

"Another day or so and I'll have it done." Crissy said, sounding like she was running. "Then I'll have to do Chase's side."

"Don't bother." Alona said. "All the action is over here. We don't even use the dining room over there—actually I'm not sure we even have one."

Beth moved the picture around on her screen, then looked the direction Michael had gone and motioned with her head. "We're going to go in the direction Michael went—it's not mapped, but I guess it turns somewhere to lead us back to Victor and his office."

"I don't know that hall at all." Crissy said quietly. "Try to remember where it turns, so I can mark it down."

"I can't believe you've been trying to do this alone." Daxx said.

"Yeah," Paisley said, "I would have gotten lost so many times."

"I have it all in my head." Crissy whispered, sounding distracted again, "it's just that drawing it out is hard to do."

"No doubt." I hissed out a breath. "I can get to the practice room, and that's about all my head remembers."

Beth pointed to the hall Michael had turned down. "Making a left turn."

"That won't lead to the offices." Crissy said, "unless it doubles back some where I don't know about."

Beth stopped walking. "Should we turn around?"

I looked at the phone waiting for an answer.

"I say go for it, see where it goes. These guys having the advantage all the time gets on my nerves." Daxx said.

"I agree with her." Alona said.

Beth shrugged and looked at me then started walking again.

"It's a dead end with only a door." I informed them.

"Door to another hall maybe?" Paisley asked.

"Could be." Crissy said. "I don't know about it though."

"It is possible there is one thing you don't know." Daxx teased her.

"There's a lot of things I don't know." Crissy laughed softly. "I need to read more books."

"Yeah, okay Miss knows-more-than-the-internet." Daxx said in a monotone voice.

We stopped at the door and looked at each other.

"So, we're guessing door to another hallway?" Beth clarified.

"Sure." Daxx answered.

"I vote hallway too." Paisley said.

"I'll vote after you open it and look." Alona said with a chuckle.

I nodded to Beth. "Behind door number one is…"

She opened it and we both leaned to look. "Not a hall." She whispered.

It was a small room, almost like a reception office with a few other doors. There were a few men standing there and one woman, they all turned to look at the door and none of their eyes were normal human eyes. I didn't pause to count the different glowing colors.

Beth started to pull the door closed when one of the doors opened and Rafael came out grinning down at a small petite woman with black hair. He glanced at us then paused.

A second later another door opened and Michael stepped out. His eyes were red.

Beth pulled the door closed and gave me a nudge to get moving, we started jogging back down the hall. "Um, guys I think we found their—diner."

"Their what?" Daxx asked.

"You found the dialup fast food pizzeria?" Alona whispered.

"Uh, yeah, we'll go with that." Beth said glancing up from her phone and pointing for me to turn down the hall. "Raf and Michael were there."

"What did they do?" Paisley asked.

Beth pointed to another hall, we kept jogging. "We didn't stick around to see."

"Your men go there to feed or whatever?" I asked, still not sure what I'd just seen.

"Troy doesn't anymore." Daxx said, now she sounded like she was running.

"Arius either." Paisley said then hissed out a breath. "How can I be lost *with* a map in my hand?"

"Victor doesn't use others anymore either," Crissy said, "he says I'm all he needs."

"How sweet. Chase is exasperating, but he can't possibly feed from others after the amount he does from me." Alona said quickly. "He'd be fat." She chuckled.

Beth pointed to the next hall. "Leone says other essence tastes like ass now, so I know he doesn't."

"How many eye colors are there?" I asked keeping my pace slow to keep up with Beth.

We went around the corner to see Alona, Daxx and Crissy running toward us.

Paisley came from the other hall then slid to a stop.

We all looked at each other, then down the hall to see Rafael and Michael striding toward us.

Daxx held out her hand. "Port to Victor's office?"

The others nodded and touched her arm. I glanced at Michael and decided this wasn't a discussion I was equipped to have right now. I grasped her arm.

When my stomach cramped, I let go and looked around. We were in a large office with a table in the middle. Troy and Chase both straightened from the desk and turned to look at us. Victor stood up from behind the desk and glanced at Crissy.

"How's the mapping going?"

She nodded. "Good."

Alona pulled the ear piece out of her ear and tucked it in her pocket.

The rest of us realized we didn't need to be on the phone with each other and took out ours.

"They look guilty." Chase said, glancing to his twin.

"Seems so, of what, is my concern." Troy replied tucking his hands in his pockets, his gaze moving over Daxx.

She grinned. "You wouldn't believe some of the things we've seen when opening closed doors."

Chase smirked and looked at Alona, "anything I should go see?"

She blushed and shook her head. "I don't think so."

The door opened, and Quinton walked in, his phone to his ear. "They're all here." He said then smirked and looked at Daxx. He nodded and hung up the phone.

Arius and Leone walked in behind him.

Leone smiled and went over and wrapped his arms around Bethany. "Get the map done?"

She hugged him, "not quite, had to pause for this meeting."

Arius' gaze didn't move from Paisley. "Caught an accelerated energy level," he smirked, "you are not planning another dance are you?"

I frowned and looked at Alona.

She waved it off. "Through their bond." She went over and leaned against Chase, "the men monitor our every move."

Chase put his arm around her. "That makes us sound like stalkers, we only do it for your safety."

Leone nodded. "Like when those creeps got into Alona's apartment."

Beth gave him a quick look. "Yes, a good reason for monitoring emotions."

I didn't know what to say to that.

"I guess you don't pick up anything from Michael through the blood bond." Paisley asked glancing up from her phone.

I shook my head. "I don't think so. Either he's void of emotion or the iceman."

Daxx snorted. "They are able to hide their emotions, unlike us poor, meek women-folk."

Troy grinned. "Yes, because that description fits," he glanced at Chase for a moment, "none of the women in this room."

Arius crossed his arms and looked at Paisley. "That didn't answer my question."

Paisley lowered her phone and rolled her eyes. "Put the beast away. I jogged back to meet them and got lost while doing it."

He frowned. "You had a map in your hand."

"It's not updated yet." Crissy said, then nodded and went and sat in the corner by Victor's desk.

Daxx shrugged and looked at Beth briefly. "Why are we meeting? Do we have a target?" She gave Troy a hopeful look. "Do I get to kick some ass today?"

I couldn't help grinning.

"Not that I know of." He motioned to me with the movement of his chin. "We need to set up who is where tomorrow. Because we won't have a location until the last minute…"

"And keeping in mind that if any of Hubert's men or women are present, the temple will have their hands full cloaking our real identities..." Chase looked back to Troy.

"So, we will go in light, just us and Emil." Troy nodded.

Daxx went over and sat at the table. "Emil is coming?"

Chase nodded. "Yes, we need to keep him actively involved right now before he goes out hunting on his own."

Alona kissed Chase, then went to the table. "I can't blame him. We had to kick him out of the apartment. Abraham is staying with Rena for a few days."

I crossed my arms over my chest, the moment feeling heavy. I'd seen so many victims in my life, but still never knew quite what to do or say.

"What about Ellis?" Arius turned to Troy.

Troy motioned to Victor. "We have him going through the files. After recruiting him once, we need to keep him out of sight."

"Your—nephew was with those people that took me?" My heart sped up.

Quinton nodded. "He got out as soon as he realized they were up to a lot more than they're telling the lower-ranked members of their movement."

"What do you mean? I thought they were taking women and..."

"They are, but that's a sideline to their main plan." He went over and sat down.

"Which is?" I looked from him to Daxx.

"Trying to bring down the barrier." She said glancing to Quinton.

"What barrier?" I paced, feeling like I needed to move.

"The barrier between the realms." Alona told me, a worried expression on her face.

"Is that possible?"

Quinton shook his head. "Not currently, but any attempts or breach would..."

"Be catastrophic to both realms." Bethany said leaning closer to Leone.

Rafael walked in the door, then Michael behind him.

His eyes immediately connected with mine.

Behind them another man walked in, he looked a lot like Arius, only with shorter hair.

He stopped, glanced around at the others and then his gaze stopped on me. "I had to go to the cells and see it with my own eyes."

I stood still, not comfortable with the way he was appraising me.

He straightened up then inclined his head. "I'm a big fan of your work."

I smirked. "Thanks. I didn't spend as much time on it as I would have liked."

He smiled.

"Autumn," Daxx motioned to him. "Emil."

Giving me an abrupt nod, he turned to Chase. "What is the plan?"

Chase motioned to a chair. "We were just about to come up with one."

Several of the others sat down. I decided to stay on my feet. Victor, Michael and Troy did as well.

Everyone turned and looked at me. I glanced to Michael.

"We need to know protocol, and your habits the day of your fights so we don't tip them off." Michael said crossing his arms and looking at me.

"Oh, right." I nodded. "Okay. I'm with Joe until he gets the location—he grabs a couple of the guys from the gym," I shrugged, "to keep the admirers from crowding me, or getting on the platform. They're with me until after the fight."

"Do they go back to the gym with you?" Troy asked.

I shrugged. "Depends on the condition I'm in. If I can still walk, sometimes I walk or jog back if it's not too far." I looked at Michael. "To keep my muscles from stiffening."

Michael turned and looked at Troy.

"What do you mean if you can still walk?" Alona asked, then raised her hand. "Never mind, I don't want to know."

Troy watched Michael for a moment, then looked back at me. "Michael and I will replace the two men that escort you."

I frowned. "And how are you making sure they don't recognize you?"

"Oh." Bethany leaned forward in her chair. "Clairee's coven can use a glamor spell so anyone without royal blood in their system will see someone else." She grinned. "I had blonde hair last time."

With my eyebrows raised, I looked around. "But I'll know to see you?"

"You have royal blood in your system." Michael said in a gruff manner.

Troy gave Michael a quick look and then turned back to me. "What are the crowds like?"

I shrugged. "Couple hundred max, sometimes less. Mine generate all the gawkers though."

"I'm part of your team," Daxx said, "I'll hold your water bottle, I don't care." She gave Troy a look daring him to object. "I want to be up front so I can see."

I smirked. "Hopefully you see me win."

"Do you lose?" Emil asked.

I shook my head. "Not often enough to keep track."

He gave me an abrupt nod. "Then you'll win." He motioned around the table. "I want to be near the back, so I can be free to move if needed."

I grinned. "The plan is to win." I looked to see Michael's expression was stony. Dragging my gaze from his, I looked over at Troy. "How can you tell if they are—" I motioned in the air, "are from here, my opponents?"

"Opponents? I thought this was one fight?" Michael scowled.

"Joe would have had to promise two, because we had to cancel the last one." I crossed my arms over my chest.

"Have you ever fought two in a row?" Leone looked concerned.

"Yeah, a few times. Usually when I've had to postpone a match because of injuries."

Michael made an exasperated sound in the back of his throat and paced to the other side of the room.

"Hey," his blue eyes snapped back to me, "I *have* to do this. Then I'll take a break, so they don't go after Joe."

"We'll know if they're from our side." Arius said quietly while Michael and I stared each other down.

"What if I were to help?" Paisley asked quietly.

I turned and looked at her. "What do you mean?"

Biting her lip, she looked at Arius for a second. "I could hold the other guys' feet still or," she shrugged, "something."

I shook my head. "You mean cheat? No." I looked at Michael, then to Troy. "I win this on the up and up or not at all." I tapped my chest. "I don't have much in my life but my integrity. I won't sink to another level." I looked back to Michael, his eyes darkened as he looked at me. Taking a deep breath, I turned to Paisley. "But, thank you for the offer."

She nodded and sat back.

"Before this gets sidetracked," Troy motioned to Victor, "lets get our placement figured out."

Victor nodded. "As we won't know the location until the last moment, this will be a general plan. Who is on watch, inside and outside." He looked to Daxx, then to Bethany and Crissy last. "You ladies will have to map out a route for Autumn to take after. Ensuring we have everyone in place."

They nodded.

"I volunteer myself to be on—overwatch or whatever it's called." Alona said. "I don't think I can, even with Chase's help, be in a crowd of so many that came to watch fights."

Chase nodded. "I agree."

Victor looked over to Crissy. "Cristy and Alona will be on watch."

Crissy nodded. "I will find the best place to watch from, after we know where."

Alona sighed. "I'm going to need climbing boots."

I studied everyone for a moment. "I'll have to go to the gym early tomorrow, so Joe knows I'm fit for the matches, other than that, there's not much else I can do with the planning." I motioned to the door. "I need to go workout for a bit, keep things limber."

Troy lifted his hand. "Of course, go do what you require."

"Thanks." I started for the door, Michael stepped in the way.

His eyes searched mine. "I've had a padded pole and bag placed in the practice room."

My jaw dropped. "Seriously?" I grinned. "Thanks. I'll go break them in right now."

The intensity of his look lightened slightly. "Just don't break anything on you."

I snorted. "Not in the plans."

Chapter Ten

I paused. I was soaked in sweat, muscles buzzing, and out of breath. I felt great, by my standards. I turned to get a bottle of water and saw Michael, Leone and Emil standing by the door like three statues, arms crossed over their chests, all void of expressions as they looked at me. Definitely related, I thought with a shake of my head.

Going over, I grabbed the towel. I had to keep moving to cool down gradually. I mopped off my face, then walked in a circle as I took a few sips. With the bottle I motioned to the padded pole, then looked at Michael. "Thanks for that. I feel great now." I held up my wrapped wrist. "For the wrap too."

He gave me a brief nod.

Emil grinned and started walking over. "I was skeptical, even after seeing what you did to those guards—but now," he motioned to the pole, "I'm in awe, and possibly afraid."

I blew out a breath. "I have to compensate for not having the bulk and size to throw around, but," I shrugged, "I get by."

"Indeed." He turned and smiled at Leone. "And you say she disarmed Rafael?"

Leone nodded. "More than once. Raf didn't even see it coming."

Setting the water down, I shook my arms, then kneaded the muscles in my neck.

"Impressive." Emil looked back to me. "I've sparred with Rafael several times. He's very good."

I rolled my head from side to side. "My biggest advantage is fighters that underestimate my size and agility." I rubbed the muscles in my neck again. "They see a cute little blonde chick and figure it will be easy."

"Have you injured yourself?" Michael came over, his brows drawn together.

I shook my head. "No. Just tight. I'm always wired before a match. I'll just take a hot shower and wrap a towel around myself to keep my muscles from tightening up. Joe has this gunk I use beforehand, keeps everything loose and limber." I lifted my hand to my mouth and used my teeth to get a hold of the wrap, so I could find the end and take it off.

Michael came over and pulled my hand from my mouth, then turned it over to find the start.

"You should give her some eufori, brother." Leone said with a smirk.

Michael turned and looked at him, I couldn't see the expression on his face.

Leone shrugged. "It works."

I shook my head. "I don't use drugs or anything that's not natural."

Emil grinned and looked at Leone. "Oh, it's quite natural."

Michael's eyes flicked to mine for a moment, then he looked back down to unwrap my hands.

Emil and Leone gave each other an odd look.

"I better go find Beth, so we can grab some z's before tomorrow." Leone saluted me and turned to the door.

Emil nodded. "I want to check in on Rena."

I gave him what I hoped was an encouraging look. "It's going to take time. She'll do what's best for her to get through it all."

He looked at me for a moment, then inclined his head to me before following Leone out.

"It must be hard for him to watch his daughter struggle through this."

Pulling the last of the wrap from my hands, Michael looked at me. "We'll do all we can to help."

I gave him a gentle look. "I know you will. Your family excels at helping others."

Balling the used wrap in his hand, he walked over and tossed it in the garbage. "We were destined to keep the balance between our realms. Any that suffer are a result of our failings," he tucked his hands in his pockets, "it is our responsibility to look out for them."

I picked up the towel, my phone and the water. "Destined or not, it's still a great thing you do." I motioned to the door. "I'm going to grab a shower and something to eat then I'll try to sleep."

"I'll walk with you." He said in a quiet tone.

We stepped out into the hallway. "So, Beth and I aren't in trouble for stumbling on your little diner?"

His mouth quirked. "Diner? That's a new term for it." He shook his head. "No. It's not a secret, it's a part of life here. Those we fed from are volunteers, they are not forced."

"It was a bit awkward." I gave him a wide-eyed look. "When everyone turned to look at us in the doorway."

He grinned. "I'm sure a few were quite excited to see two human women coming in."

I frowned, "What are we like some sort of delicacy?"

He looked at me briefly. "Oh, yes, to many."

I nodded slowly. "Got it. Don't go to the diner."

"It might be best."

"I'll give Beth a heads-up too." I patted my face with the towel.

"I'm sure Leone already has. Not that anyone would dare to feed from her."

"Oh?" I looked around trying to see if I knew where we were.

"With her mates' mark and a royal amulet around her neck, it would mean death to touch her in anyway."

I stopped walking. "Like, death, death?"

His eyes searched mine. "Yes. Some things are not forgivable, even in modern times. A true mate—" he motioned to his arm, where the others had tattoos, "is so very rare."

I glanced at his bare arm, then back to his face. "So, they get tattoos so people know? What makes a true mate different?"

He motioned for us to turn.

I did and finally recognized where we were. I wasn't sure, but I think he took a different route.

"It's complicated to explain—perhaps keeping your mind clutter free until after tomorrow would be best."

I huffed out a breath. "Yeah *clutter* free is good."

He stopped.

I looked to see we were at my bedroom. I opened the door and motioned with my head for him to come in. Unzipping the hoody I wore, I pulled it off and set it on the chair as I went past it. "Think that smelly ointment Clairee gave me will help a few tender areas?" I glanced over my shoulder to see he was standing half way across the room.

"Did you hurt yourself?"

I shook my head. "Not really, but a few spots are always tender after a workout like that."

He cleared his throat. "I'm not sure what the ointment she gave you will do." He still didn't move.

I shrugged. "Can't hurt, right? I'll try some after I have a hot shower."

He jolted like someone smacked him. "Would you like me to go get you something from the kitchen while you shower?"

I sat on the bed and undid my shoes. "That would be great. Protein and fruit if Mitz has any on hand."

He cocked his head and grinned. "Mitz always has everything."

I nodded. "She's great."

He bowed his head formally then backed up. "I'll return shortly."

Wrapping one of the large towels around me, I looked down, it went to my knees. I'd never had a towel this large before. I grabbed a smaller one and dried my hair and glanced in the mirror. My choppy hair was touching my shoulders now. I'd have to hack it off again soon. I didn't need hair getting in my way when I was fighting. I'd wanted to dye it a few years ago. Something dull and nondescript, but Joe told me the light blonde worked to my advantage. Opponents wouldn't see past my hair color and gender.

Tossing the towel on the counter, I turned to see Michael standing in the doorway. his gaze moving slowly over me.

I rubbed a hand down over the towel. "I guess I should close the doors around here."

"I should have knocked." He said quietly.

I shook my head. "No harm. This towel is big enough for three of me."

He didn't find the humor in that. Clearing his throat, he held up a jar. "Mitz uses this for Ira when he's sore after a battle."

"Oh." I walked over and held out my hand. "She really does have everything." I took it, opened it and sniffed. Making a face, I nodded. "That smells about right." Putting the lid on I handed it back to him, then asked, "Can you put some on between my shoulders? It's locked tight there."

He looked at the jar in his hand. "I could call Daxx if you'd…"

I shook my head. "The way she was making eyes at Troy during the meeting, I don't want to interrupt them." I shrugged. "I'm sure you've seen a woman's back before." I went over and stood by the counter.

He cleared his throat again. "Very well."

I loosened the towel, exposing my back. I watched in the mirror as he came behind me, his eyes were taking in my back.

Setting the jar on the counter, he dipped his fingers and touched the center of my back, rubbing the ointment around a bit. Taking a shaky breath, he used both hands to rub it in. His hands were so big, he was able to rest them against my neck and reach down with his thumbs to work the center of my back.

I sighed. "That feels good."

His gaze flicked to mine in the mirror. His eyes were red.

A shiver of awareness went through me. "Are the red eyes your natural state, or just sometimes?"

"Sometimes," he whispered.

"But you can change them anytime you want?"

He held my look in our reflections. "Yes." His hands continued to knead my muscles, moving up toward my neck.

"And now, did you change them?"

He licked his lips.

I caught a quick look of fangs.

"Not intentionally."

I closed my eyes as his hands worked magic. "Do they change when you feed?" I opened my eyes and looked back at him. "When you walked out of that room…"

"I need fangs to feed." He said in a hoarse tone.

"Right." My heart felt like it was skipping around in my chest. I needed to change the subject before I did something desperate like dropping the towel and hoping he accepted the green light. "This eufori?" His eyes flicked back to mine. "That Leone mentioned. What is it? Do you drink it or what?"

His gaze moved down the front of my image in the mirror. "No. It's the substance from our fangs when we bite someone—to dull the pain and relax them." He looked at my neck in the mirror.

"Oh. So, your brother was telling you to bite me?" I smirked.

He did not. "Yes."

I could see indecision in his eyes.

"Do you need something to relax?"

The way he looked at the reflection of my body sent a rush through me. His hands moved to my neck. "What I need—" I took a shaky breath, "to start with, is to know why your eyes are red right now, and the other times when you healed me." I touched his hand and held it against my neck. "Because if we're being honest here, I've never felt this kind of sexual tension before."

His gaze held mine.

"Don't tell me it's one-sided." I whispered.

Keeping his one hand against my neck, he used the other to tilt my head to expose the other side of my neck to him. "It's not one-sided." He leaned down, his breath brushing against my skin, his gaze never leaving mine in the mirror. "I'd like to feed from you." He took a ragged breath. "For two days I've been trying to sate my hunger and it's left me bereft and wanting."

I was having trouble translating what he was saying to make sense inside my head. I was turned on by the idea and as near as I could tell, so was he. He stood there watching me, not moving, waiting for my answer.

I prodded my mouth to move. "Yes."

Michael's eyes held mine in the mirror as he leaned down and licked over neck. My knees felt weak. Reaching around, he placed his hand on my stomach, spanning the width, then pulled me tight against his hard body.

When he bit into me, I gasped. There was no pain, only an intense feeling of need. I closed my eyes, letting the weight of my head rest in his hand. When he lifted his head and licked over his bite, I opened my eyes. Both of us were breathing fast.

"Is it always like that when you feed?"

He lifted his head and held my hip to turn me. "No. It's usually cold and methodical."

I was facing him now, looking up into lust heavy red eyes. "So, it's not sexual, normally?"

He leaned down until I could feel his breath against my cheek. "Does your broiled chicken turn you on?"

My heart was beating so fast, I was breathless. "No."

Touching the side of my face, he turned his head and brushed his lips over mine.

Leaning into him, I let go of the towel and reached up to grasp the back of his head.

He needed no further encouragement. His mouth covered mine, he took control and commanded, and I complied. I was only able to cling to him and try to keep up. I'd never been kissed like this before. Three hundred years had served him well to practice the art of kissing.

With a soft growl, he grasped my waist and picked me up, setting me on the counter. My towel slid off, I didn't care. His warm hands moved down my back, pulling me closer to stand between my knees.

I ran my tongue over his fangs and moaned against his mouth.

He pulled his mouth from mine abruptly and rested his cheek against mine. Our breathing was all over the place, rapid and shallow. Michael reached down to pull the towel back up and lifted his head away. He looked down at me with blue eyes filled with pain.

I realized then that this wasn't going any further. I glanced at the scar on his face and then reached up with a shaky hand to touch it. "What was her name? The one you wear this tribute for."

He gently took my hand from his face and held it. "Lara."

"You must have loved her a lot."

He closed his eyes and released my hand. "I did." Straightening, he looked down at me for a second. "Get some rest. I'll come by early in the morning and renew the blood bond, so you can see through Clairee's glamor spell."

I clutched the towel to me and nodded.

He backed away, then turned and quickly walked out.

I looked at the floor and sighed. "I can't compete with a three-hundred-year-old ghost."

Chapter Eleven

I paced in a circle, bouncing every few feet. Giving my arms a shake, I nodded to Daxx. She raised the pad again, bracing her feet for the hits. I stepped into it, threw a few jabs, then an elbow-jab combo. Pacing away, I rolled my shoulders.

"I prefer the upper body warmup." She said, her voice echoing through the earpiece in my ear.

No one expected me to reply. I had the earpiece in just for distraction, so my nerves didn't get to me.

Joe was sitting on the bench and watching. We were at the secret location now waiting on the go. I don't know what it used to be, but it was and old stone building with arched entryways like a castle might have had.

Rafael was outside watching for my opponents, but they hadn't arrived yet.

Troy and Michael stood just outside the makeshift dressing room I'd been given.

"I'll go see what the holdup is." Joe got up and hobbled out the door.

"Quinton you in place?" Troy asked in a quiet voice.

"Yeah, had to come in with the rush." He said quietly.

"Then you'll appear to be one of the pervs coming to see the chick fight." Leone said with a distasteful tone in his voice.

"Crystal isn't changing color, so no magic in the building." Quinton said quickly. "Other than what is used on us."

"No one familiar out here." Alona reported. "They have lookouts on the corners watching for police."

"As soon as the fight starts, you and cutie get to the building and watch the alley. Make sure they don't have backup hiding somewhere." Chase said.

"We will." Crissy answered.

"Group of large bodies coming in the south entrance." Arius said softly. "Heading to you."

"Bert-Joe is talking to some nasty people." Bethany reported. "Want me to blast them?"

I grinned to that. "He can handle himself. He's old, but respected. He didn't get that limp sitting behind a desk."

"Okay, but I'm watching them anyway." Beth said quietly. Someone chuckled.

"Easy there, sparky, no stealing the limelight from killer."

I turned to look at Daxx, she rolled her eyes.

"Less talk." Michael said abruptly.

"Joe is heading back your way." Beth said.

Michael walked in. I still couldn't believe they were walking around with swords on their backs and dressed for war and no one noticed. I wonder how he looked to everyone else after Clairee's spell. The vibes coming off Michal today were lethal. I unzipped the long hoodie I wore to warm up in and shrugged out of it.

"What the hell are you wearing?" He growled, as he took out his earpiece.

"Well." Alona said.

I looked down at the tights and sports bra I was wearing, then looked back to him. "After I got stabbed, Joe insists on no bulky clothing—so no one can hide weapons." I motioned down my body. "Can't expect them to comply if I'm in a snowsuit. We wrap our hands in front of each other too."

Someone chuckled in my ear.

Michael's gaze was still locked on me.

I pulled out the earpiece and moved, stopping right in front of him. I touched his chest. "I can't be distracted by your tense vibes." I said quietly. "I need the iceman right now."

The muscle in his jaw pulsed. He nodded and jammed his earpiece in again.

Troy stood in the door watching him carefully. He gave me a curious look.

I nodded. I was good.

"Okay guys, taking out my earpiece now."

"You got this, sis. First one is a little guy, I don't see the second yet." Rafael said.

"Thanks. I'm not worried, I'll just use the pent-up sexual frustration to my advantage." I said, watching Michael as he turned to look at me. I pulled the piece out and handed it to Daxx.

Joe came in. "Second one," he made quotes in the air, "is a surprise. First one is just a warm up."

I nodded, bouncing up and down. "Take him down fast?"

"Yeah, conserve energy for the surprise."

"Got it." I rolled my shoulders. "Let's do this."

Joe turned and almost walked into Troy. He grinned up at him. "Sure you don't want to fight?"

Troy smirked. "Probably wouldn't be good at it."

Joe snorted. "Your size doesn't need skill." He turned and led the way to the platform.

I kept my feet moving as Joe wrapped my hands and wrists.

Michael didn't take his eyes off my opponent as his hands were being wrapped.

The definition of small was still bigger than I was. Then again at five foot six, that applied to most of those I fought.

Joe finished, then turned to watch them. He shook his head. "They think twisting the wrap does more damage." He glanced to Daxx. "It does, to the fighter's hands." He gave me a quick nod. "Do your thing."

I bobbed my head, not in the mood for words.

"Second one arrived. No one could get a look at him." Daxx said quietly.

I nodded and motioned to the stairs.

Troy leaned down and spoke next to my ear. "You get knocked off the platform, you lose?"

"Yeah."

"Then don't get knocked off." He said in a low tone.

I grinned. "That's the plan." I looked at Michael. "Just keep iceman off the platform."

Michael's blue gaze was locked on mine. He gave me a slight nod, then followed Troy off the platform.

The raised platform was fifteen feet wide and just as long, not a big space if you stopped to think about it. Which I tried not to do. Rick, the guy that officiated these events didn't even stay on with the fighters.

He turned and looked, asking if I was ready. I nodded.

He did the same to the man bouncing around like he was in dance class.

When Rick stepped off the platform, the fight began. I had a few seconds to assess my opponent and pick out his weaknesses.

Rick went down the steps.

The kangaroo across from me danced around the edge of the platform, slowly working his way to the center. When he got close enough, I decided it was time to disable that hop of his. I swung my left hand, then as he went to block, I did a sweep of his legs. He was down. Before he could get up, I executed a quick crescent kick and clipped him in the jaw. He fell back, then rolled dangerously close to the edge.

It was too soon to take him out though, I knew this. A dissatisfied crowd was more dangerous then the fight.

He was back on his feet, not bouncing, as he came at me. He was mad, which I could also use to my advantage. Emotions had no place in a fight. With a growl he lunged and swung for my face. I blocked with my arm and jabbed him in the face with my other hand. Stepping out of the way of his next wild swing, I faked a side kick, then ducked to sweep his feet out from under him again. He went down hard this time.

The crowd was yelling for me to take him down, so I knew it was time.

He got to one knee, I leapt toward him, and landing in the perfect position for a roundhouse kick. My foot connected. As I snapped my head around to follow though, I saw he was only a few inches from the edge. Adjusting quickly, I landed my foot under his chin and he toppled headfirst off the platform.

The crowd loved it. Even they recognized he was a complete novice trying to impress by fighting a girl.

Rick was on the platform now. He grabbed my wrist and held my arm up, turning us slowly.

Someone caught my eye, standing back in the shadows. I turned to glance that way again, then changed my mind. I didn't want to draw attention to the fact I saw them. Pulling my arm free, I went over to the stairs. Joe reached up and handed me my water. I took it and stood up, taking small sips and checking out the crowd.

She was here.

Turning, I squatted down, handing the water back. Michael was the closet, so I grabbed the back of his head and pulled it toward me until our foreheads touched. "Red headed bitch is standing under the sign beside the entrance." I said.

His blue eyes locked on mine.

Troy put his hand on Michael's shoulder as I straightened. "We play it out, brother. Quint and Arius are close to her."

Michael nodded, his eyes connecting with mine. He gave me a nod.

I stood up. I kept moving around the platform. Glancing to the entrance, I checked to see if the second guy was coming yet. Pausing, I rolled my head from side to side. I thought I'd seen little green lights in the dark hall. Then the second opponent walked out into the light.

"Shit." I said softly. He was the size of a truck. A dump truck. I turned and frowned at Daxx. She came up the first few steps. I pranced her way, trying to keep my muscles moving. "Are there green eyes? I swear I just saw green eyes on that mountain walking to the platform."

"Fuck. Next one has green eyes." She said so the others heard.

Michael was up the stairs in two steps. He grabbed my wrist, like he was fixing the wrap, in plain sight of everyone coming up the other side. "Green eyes mean one of two things." He glanced at me briefly. "They want to weaken you to grab you later, or they have bet to win." He turned my hand over, to appear he was checking the wrap. "Do not let him touch you."

I glanced at the very large man. "Like hit me?" I scowled when I noticed he wasn't getting his hands wrapped, wondering if I could use that to my advantage somehow.

Michael gave a slight shake of his head then put his hand on my shoulder. He squeezed. "Like that, on any bare skin."

I nodded. "Okay, no touching."

"Autumn, say the word and we'll get you out."

I dragged my eyes from his serious ones and glanced at Troy. He was talking, obviously giving orders. "I'm good. We have to play this out, right? To get her."

I could see the indecision in his eyes.

"We can get her another time." He clenched his jaw and looked down at Troy.

Troy looked at me, his face clearly showing it was my call.

"I'm going to do it." I nodded. Michael wasn't happy with that but didn't say anything. I rolled my shoulders. "Stay close iceman in case I go down. Don't let him touch me."

Michael nodded and turned back to the steps.

I took a deep breath and let it out. Shaking my arms out, I turned and glanced at the crowd. If touching me would drain me, what exactly did he feed on? Bethany and Paisley stood not far from the platform now, Chase right beside them.

They had my back. I turned and looked back to Joe, he nodded. I gave him a thumbs up.

Turning around, I motioned to Rick and gave him a nod. He went down the stairs.

Okay. Get through this one and then get the bitch that had me drugged and chained up. As motivation went, that worked for me.

I moved toward the middle of the platform. This guy's arm was the length of my leg. There was no fancy dancing for him. He was hunched and leaning forward, his stance wide enough to balance his size. It was going to take an explosion to break that form.

He stepped toward me and swung up with his big paw. I stepped out of his reach and slapped his hand back.

No touching, my brain chanted.

With a snarl on his face, he came toward me again. Then dropped his shoulder and tried to use his size to slam into me and send me from the platform. He clipped my shoulder, but I managed to twist the rest of my body out of the way.

I moved back and to the side, trying to figure out where to hit him. Use your size to an advantage, he's slower, my mentor would have said. I went back at him, ducked his arm and jumped, slamming my elbow into his throat.

He smacked me away with the back of his hand like I was a bug, catching me in the side of the face. Rubbing where I'd hit him, he bared his teeth and came at me again.

When he swung, I bounced up and caught him in the throat again. I didn't clear him fast enough and he grabbed for my shoulder. Twisting, I went for a heel kick to knock him back. He didn't move far, but his hand was off me.

If I could get him to lunge again, I could catch the back of his head and throw him forward. Kick that jaw a few times and maybe I'd make a dent. To get him to do that I was going to have to let one of his swings connect, so he'd get cocky and lunge for me.

I checked my position on the platform, making sure I wasn't near the edge. He swung at me with a closed fist. I twisted at the waist so my shoulder would roll with the hit, and maybe do less damage. He caught me right in the jaw. The momentum of my own twist with the force of the blow took me to the platform.

I got to my knees fast, catching a glimpse of Troy holding Michael back. Turning, I waited until he was lunging, his center not balanced and jumped up, landing a spin kick on the back of his head. He fell forward and then caught himself with his hands, stopping himself from going over the edge.

Gritting my teeth, I turned and hit him under the jaw with a back kick. He still didn't falter. Jumping up, I used both elbows on the back of his head as I raised my knee. That one finally affected him. He shook his head and braced himself on one hand to get up.

Shit, I didn't want him back on his feet. Going around to the other side fast, staying clear of the edge—just as he straightened to stand, I twisted and touched the mat with my hand and landed a scissor-flip onto his shoulders.

Wrapping my legs around his head, I threw my body weight to the side and tucked in my arm. He went down like a tree. My entire side connected with platform, and I grunted from the force.

He grabbed my leg as I rolled to get free of him. I didn't know if the touch could work through the clothes, so I yanked on his fingers then twisted back. I heard the crunching as joints broke. He howled and pressed his hand into his chest. He should have wrapped his hands.

I scrambled away and got to my feet. As I did, he got to one knee, his broken hand clutched to his body. He had no hands out for balance. No time for proper form or footwork, I turned to the side and kicked out with all I could. My foot connected with his head and he toppled over the edge of the platform.

I dropped to my knees and tried to catch my breath. The pain was shooting through the side of my head.

Rick was beside me, holding his hand to help me up. "Had me worried." He said as I got up.

I licked the blood from my lip. "Yeah, me too."

Holding my hand in the air, he turned slowly. The crowd was going crazy.

The mountain was limping back down the hall he'd come from.

I looked down to see Beth and Paisley cheering as much as the betting crowd. Chase was holding his hand over his ear, nodding.

I pulled my hand free. "Thanks, Rick." I turned and headed to the stairs. Michael stood at the bottom. Joe stood beside him grinning and shaking his head. I went down quickly and took the towel Daxx held out.

Joe patted me on the shoulder. "I don't know how you figured taking that blow to the face was a good idea, but it worked."

I wiped the blood off my mouth. "Had to do something to get him unbalanced."

He looked me up and down. "You good?"

I nodded. "Nothing serious."

He nodded again then grinned. "I bet the house on you, girl. The soup kitchen and shelter will be eating well for months."

I blew out a breath. "Good. I need time off."

"Of course." He smiled again.

I glanced over to see two of the regulars from the gym working their way toward us.

One shook his head. "You're insane, dynamo."

I rolled my eyes. "You two make sure Joe gets his winnings back to the safe."

He nodded. "We will. You coming to celebrate?"

I glanced to Michael and figured by his expression I had about a minute before he carried me out of here. "No. I have some things to do."

He grinned at me and turned to Michael, tapping his shoulder. "Helluva woman you got here."

Michael gave him a quick glance. "I'm aware." He said making it clear he wasn't in the mood for conversation.

"Okay, Joe, go with the guys, get your money and get home." I squeezed his shoulder.

"What about your cut?" He asked, holding up his hand for the guys to wait.

I shook my head. "Keep it. I don't need it."

He frowned, then nodded. "I'll see you later. Ice that shoulder."

I dabbed my mouth again. "Yeah."

Michael lost his battle for control then and grabbed my elbow gently, steering me toward the dressing room.

We barely got out of sight, when he pulled his earpiece out and spun me around to face him. He touched my chin and looked at my face, then shoulder. When he reached for the button on his jacket, I stopped his hand.

"You can't."

He scowled down at me.

"I can't walk out of there healed up—they'll know you are with me then."

Troy stood in the door. "She's right, brother. Eunice is still out there, lets play this out."

"Fuck." Michael scowled at Troy. "Give us a minute."

Daxx came over and handed me my shoes, hoodie and phone, then she hurried out to stand with Troy.

I bent down to put on my shoes and winced. That drop on the platform was going to hurt later.

Michael hissed out a sound of frustration and knelt down, taking the other shoe and holding it out. I put my foot in and he quickly tied it. He looked up at me, pain clear on his face.

"I'm good." I told him. "Nothing is broken."

He clenched his teeth and stood up.

I pulled the hoodie on and zipped it up.

Reaching into his pocket, he held out one of the devices I'd seen on the women.

Without a word, I put it on right over top of the wrap. I'd worry about taking it off later. "How does it work?"

He popped it open. "Push that and it will take you back to a room in the underground chambers."

I nodded. "Good. Thanks." I looked up.

He reached and gently touched my face. "We're *discussing* this when we get back."

I smirked. "Whatever you say."

Leaning down he kissed my mouth softly, then licked over my lip.

I pulled my head back to see his eyes were red. Licking my fat lip, I didn't taste blood. "That's cheating."

He grinned as his eyes went back to blue.

I looked at the phone and tapped the group call button, then put the ear piece in. Pulling up the hood, I moved toward the door.

Michael grabbed my hand. "Take no chances, we don't want them getting their hands on you."

I nodded.

He put his ear piece back in. "We're heading to the North exit, then we'll split off from Autumn and circle around to follow her."

"Nothing happening at the entrance." Alona said.

"So—dynamo is it?" Chase asked.

"You heard that? Yeah that's what the guys call me at the gym." I followed Troy through the crowd.

"I like it." Chase said. "It works better than killer and I must say, after tonight, I shall strive to never upset you—ever."

"Autumn, you must teach me this fighting that frightens my mate into good behavior." Alona said quietly.

I stepped around a group of people shouting at the platform. "You're too graceful and beautiful to get dirty the way I do, Alona." I nodded to a few that gave me a thumbs up as we weaved through the people. I didn't even know who was fighting. I just wanted to get out of here.

"I adore you." Alona answered.

"Eunice is on the move. She's got five with her and the one Autumn broke." Quinton reported abruptly.

"Circling back to follow them." Rafael whispered.

"Those moves, sister." Arius said. "From now on you spar with Leone."

"Me?" Leone sounded like he was running. "Hell, no. Victor would be better."

We were at the entrance now. I hugged Daxx and smiled up at Troy like we'd discussed earlier. Then turned and stopped in front of Michael and patted his chest.

"Take no chances." He said quietly.

I nodded. "Taking the alley now." I said for all to hear.

"We can see you." Crissy said.

"I'm at the first break in the alley." Victor said. "And it would be an honor to spar with a warrior such as Autumn."

Someone snorted.

"Suck up." Quinton mumbled.

"One of their guys is taking the broken one in the other direction." Rafael said quietly. "The others are standing here. Including the red headed bitch."

After I reached the alley, I paused and stretched to the side and twisted a bit.

"Are you all right, Autumn?" Alona asked, concerned.

"Yeah." I said softly. "Just stretching out some aches. When he dropped I hit that platform, hard."

"You said you were good." Michael's tone was low.

"I am, just hurting a little. That guy was a mountain."

"He was that big?" Crissy asked.

"About the size of that guy Arius chased on the island." Paisley said.

"And you beat him, Autumn?" Crissy asked.

I grinned and started walking. "Yeah, barely."

"He wasn't as big as the one on the island." Arius didn't sound happy.

"Really? Guys, it's not about the size." Daxx said.

I put my hand over my mouth, so I wouldn't laugh out loud. I was supposed to be walking home alone, not giggling like a school girl.

"Emil, you still able to stay close to them?" Troy asked.

"Yes." Emil whispered.

I didn't know where he was, but he'd been silent since before we arrived at the site, so whatever he was doing, he couldn't talk.

"Someone just came running over to them. I don't know what they told her, but she looks very pleased." Rafael said. "They're heading to the corner. I can't follow them around it, the crowd breaks up."

"We can see where they go." Crissy said.

"We can see half the city from here. I'll be porting home from here by the way. I am not climbing down." Alona informed us.

"Okay." Crissy said. "Down isn't as much fun."

"You're telling me." Bethany said softly.

"They're in the alley." Alona reported.

"Passing the first street." I told them. "How far do you want me to go?"

"Alona, tell us when they're catching up to her." Michael sounded out of breath. "Almost to you, Victor."

"Autumn just passed. I can't see her followers yet." Victor reported.

"Beth and I are heading down the adjacent alley, we'll be at the first street soon." Paisley huffed out a breath.

"Two streets down." Quinton said breathlessly, "will be at the alley in two."

"They're catching up quickly. I'm going to say slow down before you reach the second intersection, Autumn." Alona said quickly.

"We'll be there." Chase said. "Those with porters make sure you have them ready. I want Eunice sucked into one."

I blinked, wondering if I'd heard right. "The what?"

Beth giggled. "They don't get sucked in, but it does transport them to an intake cell that they can't get out of."

I glanced over my shoulder, without making it obvious. "Yes porters at the ready please."

"Figures it's one of the few spots in the city I don't know and can't port to." Daxx said in a choppy voice.

"Heading down behind them now." Rafael said. "What's the count?"

"Four, plus the lady." Crissy answered. "Are they only fighters?"

"We don't know." Rafael said.

"Piece of cake." I said, fighting the urge to turn around and look.

"Save some crumbs for us, sister." Arius said quickly.

"Don't underestimate Eunice." Victor stated.

"She fights dirty." Michael was breathless and must have been running too. "Take no chances."

"I hate people that fight dirty." I whispered.

"Autumn." Michael's tone left no room for argument.

"I got it. Just saying if she were to accidentally fall on her face near one of you with the porter box things—it wouldn't be a bad thing." I was almost standing still now, I was walking that slow.

Someone growled through the ear piece.

"That would be a no, Autumn." Paisley said quietly.

"I got that." I smirked then remembered my swollen lip. I could hear what I thought were footsteps in the alley. "Is someone close to me?"

"I don't see anyone." Alona said. "Crissy, do you?"

"It's me." Emil's voice came through the ear piece. "Clairee cloaked me. I hurried ahead, so Autumn wasn't alone in case they ran for her."

I paused and looked around. "Freaked me out, guy."

"Sorry." He said.

"So, you were with them all along?" I whispered.

"Since they walked up to the place. Sorry, I couldn't warn you about that mountain. I couldn't speak."

"That's fine." I looked around again. "I managed."

"Indeed, you did." Emil sounded like he was grinning. "This cloaking is tricky business. I have to avoid touching anyone. That was a chore in that crowd."

I turned my head again trying to see him.

"They're catching up." Crissy said.

"How close are you to the second street?" Michael asked.

"Fifty feet." I rolled my shoulders, trying to keep them from stiffening.

"Slow down. We don't have time to get to the third street." He said quickly.

"Okay," I whispered.

"Dammit." Alona hissed. "There's a small group moving up the East alley. They're almost at a run."

"There's five of them." Crissy chimed in.

"She called for backup." Leone said.

"Should I feel flattered?" I paused and stretched my legs.

"I would. Ten people to take me down." Daxx snorted. "They're definitely afraid of you."

"No,no,no." Crissy whispered. "That's bad."

"Cristy?" Victor said firmly.

"Purple eyes." She answered.

"She's right." Alona groaned.

I knelt down like I was fixing my shoes, not sure what this meant.

"How can you see that from up there?" Chase asked.

"I brought binoculars, Chase, knowing Criss would pick the tallest building." Alona told him.

"What's purple mean?" I whispered.

"Magic user, probably a mage." Quinton growled.

"Okay, and?" I stood up, stretching my arms above my head.

"Babe, you and Beth find the one with purple eyes and keep them under wraps until one of the porters reach you." Arius said quickly.

"Will do." Paisley answered hurriedly, "hands, mouth, what?"

"Everything." Beth said.

"Got it." Paisley huffed out a breath. "We're at the corner now, behind a dumpster."

I lunged and stretched my leg muscles, glancing at the dumpster.

"Let the backup go by you," Leone said, "then I'll drop down after they do."

I frowned, he was somewhere *on* the building?

"I can see her." Emil whispered.

I straightened up and turned to look down the alley. Sure enough, Eunice was walking toward me, two men on either side of her.

She started clapping. "I admire the hell out of your fighting abilities." She slowed down.

"Yeah? I'd say thanks, but your opinion doesn't matter to me."

She lifted her hand. "Fair enough. He was supposed to weaken you and win. You cost us a great deal of money tonight."

I shrugged. "He was sloppy. Not much skill."

"He was." Crossing her arms over her chest, she studied me. "So where are my guards that were to take you?"

I realized she didn't know they had.

"No idea. They let me go." I couldn't be sure if she had a weapon or not, the dark jacket she wore hung to her knees.

"Just like that?" She tilted her head.

I shrugged. "After I beat on them some."

She smiled, that smile that looked painful. "They're such cowards now, men, not like they used to be."

I could hear her voice echoing through the ear piece and wondered if Emil had moved closer. "Some still have honor. Maybe they didn't want to be part of whatever you're planning."

She shook her head, her long red hair shifting with the movement. "I don't think that's it." She took a few steps closer. "What man would not want a chance at taming you?"

A growl went through the ear pieces. I actually recognized it at Michael's. "They can try." I told her, trying to assess the men with her.

"I think," she said looking at me from my feet up, "because of my great fondness for you, I'll make you off limits." She shrugged, "after you give birth to the next Hubert heir." She watched me for a reaction.

I raised my eyebrows. "You know you're a bit sick in the head, right?" I tapped mine. "Not quite right up there?"

I heard footsteps from the alley and turned to see her backups running at me. Shifting, I made sure I could see all of them.

"In three." Troy said softly.

"No chances." Michael whispered.

"Two." Chase said.

"Now, Emil." Arius growled

Michael and Troy came out of the alley behind me at the same moment Emil appeared behind Eunice, grabbing her by the hair.

The men in either side of her turned to him, weapons drawn.

With a sound of annoyance, Emil released her and pulled a sword from his back.

Michael moved past me to take on one of the backup guys.

"The one waving his hands, Paize." Alona said quickly.

"Got him." Paisley said.

"I'll cover her." Bethany reported.

I turned to see a man with purple eyes frozen like a statue, his arms in the air.

"Give me a sec," Leone grunted.

The brother's appeared from all directions, weapons drawn. The sound of metal on metal rang out.

I turned to look for Eunice and saw her trying to sneak away quietly. I went after her and was almost to her when she spun around, a sai in each hand. If the main blade didn't get you, the curved ones surrounding her hand would. "Were you leaving without saying goodbye?" I held my hands away from body.

"I should have drugged you again and carried you out of here." She said looking quickly over my shoulder.

I reached slowly and flipped the hood off, so I could see any movement beside me. "Where's the fun in that?"

"You would have lived like a queen with us. I'm going to hate killing you." Eunice widened her stance.

I did the same. "You can try."

She came at me fast, no tells on her direction that I could see. She jabbed at me with the sai. I kicked her hand away. She kicked out and caught me on the hip with a sloppy kick of her own. That told me she hadn't fought her own battles in a long time.

I ducked under her next swing and hit her with and elbow-fist combination.

She recovered fast and caught my side with the sai in her other hand.

It stung, so I knew it had reached my skin. I had to get rid of those, I thought.

"You're not better than me," she hissed.

I used a crescent kick and knocked one weapon from her hand. "I don't need to be." I told her.

She snarled and rushed toward me. I blocked her arm with my elbow and used her own momentum to toss her over my body. She hit the pavement hard, the other sai scuttering across the ground.

I spun to kick as she started to get up, but she rolled out of reach. Stepping into it this time like I meant business, I went down and swept her feet out as she had been trying to stand.

She howled in fury and jumped to her feet.

I stepped back and waited for her to make the next move.

She bent her knees, fists raised.

I respected that she was willing to exchange blows that way, and raised my fists as well.

Chapter Twelve

She pranced and came toward me, I watched for an opening, then she turned her hand over and blew on it.

My eyes went blurry and stung like I had never felt before. I held my hand over them, the other out from my body so I could feel if she came at me. Blinking made it burn, so I squeezed my eyes shut.

"I would have like to finish this." She said.

I heard the scrape of her sai as she picked one up.

"But it seems my incompetent men are losing."

Her voice moved in the other direction.

"Give me a second to see again and we can finish it now." I said, hoping the guys listening realized I was blinded.

"Such confidence." She sounded amused. "That's not going to clear up just like that, my dear, I'm sorry."

"We could port somewhere and finish it." I said. One of the guys with those boxes needed to get her.

"On my way." Leone said.

"She's circling you, Autumn." Alona said quickly.

"Counter clockwise." Crissy whispered.

I had to hear her movement. "Stop talking." I said abruptly, so I could hear.

Eunice laughed, thinking I had been talking to her.

Dropping my hand from my face. I crouched slightly then spun into a roundhouse. My foot connected. I recognized the sound and knew I'd hit her in the jaw. The metal clattered to the pavement as she went down. Without sight, I misjudged my landing and hit the ground myself.

"Got her." Leone said then there was a pop noise.

"Autumn." Michael was suddenly next to me. He picked me up off my knees and held me across his lap.

"She blew something in my eyes. Burns like acid when I open them." I turned my face toward him, hoping he could shed some light on it.

I felt his hand touch my face.

"It's blistering." He said with pain in his voice.

"When you said she fought dirty, I thought you meant pulls hair, bites…"

"Alona," Michael said abruptly, "call Clairee, tell her to get to Autumn's room."

"Get your mate out of here, brother, we have the last few under control." Emil said then grunted.

Michael stood up, holding me close. "Hold on." He whispered against my hair.

My stomach felt like it bottomed out and I knew we had transported.

He was walking then and set me down on a hard surface. Michael pulled out my ear piece and unzipped my hoodie and pull it away from my body. His hand touched my side near where she'd cut me.

I tried to open my eyes and then covered them with my hand. "It burns." I gasped.

"Pull your arms out. I'm going to step in the shower with you and rinse it off your face." His touch was gentle as he pulled the hoodie from my body. I heard the clatter on the floor as he shed his weapons. He scooped me up into his arms and walked across the floor.

Leaning, he turned on the taps and cool water started falling on us.

"Move your hands and let it rinse your face," he said as he turned us into the spray.

I held my chin up, letting the water spray against my face. I tried to open my eyes again and made a guttural sound of pain as the burning intensified.

"Don't open them." He said next to my ear.

"Michael." It was Alona. "Clairee is here."

He moved and we stepped out of the water. "Grab some towels." He said and kept walking.

I felt him lower me to the bed and move out of the way. The bed shifted like someone was beside me.

"Autumn, I'm going to pat your face dry so Clairee can take a look." Alona said just before soft material touched my face.

"Can I give her blood to heal up her side?" Michael asked, his voice close to my head.

"I'll get a wet clothe to clean the cut up." Alona said.

"Let me check her eyes first, Michael, blood could heal in what we need to clean out of them." Clairee said.

"What?" I asked feeling a little freaked out now.

I felt an arm go around me. "Let her look before we panic." Michael whispered then kissed the side of my head.

"Okay." I tipped my chin up.

"I've seen this blistering before." Clairee mused quietly.

"Blistering?" I went to raise my hand to feel when Michael's large hand closed around it and held it.

"Can you open your eyes?" Clairee asked.

"It burns like crazy, but yeah." I blew out a breath and then opened them slowly. It was bright, like a light was shining in them.

"Hand me a dry cloth." She said. "Autumn, I'm going to dab your left eye, so I can test what it is."

"Okay." I turned my hand and grabbed Michael's and squeezed it as she did it.

"Okay, you can close them again." She said quietly.

I did and blew out a breath trying to relax. "Did we get the bitch?"

"Yes." Michael said venomously.

"Good." I nodded. "Her and I need to have a chat once I can see."

"I will be back as quickly…"

"I'm here." Rafael said loudly his voice coming from the door.

"Port me to the temple, so I can double check my suspicions." Clairee said. "I'll be right back." She added quickly.

"Let's get you cleaned up a bit." Alona said. "I can't tell if that's dirt on your knees or blood."

I nodded.

"I got here as fast as I could." Mitz said.

"Clairee had to go test what Eunice blew into Autumn's eyes." Michael released my hand and moved from beside me. "I have to close up the gash in her side."

"I'll get towels, so we can dry her and see what we're dealing with." Mitz said.

"Autumn, I'm going to take off your shoes." Alona said, then I felt someone touch my feet and pull them off.

"Just lean back so we can look at this." Michael said, his face close to mine.

"I hope I didn't bleed all over the bed." I said quietly.

"Don't worry about the bedding, love, it will wash." Mitz told me.

Michael put his arm behind me and lowered me to lay back. I felt cloth move over my waist and side.

"It's fairly deep, Michael," Mitz said softly, "you can seal it to slow the bleeding, but she'll need blood to heal inside."

"Clairee said no blood until she knows what's in her eyes." He said, his voice shaking.

"Eunice did this?" Mitz asked, her voice coarse.

"Yes." He whispered.

"Wretched woman," Mitz said. "I'm so glad you got her, finally. I'm going to place a cool cloth over your eyes, love."

She did and it lessened some of the burning.

"Autumn took her down, even after she couldn't see." Alona said, her voice coming from the direction of the closet.

"I'm going to seal this, to slow the bleeding." Michael said, his warm hand resting on my waist.

"Hello?" Alona must have answered her phone. "Okay. I will tell them."

I felt Michael shift, then his breath was against my side.

"Clairee knows what it is, but it will take some time to make the proper ointment to counteract the effects." Alona said.

Michael made a sound and without seeing him, I wasn't sure if it was good or bad. His hot breath was against my skin again, then I felt his tongue against the cut. It stung, but I knew it was good pain this time.

I reached and rested my hand against his wet hair. "Is everyone else okay?" I asked quietly, not even sure who was in the room.

"Everyone is fine." Troy's voice came from the doorway.

"I'm going to get some hot tea." Mitz said. "She's shivering."

I hadn't even realized I was, until she said it.

"I'll grab a blanket." Daxx's voice came from the end of the bed.

Michael lifted his head, so I dropped my hand away.

"I can't give her blood until Clairee gets that out of her eyes." Michael said, getting up.

"Are you okay to sit up?" Paisley asked. "We'll get this robe on so you can warm up."

I nodded and started to rise, keeping the cloth against my eyes, then Michael's hand was beneath my shoulders helping me.

"I only slowed the bleeding, so don't move around too much.

"I don't think I'll be dancing anytime soon, all the aches are setting in." I whispered.

I felt the bed move on the other side.

"Just hold out your arm and we'll get this on." Paisley said.

"I'll get the wrap off your hands." Bethany said.

I smirked, then remembered my fat lip. "The gang's all here, huh?"

"Everyone except Rafael and Arius." Daxx said. "Arius went to check on his celebrity guest in the cells."

I snorted. "I hope she landed on her face when she was ported."

Someone chuckled.

"She certainly did when you knocked her flying with that kick." Leone said. "It was a thing of beauty."

"Good. I'll have to work on my follow-through with my eyes closed. My knees are really reminding me of how I landed."

"What happened to take no chances?" Michael asked quietly.

I switched hands holding the cloth, so Beth could take the wrap off my other hand. "I was staying out of it, admiring all of your actions when I noticed her sneaking away. You guys were busy, so I thought I'd slow her down."

"And," Arius' voice boomed from the doorway, "she is pissed. Like, livid, we may have to tranquilize her."

I grinned and touched my lip when it split open because of the movement. "That makes me feel better." I lowered the cloth from my eyes and heard a few hisses in the room. "That pretty, huh?"

"What is taking Clairee so long?" Michael sounded like he was in pain.

I held out my hand in his direction. "Michael. Help me up, maybe one of the girls can help me change out of these wet clothes?"

He took my hand, then I was scooped up into his arms.

"Or that works too." I said wrapping my arms around his neck. I leaned the side of my head against his as he walked into the bathroom. A warm feeling moved down my side. "I think I'm bleeding again."

He set me on the counter and pulled the robe open. "Fuck." I felt him hold a towel against it. "Leone." He bellowed.

"What's wrong?" I asked.

"What?" Leone asked from the door.

"Where are Eunice's weapons?" Michael asked.

"I dropped them at the armory." Leone answered. "Why?"

Michael pressed the towel harder into my side. "I think they were laced with something. I've been trying to figure out the bitter taste in my mouth, and she's bleeding heavily again."

"I'll go get them and get them to Clairee." Leone said quickly.

"What's going on?" I asked clutching Michael's arm.

"Michael?" Troy was in the bathroom now. I heard him come over and the towel move slightly. "Autumn do you know your blood type?"

I frowned. "Uh, yeah, but it's rare." I started shaking harder.

"How rare?" Michael asked touching the back of my head.

"It's B negative." I said, grasping Michael's wrist. "What's going on?"

"I'm B negative." Paisley said slowly. "Well I was, does the full blood bond with Arius change that?"

"No." Troy answered. "Quinton, go get the doctor."

"Be right back." Quinton said from the door.

Michael rested his forehead against mine. "She had coated something on her weapons, so when she cut you it won't clot and heal." He said softly, his voice rough. "We have an antidote, but it will take time and you're losing too much blood."

I grasped his hair, holding his head. "Okay, do what you have to."

He hugged my head for a second, then straightened away.

"Doctor's here." Arius said from the doorway.

"Let's get her back to the bed." Troy said. "Paisley will give her blood, Arius can keep her strength up with his own."

Michael picked me up into his arms and started walking. I felt him put me on the bed, and sit behind me, while still holding the cloth over my side.

"I may have to break her face after this." I said in a shaky voice.

"I'll help." He said in a cold tone.

"I have to put a needle in." A man said from beside us. "We'll get the blood started, then I can give her the treatment to counteract the agent's circulation."

"Get on with it." Michael said abruptly.

I felt cold hands on my arm.

"Paisley's is in." Alona said.

"You're a nurse?" The man asked.

"I helped in the hospitals during the second world war." Alona answered.

I hadn't realized Alona's age until now.

"I need to distance myself a bit now, sorry, the pain is getting to me." She said quietly.

"Of course, my queen, her injuries are quite extensive, no need for you to suffer as well." The doctor said.

There was a soft growl near my head.

"Hey," I said breathlessly, "nothing's broken."

"Eunice Hubert do all this damage" I felt a pinch against my skin and then the burn that goes with a needle being inserted.

"Occupational hazard." I whispered.

"She's retiring." Michael said gruffly.

"She fought two men before taking out Eunice." Daxx said.

"I will ensure you recover." The doctor said, his cool touch leaving my skin. "I have been cleaning up her carnage for too many millenniums. You will be a hero to all of Alterealm once word gets out." I felt the bed shift. "You'll feel a bit funny as the blood starts." His voice was on the other side of the bed now. "Is Clairee looking after the antidote for her eyes?"

"Yes." Michael said, his head touching against mine.

"My prince, I must insist you take the oral antidote and go feed." The doctor said.

"I will after…"

"Now, Michael." Troy said bluntly. "She's going to need your strength when you can give her blood."

Reaching with the hand that didn't have the needle in it, I touched the side of his face gently. "Go do what have to do. When we tag team Eunice later to wreak vengeance, I need you five by five."

He clasped my hand and moved it to kiss my palm. "Vengeance is the last thing on my mind for the first time in three hundred years." His voice was shaky.

"My prince, your coloring is not good. You need to do as instructed." The doctor said.

"We won't leave her." Daxx said.

"We're right beside her, brother." Arius said quietly. "Go."

I felt Michael's chest rise and fall. "I won't be long." He kissed the side of my head.

"I have what we need for her eyes, but I'll wait until the doctor is done." Clairee said quietly.

"Ira has increased the guard around the chambers." Mitz said coming in the door. "In case Willis gets any ideas."

"I'll go check in at the cells, brother." Chase said.

"Let me know." Arius said.

Michael shifted and rested me against pillows.

"I'll hold the cloth on her side." Bethany said.

I felt the change in pressure.

"Drink this. Go shower and feed." The doctor said. "Your mate won't even notice you missing shortly, after I give her this to purge the poison from her system."

The word purge didn't sound like it was going to be a good thing.

"I'll be back shortly." Michael said.

I nodded, my head feeling light. "I'll be here." I said quietly.

Purging turned out to be as much fun as I'd feared. I threw up, hurt like I'd been put through a meat grinder and then to add to the fun, the drops for my eyes burned like I was rinsing them with gasoline. I'd had to do all of this attached to Paisley through the I.V. the whole time. Eunice had better be praying they never let me see her again.

"We can stop the transfusion now." The doctor said, then I felt his cool hands on my arm.

"I've had some food and juice put in your room." Mitz said.

"Thank you, Mitz." Paisley said sounding tired beside me.

"Go brother, tend your mate." Michael said.

"Keep us informed." Arius answered, then the bed shifted.

"Thank you," I whispered barely able to form the words.

"Guess we're blood sisters now." Paisley said giggling quietly.

"Try to get some tea into her." The doctor said.

"I can't give her blood yet?" Michael asked.

"Not just yet." Clairee answered, "we need to flush her eyes a few more times."

"Oh good." I moaned, not looking forward to that.

"You can heal that wound on her side now, it will stay closed." The doctor said. "I will check back shortly."

"Thank you." I whispered.

"It is my pleasure to care for the woman that took out Eunice Bosworth, my princess." He said formally.

Someone cleared their throat. "I need to go deal with a few things." Troy said. "Quinton, I may need your assistance."

"I'll check in when I get back." Quinton said. "I'll grab some food for you on the way back, brother."

"Thanks." Michael stood beside the bed now.

"If you don't make her my sister, I'm adopting her." Daxx said abruptly from beside me.

"We'll be back." Troy said, his voice near the bed now too.

Later when my head didn't feel like sludge, I'd have questions.

"Let's rinse her eyes again, then you can heal that wound on her side and put her in a warm bath," Clairee said moving closer to the bed, "she must feel like she's been crawling through mud at this point."

"She's in so much pain, I can barely keep it at bay." Michael said.

I moved my head, in the direction of his voice. "You're doing that? Making me feel kind of numb?"

"I'm trying." He was beside my head again.

"You'll need to feed again soon, brother." Rafael said quietly.

"I'm aware." Michael said in a low tone.

I felt him lift my head, a towel in his hand.

"How many more times do we have to do this?" I asked, trying not to sound like a wimp.

"Until your vision clears." Clairee said. "I'm sorry, but it's the only way to flush it out without damaging your vision.

"That's okay, the visions of what I'm going to do to Eunice when I see her again are keeping me happy right now." I whispered.

Someone snorted.

"Victor said she's still going crazy in the cell." Crissy said from the other side of the room

"Good." I said. I felt Clairee touch my face and blew out a breath, knowing what was coming next.

"Sorry." She whispered, just before I felt the drops hit my eye.

I gritted my teeth and blew out a breath between them.

Michael's hand shook as he held my head.

"Do the other one." I said trying not to squeal.

She touched my other eye and the drops hit it.

I groaned this time, then squeezed them shut, panting through the pain.

"I'll come back in a few hours and do it again." She said quietly.

I felt the bed shift as she got up. I wanted to thank her but couldn't speak right yet. I just lay there, holding Michael's hands against my head, breathing in and out slowly.

"Mitz and I can help her get ready for a bath." Bethany said.

Michael slowly released my head.

"We'll put her in something so you can join her, Michael." Mitz said quietly.

I felt his weight shift as I he got off the bed. Then his arms were under my legs and I was being lifted.

He went into the bathroom and set me on the counter.

"I want to heal this closed now." He said softly, pulling the robe open.

I put my hand on his shoulder as he leaned down, his hand on my back, so I could lean back. I rested my hand on his head as his mouth moved over the cut on my side. His touch was gentle. It didn't sting like it had, but I suspected he was still doing whatever it was to help me with the pain.

When he lifted his head, I touched his jaw. "Don't make yourself weak for me."

He dropped his head into my lap. "You shouldn't have been there."

I tugged on his hair gently, wishing I could see his face. "Hey," he lifted his head, "I don't regret any of if, well except my landing at the end, but I'll heal."

He stood up and leaned over me. "I'll let the girls help you change." His voice was shaky, he kissed the top of my head then straightened.

"We've got her." Bethany said from beside him and I felt her touch my shoulder to keep me upright on the counter.

"I'll be right outside the door." He said.

"I found something." Crissy said coming into the room.

I heard the door close. "Who all is in here?"

"Mitz, Crissy and I." Bethany said.

"Okay, good, because I'm not sure I can stand or walk right now." I leaned back against the mirror. Someone turned the water on in the tub.

"We'll make sure you don't hit the floor." Beth said.

"Appreciate it. I don't think I can handle another bruise right now." I moved my arms as someone pulled the robe off my shoulder.

"You are so many shades of red and purple right now." Bethany whispered.

"Yeah, I bruise easy, which since I'm a fighter means I'm always multi-colored." I said hissing out a breath as I lifted my other arm.

There was a quick knock on the door.

"Came back to help. Troy is barking orders at everything that moves." Daxx said.

I heard the door close.

"They are all going to be restless for a while, love, it affects them all when one of you women get hurt." Mitz said.

"Help us get her standing. I think we're going to have to rip open the scabs on her knees to get these pants off." Beth said sounding distressed.

"Awesome. More pain." I mumbled.

"Michael will be able to give you blood soon." Daxx said as I felt her put her hand under my arm.

"I'll get the other side." Crissy said. "Victor's aura is swirling right now. Someone is going to get raged on." She said softly as she took my other arm.

I managed to get to the edge of the counter, but my knees buckled when my feet hit the floor.

"We've got you." Daxx said.

"Better be quick." I said huffing out a breath. "I have no strength right now." As they peeled the pants down my legs, I concentrated on keeping my knees locked. When they pulled them over my knees, I hissed out a breath.

"Daxx?" Michael was on the other side of the door.

"Not yet, Michael." She adjusted her hold, so I could try to lift one foot out. "The spike in pain was just getting the leggings over her scraped-up knees."

I could hear mumbled voices outside the door. I needed distractions as they helped me lift feet and pulled some kind of shorts up my legs. "What's this mate, princess stuff?"

It was totally silent for a moment.

"Michael warned the other males to keep their distance, so I guess you're his." Daxx said quietly, her response hesitant.

They leaned me back against the counter, so we could take my sports bra off. "Maybe he was afraid I'd hurt them." I blew out a breath, feeling winded from doing nothing.

"Try to lift your arms, love." Mitz said quietly.

Daxx and Crissy lifted my arms.

"No. You're Michael's. For sure." Crissy said. "The prophecy couldn't be for anyone else."

I felt material moving down my arms.

"What's it say, Criss?" Daxx asked

"It's a tank top." Bethany told me as they worked it over my chest.

I nodded, too breathless to speak.

"The keeper of peace will find his mate in a woman that is a champion for the meek." Crissy said quietly like she was reading it from a book. "A woman without fear will bring justice to any whose morals faulter."

Daxx snorted. "That is definitely you, Autumn."

I blew out a breath. "I don't know about any of that. I just do what needs to be done."

"Exactly." Beth said. "Okay let's try to get you over to the tub and into it."

I nodded. "So, mate, like you girls and your tattoos kind of thing?" I needed to take my mind off how much more moving around was hurting.

"Yes. When you're feeling better, we'll explain." Daxx said supporting more of my weight.

"Okay. Let me kick off my shoes and step in, so I can balance you." The water turned off.

"Can you lift your leg, love?" I felt Mitz reach down to help me.

"I think," I huffed out a breath, "you're mistaken." My foot touched the water.

"Other one." Daxx said.

"He wears a scar on his face," I grunted trying to force my muscles to work, "for another woman." My other foot was in the water.

"Okay, let me get behind her." Bethany said.

"That was a long time ago." Mitz said softly.

Bending was, to put it mildly a bitch, my whole body was shaking when I was finally sitting. "Not to him," I whispered. "Every time he's close to me I see the regret in his eyes."

"Oh?" Daxx said in a strained voice.

"Then he freezes and leaves." I put my head back and rested it against the tub. "Don't let me slide under and drown."

Bethany laughed. "I'll stay and support you until Michael gets here."

"We'll corner Quinton later and get the full story, he was around then." Daxx said.

"So was Victor, but he will just clear his throat and go find something to be busy with." Crissy said.

Daxx snorted. "Another trait shared among the brothers."

"Daxx?"

Michael was at the door again.

"You can come in now." She said.

I heard the door open.

"Bastard, you could have used eufori." Rafael said by the door. "And closed the marks."

"You'll heal." Michael said coming into the room.

I heard the door close and knew he was in the room, I could feel his eyes on me. "Did you just bite your brother?"

"He offered so I didn't have to leave." His voice came closer to the tub. "Showing him how to feed when he was fifteen was painful."

"I remember." Mitz said. "You boys would draw straws to see who went next." She laughed. "Except Chase, he said it was a fang problem."

"Mmm," was his only reply.

I heard movement but couldn't tell what was going on.

"Oh. Okay. We'll go now." Bethany said, the water moving as she got up.

"Yep." Daxx sounded like she was at the door.

"Bye." Crissy said.

"Don't keep her in there too long, love." Mitz said. "I'll send some food."

I heard the water splash around. Then the water level rose.

"Thanks, Mitz." Michael said quietly from in front of me.

He was in the tub with me.

I heard the door close.

"Are we alone?" I asked, my voice barely functioning.

"Yes, just relax. I won't let you slip under." His voice was low. "I'm going to heal any areas I can without blood."

I relaxed my hold on the edge of the tub. I felt his hands touch one leg, bending it slightly. Before I could ask how bad it was, his mouth moved over my knee. Anything I was about to say vanished. I wondered if he'd taken his clothes off or if he'd climbed in dressed like he had with the shower.

Finishing with that leg, he touched the other one, bending the knee.

"Are your eyes red?"

"Mmm," was his replay as his mouth touched my leg.

"If I weren't half dead here, I'd be enjoying this—I'm sure it's every girl's dream."

He lowered my leg, then I felt him move closer.

I could feel his skin against my legs.

He took my hand and his mouth moved over my fingers, his tongue healing cuts I didn't know I had.

"I especially appreciate it because I know being too close to me bothers you." I whispered.

His mouth paused. "You're like this because we allowed you to use yourself as bait to lure Eunice out."

"I did what I had to."

He moved again, his large body against most of mine now.

I felt his breath on my jaw as he tilted my head to the side. "So, you're just grateful that I got her?" I whispered.

His lips, then his tongue moved over the corner of my mouth. "It's not like that, Autumn. I can't explain right now." I could feel his hair brush my forehead. "I'm already struggling with my instinct to go slit her throat, seeing you like this."

I reached up and touched the side of his face. "We'll have this talk when I can see you." I whispered.

He licked over my swollen lip. "Shh, just rest and let me help you." His large hand cradled my head gently.

I relaxed into it.

The next thing I knew, I was being woken up.

"Autumn," Michael's voice was next to my ear. "Clairee's here to rinse your eyes again."

I opened them. I could see light and some blurry images.

"Can you see us?" Clairee asked.

"Just blobs, but they don't burn now when I open them."

"Oh, good. You should be able to give her blood after this. It would probably clear up on its own without this treatment, but I want to be sure—after what we went through with Crissy." She said softly.

"I agree." Michael said and then I found my head being lifted into his big hands.

"Hold this towel, so we don't soak her pillow." Clairee said.

"Is it going to burn again?" I asked when she touched my face.

"Probably, sorry."

"Go for it." I blew through the stinging, holding onto the fact that I'd be able to see again. "I was a little worried at first." I confessed when she was done.

"I can imagine how frightening it must have been."

"Yeah, not to mention learning how to fight all over again."

Clairee chuckled. "I think you should consider a career change."

I blew out a breath as she wiped the side of my face. "This is who I am."

"I think you're amazing." She said, then the bed shifted. "No bright lights for a few hours, but you can give her blood now to heal—everything else."

Michael got off the bed. "Thank you, Clairee."

I heard the door close and lifted my head, trying to see. Everything was a blur, the only light coming from the bathroom.

"Do you want some juice or tea?"

I shook my head on the pillow. "I'm just too tired to try right now."

I felt the bed shift again. "I want to give you blood a few times before morning, to make sure everything is healed." He lay down beside me, then pulled the covers higher up on me.

I realized I was naked under them.

"Mitz took off your wet clothes after the bath." He said quietly.

Pulling my arm out, I reached and touched his waist. "Thanks for looking out for me."

He didn't say anything for a moment. "Blood and then rest."

I could feel him moving, then he grasped the back of my head gently, pulling me toward his chest. I opened my mouth, using my tongue to find the cut in his flesh.

He inhaled sharply, his hand flexing in my hair. When it closed, he took a ragged breath. "Again." He said in a rough, gravelly voice.

Chapter Thirteen

When I opened my eyes this time, I could see Michael's face as he slept on the pillow beside me. The dark lashes against his skin made twin crescent moons on his face. Lifting my head, I looked down over his bare chest. I was very thankful I could see right now. I touched his chest and ran my hand slowly down it. The muscles clenched under my touch, so I knew he was awake and aware of what I was doing.

As I reached his waist, he caught my hand and held it still. I looked up to see sleepy blue eyes watching me. "Morning," I whispered and leaned up on my elbow.

His eyes searched mine, then my face.

"I can see perfectly." I said.

Relief showed in his expression. "You need to eat." His voice was heavy with sleep.

"I will shortly." I moved closer.

He watched me with a wary look in his eyes.

Stretching the last few inches, I kissed his mouth softly. "Thank you." I hovered by his mouth for a moment, our eyes locked on one another.

He blinked. "I have to go feed."

I moved back and tilted my head, exposing my neck. "You can from me."

"You were…"

I put my hand over his mouth. "I'm fine now." I smirked, "and I find it kind of sexy. Don't deny me that. You licked my legs last night and I couldn't even enjoy it."

His eyes flicked from mine to my throat, then back.

I moved my hand and lay back down. "Please, Michael, let me do this for you."

He rolled onto his side, his hand resting lightly on my hip. "I shouldn't." He whispered.

"I want you to." I moved closer, resting my hand on his chest.

Raising up on his elbow, he looked down at me. I could see his eye color hovering between the blue of the man and the red of the primal being. With a soft sound, he leaned down, his breath brushing over my throat. He inhaled deeply, pulling me against his chest.

When he bit into me, I moaned. I didn't know what it was about this man, but every touch from him did it for me.

As he lifted his head, I leaned my head back and looked up to see red eyes watching me. Giving him a gentle shove, he rolled onto his back. I shifted to lay across his chest. Michael grasped my waist and lifted me, so our mouths could reach each other's.

They clashed in a frenzy of passion. His hand wove through my hair, holding me as he took control of the kiss. I may have been on top, but he was completely alpha now.

I ran my tongue over his fangs. He groaned and broke the kiss, then flipped us over so I was laying under him. He kissed me again and I felt a fire ignite inside.

I struggled to free my legs from the covers.

He lifted up on one arm and yanked them out of the way.

I took that opportunity to undo his jeans and shove them down his hips.

His red eyes held mine.

"Don't stop." I pleaded softly.

With a growl in the back of his throat, he lowered his head and nipped across my shoulder with his fangs.

I shoved at his jeans, pushing them down. Once I got them low enough, I used my heels to shove them down his legs.

He moved back to my mouth and kissed me so passionately, I was sure there would be steam coming from us.

Everywhere I touched was muscle. I was easy, a finely toned body did it for me.

Reaching under me, he lifted my hips to align our bodies. I wrapped my legs around him, making sure he wasn't going to change his mind.

He broke the kiss, I was gasping for air. He lifted his head up, his red eyes capturing mine as he thrust into me.

There was no gentle beginning for either of us. The tension and heat between us had been building far too long. I moaned, deeply satisfied, as he held my hips and rocked into me. Normally I wasn't the submissive one in bed, but he was playing my body with such mastery, I didn't have to control.

When I felt like I couldn't take a moment more, he leaned down and bit my neck again. It was the right combination of pain and pleasure. I crashed over the edge, moaning as my body erupted for him.

Not pausing to let me catch my breath, he increased the speed and intensity of his movements and I was gasping and moaning, my whole body shaking.

He stiffened and growled against my throat. With a gentle touch, he licked over his bite and then rested his head on the pillow beside mine.

Both of us were trying to bring air into our lungs. I ran my hands up and down his back in a lazy motion.

"Did I," he panted, "hurt you?"

I shook my head slowly. "No." I inhaled, trying to get a handle on my breathing.

Taking a deep breath, he let it out slowly and then lifted his weight onto his elbows. His blue eyes stared down at me. Leaning down, he kissed my mouth tenderly. Moving off me, he glanced at me quickly. "I have to go." He whispered.

Rolling, he stood beside the bed, his pants in his hands. "Go get something to eat."

Then he vanished.

I dropped my hands to the bed. Turning I looked at the bathroom. "Shower. Food." Nodding, I sat up slowly. My breathing still hadn't slowed. I'd had guys bail right after, no cuddles, but usually we'd at least caught our breath. I looked to where he'd stood. "Yeah, no commitment issues there."

Showered, dressed, and absolutely starving, I opened the door. A large bald man with a red beard stood outside the door.

He inclined his head briefly. "I'm to take you to the dining room."

"Oh." I close the door. "Good, save me following the map." I put my hand out. "Autumn."

He looked down at my hand, his brows furrowed. "Woodrow." He shook my hand quickly, like he shouldn't be.

"Woodrow. So, what do your friends call you?"

We stared walking down the hall.

"Woods, mostly."

I nodded. "Okay, Woods."

"I'll be your personal guard."

I looked up at him. "I need a guard?"

"My king's orders." He said quietly.

I shrugged. "Well, okay then."

We turned and went down a hall I recognized. "Maybe we can spar after breakfast, if there's nothing gong on."

He inclined his head. "If you wish." He motioned to a door and stopped.

I looked at the door. "You're not coming to eat?"

"In the royal dining room? No."

"Okay. I'll see you later."

He nodded.

I went in to see everyone was at the table, except Michael. Emil sat at the end, so I sat to his left, still close to the door.

"Well, you look much better." Alona said with a smile.

"I feel great—and I'm starving."

Mitz came out with a plate and cup. She rushed down to me and set it down.

I looked at it, my mouth watering. "Thanks, Mitz. I'm famished."

She leaned down and grasped my face then kissed my forehead. "I'm just happy you're all right, love." She turned and rushed from the room.

I glanced down the table to Daxx, then to Michael's empty chair.

"Michael and some of the guards went out first thing."

"Oh? Just looking or did they find something?" I stabbed my fork randomly at my plate, taking a bite of the first thing I speared.

"Not sure." Quinton said leaning by Rafael and pouring some juice in my glass. "He's got a fire under his ass this morning."

I nodded. "Thanks."

"It may be because we've barred him from going near Eunice." Chase said. "At least until we get something useful out of her."

I shrugged. "That would do it." I turned to see Arius watching me with an odd look on his face. "What?" I patted my chin worried I had food on it.

He shook his head. "Just happy to see your eyes today."

I snorted. "I am thrilled to see anything today. Yesterday was intense."

"Oh, speaking of intense." Daxx pulled out her phone, tapped the screen and slid it down the table toward me. "Got a couple pics you may like."

Reaching I picked it up and looked. It was me kicking the mountain with green eyes. "Cameras aren't allowed. How did you manage this?"

She shrugged. "I had Troy and Michael behind me, they're great blockers."

I slid my finger across the screen and looked at the second one. She'd captured it perfectly. "Wow, I look like I know what I'm doing here."

Emil chuckled. "If that was you bumbling, I do not want to see you confidently attacking."

I grinned and slid the phone back toward her. "I was trying to get him to my level. His only weakness was his head."

"I think I held my breath the whole time." Paisley said.

Bethany nodded. "Me too."

"Took a lot of constant chatter to keep Michael off that platform." Chase said.

"Yeah," Leone nodded. "I thought we were gong to have to drag him out a few times."

"Did you really take that hit on purpose?" Troy asked.

I nodded. "I had to get him to think I was down, so he'd relax his stance and lean for me. Of course, I questioned that for hours as my jaw and mouth throbbed."

Arius pulled out his phone. "Eunice has finally exhausted herself." He pushed his chair back and nodded to Troy. "Want to come take a look now?"

Troy leaned over and kissed Daxx. "Love to."

Chase jumped up. "I'm not missing this."

"I'll come with." Emil stood up.

Victor and Leone also got up. Rafael grabbed his cup. "Wait for me."

Arius looked down at Paisley. "I'll call if we need you to hold her."

She nodded. "Okay. We'll be in the cave."

After they left, I pointed to the door. "I opened my door to see I had a personal guard."

The women nodded.

"Yeah, we all have one." Daxx said.

Crissy sighed. "Anytime we go…"

"Anywhere without…" Beth smirked.

Alona made quotes in the air. "One of the brothers…"

"Our guards are to be our shadows." Paisley shrugged.

Quinton started laughing. Then stopped and looked around like he just realized he was the only man left.

Daxx motioned to the door. "Aren't you going to stare at Eunice too?"

He shook his head. "No. I've seen her enough in my lifetime. I'm good."

I leaned forward and looked at Daxx.

She smiled at Quinton. "That's great, saves me hunting you down."

He frowned, then looked around the table. "For?"

I set my cup down. "What can you tell me about Lara?"

He looked at me for a second, then pushed his plate away. Exhaling a deep breath, he looked at the table. "She was soft, delicate, graceful." He looked at Daxx who rolled her eyes. "And spoiled, privileged, and wanted Michael to make her a princess."

"Were they officially mated?" She asked.

He shook his head. "No."

"What happened?" Alona looked at him.

"We were on lockdown, not to leave the palace. Michael had Lara and her parents moved up to a guest wing—for their safety, so Willis couldn't use them against him." He sighed. "Lara was whining about being confined."

"Yes, being confined in a palace on a mountaintop is very trying." Alona said glancing to Daxx.

"She talked him into going for a ride—just the two of them. He was so smitten with her, he agreed." Quinton picked up his cup and looked in it. "Eunice and some of their followers ambushed them. Lara died while Michael was fighting for his life. If the patrol hadn't come along, he would have died also."

Alona covered her mouth.

Quinton took a drink and set the cup back down. "By the time he recovered, she'd been buried, and her parents had moved, wanting nothing to do with the royals ever again."

I looked around at the others, no one moved or spoke.

"You have to remember at that point, there was just Victor, Michael and I." He shrugged. "We had no idea we were the men in the King's sons numbering nine prophecy. We didn't know that until our father told us about his ninth son born on the other side."

"Emil." Crissy said when I looked at her.

"That was only a hundred and sixty years ago. Michael had a hundred and forty years of thinking he lost the love of his life." He finished quietly.

"Well that puts things into perspective." Alona whispered.

"And true mates?" Daxx gave me a quick glance, "do people actually resist that attraction? Do they fight fate and win?"

Quinton glanced to me briefly then to Daxx, his brows furrowed. "It's happened. Usually when one is already officially mated to another."

"So, love can conquer fate." Alona said softly.

"I guess." He frowned. "Now why are you asking me all of this?" He looked back to me. "Michael say something?"

I shook my head.

"I know he has a blood bond with you. Your essence is different, and you're healed."

He could smell that? "Just," I looked at my hands folding in front of me, "just curious."

"You should ask Michael all of this, not me."

"Well it would help if he didn't run from her like his ass was on fire." Daxx told him.

Quinton rubbed the back of his neck. "Well, figure out how to stop him from running."

Paisley and Beth exchanged a look. "We'll work on that."

He nodded and stood up. "Let me know if I can help. Tormenting younger brothers is one of my favorite pastimes." He walked out of the room.

"That wasn't helpful at all." Alona said with a sigh.

"Soft, delicate, graceful." I said, then covered my face. "A three-hundred-year-old *perfect* ghost."

"Get in his face. He can't run then." Daxx looked around at the others. "He can't resist forever." She frowned, "if he does, I'm stabbing Troy."

I gave her a puzzled look, then sighed loudly. "He didn't *resist* this morning when we woke up. But he also made the fastest exit I've ever seen."

"You two—" she glanced to Alona quickly, then back to me.

I nodded.

"And he ran out the door after?" Alona asked.

I snorted. "Oh no. He didn't use a door. He jumped up and vanished."

"Holy shit. That's a smack in the face." Daxx said with shock on her face. She recovered quickly. "Okay, first you have to avoid a repeat of this morning while we'll all try to figure something out."

"We need to get her gloves." Crissy said.

Alona nodded.

I had no idea what that was about. "I'd like to go check on Joe." They all turned to look at me. "Make sure he made it back all right and grab my stuff, I mean, I can't stay there right? They'll come looking for me again."

Daxx stood up. "Let's go catch Troy and maybe he'll allow us to go with our guards."

"We'll be in the cave. Let us know what's going on." Alona stood up.

"I'm going to my tower. I have to figure out these flashes of light." She grabbed her pack and ran from the room.

"That doesn't sound good." Bethany said quietly.

Daxx nodded. "Probably isn't, but if she can give us a location—that's more from team bad in our cells."

"Team bad?" I stood up.

Paisley nodded. "As in they are so bad, we couldn't come up with a better name for them."

Alona laughed. "I think it was Rafael who called them that first." She headed to the door.

I looked down at my plate.

"Leave it this time." Daxx motioned to the door. "If we don't catch Troy at the cells, we'll be chasing him all over Alterealm."

I followed her out. Woods stood there and started following us. "Can't we just port there?"

She shook her head. "Can't port in the cells. Which makes sense, so people can't get in and out that shouldn't be."

"Oh, good point."

We weaved through the halls, Woods right behind us. I wasn't a big fan of someone walking behind me. "So, where's your guard?"

"He hangs out at the guard's training yard until I message him." She said and motioned for us to go down a sloping hall.

I stopped abruptly and turned to Woods. "You could do that. Go hang out with—" I looked at Daxx.

"Tim," she shrugged, "Sith, Bronx, Mac, Felix." She rhymed off.

He looked from her to me again. "I was…"

Daxx stepped beside me. "Go. We'll be in the cells, then we might go on a field trip to the other side. We'll call if we are."

He inclined his head. "My huntress." Then turned on his heel and walked the other way.

She shook her head. "It pays to have rank around here sometimes."

I nodded. "I guess you are a queen."

She snorted. "Only when they make me wear a gown."

"A gown?" I followed her.

She nodded.

"For what?" I frowned. I didn't do dresses.

"To make me look like a cake topper mostly." She stopped and opened a door.

Once inside the cells I was gobsmacked. It seemed like miles of clear rooms. Daxx seemed to know where she was going because we made our way through them quickly. When we reached a large open area, we found all the men standing there, except Michael. Even Quinton was there now. He shrugged when Daxx gave him an odd look.

Inside a smaller space were Arius, Troy, Victor and Eunice. They'd put her in one of the grey jumpsuits. I didn't want to be petty, but that brought me quite a bit of satisfaction to see her in it.

"How are they doing?" Daxx asked Leone.

"Not good. Troy can't get anything useful from her." He said crossing his arms and watching.

"Is she blocking him?" She moved closer to the wall and looked at him.

"No. More like garbled crap." Rafael said. "He can't see anything useful as long as she does that."

I stood beside Daxx. "Can she see us?"

Daxx shook her head. "No. They can make it so she could but seeing us standing here won't help him see anything clearly in her head."

"What if she could see me?" I whispered.

Daxx looked at me.

I motioned to Eunice. "She had big plans for me."

She turned and looked at Quinton, then Chase.

"It could work." He said. "Distract her from doing whatever she is it to disturb access to a clear thought."

Daxx nodded. "You guys move out of sight." She pointed to the center of the wall. "Stand there." Then she went over to the end by the door.

"Ready?"

"Yeah," I nodded, "lets do it."

"Okay. She can't hear us, but she'll see you."

I nodded again. When Daxx did something on the pad, Arius looked at me and straightened from where he was leaning. The other two men looked at me as well. Eunice turned slowly. Her blank expression changed to something harder. One side of her face was swollen and bruised, with just enough road rash to let me know how well I'd connected with that blind kick. She grinned that broken smile and continued to look at me.

Victor said something to her. She glanced at him and answered, then turned to look at me again. She puckered her lips and blew me a kiss.

"Eww." I whispered.

Troy nodded and went to the door. The other two followed.

"Okay, she can't see you now." Daxx said.

"That was brilliant." Troy said coming in.

Daxx pointed to me. "Her idea. Did you get anything?"

"A few things. I need to think about them and try to make sense of them, but," he smiled at me. "it's a place to start."

"I think Eunice wanted Autumn for herself, not a grand plan." Chase said with a smirk.

I shuddered. "Just—yuck."

He chuckled. "What brings you ladies down here to the depths of hell?"

Daxx smiled at Troy. "I needed to ask my king something."

Troy looked at Chase then back to her.

Chase grinned at him. "She's batting her eyes, brother, you're in trouble."

Troy raised an eyebrow as he looked down at her.

"Shut up, Chase." She said without looking at him. "Autumn wants to go check that Joe made it back okay and get her stuff." She crossed her arms over her chest. "She wants to remove all traces of her being there so if they come looking, they can't take it out on Joe."

Troy rubbed his hand over his jaw. "I can't go right now." He glanced to Leone. "Michael say when he was coming back?"

"Don't mention his name right now, or I'll stab you." She said glaring at him.

He gave her a shocked look.

"I'll explain later. We'll take our guards. I can port us in and out." She nodded.

He turned and looked at his brothers.

"Troy—why give us giant guards if we never use them, because we never go outside these chambers?" She glared at him.

He took a deep breath and looked from her to me. "In and out, no side trips."

She nodded.

"Wear your devices."

She held up her wrist and showed him hers.

I did the same. I'd put it back on this morning, deciding I was wearing one for the rest of my life, after being taken once.

"Call me when you leave and when you get back." He said, his eyes moving over her face.

Smiling, she leaned into him and rubbed her hand on his chest. "We will."

Arius cleared his throat. "Are just you two going?"

Daxx rolled her eyes. "Yes, your mates are safe in the cave. You guys really need to lighten up."

Chase hissed out a breath. "Because you would never find trouble."

She rolled her eyes. "Not intentionally."

Victor rubbed a hand over his brow. "No, but it finds all of you well enough."

Daxx turned to me. "Ready to go? The testosterone in here is getting a little deep."

I grinned then looked at Troy and covered my heart. "I will kick anyone's ass that goes near her."

"I believe you would." He grinned. "Go, before I clear my schedule to come with you, and she stabs me."

Chapter Fourteen

I grabbed Daxx's arm before she opened the back door to the gym. "Wait. I can't go in like this."

She turned and looked at me. "Like what?"

I motioned to my face. "Without a mark on me."

Her eyes widened. "Shit."

I looked up at Woods. "Hit me." I tilted my face up.

He looked horrified. "I—my king—"

Daxx shook her head. "They won't do it."

Tim snorted. "The law wouldn't take that well."

I frowned. "The law?"

"He means Michael." Daxx said biting her lip.

I shrugged and looked at her. "Okay. You do it. Queen trumps the law, right?"

She opened her mouth, then closed it. "I suppose." She looked at my mouth. "Fat lip, that's all I can bring myself to do."

I nodded. "That will work." I turned my head so she could catch as much of my mouth and jaw as possible in one shot.

Stepping inside, Daxx mumbled. "Don't ever tell Michael I did it."

I licked the blood off my lip. "I won't."

Joe came out of his office and limped toward me. He stopped when he reached me and looked at my mouth. "Guess he hit like a girl." He looked me up and down. "You don't even look like you fought."

I shrugged. "First guy was a joke."

He nodded. "Second one was all bulk, no skill." He glanced to Woods and Tim. "You want to tell me what you're into?"

I sighed. "I got some people after me, trying to get me into things that don't sit well."

"I figured something was going on." He said quietly.

I nodded. "Yeah. I need to lay low," I motioned to the end of the hall, "going to grab my stuff and erase myself from here." I touched his shoulder. "I don't want them coming after you."

He looked at me for a moment, then to the men behind me. "Keep her safe."

Tim and Woods nodded briefly.

We started walking toward the gym. "You get the money tucked away?"

He grinned. "Yeah, took half to the shelter this morning. I'll go to the kitchen later." He motioned to Pete where he was working on the bag. "Pete will go with me."

I nodded. "Good."

"Dynamo." Someone called out from the ring in the center of the gym.

I turned to see Smith, one of the regulars leaning on the ropes. "You keeping your jab tight?"

He nodded. "Of course. Heard you impressed last night. Fought a beast."

I shrugged. "More of mountain, he had no bite."

He motioned to the men walking behind Daxx and I. "You cheating on us with another gym?"

I laughed. "No. I'm helping some friends out."

He nodded and motioned to the ring. "Got a minute to check out what I'm working on?"

I looked at Daxx, she shrugged. "Just a few." I went over and climbed into the ring with him. Going over I picked up the punch mitts and put them on. Turning, I held them up. "Show me what you got."

Daxx and I went around the corner of the hallway.

She grinned at me. "It's great that they respect you like that." She rolled her eyes. "It's not easy to take a bunch of men and get them to see you in that light."

I laughed. "I had to throw each one of those guys down to earn that respect."

She stopped walking.

I glanced to see what she was looking at. Michael and Troy stood outside the door of my room. Troy's arms were crossed over his chest as he spoke to his brother. Michael's posture said he was having nothing of what Troy was saying.

"This can't be good." Daxx said then started walking again.

I hefted my bag on my shoulder and followed her, watching Michael as we walked. His hair was wet, like he'd just had a shower. My brain prodded me with images of what that would look like.

Troy frowned as we got closer. He was looking at my face. "Do we need to get you a face mask to protect your mouth?"

I smirked, then licked over my fat lip. "No. But I'd love some safety glasses or something so yesterday never happens again."

Michael was in front of me, tilting my chin up. He was not happy. "What happened?" He glanced to Troy. "You said they went to grab her belongings."

I jerked my head out of his grip. "It's nothing."

Daxx gave me a quick look and glanced to Troy. "You should see the way these fighters hang on Autumn's every word. You all could take lessons from them."

As far as changing the subject went, that worked well, I thought.

Daxx waved her phone. "Got your message. What's up?"

He dragged his eyes from his brother then looked down at her. "We're going to meet and go over a few things I picked out of Eunice's head."

Michael pointed at me. "Why would you flaunt Autumn in front of Eunice?"

Troy looked at his finger pointing to Daxx and then turned to Michael. "She didn't flaunt her. The mere sight of her on the other side of that wall stopped Eunice from scrambling her thoughts and allowed me in."

"I think Eunice has a thing for women." Daxx said.

I made a face. "Let's not go there. The way she looked at me—" I shuddered.

"So, what did you see?" Daxx looked up at Troy.

"The caverns." He said quietly.

Daxx looked from him to Michael. "Caverns?"

Michael finally looked somewhere other than at me. "Yes. Under the palace there are caverns and tunnels throughout the mountain."

Daxx huffed out a breath. "Awesome not just rodents to worry about, but wild animals." She shrugged. "When do we leave?"

"We're meeting the others at the practice room in a few minutes." Troy said.

Michael looked at me, his gaze moving to my mouth. "We'll be along shortly."

I glanced up at him, then to Daxx. Him healing my mouth was not going to help. I was finding it difficult to not daydream about this morning. I shook my head. "No, we'll come now." I opened the door and tossed my bag inside then turned and started walking in the direction of the practice room, at least I hoped I was.

When we walked in a few of the men stood there leaning on wooden practice weapons.

"Clairee said she can send someone to cloak us, as long as we keep the numbers down." Rafael said.

"Why can't we just port in?" Bethany asked.

Victor shook his head. "Too many unknowns. We won't know what we're dropping in on."

Leone grinned at Beth. "I won't let you fall off the horse."

We walked over to the group. "Horses?"

Quinton nodded. "Be easiest to ride in undetected."

I glanced at Michael, remembering my last and first ride. "Oh." I shrugged. "Has to be easier not chained up, right?"

Leone grinned, then stopped when he looked at Michael's scowl. "Yeah."

"We don't know what we're going to find." Michael said crossing his arms and bracing his legs. "I think it's best Autumn stay here, she's not experienced with our sort of fighting or weapons."

I looked at him, then to Daxx, her eyes were wide.

"I don't know about the rest of you," Alona said, "but if we're skulking around in dank caves and caverns under a mountain—" she motioned to me, "I will feel much better having Autumn beside me."

Paisley nodded. "I agree."

Daxx glanced to Troy, then to me. "Add her skills to what the rest of us women have and we'll be a force to be…"

"She stays here." Michael said in an abrupt tone.

I huffed out a breath and stepped in front of him. He looked down at me, his eyes holding mine with a cold look. "I'm going."

"You're not taking chances…"

I lifted my arms out from my body and glared at him. "Look, just because we had sex, that doesn't give you proprietary rights."

Everyone stopped talking.

"Oh boy." Quinton muttered.

I glanced around. Rafael looked at the ceiling when I turned. Shaking my head, I took a deep breath and looked back up at Michael, the hard look had changed, but I didn't know what it meant. "You've made your feelings on all fronts quite clear." I waved a hand up and down my body. "My body, my choice. I'm going."

The muscles in his jaw pulsed as his blue eyes locked on mine. He inhaled deeply through his nose, then flicked his eyes to Troy. "I'll be at the stables. We leave in an hour." With that he spun on his heels and stormed out the nearest door.

I stood there with my back to the rest of them, staring at the door he exited through. Sighing, I turned. "Sorry. I didn't mean to cause a spectacle."

Chase waved his hand at me. "Not at all, we all enjoy a good spectacle from time to time."

I blew out a breath and motioned to the weapons wall, then looked at Rafael who was watching me warily. "Help me find something that won't hinder my movement, but will *weaponize* me."

He glanced to Troy for a second, then nodded. "Yeah. Okay. Maybe something compact on your back?"

I nodded and followed him. "Yeah, something no longer than a baton, but pointy and easy to work with."

He glanced at me, then went down the wall. "Maybe a kama? It's the same length as a baton, but you have the blade as a backup." He pulled one down. "Of course, the blade on the real one is steel." He flipped it back and forth in his hand, changing from offensive to defensive. "You can use it to block and disarm," he smirked, "like you did me. Or," He flipped it so the hooked blade was turned out, "when you mean business." Holding it out to me, I took it. "Trick is to keep that blade away from your body while in motion."

I flipped it a few times. "Yeah." I looked over to the others, then back to him. "Can I practice for a few minutes?"

Crossing his arms, he nodded. "We've got time." He motioned to the mat. "Usually they're used in pairs, so navigating with one shouldn't be too difficult." He paused and rubbed his jaw. "Do I want to know what happened to your mouth?"

I licked over the puffy lip, then glanced over at Daxx. "Probably not." I said quietly, then stepped back a few feet. "Help me get this down so your brother doesn't try to bench me again."

He snorted. "He's going to keep trying," he motioned to the other men, "they all do and fail every time." He motioned with his arm behind his back. "Find the angle that will be easiest for you to access it quickly." Rafael put his arm behind his back a few times and pulled out from different directions. "Over your head works best," he did it a few times, "because then you've got that downward swing to use to your advantage immediately."

I held the kama above my head and bent my elbow. "And how to I not cut my head off pulling it out?"

Quinton came over with a leather case and strap. He motioned for me to turn around. "It takes practice, you don't want to know how many nicks we got in the beginning, getting those swords past our heads."

Rafael grinned, "My head wasn't the issue, it was other body parts with our knives."

Nodding, Quinton placed the strap over my shoulder. "Left or right?"

I looked up at him. "Can't I do either?"

He glanced to Rafael, then cocked his head to the side. "Not if you're pulling over your head. The handle will have to rest against the back of your neck and might impede your motion."

I bit my lip and reached to my lower back with the hand not holding the wooden weapon.

He shook his head, "blade will have to be against your shoulders, one wrong move and you stab yourself."

I huffed out a breath and looked at them.

Chase came over and held up his hand. "We have something similar to a kama, same curved blade, but retractable."

Rafael's brows drew together. "We do?"

Chase nodded. "Alona has been working with our armory staff to make weapons for the girls, so they're small and concealable, but deadly when needed." He smiled at me. "Would you like to test our new design?"

I grinned. "Oh yes I would." I looked at Quinton. "Then I could wear it so I'd pull from the bottom?"

Quinton nodded. "Without the blade, you could wear it anywhere you wanted."

I nodded to Chase. "I'll test it."

He inclined his head. "I'll bring it to the stables." He motioned to Alona. "The girls are going to get changed now, I believe they're waiting for you."

I handed Rafael the kama. "Thanks."

"Just don't use it on my brother." Chase said tilting his head to the side. "Regardless of how much he deserves it."

I sighed. "I'll just use my feet on him." I winked and turned to go with the girls.

I tapped the end of the baton again and watched the blade flip out of the other end.

"That is cool. Scary, but cool." Paisley said.

I nodded and pushed the blade back in with the heel of my boot. "I feel like a kickass ninja." I grinned at her.

She looked at my outfit and nodded. "You look like one too, with that hood up."

I pushed the hood back. "Mitz somehow knew I needed to feel unseen."

"Mitz knows everything." She laughed.

I turned to see Troy and Arius watching us. "What's up with your guy today? Every time I turn around, he's watching me like I've done something wrong."

She turned and looked over at him. "I'm not sure, but I'll ask on our ride." Paisley cringed. "I haven't been on a horse in my life."

Leone walked out of the barn and handed Bethany a pouch. She smiled up at him and then stretched up to kiss him. Turning, she came in our direction.

Daxx and Alona came over. "Just once I'd like to take a car somewhere."

Alona nodded. "At least it's not a boat."

"I want to take a plane." Crissy said.

We all looked up to see her on the branch above us. She waved, then flipped over and jumped down.

Bethany shook her head and put her hand in the pouch. "Leone and I have been working with Elder Arian on these." She held up a small plastic case about the size of a battery. "They're signal amplifiers," she looked at Alona, "so we don't end up in some dark place with no signal on our phones again."

"Oh." Alona took it and turned it over in her hand. "This is wonderful."

Beth handed each of us one. "It's mostly to keep us connected, not so much for making calls or," she looked at Paisley, "downloading music." She turned it over and pulled a short thin cord from it. "It can also be used to charge your phone, but the battery life on it is only good for about an hour." She shrugged. "For now."

Paisley clipped hers to her waist. "I'm good with not being stuck in the dark with no phone again."

Beth nodded. "We'll turn them on when we get there, and don't forget to charge them again later."

I clipped mine to the strap on my shoulder. "Sounds like you guys have had some adventures."

"That's one word for it." Alona rolled her eyes. "Ah, my man is ready to go."

We turned to see Chase riding toward us.

"Is it just me, or do they all look hot in their gear?" Paisley asked watching Arius get on his horse.

Alona smiled. "Yes, and they know it too."

"Wouldn't surprise me if they fought like that so they could look like warriors with those swords on their backs." Bethany said watching Leone get on his horse.

I shook my head. "Having attempted to wield one of those swords, sexy or not, they have my admiration for using them."

"And I'm sure all you think is admiration when you see Michael looking like that." Daxx said.

I turned to see him on the horse. He looked larger than life and sexier then words. "Yeah. Admiration doesn't come to mind right now." He was riding this way. "Shit, I can't ride with him."

Daxx nudged me, I turned to see Quinton going by.

"Quinton, can I ride with you?" I said quickly.

He stopped and looked at me, then glanced to Michael heading this way. Sighing he held his hand down to me. "Sure, I've lived a long enough life."

I went over and clasped his wrist and vaulted up, although with his strength it wasn't hard, he could have tossed me right over to the other side. Settling behind him, I looked and grabbed the strap on his waist, then decided that holding on with two hands would be better, and took the other one.

Michael stopped his horse and looked at me. His eyes moved to Quinton. I didn't know what look he gave him, but Michael inclined his head to his brother and then prodded his horse and rode in the other direction.

"That wasn't tense at all." Quinton said quietly. He looked over his shoulder at me. "When I said I'd help you girls, I didn't mean at my own peril by the way."

I shrugged. "I just needed to make a point."

He snorted. "You succeeded." He turned and looked down at Daxx. "Don't toy with fate too much, it could get messy."

She grinned at him. "Just enough to make him think."

Shaking his head, Quinton turned the horse and followed Michael.

As soon as we started moving, I decided holding onto his waist would be better than a strap.

"Just don't smack your face on my swords." He said over his shoulder. "Your mouth can't take many more hits today."

Chase and Alona caught up to us, she sat in front of Chase, sideways like Michael had done the day they'd found me. Chase paused and looked at me behind Quinton and shook his head. "Don't play with the devil too much, dynamo, he's been known to bite." With a smirk he turned and followed Troy and Daxx.

I looked around to see all the other women riding in front of their mates, except the tiny woman with Rafael, she rode behind him like I was.

Quinton shifted and turned so he could look at me. "The one with Raf is the witch, she's cloaking all of us and the horses, so no one can see us." He looked at Michael at the front of the group beside Emil, then shook his head and turned back around.

"Why do I feel like I'm missing something here? I realize with this many of you, there has to be some sort of pact so you don't steal each others dates, but—"

He snorted. "Oh, we've been there more then once over the years." Quinton let the horse walk so we were behind the others. "It's not for me to explain, I'm sure the girls will if you pull out a bottle of wine, but just be thankful your arm isn't adorned with a tattoo right now." He gave an abrupt nod. "That will put it into perspective a bit." Prodding the horse, he caught up to the rest.

I looked at my arm, not knowing what he meant by that. I knew the couples had theirs done to match, it was cute and an original tradition, but what it had to do with Michael and I, I had no idea. When he nudged the horse into a full run, I decided I'd just hang on and think about things later.

Chapter Fifteen

"Is anyone else having a Lord of the Rings moment? I feel like we're walking into a cave filled with dangerous creatures." Bethany said quietly.

Paisley nodded.

"The dangerous creatures should feel lucky to have our attention." Chase's voice echoed through the headset as he went past me.

"I was thinking you men were the dangerous creatures," Alona said watching him walk past, "perhaps I misunderstood."

"When I suggested testing our mics, I was thinking more of a check from everyone." Quinton said, then sighed.

"Cheap bastard, you always want someone else to get the check first." Leone said grinning at Quinton as he walked by him.

I looked at the woman with the horses. "We're leaving her out there alone?"

"She's a witch and no one can see her but us." Daxx said, then followed the men into the cave.

"Right." I went in after her.

"Victor, you're leading this adventure," Troy said, "I believe you grew up in these."

"Are you saying I'm a caveman?" Victor asked giving Troy an amused looked as he went in.

"What? No?" Troy realized he was kidding and motioned for him to go in.

"I sometimes think I've ported into a sitcom and not a royal family." Emil said calmly. "Which I haven't decided if I'm good with or not."

"Says the brother that was humming the Star Wars theme while beating every guard in the yard last night." Arius chuckled.

"I couldn't get the damn thing out of my head." Emil told him.

"I have that problem with that Muppet song when I hear it." Crissy said. "The one that…"

"Crissy. Do *not* hum that song." Daxx warned. "It will haunt me for days."

"Okay, but it's a good song." Crissy said.

"Are we finished?" Michael asked. "Shall we break out and dance as well? If anyone were here, perhaps they'd join us— as we're announcing our presence and these caverns echo."

I glanced ahead to where he was walking. I felt like his mood was my fault. I turned and looked at Daxx over my shoulder. She shook her head as if she knew what I was thinking. "Is there one main tunnel or does it break off?" I asked.

Michael stopped and turned around and looked at me. "We are not separating."

"Just asking." I said slowly.

"Damn, brother, do you need a nap or something?" Leone asked and motioned to us women to do ahead. "Michael and I have the back of the line."

Michael stood there, his gaze was locked on me as everyone went past.

I stopped in front of him. "You due for a thaw soon, iceman? We get you're pissed I'm here, but get over it, and let's get this done."

He continued to stand there and look down at me, then inclined his head and motioned for me to go.

"Fearless." Daxx said quietly into the mic.

"I'm a big fangirl." Alona whispered.

"Cristy, if I'm to lead, that usually means you follow, not race ahead." Victor said quietly.

"Sorry, I'm excited. I'm in tunnels, under a castle. I've never seen them, in or out of my head." She whispered. "Can we climb these?"

"No." Leone said, "no proper footing."

"Too bad." She sighed.

I had my own moment after she said that. We were in a castles' underground caverns. Caverns that could be filled with people responsible for taking women. Yeah, that last part ruined the illusion for me.

Everyone stopped and crouched. I pushed the hood off and tucked it into the strap on my shoulder.

"Someone has been in here recently." Chase whispered.

We moved into a large, open area. Leone and Rafael went over to stand by two tunnels leading out. I took a moment to look around. The walls were a combination of natural and manmade creation. I was going to ask how old they were, but decided I might not like the answers and it probably wasn't the time for an Alterealm history lesson.

"Where do these tunnels lead?" Arius asked.

"Left goes up, the right leads down and to the other side of the mountain." Michael said quietly.

"Leone, you and Rafael go down, see if they've been that way. Do not engage if you find anyone." Troy told them.

"On it." Rafael whispered.

"Got it." Leone said.

Victor pulled his hand out of the ashes and nodded to Troy. "Still warm at the bottom."

"Crissy can you remember these tunnels as we go?" Quinton asked.

"Yes, I can." She nodded at him.

Quinton nodded at her. "Good. We may want to send patrols to check them daily."

"Let's keep moving up." Victor suggested, "we have quite a way to go."

"Where does the main tunnel come out?" Chase asked.

"Behind the courtyard." Michael answered without hesitation.

"There are a few smaller ones that lead to other areas, but we had the bridges removed so people couldn't access the main building, after we moved to the current underground chambers." Victor talked quietly so his voice wouldn't carry.

Every fifty feet there were small areas carved out. I wanted to ask what they were for, but too much chatter would make it harder for us to hear other movement.

"Leone, how far are you?" Michael inquired.

"We can see the end. Nothing so far." Leone answered.

"Is there light at the end of the tunnel?" Quinton asked, then cleared his throat. "I'm being serious."

"Yes. Should there be?" Rafael asked quickly.

"No." Michael answered. "That entrance has a solid gate that should be sealed closed."

"Okay. Going silent until after we look." Leone said quietly.

It was getting darker the further up we went. I stopped and stood when it dawned on me that we were literally standing under millions of pounds of earth. I was okay with tunnels, usually, I didn't know how far down they were or what sat over me. I took a few deep breaths, trying to shake the feelings that were swamping me. My heart felt like it was beating in my throat.

When Michael stopped in front of me, I realized how long I'd been standing there. His brows creased as he gave me soft look.

I'd forgotten the blood bond and that he could sense my emotions. I was going to tell him not to worry when a warm feeling came over me, a comforting one, like a hug of encouragement. He had done that for me.

Quinton reached us and gave us a look that said now was not the time for a staring contest.

I started walking again, forcing my heart and breathing to settle down. Why would Michael do that for me? He'd made it clear he didn't want much to do with me—whenever it was possible. Scowling, because he was distracting me, I picked up the pace to put some distance between us. He'd probably done it so I wouldn't hold them up, or to keep me from freaking out and alert them to our presence. I bit my lip, then winced, forgetting it was swollen. I was being stupid walking through here this distracted.

"Hold up." One of the men whispered so faintly I couldn't tell which one had said it. I looked ahead to see everyone looking back and turned to see Michael and Quinton both poised and ready, facing behind us.

I checked my position where I stood, needing to know where I was in case anyone came at us. We were close to the next carved out area, so I had room to maneuver. I thought I heard a noise, a scuffling like a foot dragging along the stone. Turning my head, I listened again. I moved toward the small concave area, it went back further than the rest had.

With silent movements, I stepped inside. A small tunnel, no taller than I was showed movement and light. I went toward it carefully and looked through the opening.

I looked behind me to see Bethany had stepped in and was watching me.

Pulling the kama from my back, I stepped into to the tunnel, crouching low. I hadn't been seeing things. There was a small wooden bridge across a ten-foot opening, with narrow stone stairs at the far end.

"That's a dead end," Michael whispered, "we destroyed the bridges."

I looked again. "Michael, I'm looking at a bridge." I glanced back to see him coming toward me.

Sheathing one sword, he pulled a shorter knife from his hip. I moved out of the way, trying to figure out how he'd fit through the space built for far smaller bodies. Turning sideways, he put one foot through and ducked, sliding in like it was a larger entrance. Obviously, this wasn't his first time.

"They rebuilt them." He whispered.

"That's how they got in the throne room to put up the barrier." Arius said in a low tone. "Only royal blood could access that room if the door was closed.

"Go up?" Michael inquired.

"They'll have a barrier at the top." Victor said.

"We'll have to check the rest," Quinton motioned for me to come back to the large tunnel.

"I heard something. That's why I went and looked." I said as quiet as possible. "There were shadows in the light."

"We're not alone." Daxx whispered.

Michael looked down at me, then headed to the rest.

Chase motioned to the area we'd just come out of. "Michael, you and Autumn go check it out. See if there is a barrier at the top." He looked at Troy. "They could be cocky enough to not put one."

Troy nodded. "Anyone that breaks off from the group goes with someone that has a porter."

Michael didn't look happy, but still motioned for me to go back inside.

I did, sheathing the kama on my back. If I met up with anyone, I wanted my hands free. I didn't wait for him to go through first, I stepped through carefully and moved to the side, so he could get his large frame through the opening. Once he stood beside me, I made my way across the bridge, making sure not to look down. I didn't want to know what was, or wasn't, under it. The stairs were old, very old, and made from stone. I didn't turn around but was guessing his shoulders were probably wider then the stairs were. All I could see when I looked up were more steps. I was thankful it was a gradual climb and not a tight spiral.

Looking around I tried to figure out how it was lit. I glanced behind me to Michael.

"Witch's lighting." He whispered. "As soon as someone steps through, it lights up."

My eyebrows went up.

He offered a slight shrug, before motioning for me to continue.

There was so much I didn't know about this realm, the people here—different classes or races of people meant much more than it did on my side. On my side it meant poor to rich. Here they were actually different classes of people based on abilities or more.

I squatted lower and looked up. The light had flickered, like someone moved in front of it. I pointed up for Michael to see, then looked back at him. He jerked his chin telling me to keep going.

"Where do these stairs lead?" Troy asked.

Michael paused on the stairs waiting for an answer.

"Our parents' room." Victor said.

I turned to see Michael following again.

"Daxx and I will go see if we can access it." Troy said in a hushed voice.

The light above us flickered again, like a candle does when someone moves past. I paused and pointed. Michael came up behind me and looked up. "Someone is at the top." He whispered more in my ear than the mic.

"We have a situation." Rafael said with an urgent tone.

Michael touched my arm, so I'd stop.

"There's fifteen men heading our way. With three women—in jumpsuits." Leone said with a venomous tone.

"Can you hide somewhere?" Chase asked. "Let them pass then block them at the first cavern."

"Yeah we can." Leone said quickly.

"We'll head back down." Michael said. "Try to get down further so Leone and Raf have more help." Turning, he hurried back down the steps.

All I could think about were those women with the men.

"Alona, you, cutie, sarg and sparky get those women." Chase said quickly.

Later when I was trying not to slip down the steps, I'd have to find out why Chase insisted on calling all of us by nickname.

"We will try to separate them." Alona said.

"Leave that to us. Beth and I will clear out anyone near them." Paisley whispered.

Michael cleared the last step and waited for me before crossing the narrow bridge. I didn't even think when I accepted his hand as we hurried across.

I was about to go back through the opening, when he tugged my hand so I'd turn. Before I could ask him why, he leaned down quickly and licked across my lip. I pulled my head back and looked to see his eyes were red. Remembering the mic, I didn't say anything but hoped my look conveyed we'd be talking about that move later.

Slipping back out the opening, we ran toward the large cavern.

"Daxx and I will block the other exit." Troy said sounding out of breath.

We reached the large cavern right behind the others and hurried into the small concave space on the opposite side. After they were in the cavern, we could block them from turning back. Daxx and Troy went into the tunnel we'd taken from the outside. The others stood in the tunnel leading up to the main floors.

"We're in place, Leone." Victor said softly.

The men weren't even attempting to be quiet. They had no idea we were here.

"You should feel special, you're the first of our guests, ladies." One of the first men entering the cavern said.

Standing and waiting for all of them to clear the tunnel felt like it took hours. The women were scared and walking close together. None had shackles on. When the last came through, I went to step out, but Michael put his hand out to stop me.

"Warrick, you traitorous bastard." Quinton stepped out of the shadows. "I wondered where you had disappeared to." He looked at the man that had spoken.

Warrick stopped and turned around. "You didn't expect me to stay loyal to a guard that tossed me out did you, *prince?*"

Quinton moved toward the middle of the cavern. "You were tossed out because you couldn't follow orders." He kept walking slowly.

I realized he was trying to get them to turn so they wouldn't notice people in the tunnel leading up.

"Orders that endangered my life." The man snarled.

"As a guard you take an oath to protect others, even at the cost of your life." Quinton stopped moving and stood there, a large sword in either hand, casually holding them, tips pointed toward the floor.

"You should have brought help, prince." Warrick snarled as he pulled a sword from his hip.

"What makes you think I didn't?" Quinton asked calmly.

"So, this is where the dishonored guards end up." Rafael walked into the cavern.

The men jolted, pulling weapons out as they turned to face him.

"I see more than one familiar face." Leone came to stand beside Rafael.

"Three against all of us? Royal or not, you're no match for us." Warrick smirked.

"Enough talk." Daxx stepped out, Troy right behind her.

Michael dropped his hand and moved into the light. I was right beside him.

Someone chuckled.

"You brought little human women to fight?" A scruffy man with dirty clothes said with a grin.

I looked at Michael, he shrugged and motioned toward them. With a smile, I looked back at the man and took a few steps toward him.

He lifted his sword and pointed it at me, stepping in my direction.

"Try it. I will beat you ten different ways from tomorrow." Reaching, I pulled the kama from my back, leaving the blade hidden.

"Is she a relative of yours, kitten?" Chase asked as he stepped out into the light.

Without taking my eyes off the man, I spoke to Michael. "Have your little box ready." I didn't give any other warnings. I stepped toward the sword, ducking down as he swung. Rising up, I blocked his elbow and twisted. His sword hit the stone at his feet. I put my foot behind his and swept his feet from under him. He went down. As I side stepped I heard a pop. He vanished.

Michael straightened and swung his arm, using his sword to block the swing of the man next to him.

Taking a quick step, I grabbed Michael's free arm and used it as leverage to gain the height to land a scissor kick on the man's chin. He stumbled back. Michael hooked his foot and down he went.

Turning, I saw Beth and Paisley knocking men back from the women using their abilities. I rushed over and hit the one that grabbed one of the captive woman's arm with a jab-elbow combination. "Go." I told her as he recovered and came at me, sword swinging. I ducked and whacked the back of his knee with the baton. His leg buckled and I was able to knock him off balance with a fast crescent kick.

"Got him." Daxx slid in with a box in her hand, then he was gone. "Get the women outside with the horses." She said quickly.

I turned to see Alona swinging nun-chucks to keep a man from following Crissy, Beth and Paisley as they led the women to the tunnel. I ran toward her.

Quinton kicked another one so he stumbled back. "Autumn." He said as I approached him, he bent down, one knee out. I put my foot on his knee and launched myself over his back, using the extra height and momentum to spin and kick the man in the back of the head.

Alona swept his legs out at the same moment, taking advantage of the distraction.

Leone was right there, box in hand and the man was gone.

Alona gave me a quick nod and headed out the tunnel.

I turned to be sure the others had things under control and went after her.

Chapter Sixteen

I watched as Quinton and Arius reappeared.

"They're with Liza now." Quinton said.

Liza, I'd found out, was running the safe houses Alona paid for, so the women they'd rescued were in secure locations and couldn't be taken again. This family was amazing. The lengths they went to protect others, it made me proud to be helping them.

"I only removed the porting from their minds." Arius looked at Troy.

I wasn't sure if I was amazed or scared that he could do something like that.

Troy nodded. "We'll have to get more details from them later."

"Check the database and see if their names were on it." Chase said to Alona.

"I will, when we get back." She had such a sad look on her face.

"We need to do something about these tunnels." Victor's words sounded like a command, harsh and not to be ignored. "We could have Romulus seal them." Rafael suggested. "Or don't, and have him place an alarm on them so we will be alerted when someone is here.

I glanced to Beth, wondering if they could do something like that. She nodded.

"Or," Paisley looked around at the men, "we could go and place motion activated cameras, non-magically at the entrances."

Arius smiled at her. "They wouldn't be checking for that."

Victor looked from his brother to her. "We'll do that."

"Are we going to see who is up there?" Daxx looked up the side of the mountain.

Troy glanced to Chase for a moment. "Yes, but you probably won't like the how."

Daxx frowned. "How?"

"There's a trap door on the roof. Only members of the royal family know about it." Michael motioned to Victor and Quinton. "The last three that lived here are standing right here."

"The roof?" Paisley looked at her man.

"You'll be fine, it's large, not a ledge. We're porting there, then going inside." He spoke quietly, a soft expression on his face.

She didn't look happy.

"Where does it come out?" Alona asked.

"Our parents' room." Quinton said quietly.

"We should check the roof and make sure they don't have the area warded." Leone looked to Arius. "You said the throne room is."

"I'd feel better knowing we could port there." Bethany said then bit her lip. "I mean what happens if you can't? Do you come back or—"

Leone held up his hand, so she wouldn't go further with her thoughts.

"I'll go." Victor said abruptly.

"Take this." Daxx pulled the porter off her wrist. "In case you end up in some strange place."

Victor looked offended momentarily, and then accepted it and put it on his wrist. "I'll be right back." He vanished.

Crissy stood there looking up the mountain.

The entire group was quiet, waiting.

Victor reappeared. "It isn't warded. And the door is still sealed."

"So, we're good?" Quinton asked.

Victor nodded and held out his hand to Crissy. She took his hand and then reached out and took Daxx's, who was holding Troy's. Rafael stepped over and put his hand on Victor's shoulder.

All of them were gone.

Arius pulled Paisley closer. "You'll be fine." He kissed the top of her head and put his hand on Quinton's shoulder.

Emil moved over and put his hand on the other shoulder.

Chase hugged Alona to him and then put his hand on Michael's shoulder.

Michael held his hand out to me. I took it and stepped closer to him.

"Oh good, I haven't wanted to throw up in a few hours." Bethany whispered as she hugged Leone while he touched Michael's other shoulder.

My stomach clenched. Before I could complain, I noticed the breeze on my face. I moved away from Michael and looked around. "I'm standing on a palace." I said quietly.

Crissy grinned, nodding enthusiastically. Then her face sobered. "I think this is where the flashing lights were." She looked at Daxx.

"What kind of flashing lights?" Daxx asked.

"A storm?" Rafael was looking at the sky.

"I don't know, but it was surrounded by badness." Crissy whispered.

"Everyone take care, don't rush a single step." Troy was looking all around the roof.

"Where's the crystal, Raf?" Quinton bent down beside the trap door and held out his hand.

Rafael pulled out a clear crystal and handed it to him.

Quinton held it over the trap door. It didn't do anything. Opening the door, he held his hand inside. "It's not sensing anything."

Troy held out his hand. "I'll keep it visible as we go."

Nodding, Quinton handed it to him. "Watch your step. This hasn't been used in a long time." He climbed down into the hole.

Not wanting to be left behind, I went over and went down next. The rungs were in good condition, I hadn't felt any of them so much as slip. Jumping the last few, I landed beside Quinton and turned to check out the room. It was huge, ornate, and very empty. I moved over to the door and stood beside it. If anyone came through, I'd be ready.

Michael and Victor were down now.

Paisley and Alona were coming down next.

Michael tapped his ear. I remembered I needed to reconnect to the call and did it quickly.

"Ugh, will I ever get used to porting?" Paisley said looking ill.

"Might be the altitude. I'm feeling a bit off too." Alona said quietly.

"Must be." Daxx said coming down the ladder. "I feel ill, like I haven't since my first few ports."

Crissy was right behind her. "I feel funny too, and I'm used to high places."

"What do you mean?" Victor was to the ladder in one step, lifting her down quickly.

"I just feel wrong." She told him. "In my head." She pressed her palm against her forehead.

Paisley nodded. "Mine too."

Emil, then Rafael came down.

"Pressure from the storm coming in?" Rafael rubbed his temple. "It's got me too."

Leone hopped down. "I feel okay."

Bethany was right behind him. "I must be susceptible, because I have pains stabbing through my temples."

Chase climbed down quickly and went to Alona. "Are you picking this up from everyone else?"

She shook her head. "No, this is all me."

Arius almost jumped from the top. "Is it the room? I was fine at the top." He pushed his hand against the top of his head.

Troy jumped from the ladder. "I've got knives stabbing though my skull." He held out his hand with the crystal. It was red. "What does red mean?"

I looked at Rafael.

He was squeezing his temples with a hand across his forehead. "It's not good. Blood magic."

"Blood magic?" I turned to Michael, his brows were drawn together.

"I'm not feeling anything." He looked around at the others and then to me.

"I'm fine." I told him.

"Uh." Daxx grabbed her head. "Something isn't right."

Troy winced and nodded.

"It's making me feel sick." Beth whispered and leaned into Leone.

"Why is it only affecting some of us?" Emil looked to Michael.

"I don't know." Michael looked at the crystal again.

Alona and Paisley looked like they were going to pass out.

"Abilities." I looked at all of those affected. "It's only hurting those with an ability."

"I don't have one." Daxx squatted down and held her head.

"You're immune to abilities." Michael said. "That's considered one."

"Lucky me." She groaned.

Arius hissed out a breath. "We have to get out of here."

"Port to where the horses are." Victor said, scooping Crissy into his arms.

"Can't." Troy mumbled. "Can't focus on anything."

"Same." Rafael said.

Troy pulled Daxx to her feet and stumbled over to Victor.

"Come, Rafael, Alona." Victor said harshly.

Chase helped his mate over. "Go." He kissed the top of her head. "We're right behind you."

Leone helped Bethany over to Victor as Arius held his hand out to Paisley.

All of them managed to crowd around Victor.

"Let us know if it clears once you're out of here." Michael said looking concerned.

Troy dropped the crystal as they vanished.

I looked at Michael, his expression was hard.

"We need to check the rest of the floor." Chase was scowling.

"Do you think it will affect mages?" Quinton was looking around the room. "How do we remove it, if it does?"

"I don't know, brother." Chase answered quietly.

"They're still a bit off, but it does clear once leaving that space." Victor's voice came through the ear piece. "Ms. Tremon says the crystal turning red is not encouraging."

"Can it be removed?" Chase asked.

"It's complicated." Troy sounded drained.

"How did they place the wards if those with abilities can't be in the same space?" Quinton glared at the bedroom door.

"I don't know." Troy answered.

"You can't go exploring with so few people." Arius said quietly.

"He's right." Rafael's tone was very quiet. "It's what they want. To take out most of us, leaving the rest outnumbered."

I glanced to Michael and nodded, telling him I agreed with Rafael's theory.

"So, we go back and prepare for this?" Chase didn't look pleased.

"We have to find a way to remove it." Arius said in a monotone.

"That did me in." Paisley whispered.

"Me too." Crissy sighed.

Emil shook his head and looked at Michael. "I'd feel better if we knew what we were dealing with before going further."

"We could put a camera here too." I suggested. "Maybe one outside the door."

Leone nodded. "I think we should set as many in here as we can."

"First we need to get our strength back." Troy's tone was more commanding now.

"We'll come down." Chase motioned to the open trap door. "As soon as we close the door."

"I'll go up and pull the ladder so it's hidden again." Quinton started up it.

Michael picked up the crystal and looked at it, then went over to the door. He held it against the door knob. It lightened, but still didn't clear. Using his other hand, he touched the door. Sparks came off it. "Door is warded. We can't exit this room."

"Guess Romulus is going on a field trip." Quinton said, amused. "He loves those."

"Let's get back and get the cameras installed in the caverns before they think to ward those as well." Victor said.

"We're going to port back, someone bring the horses." Troy told us.

"I'm going to quickly check other entrances." Quinton said sticking his head down in the hole in the ceiling.

"Be careful, brother." Victor warned.

"I'm checking from outside the building." Quinton closed the hatch in the roof.

"Those that weren't affected will bring back the horses." Michael said, his tone leaving no room for argument. "No one goes anywhere alone."

I looked at him, his eyes held that haunted look. His ghosts were chasing him. He held out his hand to me. I took it without hesitation.

Chapter Seventeen

We sat around the dining room table waiting on the others to arrive. The mood was somber with very little conversation. The men all looked in deep contemplation, and I was right there with them. I knew nothing about magic or spells, but I did understand that if we couldn't get into the palace, all of us, catching those who were taking women would be impossible. All the entrances had been checked and Quinton couldn't get in. With those wards, or whatever they were all over the palace, once the abducted women were in there, we wouldn't be able to get them out.

"We can't send anyone in under cover," Emil said quietly, "because they wouldn't be able to get out."

"Kinsley's out for good." Michael said. "She has an ability, and if they're blocking those, they would know right away."

"If it's blood magic, would it only affect us though?" Quinton rubbed the back of his neck. "Did you talk to Romulus?" He looked to Michael.

He nodded. "Briefly. He was going to look up a few things and then one of us can take him over, so he can test things out."

"Is everyone else all right?" I touched my finger to my swollen lip.

Michael watched my hand for a second. "Yes, they'll feed and exchange blood and they're back to full strength again."

"That was unnerving." Emil leaned back and crossed his arms. "What about getting the cameras installed?"

"I'll take them to the caverns once I see everyone is doing okay." Quinton told him.

"You take at least four guards when you go." Michael pointed to him. "That's from now on, not just to install cameras."

Quinton nodded. "I agree with that. I'll make sure everyone has porters on too."

Emil sighed. "Is this getting better or worse? I feel like this is a pivotal moment."

"We've cut down their numbers by hundreds since this started. I know it might not seem like it, but right now they're desperate." Michael glanced to Quinton. "For them to be bringing their hostages over here must mean they're running out of places to hide on the other side."

Quinton turned to Emil, "finding them on this side will be easier, we know the lay of the land."

Emil pulled out his phone and looked at it and sighed. "Rena is having another bad spell." He looked to his brothers, then to me. "I'm going to go see if she needs anything. Abraham isn't all that good with nauseous women."

I offered him an understanding smile. "I'd like to meet her, when she's having a better day."

He stood up. "I don't know when that will be, just keeping anything down right now is a challenge."

"Peppermints." I tilted my head. "The woman that used to visit all the pregnant girls carried a bag of those white mints with her, said it helped."

"I will give that a try." Emil inclined his head.

"Talk to Clairee and see if she has any safe herbs to use, too." Michael rubbed the back of his neck. "She'll probably have suggestions for everything."

"I'll speak to her when I get back." He turned to the door. "Don't go into battle without me."

Crissy and Victor came from the kitchen. She smiled. "I feel better." She went to her chair.

Victor sat down and picked up the coffee urn. "I just spoke to Elder Arian, she's charging remote cameras, as many as she can get her hands on."

"Good. Quinton is going to take some guards and one of the science techs to go put them in the caverns." Michael took the urn when Victor held it toward him.

"Am I trying a few other spots? Balconies or entrances?" Quinton stood and went down the table to pick up the water pitcher.

"I have mixed feelings about that." Victor said. "Perhaps try the other areas once we have the mages check them out."

Crissy nodded. "And stay off the roof. Those flashes of light are either on or near it."

"Do you know any more than that, heart?" Victor inquired.

"I've been trying to fit them together." She shook her head. "I'm missing a piece."

Victor squeezed her hand. "Perhaps some quiet time in your tower will help."

She nodded. "I'm going to go there after I eat something. My stomach is gurgling."

"Romulus will have to go onto the roof to determine which spell was used in our parents' room." Quinton said, "but we won't linger any longer than necessary."

Crissy nodded. "Okay." Frowning, she looked at me and then back to Victor. "I need to talk to witches and mages."

Victor's eyebrows went up.

"Autumn was right." She smiled at me, "the herbs I keep seeing aren't from here." She paused. "or there, my side. I think I know what they are." She nodded, "and I think they have something to do with the spell that made us sick." Nodding again, she dug in her pack and pulled out her notebook. She flipped through the pages and then held it up. "This is the plant. I couldn't find it in any of the books." She bit her lip. "Even the old ones." She poked it with her finger, shaking her head, she looked at Victor, "don't you find that strange?"

Victor glanced to Michael, who held up his phone. "I'm on it."

Michael got up and went into the kitchen.

I wondered what it was like to remember everything you read. Had she been sitting there flipping through books in her head?

"As far as days go, today is a ten on the scale of suckage." Daxx said walking in with Troy.

"It wasn't fun." Crissy agreed.

Mitz came out with a tray and set it on the table, then hurried back through the door.

I got up and followed her. She went past me with another tray before I could get through the door. I shook my head at her speed and hurried to get the last tray on the counter. When I turned, she took it from my hands.

"Thank you, love." She looked at my swollen mouth, "It's a joy to have you around." Turning, with the tray, she went back into the dining room.

Arius and Paisley came through the door on the far side.

"That," Paisley waved a hand around, "was an epic fail for our team."

Arius wrapped his arm around her. "We did free those women and get a few more traitors."

I pointed to the dining room. "Crissy is onto something."

Arius' eyes lit up. "Hopefully it leads to retribution." He nodded. "I'm definitely in the mood for that."

Rafael came in the door behind him. "With you there, brother." He looked around the kitchen. "Food on the table?"

I smiled, then remembered my fat lip. "When isn't there food on that table?"

They went back out to the dining room. I watched Michael tuck his phone back in his pocket. "Is that possible?" I motioned to the door. "Using some kind of plant to make the others so sick?"

He sighed. "I have come to learn that just about anything can be, with magic and," he waved his hand in the air, "spells, and ill intentions."

"Will Clairee know?" I crossed my arms, so I wouldn't do something stupid like touch him.

Michael's gaze was on my swollen mouth. "If she doesn't, she will find someone that does."

I shook my head. "Before those jerks grabbed me, I never would have believed any of this is real."

Rubbing a hand on his jaw, his eyes locked on mine. "About this morning…"

I held up my hand. "Now is not the time to talk."

Inclining his head, he motioned to the door. "We should go back out. This is going to take quite a bit of planning."

I nodded and turned to go when he grabbed my chin.

"Could you *please* stop using your face to block punches?" His voice was barely a whisper.

I looked up into very serious blue eyes.

"I'm fine, Chase." Alona said quietly as they came in the door.

Michael released me and stepped back.

Chase walked past us, giving Michael an odd look and ushered her into the dining room.

I followed him quickly, remembering that Daxx had said to not be alone with him. I won't mention that when I was near him, my heart skipped in my chest like it did after a five-mile run.

Chase stood there, looking at the others seated at the table. "Tell me we know something."

I moved to the far end of the table and sat down.

"Crissy may have a lead on what they used to disable everyone." Quinton said around a mouthful of food.

Chase looked to Crissy. "I don't suppose you glimpsed the person responsible?"

Crissy shook her head. "No faces."

Sitting down, Chase gave Troy a hard look.

Troy nodded. "I'm with you there."

"I will blast them through a wall if I find them." Bethany growled as she came into the room.

"You might have to get in line." Leone said as he came through the door. He watched her sit down, then looked around. "Do we know how they did it yet?"

"We're waiting for Clairee and Romulus." Troy informed him. "Crissy saw what they used, we just have to find out what it means."

Leone gave an abrupt nod. "Good, because when I find out who the sick…"

Arius snorted, "agreed."

Shaking his head, Leone sat down.

"This is going to take meticulous planning and coordination, with a very short time line." Victor said while looking at the brothers.

"We're going to have to block off the secret stairs." Michael put food on his plate.

I had to wonder if anything stopped them from eating. My stomach growled as I had the thought. Okay, so eating right now would be all right, I supposed.

"All exits and balconies will need to be covered." Leone nodded, then reached over to pick up a tray so Beth could get food.

Arius got up and poured a coffee. "I think we need to monitor the cameras for a few days to see what we're up against."

"Agreed." Victor took a bite from his plate.

"What about the tunnel entrances? We'll need those closed off, or something else to stop their help from arriving." Daxx looked at her plate but hadn't yet taken a bite. "Or do we want more hostages to arrive? They think they're safe here."

"While we're figuring out all that, we need those cameras placed and to find a way around that spell and the wards on the doors." Rafael nodded to Leone when he held up a tray. Taking it from his brother, he started to fill his plate. "Are the wards and spells to keep us out, or others in?"

Michael pointed his fork at him. "I've been wondering the same thing."

Quinton shrugged, "we could drop Romulus down in the bedroom and see."

Leone smirked. "I don't think that would help him solve the problem."

Daxx snorted. "Great motivation though."

Clairee walked in with another woman. "It took me a few moments to locate Roberta." She motioned to the petite, black-haired woman beside her. "She is our specialist in herbal magics."

Crissy stood on her chair and held out her notebook. "They used this to make all of us sick."

Frowning, Clairee went to her and took the notebook. She looked down at it then to Roberta. "Is this what I think it is?" She turned it and held it for her to see.

Roberta went to her quickly and snatched the book from her hand. "Oh dear, it is." Her brows furrowed. "It shouldn't exist."

Daxx threw up her hands. "What? What is it?"

Roberta handed the notebook back to Clairee. "The common name is Witch's Curse. I had thought it was eradicated centuries ago."

"Witch's Curse?" Bethany looked from her to Clairee.

"It has an almost unpronounceable Latin name, but yes." Clairee said with an abrupt nod.

"And it does what, exactly?" Beth sat forward in her chair.

Roberta looked at her for a moment. "You know in the movies where they use wolfsbane on werewolves, and vervain on vampires?"

Bethany nodded, her eyes wide.

"This is the botanical option for blocking magic and abilities. The side-effects can be lethal if exposed too long."

"Son of a bitch." Arius whispered.

"So where would they find it if it was eradicated?" Chase looked to his twin.

"We'll have to test to be certain…"

Victor cleared his throat. "If Cristy has seen it, we can be certain."

Clairee nodded and looked to Roberta. "The fates never mislead her."

Crissy sighed, "no, they just don't send explanations."

"So where did they get it?" Leone put his arm around Beth's shoulder.

Roberta looked at Clairee and a look passed between them. "We have samples in the archives, for reference. In case it reared its ugly head in the coming centuries…"

Clairee rubbed a hand across her forehead. "To our knowledge, and searches we cast periodically, there are no other plants of that kind out there—in any realm."

Troy sighed and glanced briefly to Chase. "Are your samples still secure? Marcus has had many traitors hidden among us."

Roberta shook her head. "It would take fifteen years or more to cultivate a single plant strong enough to use, to affect as many of you that it did, that quickly—it would take several decades."

Quinton sat back and gave her a bored look. "Willis Hubert has had centuries to plan this, waiting a decade for a plant to grow seems likely."

Roberta's eyes went wide. "I'd heard rumors that the Hubert line was at it again, but," she looked to Clairee, "I'm going to go check the archives." She rushed from the room.

Clairee handed Crissy back her notebook. "I looked into the blood magic spells, that they could have used on the wards." She looked to Troy and then Chase. "Romulus will know more about the warded doors, but I believe it is geared toward Royal blood and breaking it is not going to be easy."

"And they'd have to have samples of our blood to make the spell?" Leone asked glancing at his mate for a moment before looking back to her.

Clairee nodded. "Most definitely."

Troy rubbed the bridge of his nose. "Only places that have our blood are your temple, the doctor's records, and the registry vault."

"More spies?" Crissy looked to Victor.

"It would seem so." He clasped her hand kissed it, and then released it. Grasping his phone in the other hand, he dialled it with sharp movements.

This was the first sign I'd witnessed where his emotions were showing. With a seasoned, disciplined warrior like Victor, that wasn't good news for those causing that emotional tell.

"I need a list of all those with access to the medical records and registry vault." His tone was cool as he glanced to Michael briefly. "Today." He hung up and looked at the nervous witch standing behind Daxx. "Clairee, I need you to find out who has access to your archives and the blood samples you have on hand that are used for seeking spells."

Clairee nodded. "I'm just going to go discuss the blood magic with Romulus and then I'll get those names to you." She nodded again and left.

Crissy looked at Victor. "I don't know if I can see good or bad in people with magic." She gnawed on her bottom lip.

He gave her a soft look. "You can see Bethany's."

Turning she looked at Beth, or more around than at her.

"Yes." She bobbed her head. "I can very clearly. It's good with some," she moved only her eyes to her mate for a second, then back to Beth, "anger mixed in."

"That's all we need. Those you can't make out, we'll use other means to check."

I felt like I'd missed something important. "What is she doing?"

Daxx looked down the table at me. "Crissy can see a person's aura?" She glanced to Beth who nodded. "Around them. She found spies before because theirs were dark and…" lifting her hand, she shrugged, "I don't know what, but we found them."

"Oh." I grinned at Crissy. "Do I have one?"

Crissy bobbed her head again and looked above me.

I had to force myself not to look up.

"Yes. Yours is pure, but fierce."

I frowned, not knowing how that would look. "Pure?"

"Good." She smiled. "Pure heart." She turned to Victor. "I'm not going to my tower. I'm too distracted with wanting to know what Clairee will figure out."

"We could go over more records and search for more women." Alona suggested.

Chase rubbed under his chin as he gave his twin a quick look. "I'm not sure sending any teams out is a good idea right now."

"Until we know more." Troy finished for him.

"So, all of Alterealm is benched?" Daxx pushed her plate away, scowling.

"Our teams don't go without one of the brothers accompanying them." Arius said quietly.

Paisley leaned her head on his shoulder. "Until we know how they did that spell and the blood magic, I agree, we're not taking chances with any of us."

Several of the others nodded.

"So, what are we to do? Sit and twiddle our thumbs?" Alona turned to her mate. "I know nothing of planning, or tactics…"

"We can work on the hall map." Crissy suggested.

Alona sighed. "I suppose it's better than pacing."

Arius picked up his phone and looked at it. "They found something odd on the men we brought back from the caverns. Some sort of device that actually came through to the cells." He leaned over and kissed Paisley. "You go nowhere without Felix." She nodded. Standing up, he looked at Troy. "May need a hand getting into their heads."

Troy set his fork down and picked up his cup. "Did they isolate the devices in case they are trackers?"

"Immediately." Arius picked up his plate and started for the door.

"Right behind you." Michael said and got up. He paused and looked at me. "Your guard stays with you." He gave an abrupt nod, then looked at the other women. "All of you." He picked up the plate and motioned to his brothers. "None of us will be moving around alone either, unless it's porting to and from secure locations within the chambers." He left carrying his plate.

Victor lifted his phone. "I've just sent word to Ira to send all the women's guards here, and to post additional guards at any entrances to the royal chambers." He leaned over and kissed Crissy's head. "He's meeting us at the cells." He stood up.

One by one we watched the men leave.

"Never thought I'd agree with the constant guards, but after what the plant or spell or whatever did to me, I'm waiting for Tim to get here." Daxx said playing with the food on her plate with her fork.

"I definitely don't want to feel that ever again." Bethany agreed.

"It was almost as bad as the burning on my back was." Crissy's eyes were huge. "Almost."

Chapter Eighteen

"It's just another utility closet." Alona said, disappointed.

"At least we know the housekeeping staff don't have to travel far to do their job." Beth's voice came through the earpiece.

"Has anyone ever seen them cleaning?" Daxx asked.

I glanced around to see Woods ten feet behind me. I still wasn't fond of the constant shadow but accepted that I had backup if needed.

"Never." Alona answered.

"Me either." Crissy replied in her distracted way.

I stopped by the next door. "Someone cleans. This place is always spotless." Grasping the handle, I opened the door and looked inside. "My door is an empty room."

"Only spotless when there's no mud pits." Crissy mumbled.

"How big is the room?" Paisley asked.

I stepped in. "About the size of the bathrooms."

"That's pretty big." Beth mused.

"Good to know there are a few extra rooms if there's ever a need." Alona offered.

"Any doors yet, Beth?" Crissy asked.

I closed the door and started walking again.

"I see one finally. This is a long hallway… wait." She paused. "Mac says this hall leads to the outside on the South."

"So, the door will be keypad access?" Daxx asked.

"Yes, it is." Beth replied.

"That hall is complete now." Crissy sounded excited.

"I feel like we may soon have a complete map." Alona paused. "I turned the wrong way, I have to go back."

"Good call on splitting up, Autumn, we've covered a lot more this time." Paisley almost sang into the mic.

I looked back at Woods. "With our shadows following us, I thought we might as well." I stopped outside the door. "I'm at the last door in this hall."

"Don't keep us in suspense." Alona whispered in a dramatic way.

I grinned and opened it. "Holy." I pushed it open further and reached along the wall for a light switch.

"What?" Daxx said hurriedly.

"Autumn? What have you found?" Alona spoke louder than normal.

I stood with my hands on my hips. "The biggest hot tub I've ever seen." I shrugged, "not that I've seen many."

"She found *the* hot tub." Daxx laughed.

"How many will it fit?" Alona asked. "Is there a wading pool? Cool water after a hot soak does wonders for the pores."

I looked around. "I don't see anything like that, but there is another door."

"Don't open it. Wait for us." Bethany said, sounding like she was running.

I went over to the large tub. "This thing would easily fit fifteen people."

"I'm stopping by the cave for wine." Alona's tone was excited.

I frowned. "You know drinking while in it will…"

"Shh. It's a wonderful way to unwind." She said quickly. "And I don't know if you've noticed, but it's been a little tense lately."

I smirked. "I noticed."

"So where do I turn after the second left turn?" Paisley asked.

I looked at the phone and moved the map. "You don't. Keep going to the end."

"Yes. I'll be there soon."

I shook my head when Alona offered me wine again. "I've never been a drinker." I shrugged, "that can end badly when you live on the streets."

The others nodded.

I smirked, ignoring my lip. "And I can't see straight after one drink."

Alona laughed. "I have a high tolerance."

"Is that because you're part," Beth waved her hand around, "whatever?"

Alona pursed her lips together. "I've never thought about it, but it could be."

"I'm going easy this time in case we have to kick ass on short notice." Daxx said taking a small sip. "It's hard to fight when you have to close one eye to see the target." She motioned to me with the glass, "whereas Autumn needs no eyes, I need two."

"Eyes. I can't believe I forgot." Paisley gasped.

"You forgot eyes?" Crissy looked confused.

"No." She laughed. "Before we went to the caverns, Arius kept giving Autumn strange looks, so I asked why." Paisley took a sip.

"I don't get the connection." Daxx frowned.

Paisley gave Daxx a blank look and then turned to me. "He says our eyes are too similar for it to be a coincidence— add that we both have the same rare blood type."

"Arius thinks you're related?" Alona sat forward.

Paisley nodded, looking excited.

Beth looked from me to her. "Go sit beside her."

Standing up, Paisley came over and sat beside me.

I looked at her eyes closely. I didn't see it.

She studied mine.

When I turned to say that, the other four women were right in front of us.

"Oh my. There are amazing similarities." Alona said softly.

"Hold on." Daxx went back over to where she'd been sitting and grabbed her phone. "Let me take a picture and show you what we're seeing."

Paisley and I looked at each other and then to Daxx. She took several pictures, then held out the phone.

"Eye shape and brow lines are the same as well." Alona mused.

"How did we not notice this?" Daxx asked.

"With the injuries Autumn has to her face, it's been hard to spot." Beth nodded.

Paisley held the phone up and made the picture bigger, she slid it back and forth so we could see our eyes. "I think he's right," she whispered.

"Is that possible?" I'd never had family. Real family.

She handed the phone back to Daxx. "My *grandfather*, she made quotes in the air, "disappeared—I've been thinking about it a lot and I think my grandfather was actually my father and Elder Roan's son. Arius agrees that something is off, and has someone doing research to see what they can figure out."

"So—," I looked from her to Beth, then back to Paisley again, "so—how do we find out if we're related?"

"How old are you?" She studied my face, a hopeful look in her eyes.

"Twenty-five, roughly. I don't know when I was born."

"We could be half sisters." She covered her mouth, then lowered her hands. "My, or maybe our great," she shook her head, "our grandfather is on the elder's council and there are so many other relatives."

My heart was pounding in my chest. I didn't know what it was like to have family. Sure, there had been people in my life that I thought of as family, but blood relatives—what was that like? "How do we find out?" My throat was tight with emotion.

Paisley looked at Daxx. "They should still have the results from mine right? Couldn't they compare it with that?"

"I would think so." Daxx glanced to Alona.

She snorted. "Don't make me ask Chase—he'll go off about Elder Roan, again."

"Have Arius check with the lab," Beth suggested.

"Sisters!" Crissy stood up, water splashing all over as she climbed out of the tub. She went over to where she'd dropped her bag and started digging in it. "Was it before or after my rune tattoo or Daxx's tattoo?" She shook her head. "I don't remember when, but there were sisters. One light, one dark—not bad dark, just opposite. Their eyes were the same."

I turned and looked at Alona, she didn't look surprised.

Crissy flipped through the notebook, trying not to drip on it. She tapped a page. "The light and dark, it was their hair, but the eyes were the same." She stood up smiling. "I saw you. You're sisters—but not twins, or if you are, not identical."

I opened my mouth, then closed it and looked at Paisley. "If we were, wouldn't we have been raised together?"

She bit her lip. "I don't know. I don't have a lot of information on what happened before I was born."

"I say check with the labs, then tell Elder Roan." Beth said quietly. "Can't be easy for him with his son vanishing and not knowing."

Paisley nodded. "That's what we'll do."

Music started playing. Paisley ginned and turned to reach for her phone.

"Beauty and the Beast?" Beth laughed.

Smiling, Paisley answered the phone. "I'm fine." She rolled her eyes. "Not a bad reason."

I needed to find out more about this bond thing. The men were totally tuned into their women.

"I was just talking to Autumn about your suspicions that we're related." She continued.

"I seen it." Crissy blurted out.

Paisley nodded. "Crissy had a vision of sisters before, one with dark hair, one with light." She bit her lip. "No. We'd like to talk to the lab and see if my grandfather's blood is required again or—" She laughed softly, "yes, to avoid you having to see him. That would be great."

"Do they know anything yet?" Daxx whispered.

Paisley nodded. "Has Clairee figured out anything?" She frowned. "What about those devices?" Her eyebrows went up. "Oh? Is that good?" She nodded. "Okay, I'll tell the girls." She hung up and looked at me. "Arius will talk to the lab, but he says a sample of your blood should be all they need."

I bit my lip, then winced, forgetting again that it was swollen. "I have to admit I'm a little freaked out thinking I might have actual family."

Daxx snorted. "And then some, you're Michael's mate, so you have family—Royal family to no end."

"Which includes us, so you should feel privileged." Alona added with a big smile.

I nodded slowly. "A pretty kick-ass family."

"What did Arius say about the spell?" Daxx picked up her empty wine glass, then put it back down.

"Clairee and Romulus are talking to the kings right now."

Daxx picked up her phone and checked it. "I'll give them five minutes before I interrupt."

Paisley leaned back. "Those devices have something to do with blood. Arius said the science techs and a mage are testing them."

Everyone looked at her.

"Why do I feel like that's bad for us?" Daxx asked.

"Because it involves blood?" I rolled my eyes. "Any movie with blood magic, spells, or curses, is never a good thing."

Beth nodded enthusiastically. "She's right."

Alona waved her glass around. "Not always. Fangs get a bad rep in movies as well and they're not." She shrugged, "at least Chase doesn't think so."

I watched the others' cheeks flush, then remembered when Michael had bitten me. I smirked. "I didn't find anything bad with them."

"We need to get her gloves." Crissy all but sang then she looked at me. "Unless you want to be marked, then you don't need them."

I looked around at the other women. "Which means what?"

"Damn, I should have brought more wine." Alona sighed, then held up her left arm. "This is the mate's tattoo, it appears," she nodded, "all by itself if your left palms are touching during," she shrugged, "sex with your true mate."

I dragged my gaze from hers to her arm for a moment, then looked at the other women's inked arms. "They appear?"

Daxx nodded. "Yes." She held up a hand, "and you do not want that if you are not willing to seal the deal with a full blood bond. Believe me, that's no fun."

I raised my eyebrows but couldn't find the words to say.

"Does she really want to take a chance and be mated to a man hung up on a ghost?" Paisley asked.

I pointed to her. "That. Yes. He may be attracted to me, or whatever this mate thing is, but he regrets being near me each time." Later when I had some time to process the new information, I'm sure I'd have to ask myself why the whole mating thing didn't have me packing up and running far away.

A silent understanding passed between them.

Alona turned to Crissy. "Better get her gloves."

Crissy nodded. "I'll talk to Mitz."

"So, I wear gloves, then what?" If they had answers, I was willing to listen.

"Honestly? I don't know." Daxx said. "The fact you weren't marked already is surprising—well, not completely as it seems the only one *without* control among the brothers is Troy."

I couldn't keep the surprise off my face.

She snorted. "Let me tell you how I…"

All of our phones rang at the same time. It was the group call.

"I'll answer." Paisley said. She picked up her phone and tapped the screen. "Hello?"

I looked at my phone and reached over to decline the call so it would stop ringing. The others did the same.

"Are all of you together?" Troy asked.

"Yes, we are." Daxx said loud enough they'd hear.

"We're meeting in Victor's office as soon as you ladies can get here." That was Chase.

"We'll just have to go change out of our wet undergarments." Alona said with a grin.

"Are you wine tasting in the tub again?" Chase asked sounding amused.

"No." Beth said. "We're in the hot tub."

"They found the hot tub." Leone whispered.

"There goes the quiet spot." Quinton joked.

"When you're finished clowning around, go change and meet us." Michael snapped.

"I don't know who you are or what you've done with Michael, but I'd like him back now." Rafael sighed loudly.

"Cristy, come to my office in short time, please." Victor wasn't fooling around.

"I'll be there soon, Vic." She stood up.

"See you shortly." Paisley hung up the call.

"I have knots in my stomach." Alona said as she stood up. "I fear it's not good news."

"Story of my life." Daxx said as she pulled her jeans over wet legs.

"I think we need to have towels stocked here." Alona mused as she put her blouse on over a wet bra.

"Or robes." Bethany suggested.

I pulled on the track pants and looked down at the water soaking through. "I'm going to change and get Woods to show me the way to Victor's office." I didn't wait for answers, just turned to the door. I had a lot to consider before this meeting. I might have a sister, relatives—not to mention a man I was somehow fated to be with that didn't want me. Or perhaps want to want me was the better explanation.

Chapter Nineteen

I glanced to see the women were looking as confused as I was. I felt less like an outsider. I turned back to the man with the glasses, he vibrated where he stood, like he'd had way too much coffee. "You lost me at blood key."

He pushed his glasses up and nodded his head quickly. "It's quite brilliant, the concept." He paused when Troy gave him a look of censure. "Al-although, very much illegal."

"What is it for?" I crossed my arms and leaned back against the wall.

"We don't know yet. We're still running tests, but as it's a key…" He nodded again. "It will open something."

"Whose blood is it?" Daxx looked as impressed with his vague answer as I was.

"We're testing that right now." He tucked his hands into his pockets, then pulled them right back out to adjust his glasses once more.

"Could it be to bypass the throne room doors?" Paisley asked looking up from her phone.

"It's possible, although that means it would have to be the blood of the royals in it—" He held up his hand. "I must go." He rushed from the room.

Everyone was silent, as we stared at the door he'd all but run out.

"Science geeks." Rafael muttered, shaking his head.

"Well, that was—" Troy glanced to his twin.

"Energetic." Chase finished.

"Perhaps we could hear what Clairee and Romulus have discovered." Victor suggested.

"At least they're not vibrating like they're on caffeine overload." Quinton rubbed the back of his neck.

"I fear we're not going to like the conclusions." Troy said, then turned and went over to lean against the desk beside his twin.

"Why?" Paisley looked at Romulus.

"I can't break the ward without having the blood used to make it." Romulus said solemnly.

"How do we find out whose blood it is?" Alona inquired.

"We're working on that." Romulus answered, pushing his greasy hair back as he glanced to Clairee. "Even if we find the answer, I have no doubt that there will be a ward hidden to combat royal blood," he sighed, "actually, I'm about ninety-eight percent certain there will be."

"So, even if you know whose blood the ward is bound to, we won't be able to get in because of another ward?" Michael clarified.

Both Clairee and Romulus nodded.

"What is it about that plant that made us sick?" Crissy asked with a worried look.

"That is complicated, but easier to work around." Clairee said.

"But we'll be able to go in?" Leone turned in his chair to look at them.

"Not right away. No." Clairee said looking nervous.

"What do you mean?" Arius straightened in his chair.

"It is going to have to be deactivated, the spell and the herb dust must dissipate before any with an ability can go in safely." She answered quickly.

"Which bring us back to the problems with the ward." Romulus finished.

"Are you saying we're screwed?" Daxx put her hands on the table and glared at them.

"Not entirely." Romulus glanced to Clairee again.

She rubbed her hands down her arms. "If we're able to figure out the blood key, it will still take someone with no ability and no royal blood in their system to go in and take down the wards to clear the spell." She motioned to Romulus, "which means this person can't be any skilled person from either of our factions."

Quinton blew out a breath so loud it sounded like he was in pain. "How risky is it for someone that doesn't know what they're doing?" He motioned between them, "with no magical training?"

Clairee sighed. "It will be quite risky. One misstep—" She didn't finish.

"But you can teach this person?" Beth asked.

"Even if they do break through," Troy glanced to Chase, "we don't know what is on the other side of that door."

Leone shrugged. "So, we teach one of the guards—"

Romulus shook his head. "This warding, if it's as complex as I fear, will have a fail safe, or will backlash. Someone large," he motioned to Sith, "would be an easy target for the secondary spell."

Emil looked to Troy, then Chase. "I feel like we're backpedalling here."

"Does this blood key override the throne room to bypass it, allowing only those with royal blood to open it?" Michael crossed his arms and waited for an answer.

"That would be the logical explanation." Clairee nodded.

"Or," Romulus looked around the room at everyone, "it has a dual purpose, to get through the new ward and break the royal one."

"If it is dual purpose, I'd be willing to bet Eunice's blood was used." Michael's blue eyes connected with mine.

I nodded. "She's arrogant enough to do that."

Romulus frowned. "I doubt we have any Hubert blood samples on file. They've been in hiding for many millenniums. We'll need a sample."

"That won't be a problem." Arius said. "Paisley and I can take care of that."

Paisley nodded. "I'd love to freeze her so you can jab her with a needle."

Arius smirked.

Chase chuckled. "Aside from that entertainment," he looked back to Clairee, "who do we need you to start training, to rid this spell that made everyone ill?"

Clairee looked from one king to the other, then she stared at the floor. "They'd have to have no abilities, and no royal blood in their system." She glanced to Victor. "Which leave out any of the guards sworn by a blood oath." His eyebrows raised, she continued. "They'll have to be agile and fast on their feet in case of backlash."

"Trained for combat wouldn't hurt, depending on what is on the other side of that door." Romulus added.

"Yes, that, too." Clairee agreed.

"That leaves out everyone here." Rafael said.

I shook my head. "Not all of us."

Michael's head snapped around, he glared at me.

I looked to Victor. "I can do it." I motioned to Clairee. "If they're able to teach me what I need to know."

He studied me for a moment, giving Michael a quick glance before nodding his head and turning to the twin kings. "It would ensure someone we trust gets inside."

Both kings looked at Michael.

He shook his head. "Absolutely not."

"Michael, we have to get in." Rafael said slowly. "Autumn won't walk us into a trap."

Michael scowled at him. "And if something goes wrong?"

"We get her out." Victor answered.

Michael shook his head again. "There has to be someone else."

Leone blew out a breath. "Who? Who do we know we can trust aside from those in this room?"

"Personal guards." Troy shrugged, "but they've taken a blood oath—they may not have ingested royal blood, but we can't be certain it wouldn't be sensed somehow."

Rafael shrugged. "Autumn can do it."

"It wasn't a question of her being able." Michael said in a low tone. "But, should she? We don't know what lies in wait for us."

I straightened from the table. "Then be there to watch my back."

He turned his hands on his hips and his chest puffed out as he studied me for several seconds, while clenching his jaw.

Stepping away from the table, I went over and stood in front of him. "I can do this. Let me." I motioned to Emil, "so no other woman has to suffer as your niece has."

Michael's eyes held mine, I could see the battles taking place inside.

The tension in the room was palpable as everyone held their breath waiting.

He spun and pointed to Clairee and Romulus. "You train her for every possible contingency *and* you train another person for backup. If anything happens to her, it's *your* lives if I can't get to her." Michael turned on his heel and stomped out of the room, slamming the door behind him.

"Well, that went better than I'd imagined." Troy said quietly.

"I anticipated bloodied faces, at the very least." Chase nodded.

Daxx gave her mate a curious look. "You two knew about this?"

Troy shrugged.

"Not entirely." Chase said giving Alona a wary look. "We were going to suggest Autumn, then she volunteered."

I turned to Clairee. "How much time will it take? To show me what I need to know."

She brushed her hair back from her face. "A few days, we have some ideas for cheats to get it done."

I nodded. "Normally, I'm not into cheating, but if it gets us inside there." I glanced to Victor, who inclined his head. "I'll do it."

Romulus motioned to the door. "We have much to do."

Clairee nodded. "Meet us at the temple in the morning and we'll get started."

"I'll be there." I didn't know where the temple was, but Woods probably did.

"I'm going to monitor the cameras." Quinton stood up. He gave me a quick nod and left.

Arius got up. "I'm going to see if the science techs want Eunice's blood." He looked at me. "I called the lab, they just need yours to check."

My eyes widened. I'd forgotten I might have a sister.

"Check her for?" Victor asked.

"To see if she's Paisley's sister." Crissy grinned at him. "It was a long time ago, but I think they're the light and dark sisters from my head."

Victor looked from me to Paisley. "There is a resemblance."

"What is this?" Chase moved away from the desk. "We may have another Roan in the family?"

Alona smirked.

"Has anyone informed his elderness?" Chase looked to Arius.

"Not yet, brother. We'll wait for the facts, then tell him." Arius looked amused.

"I insist on being there when you do." Chase smiled at me.

I shrugged. "Whatever makes you happy."

He pointed to me. "Yes. I like you. Smart answer."

Alona stood up and took his hand. "That smart choice would be the two of us going to get some sleep."

Chase gave her a soft look, then pulled her close. "I doubt I'll be able to, while waiting for news, but if you're tired, beloved, we will retire." He grinned at me and held his hand to his ear like he was holding a phone. "Be sure to call and let me know as soon as you do."

I nodded as Alona pulled him from the room. "That wasn't weird at all." I mumbled.

Leone and Rafael both got up. "We have to get to work on the planning, we're meeting Ira in the yard." Leone looked to Victor.

Victor kissed the top of Crissy's head. "I have a few ideas there."

Troy looked to Daxx. "Want to sit in on this?"

Daxx looked surprised and got up quickly. "Yes."

Emil nodded. "I'll tag along."

"Beth and I are going to go to the practice room to work on some new moves." Paisley motioned to the door.

"Gods, that's just what we need, a scarier tag-team move." Leone winked at Beth.

"I'm going to my tower." Crissy grabbed her pack, then looked at me. "Want to come sit in my tower? The stars are peaceful."

Normally star-gazing wasn't my thing, but my mind was spinning faster than a roundhouse kick. I might have a sister, and other relatives—and I'd just volunteered to break a spell and blood ward… peaceful stars might be just what I needed.

Chapter Twenty

It was an actual tower. Like a medieval guard tower. I don't know what I'd expected, but this hadn't been it.

Looking down at the roof, I tried to see how far down it was. Fifteen, twenty feet, it was hard to tell in the dark.

Crissy was hunched over her notebook drawing something, while I stared out into the dark night. There wasn't much light in the direction I was looking. I could have gone to the other side and seen more with the lights that way, but the calm of the darkness was what I needed right now. The moon was just big enough to cast shadows along the land, but not bright enough that you could see anything in detail.

"You can talk. I'm very good at doing more than one thing." Crissy said quietly.

I turned and looked down at her. "My head is kind of spinning right now. Too much to process."

She giggled. "I know what that's like." She held up her hand. "Want my ball to bounce? It helps focus."

I looked at the red ball in her hand. "No, I'm good, but thanks."

"Okay." She continued doing what she was doing.

I looked back into the night. How did I ever begin sorting the clutter in my head? There was so much, I didn't even think a workout would help, and that was a first for me.

Thoughts of Michael invaded my mind again. That was a dead end, I kept reminding myself. Even if he wanted me, the sparks between us were almost real enough to burn—but he wasn't going to let his body cheat on the ghost in his memory.

I studied a spot along the trees, thinking I'd seen something. When I couldn't see anything out of place, I took a deep breath and exhaled slowly.

"I have to know what the lightning means." Crissy said softly. "I know it's that roof."

I glanced at her, she wasn't looking at me, so I wasn't sure if she was talking to me or herself.

"You'll be on that roof, so I need to know." She continued softly.

Looking back toward the trees, I tired again to make out the shapes I'd seen. "I'm all for any inside info possible."

"Something hidden or unknown." She stood up beside me, "that's all I know, but don't know what the lightning has to do with it."

I squinted, trying to see in the dark. "Maybe it's just a stormy night." I could have sworn the shapes moved. "Can we turn off your lamp for a minute?"

"Sure." She moved away. "And it's not a storm. I checked the forecast for the next week or so."

I blinked a few times, letting my eyes adjust to the darkness. "That's not encouraging. Maybe ask the magic folk if it's significant?" Something was moving in the dark, it wasn't my imagination. "Don't suppose you have binoculars or something?"

"I do." I heard her moving around behind me. "Victor got them so I can see far. What do you need to see?"

Taking them, I held them up and looked. "Probably just an animal, but my guts are nagging at me." I adjusted the focus.

"Guts can do that?" She was beside me again.

"A feeling, not your guts." I started to lower the glasses, then something flashed in the same spot I'd been looking. I froze, paused on the shapes, waiting. If whatever it was moved a few feet, the moonlight would make it easier to see.

"Oh, I get those feeling. A lot. They tell me to hide."

"Hiding is an option." I said quietly. The shape moved and I glared through the glass when I realized it was a man. "Guards patrol by those trees at night?"

"I don't think so. It's not near the border." I felt her move away. "Maybe it's someone taking a break?"

I moved my head slowly, trying to watch where the moonlight met the shadow. There was more then one figure moving down there. "If you follow the treeline toward us, what is there?" I asked quietly, hoping my guts were just confused from the information overload the last few hours.

"One of the outer tunnel entrances to the royal chambers."

My heart sped up. "What's near it?"

"The cells." She whispered with a note of confusion in her voice.

I watched as five men moved out of the shadow and hurried toward the next dark spot. "Shit. I think they're planning to try and break Eunice out." Four more men followed them. "Crissy, close all the other shutters except this one. Quietly." Another two, "Just leave me enough space to see."

"Okay."

I heard them being closed, but didn't want to look away, I needed a head count. "Fifteen so far." I told her, still watching. "Open the door and tell Woods and Bronx to get a hold of the guards."

"Okay."

I heard her whispering, but stayed focused on the people hoping to break in. I didn't see any more, but that didn't mean there weren't more somewhere.

"Autumn, put your ear piece in. We have to tell everyone. Here's your phone."

I looked away long enough to take it. Trying to keep them in sight, I fumbled to get the ear piece in.

"What's going on?" Chase sounded half asleep.

"Autumn and I are in my tower," Crissy whispered.

"There's at least fifteen heavily armed men slinking their way toward the…" I didn't know the direction.

"West tunnel entrance." Crissy said quickly.

"I can't see if there are more in other directions." I looked back to the treeline.

"Bronx has called the guardhouse." Crissy added.

"Shit. Keep an eye on them." Rafael said hurriedly. "Most of the patrols are out right now."

"They probably know that." I checked how close they were getting. "They're taking their time."

"On my way to the armory." Arius said.

"Where do you want us?" Daxx asked.

"Head to the entrances, take your guards. Check for tampering." Troy said sounding like he was jogging.

"Get your weapons first." Victor stated.

They weren't going to make it. I watched as the men moved forward more often, not cautious, clearly knowing most of the guards were sleeping or away. Lowering the binoculars, I looked down at the roof. Too far to jump.

"Porting to armory." Michael said.

"Right behind you." Quinton said in a clipped voice.

I pulled the earpiece out and tapped Crissy on the shoulder. "Do you have rope up here?"

She shook her head. "I have my box, I don't need rope."

I didn't know what that meant but nodded. Putting the piece back in my ear, I tucked the phone into the pocket of my hoodie. "I'm going down to see what they're up to."

She took off her belt and held it out to me. I took it and put it around my waist. Then she handed me a box and pulled out a strap and hook.

"Autumn, you should wait." Leone said.

I watched her attach the strap to the pillar beside the window we'd left open. She came over and took the box out of my hand and clipped it to the belt. Pushing a button on it, a cable came out, she went over and attached it to the strap.

I nodded and pulled myself up onto the ledge. "If I can stall them, I will." I swung my leg over the edge. This couldn't be that different then climbing a rock wall, only I was going down.

"Alone?" Paisley asked.

Crissy held out fingerless gloves. I took them and put them on. Later I'd have to tell her how awesome she was for being so prepared. "Maybe seeing me will make them pause long enough for you guys to get there." Grasping the ledge, I lowered my body down far enough until the cable was tight.

"I think she should wait." Rafael said.

I grabbed the cable and leaned back, trying to get a feel for how this box worked.

"Wait for what?" Michael had reconnected to the call.

"Autumn is going down to see what they're up to." Alona said with concern.

"Down what?" His tone was abrupt.

"The outside of my tower. I gave her my rappelling box, Michael. She's doing good." Crissy looked down at me and nodded.

I looked behind me and figured I still had ten feet to go. Hopefully I had enough cable.

"Cristy, when she's down, go with Bronx."

"Okay, Victor." Crissy agreed hurriedly.

"Autumn. Go back up." Michael's tone let me know he wasn't asking.

I wasn't in the mood for orders. "I'll be—" My foot slipped on the stone blocks, I spun around like a ball on a string. My shoulder connected with the wall of the tower. I clenched my jaw so I wouldn't yelp on the group call. Kicking out with my left foot, it hit the wall and stopped the turning. I heard the clatter of my phone hitting the roof below me, then sliding down it. "Dropped my phone." I said quickly as I tried to right my position again.

"As long as it didn't break, you should…"

Paisley's voice cut out, confirming my phone didn't survive the fall.

Pulling the earpiece out, I put it in my pocket and jumped the last few feet to the roof. As soon as I undid the belt, it started moving up to the tower. Crissy was wasting no time.

Squatting down, I checked the slope of the roof. It had been a while since I traveled along the top of a building to stay out of sight. I was much bigger, but definitely more coordinated then the last time I'd done this.

Staying low, I began to make my way along. I had to find a quiet way down. I also wasn't sure of the distance I would have to drop. What I didn't need was a sprained or broken leg.

Before I ran out of roof, I moved closer to the edge to look for a way down. There was no light, which was the reason I was up here in the first place, all entry points should be lit. You would think with men as tactically aware as the brothers, they'd know this. Someone was going to hear about this later. Now though, I had to get down.

I couldn't see anything to use to get down. At least, they'd managed to prevent people from getting up onto the roof.

I looked at the gloves on my hands, hopefully they'd help me grip tight enough to swing down and drop to the ground. Landing in a crouch, should absorb most of the impact—I hope.

Turning, so my feet went first, I crawled backwards toward the edge. I was taking too long, the entire guardhouse would be here shortly and I'd be dangling from the roof. I pushed myself over the edge, then balanced with just my shoulders, arms and head still on the roof. Inhaling a breath for courage, I swung my legs out and let the momentum pull me off.

I dropped down into a crouch, stinging radiating through my ankles into my shins. The force of impact sent me off balance and I fell on my butt. Darkness was good, I paused to think, no one could saw that failed move. I looked up, then again with the distance there could be worse then a dusty bum.

Getting up, I hurried in to the end of the wall. The armed men were almost there. I stopped and looked at the door, wondering briefly why someone wasn't posted on the outside. Another thing to bring up to the brothers.

Hearing the sound of boots behind me, I turned and gave the closest one a half smile for a half a second. "Do you know what time it is? I dropped my phone."

"No." He answered abruptly.

I glanced to the man beside him. The expression on his face was void of any emotion. "Really? Not one of you have a phone or watch?" They were big. Size of the brothers, big. Why was everyone so big lately? I glanced to see a few devices on wrists and made sure my cuff hid mine. I shrugged, "I'll just wait for the guard to come back." I looked at the door, but wasn't about to turn my back to these ogre-sized jerks.

"You should move on." The one at the front said.

I shook my head. "I'd rather wait. It's really dark out tonight." I wasn't a good actress, so playing the helpless female wasn't going to work for me. I motioned to the door. "You guys waiting for the guard too?" Later, I'd have to ask why the brothers couldn't port here. I pictured them running through the tunnels. The two men at the front of the group exchanged a brief look. The kind of look that had me widen my stance and drop my arms to my sides, ready.

I was about to get an unscheduled workout.

Ogre number two lunged for me, his big paws swiping in my direction. I jumped back and landed a scissor kick to his face. He stumbled back, swearing. I would have liked to see how much damage I'd done, but that move spurred the rest of them into action.

The next few moments became a fast-paced burpee exercise routine. I squatted, ducked, sprang up to avoid hands and arms from grabbing me. Unfortunately, doing this moved me away from the door into the darkness.

As I hopped over the next attacker's attempt, my hope for this fight remaining weaponless was squashed. I heard the blade clear its case and leapt back to give myself more space to see the one wielding it.

The loud clang of metal on metal let me know the Calvary had arrived, changing this whole scene from one of stalling to taking them down. The one that had just tried to slice me with his knife paused long enough to glance over at the new commotion. Using his distraction to my advantage, I kicked his hand holding the blade. It hit the dirt. His head snapped back to me, his eyes promising retribution.

I backed up, rolling my shoulders. "Don't make promises you can't keep." I told him quietly.

He grinned, a possessed, or fanatic's type of grin. Reaching behind him, he pulled out a device. I had no idea what that was. Then it must have pushed a button because sparks arced from it. He planned to zap me like a bug.

Why a giant of a man had to carry a women's defense device, I had no idea. I couldn't assume he was a complete idiot and use the same move I'd used to knock the blade from his hand. But, I could take advantage of the fact that he was probably using his dominant hand to hold that taser, which meant any actions I took, he'd have to block with his off hand. Unless of course he was equally strong in both, and then I was in trouble.

I backed up, then lunged and went down to sweep his feet out from under him. He stumbled back but had fast recovery. Before he was completely balanced, I went for a kick to his chest, I just had to keep him off balance long enough to find an opening to get rid of his little toy. I'd never felt the jolt from a taser and was good with not adding that experience to my list.

My efforts only pushed him a few steps back, meaning he knew how to fight with proper balance. Out of the corner of my eye, I could see images moving in the dark, could hear the grunts and hisses as the others fought. I just had to stall this jerk long enough for one of the guys with their port boxes to get here.

"Get the girl." Someone called out.

I didn't have time to stop and take a head count of how many women were out here, so I'd just have to assume I was *the* girl. He dove toward me, his empty fist raised. I crouched and blocked the attempt with both forearms. He outweighed me by a lot, the brunt of his hit radiated up to my shoulders. Not pausing to whine about it, I kicked out at the side of his knee, hoping to break it, or at the very least, make him back off. None of those happened, by the time I was on my feet out of arm's reach, he was coming for me again.

Bouncing to get enough spring into the move, I went for a fast roundhouse, hoping there was momentum enough behind it to do some damage. My foot connected with his face and I was rewarded with the grunt of pain. I landed and prepared for a second move while he was shaking his head. Kicks to the head were the worst, your whole brain buzzed. With no warning someone slammed into my side. The breath left my body as it became one of those split-second slow-motion moments. I hit the ground. Hard.

Fighting through the pain of broken ribs, I pushed up on one hand to looked to see who had hit me. It was ogre number one and he currently had his hands full with a very angry Troy. The jerk with the taser had Michael all up in his face, and I half hoped he'd get to feel the jolt from his own toy.

"Daxx. Get her out of here." Troy barked.

A blurry Daxx appeared in front of me as I fought to not throw up. She didn't pull me to my feet, just dropped down beside me and grabbed my shoulders.

Chapter Twenty-One

My stomach lurched. I squeezed my eyes shut and tried to inhale slowly.

"Are you all right?" Daxx was right beside me.

I opened my eyes and realized we were lying on the floor in my room.

"Yeah, I was aiming for the bed, but missed." She said as she moved to hover over me so I could see her. She offered her hand.

I shook my head. "Just give me a minute."

"Ice pack?"

I nodded. "Good start."

"I'll call Mitz." She moved away.

I lay there staring at the ceiling, taking slow, shallow breaths as I tried to assess how bad my ribs were damaged. The pain radiated through me with each breath, that wasn't a good sign. This was probably the worst timing ever. In a few days time I had to break a spell doing things I didn't know anything about, and now I was going to have to do it with taped up ribs.

"Are you out of your mind?" Michael's voice boomed from the direction of the door.

I turned my head to see him stomping in my direction. Before he reached me Troy literally appeared behind him and rushed forward to put a hand on his shoulder.

Michael stopped and shrugged it off.

"While I don't encourage what she did, it gave us the time to get there." Troy said evenly. "If she hadn't, we don't know if they had the means to get through the coded door."

Michael glared down at me, then huffed out a loud breath and turned to his brother. "They knew our guard rotation, our patrol routes…"

"I know." Troy answered.

"Mitz is bringing ice and painkillers." Daxx said coming out of the bathroom. She stopped and looked at her mate, then to Michael. "They knew our weakest points. How? We changed up the routine."

"I don't know." Troy said through clenched teeth.

Michael stared at me, I couldn't quite determine what level of pissed off he was, his facial expressions betrayed nothing.

"Hey." I said as loud as I could without pain. "I didn't block with my face." Breathing hurt, so I didn't even try for a quiet laugh.

"How bad is it?" Troy asked coming over to look down at me.

I now know what an ant feels like. "Broken ribs, probably a few other strains from the impact." I inhaled slowly.

Michael knelt beside me, his emotions bouncing from vengeance to concern. He undid the strap holding his blades to his back.

Troy put his hand on his shoulder. "You can't give her blood, brother."

Scowling, Michael looked up at him.

"She can't have blood in her system when she enters the palace in a few days." Troy said in a whispered tone.

Michael motioned to me. "She can't even get off the floor, you really think she's going to be climbing ladders and breaking wards in a few days while she's weak?"

Daxx came over. "Let's get her up before we start deciding what she can and cannot do."

I didn't want to get up, I knew how that was going to feel, but I also didn't want to be taken out of the game. "Leave me here. I'll move after the ice gets here."

Rafael and Quinton came in. "The entrances are secure." Rafael stopped and looked down at me, then gave Michael a curious glance.

"She thinks a few ribs are broken." Daxx went and sat on the bed. "One of them body-slammed her to the ground." She gave me a sympathetic look. "And we can't give her blood."

Rafael pulled out his phone. "I'll call Clairee, see if she has anything."

Quinton pulled out his. "I'll get the doc here."

Mitz came running in. "I brought ice packs." She stopped short and looked at me on the carpet. I didn't get a chance to say a word before she dropped to her knees beside me and moved the hand holding my ribs.

I sucked in a breath when she put the ice on my ribs, which was the wrong thing to do as the pain to radiated through me. Blowing out tiny breaths, I watched as everyone else arrived. "So," I blew out another breath, "why aren't there guards outside the entrance?" I felt like I was whispering but couldn't speak any louder without crying.

"What do you mean?" Victor moved over and looked down at me. "There are guards posted at all entrances."

I shook my head slowly. "There wasn't." I glanced over to Troy, "and why isn't there some sort of light out there?" I snorted, then hissed in pain. "I'm surprised you haven't had break-in attempts before."

Troy stood there, his arms crossed looking at me. I couldn't tell what he was thinking from his expression. "You have a good point."

"She does." Leone said. "We need to update our thinking and protocols."

"Why wasn't there a guard?" Quinton looked from Victor to Michael.

Victor scowled and pulled his phone out of his pocket. "I'll call Ira and see who is responsible."

"I don't think it was a lapse." I said quietly. "They knew no one would be there." I winced when I forgot and took a deep breath. "They knew every shadow out there, to hide in."

"If Autumn hadn't seen them, they could have gotten in." Daxx got up and sat on the end of the bed. "All the door codes should be changed."

Clairee came rushing in. She zeroed in on me. "I have a poultice that will help healing." She stopped and looked from me to the bed. "Would you like to get up on the bed?"

I shook my head. "Firm support of the floor is better."

Michael made an exasperated sound and got up. Going to the bed, he pulled off the pillows. Coming back, he knelt and put one under my head. Without a word, he put his hand under my knees and lifted them, slipping another pillow under them.

I was able to breathe easier. "Thanks."

He held my look for a moment, I honestly didn't know if it was pain or anger in them.

"Okay, we can apply the poultice and then put the ice back on." Clairee knelt down beside me and opened the bag she carried. "I'll get it ready."

"I was told I was required."

I turned to see a man that had to be a doctor standing in the door.

"We believe Autumn has a few cracked ribs." Troy motioned to me.

His brows drew together. "Princess Autumn, have you ever considered a different hobby?" He came toward me.

I ignored the princess when I realized it was the same doctor that had helped the last time, I just hadn't been able to see him. "Taking down bad guys is kind of my thing, Doc." I offered a slight smile.

He stopped beside me and looked down at me. "For that, we are eternally grateful." He slowly knelt beside me, forcing Michael to move toward my head to make room. "I have been spreading the word of your capture of Eunice Hubert."

I smiled. "Good, tell everyone if they step out of line, I'm coming for them." I winked at him.

"I shall." He motioned to my ribs. Clairee nodded as she did whatever she was doing to the cloth beside me. "I apologize for the pain this may cause, my princess."

I nodded. "Just stop the fancy names and we're good."

He glanced at Michael and then gave me a brief nod. "Very well."

When he pulled my top up, I put my arm over my face knowing how much this was going to suck. He started low and did that push, circle motion doctors like to do when they examined body parts. I knew he had to do it so he could feel, but he may as well have been wielding a sledgehammer at this point. I closed my eyes, blowing out shallow breaths, hoping to not whine like a puppy as he moved closer to the injured area.

Someone took my other hand, I knew without looking it was Michael. He knew I'd tough this out, but it was a nice gesture. When the doctor hit the injured ribs, I squeezed Michael's hand as hard as I could.

"The coloring and inflammation tell me all I need to know, I won't cause you anymore discomfort, my— Autumn." The Doctor said quietly.

"Can you do anything to speed the recovery?" Daxx asked.

"Ribs are…"

"We have a chance to get to Willis Hubert in a few days time," Troy interrupted, "and Autumn is instrumental to that mission."

"Oh. Oh, I see." The doctor nodded slowly. "Ending the tyranny of the Hubert line would indeed be wonderful." He leaned back on his heels. "We do have something that we use

in emergency situations to expedite healing of important—"
he looked up at Troy, "when there isn't royal blood available,
but," he looked back at me, "there is no guarantee it will
work on a bone injury." He paused, his brows furrowed, "it is
also quite painful."

"What is it normally used for?" Michael asked him.

"Deep tissue injuries, fatal ones." The doctor told him
with a serious expression.

"So, it might not work?" I asked, trying to ignore the pain
he'd mentioned.

"There is that chance." He knelt there patiently.

"Oh, the hyper-nostrum elixir you were testing last year?"
Clairee inquired.

He nodded. "Yes, it's been quite successful."

"I don't recall this elixir." Troy stood there, arms crossed,
looking very king-like.

The doctor stood up and turned to him. "It's been in the
works for many decades, a failsafe in case one of the royals
were injured and there wasn't another around to aid in their
healing." He bowed his head and stayed that way. I wasn't
sure if it was out of respect, or if he thought he was in
trouble.

"Should we be flattered you want us to live forever?"
Chase asked from where he was leaning across the room.

The doctor looked over at him. "We thought it prudent, as
none had found a mate for so many years."

"Ah, you just want new twin kings." Chase smiled.

"That-that wasn't," the doctor looked from Chase to Troy,
a panicked expression on his face as his mouth worked like a
goldfish.

"Relax, doc, he's pulling your chain." I said, then tried to
clear my throat without straining and moving my ribs. "When
you said painful, how painful are we talking?"

Clasping his hands together, he gave me an apologetic
look. "I can't be certain, as I said it was never tested on bone,
only deep tissue injuries."

"Awesome." I whispered. I met Michael's somber look. "All right, lets give it a test on bone." A pained look went through Michael's eyes.

He turned and looked at his brother. "Is there no one else able to break the wards?"

Troy glanced from me back to Michael. "We haven't been able to find anyone else we trust completely. Autumn is the only one so far." He glanced briefly to me then back to his brother, "we're still looking."

My eyebrows went up, I hadn't heard that there wouldn't be a backup trained to break the spell and ward.

Michael closed his eyes, his jaw clenching.

"What about eufori?" Beth blurted out.

Michael looked at her.

"To help with the pain of this miracle mix or whatever." She looked at Leone, then back to him. "It's not royal blood and wears off fast—" She turned to Clairee, "right?"

Clairee nodded. "It would be out of her system within a few hours."

I looked from Beth to Clairee, then to Michael. I was all for fast healing with less pain, but I wasn't going to ask of it from him, when he wasn't able to decide what he wanted. This decision had to be his.

All movement in the room stopped, every eye was locked on Michael. His blue eyes were moving over my face.

"I could sedate her." The doctor suggested quietly, "but, we've had a few adverse side effects and she could aspirate if she were unconscious and vomited."

I grimaced. "No sedation, thanks."

"Go get your miracle cure." Michael growled in a low tone, not sounding happy about his own decision.

Rafael came over quickly and touched the doctor's shoulder. "I'll take him." They vanished without another word.

"I'll go get a basin and some tea made." Mitz got up and walked toward the door.

"Maybe we should help her get onto the bed." Paisley came over, and gave me a sympathetic look, "so if you do throw up, you can roll on your side."

"Sounds like fun." I blew out a breath. "Yeah, help me up."

Michael looked down at me, the nerve in his jaw pulsing. "It will hurt less if you walk, then if you are carried."

Holding the ice pack with my elbow, I held up my free hand.

Michael reached under my shoulders with one hand while holding mine. "Ready?"

I nodded and focused on holding my breath. I locked my elbow, my grip on his hand tightening as he pulled me to my feet. Even with his help, more muscles tightened and the throbbing turned into jolts of pain through my chest and abdomen.

Dropping my head forward, I rested it against his chest until I was able to breathe again. Lifting my head, I nodded. "I'm good."

He continued to hold my hand as I walked over to the bed. Truth be told, I was glad he did, I wasn't very steady.

When we reached the bed, I looked down at my shoes.

"I'll get them." Beth scrambled across the bed. She dropped off the other side by my feet. "Having recently broken," she paused and gave me a look of pain, "everything, I know your own feet seem a mile away right now." She undid them and pulled them off as I lifted each foot as high as I could.

"Here's the basin." Mitz came jogging in and came over and set it on the table beside the bed. She paused and touched my cheek. "I'm going to steep some relaxing tea. To help you rest, love." She gave me a brief look, then hurried back out the door.

"Whenever you're ready." Michael said with a soft tone.

"Let's get her jacket off." Bethany rushed back over and held my sleeve, like she was helping a child. She moved around me to the other side with my hoodie in her hand and just pulled it right off my other arm.

"My earpiece is in the pocket. I don't think my phone survived the fall." I looked up to Michael hoping he wasn't mad I'd killed my phone.

"We have more." He said drily.

I gave him a slight nod, then took hold of his arm. Down was going to suck as much as up had.

Mitz came rushing back in the door. "Everyone out, she doesn't need an audience for this." She glanced at Clairee. "Clairee and I will stay."

I didn't wait to see if the others griped or complained about being kicked out, just looked up at Michael and gave him an abrupt nod.

He grasped my hand and put the other behind me as I blew out steady, even breaths and sat slowly. That wasn't the bad part, laying back was going to be worse.

"Rest your weight against my hand, I'll do the work." His eyes held mine as I did what he said.

It still hurt and I tensed, making it hurt more, but it was much better then if I'd used my own muscles to get me on the bed. Releasing my hand, he turned and gently lifted my legs onto the bed. I looked up at the ceiling and let my body settle into the mattress.

Michael sat down carefully and looked down at me. I could see the fear haunting him.

"Flashbacks?" I watched his look change to surprise. I sighed. "I asked Quinton to fill in a few blanks."

"I see." The nerve pulsed in his jaw as he studied the headboard above me.

"Hey," he glanced back to me, "I'm not her. I'm still here." I scowled. "If that jerk hadn't of slammed me like a schoolyard bully, I'd be dancing on his face right now."

The serious note in his expression lightened slightly. "I know…"

"I'm back." The doctor rushed in the door and stopped at the end of the bed. "I can't persuade you to use blood healing and postpone this task that requires our heroic princess to suffer?"

I shook my head. "Can't do, Doc. Time is of the essence and all that. Can't let the bad guys get away."

He inhaled loudly and then nodded. "Very well." He walked around Michael and set a container on the table beside me. "I do apologize for the pain this is going to cause."

"Not necessary. How bad can speed-healing some ribs be?"

Famous last words.

Chapter Twenty-Two

It was bad. Worse than any other pain I'd ever experienced. I had nothing to compare it to. It may have been better without the vomiting, which meant moving and muscles clenching—but the internal pain, *that* was off the charts. I panted quietly, trying not to breathe too deeply.

"The initial shock is over, you should give her more eufori, my prince, it's not completely finished." The doctor released my wrist after checking my pulse.

Mitz climbed across the bed and moped off my forehead and face. "None of us knew it was this bad, love." She whispered.

I opened my eyes to reassure her but only gave a slight shake of my head, still not sure if I could speak without throwing up.

"I'll go get the tea and fresh ice packs." Mitz got up.

The doctor looked at Michael. "Check for a fever and swelling for the next twelve hours, call me if you have concerns." He gave me a pained look, inclining his head. "I hope our next meeting is under more pleasant circumstances."

"Thanks, Doc." I said barely louder than a whisper. I wasn't thanking him for the pain, but he had only done what we'd asked, so despite how I felt I couldn't be rude to him.

I didn't watch to see if he left, I looked at Michael. He hadn't moved throughout the whole thing. He wiped the hair back from my eyes, pain etched in his face. "I'm going to give you more eufori and hopefully you can rest a while."

If I wasn't feeling like I lost a battle I would have questioned why he was helping me. Another twinge of agony from this internal miracle cut through me. I took a sharp breath, all thought of needing answers gone.

Michael knelt beside me and leaned closer, "just close your eyes and breathe it away." He moved the hair from my throat and tilted my head gently.

I closed my eyes when his fangs pierced my skin, the floating feeling washed over me immediately. Later, I'd ask if he could control how much or how that worked—but for now I'd take the break from the throbbing and nausea from the pain.

When he lifted his head, I opened my eyes to see him looking down at me. I gave him a loose smile. "Thanks, iceman."

His mouth moved to resemble something that may have been a half-hearted smile. "Try to relax."

I wanted to laugh but didn't want to ruin the buzz with pain. "Relaxing is all good now."

"Is it okay if we come in for a bit?" Bethany was peeking in the door.

"Sure. Come on in." I nodded my head. "I think I'm done throwing up."

She came in, some of the others following her. "We were in the hall, we heard."

"Yeah?" I looked at Troy as he entered. "Did you hear iceman swearing at the doctor?"

Troy glanced at Michael. "Heard it, felt it."

"That's right, you all have that brother connection thing going on." I smiled at Arius. "That's cool."

He grinned at me, then turned to Michael when he stood up. "Spoke to Ira."

Michael's posture changed, stiffening.

"Guard didn't show up." Arius looked over at Quinton where he stood by the door. "They're headed to his place now to see if he's there."

Michael gave an abrupt nod. "Let me know." He motioned to me. "Unless he's dead, there's no reason why he wasn't there. If he had been, Autumn wouldn't be injured now." His tone was murderous.

Even in my current stoned condition I recognized that tone and what it meant for that guard if they found him. "I will kick his…"

"Pardon the interruption."

A thin man with grey hair stood in the door.

"Elder Roan?" Arius straightened up from the dresser he was leaning on.

"Prince Arius." The man smiled at him. "I was looking for my great-granddaughter." He looked at me in the bed, then back to Arius. "Is this Princess Autumn? The one responsible for Eunice Hubert being in the cells?"

Arius nodded. "Yes." He motioned to the door. "Paisley will be back shortly, she went to get Autumn something to eat."

He stepped into the room. "Is she injured?"

I waved my hand at him. "Just some busted ribs, the doc used a miracle cure to fix me up."

The elder looked to Troy, who nodded. "Wouldn't blood be less painful? I've read the reports on that hyper-nostrum concoction."

Troy rubbed the back of his neck. "We couldn't use blood healing, because of the wards on the palace."

"Yes, yes. Elder Arian was explaining that situation to the council." He motioned to me, "Princess Autumn is the one needed to enter the palace and break the wards?"

"That's the plan." I said loud enough to be heard. I looked at Daxx, then back to him. "So, you're Paisley's great-grandfather?" I pointed to him. "I heard about you." I smiled and looked at Arius for a moment then back to him. "Guess we find out soon if you're mine too." I sobered. "I think. I don't know how long the lab will take."

The expression on his face was like someone had just landed a spin kick against the side of his head.

Paisley came in the room carrying a tray, Alona and Chase right behind her.

"Elder Roan." Chase grinned and looked at Paisley then to me. "To what do we owe this…" Chase frowned. "Are you all right? You look like you've just been struck."

The man gave Chase a harsh look, then turned to Paisley. "Is this true? That Princess Autumn may in fact be…"

"We don't know yet." She hurried over and set the tray down, pausing to smile at me before turning back to him. "It was just a possibility suggested by resemblance of some of our features, but Crissy saw it."

"The Seer of Truth saw the both of you?" The gobsmacked look was gone, replacing it was a look of elation.

"Yes, Elder Roan, she did." Alona went over and stood beside Chase.

I don't know if it was the pain, the eufori, or everything combined, but it finally hit me. I had family. *Family.* Actual relatives. The realization made my chest ache in a strange way.

Michael sat on the edge of the bed slowly, his back to everyone. He gave me a look asking if I was all right.

I inhaled slowly and nodded. I wasn't, but I was in no shape to try to deal with this sort of thing right now.

He studied me for a moment, his gaze moving over my face slowly. He stood up. "I think Autumn should rest now."

"Oh. Of course." The elder walked to the end of the bed. "I wish you a fast recovery, Princess Autumn. I'm sure we'll speak soon." He bowed his head and then turned around. "Your majesties." He bowed his head and walked out of the room.

Chase pointed to me, a big grin on his face. Before he could speak, Alona grabbed his hand and shook her head. "Later, Chase, she needs to rest now."

Everyone said a quiet goodbye and left.

Michael sat down on the bed. "How are you doing?"

"Head's a bit of a mess if I'm being honest." I took a short breath. "Physically, not much better."

"Do you want to try to eat?" He motioned to the table.

I shook my head. "No, I think I'll just close my eyes and rest while the pain is dulled."

He nodded. "I'll stay close so I can give you more eufori if you need it. Hopefully you'll rest all night."

I touched his arm. "Thanks, iceman." I closed my eyes and left the thoughts of relatives float away, replaced with the haze of the high feelings still filling me. Rest now, think later.

I came to slowly, dazed and unsure of where I was. The first movement brought a shot of pain through my ribs, and everything came back to me. It was dark in the room, just a bit of light from the bathroom. I looked at the ceiling, debating if I wanted to get up, then I realized I wasn't alone.

"You have to make a decision, love, you can't keep going like this. It's not fair to either of you." Mitz said in a hushed tone.

"I know." Michael answered quietly.

"It was long time ago. I know you've realized it wasn't what you thought at time—"

"It's not that. I figured out that my title and all the money in the realm mean nothing to her. I know she isn't anything like Lara," he made a hissing noise, "so far from anything like her."

I knew I should alert them to the fact I was awake, but wasn't sure how to go about it, and part of me wanted to hear this conversation.

"Then what is the problem? I'm not seeing it. What I *have* seen is how you are with her, Michael. You know what fate has brought you…why are you so conflicted?" Mitz was asking the questions I needed answers to, more points for her.

"I just," I heard him move, probably standing up, "I don't think I can. She is fearless, throws herself into any situation, even when she shouldn't…"

"She's noble and honorable."

I really liked Mitz.

"You should see how she fights…"

Mitz made an odd noise, "no I don't think I'd like to, just hearing the rest of you talk is more than enough for me."

"That's it exactly. There's no way I can hinder her, or ask her to heed to my wishes. I can't form a complete bond because she has to jump in regardless of her own personal safety…"

"Sounds like you're like every other mate out there and fear what they fear—to lose one." Mitz's voice held soft understanding and a motherly tone. "Your brothers fear the same thing, Michael, but cherish what they have been given."

"I can't go through that again, Mitz, ever." Michael sounded so sad. "The circumstances of Lara's death will haunt me forever, but to lose my true mate, I can't survive that."

"Do you think if you don't it won't hurt as much if, gods forbid, something happens to her and you're not fully bonded?"

You tell him Mitz, I thought. I still didn't know if this full bonding and mating thing was for me, but I did know Michael meant something to me that no one else ever had… and in this weak moment I could admit I didn't want to lose that. I closed my eyes, trying to think beyond how crappy and drained I felt. What was he saying? It wasn't the perfect ghost of Lara causing him to run, it was the fact I was his mate? It wasn't me he had a problem with? Thinking wasn't working for me right now.

"I don't know." Michael whispered.

I opened my eyes and decided I couldn't lay here and listen in on any more of this conversation. I pushed up using the arm on my good side, hoping I could pull it off without muscles moving. The shift in position wasn't approved by my body. I groaned out loud when the twinges of pain shot through me. At least they were twinges, and not the knives stabbing through me now.

"Autumn." Michael rushed over and put his hand behind me, helping me sit up.

No. This position hurt more.

"Take it slow." He said softly.

Mitz was beside the bed now. "How are you feeling?"

"Well," I waited for Michael to help me swing my legs over the side, "I won't be sparing anytime soon."

"You need to eat to build up your strength." She knelt on the bed.

My guts felt like they'd been put through a grinder. "Are you sure whatever that miracle cure was is done with my stomach?" I truly felt awful. If my body wasn't telling me I needed to go to the bathroom, I would have laid back down.

"It's been four hours, you're through the worst of it." Mitz said as she got up and turned on a lamp.

"I was out that long?" That could explain why my back was numb.

"You needed it." Michael squatted down in front of me, his hand resting on my shoulder like he was afraid I'd do a face plant.

The way I was feeling, that wasn't out of the question. "Right now, I need the bathroom." I said quietly, still feeling groggy.

Mitz was on the move immediately. "You help her to the door, Michael, and I'll assist her after that." She went to the bathroom and opened the door.

Michael stood up and offered his hand. I had to give him points for knowing I needed to get on my feet myself. I took it and locked my elbow while mentally preparing my body for movement. My legs felt disconnected, so I wasn't even sure I could stand up.

Without being obvious, Michael pulled up enough that I only had to straighten my legs. The whole room tilted, like I'd been kicked in the head.

He wrapped his other arm around me, careful to not touch my side.

I felt weak. I hated admitting it, but had to rest my head against his chest and let him balance me until the room stopped moving.

"Don't rush it. That elixir puts your body through accelerated healing. A week's worth in a few hours." His hand moved across my shoulders in a soothing motion

I listened to the to his voice rumble through his chest. "Talk to the doc when I passed out?"

"I did."

Lifting my head slowly, I paused to see if the room was steady. "Is he still breathing?" There had been a few moments when I was practically screaming when I wasn't heaving, I'd thought Michael might kill the man.

"He is." His muscles tensed beneath my hand.

I looked up at him slowly, still afraid to move too much. "I know you don't agree with this, but thanks for seeing it through."

Michael stood there, looking down at me. Too many emotions going through his eyes for me to catch them all. "Ready to try walking?"

I grimaced. "No, but I have to." I smirked. "Just don't let me do a face plant. I know I'm not strong enough to go through that accelerated healing crap again."

He took my hand and stepped back. "Your strength is unwavering, little warrior."

As compliments went, that was probably the best I'd ever gotten. My eyes watered. I cleared my throat and took a careful step. Stupid elixir junk was making me all emotional too. "I smell like a back alley, but don't think I can stand long enough to rinse off." I looked toward Mitz standing in the bathroom door, she gave me a soft smile.

"I'm sure we can find a way to hose off some of the stench." She looked to Michael. "You can pop to Alona's apartment and get the stool Bethany used."

"After I am sure she's steady enough to leave." He said, as we took another slow-motion step.

By the time we reached the bathroom door, I felt like I'd just gone ten rounds in the ring against a much larger opponent. I was out of breath, shaking, and the sweat was rolling off me without pause. "Whew." I held onto the doorframe. "That was exhausting."

Mitz took my hand when Michael released it. "We'll get you cleaned up and get some food into you." She nodded. "You'll be at the top of your game in no time."

I blew out a breath. "Definitely can't get any lower." Feeling weak wasn't something I was used to. I took a few steps toward the toilet. "Anyone know how long I'm going to feel like this?"

"Doctor said it would take about two days to recover." Michael spoke from the doorway. "Just as long as you rest and behave, it will be nothing more than bruised ribs by tomorrow."

I nodded and took another step. "I don't plan on doing anything to slow down this recovery. I want to get that palace cracked open, and put a stop to those sickos and their whack plans."

Mitz beamed at me. "I'm sure you'll accomplish all of that." She looked over my shoulder. "Go. Close the door and get that stool."

I kind of had a girl crush on Mitz, how she spoke and the men around this place listened without question. I heard the door close and blew out a breath. "He's a little more intense then normal." I said under my breath.

She chuckled. "Yes. You've taken his rock-solid resolve and scrambled it good, love." She gave me a huge smile. "It's about time too. He needs to be set right."

I rolled me eyes. "I don't think I'm the one to do it." I finally reached the toilet. It felt like a victorious moment.

Mitz helped me get turned around and the track pants I wore situated, then she backed up and stood patiently. "You are the only one to do it."

Normally I'd be a bit shy about sharing space with someone at a time like this, but my body was at the point it really didn't care.

"Don't try to get up. Let me run and grab a robe." She spun to the door, her movement blurred.

I wasn't going anywhere.

She was back before I had time to process a single thought.

Setting the robe on the counter, she came and held out her hand. "How much of that conversation did you hear?"

I gave her a quick look, not sure how she'd known I was awake. "Enough to know that iceman wants nothing to do with me or this mate stuff."

She chortled. "*Iceman* doesn't know what he wants, and that is the problem." She held me steady while I kicked off the pants. "The brothers, all of them, have lived," she paused, a look of thoughtfulness on her face, "essentially alone with their thoughts for far too many years. They don't do change well." Pausing again, she looked at some bruising on my hip, with a shake of her head she straightened up. "Each of my boys stared at their prophecy, dreaming of the day theirs came to be, and yet are shocked when it does." She took my hands, watching to see I was still able to stand. "For a man that doesn't want something, he can't seem to stay away from you."

I looked at her for a second, then let go of her hands and carefully pulled my arm out of my sleeve. "I don't know if I'm all into this fated mate thing." She pulled the shirt away from me, so I could slip my arm free without too much movement, "but the hot and cold thing is driving me crazy."

Mitz pulled the shirt over my head and tossed it across the room. "Hot and cold?"

I wasn't about to tell her Michael and I had sex and he vanished right after. "He'll be stomping around giving orders, avoiding me, then lick my fat lip or heal my injuries." I rolled my eyes, "not to mention sending me these warm fuzzy feelings through the blood bond."

She smirked as she went over and grabbed the robe. "Would you like some advice from someone with a few years of experience?"

I turned around slowly. "How many years are we talking?"

She smirked. "I'm much older than all the boys."

I grinned. "You don't look a day over fifty."

Mitz laughed. "You're a joy." She sobered. "Absence. That's the key. We'll find somewhere to tuck you away for a few days while you recuperate. It might be the nudge Michael needs to make a decision."

I moved in slow motion getting the underwear off under the robe. "Yeah? Where are you thinking of tucking me?"

She motioned for me to go sit on the edge of the tub and walked beside me as I did. "I think a fresh face for Rena might be nice." She grimaced. "Instead of a brooding brother, seething father, and an empath that has to visit at a distance."

I nodded. "I do want to meet her." I shrugged one shoulder. "I've never been in her position, but I've seen a lot of crazy sh-stuff happen."

Mitz gave me one of her motherly smiles. "I think you're just what each other need."

Someone knocked on the door. "Mitz?" It was Michael.

"Come in we're decent." She smiled at me.

Michael came in carrying a stool. "Sorry I took so long, I checked with Leone to see if they found that guard yet." His gaze moved over me while he spoke.

"Did they?" I wanted to have a chat with him if they had.

He shook his head. "As far as his family knows, he left for his shift and they haven't heard from him since." He took the stool over and set it in the shower stall.

The stall was glass and sparkling, nothing like the showers at the gym.

"Oh dear." Mitz gave him a worried look. "I hope nothing has happened to him."

Michael rubbed the back of his neck. "He has a mate and three children at home. Ira say's he's solid, so him voluntarily doing anything to help the Hubert's is a long shot."

"Oh." She covered her mouth, her eyes reflecting concern.

Michael shook his head. "His mate doesn't sense loss, but also can't pick up anything helpful."

"That's reassuring, I suppose." Mitz waved her hand at the door. "Out. Autumn can't wait for much longer."

She wasn't wrong there. I felt like I was close to sliding to the floor. I went to stand up and could barely find the strength.

Michael rushed over and took my hand, once again pulling me up far enough for me to get my legs under me. He led me to the shower and didn't release my hand until I was perched on the stool.

"Thanks." I gave him a straight look. "I really hope I come across this Hubert guy."

He grinned, but not in a pleasant way. "I'll hold him for you."

I nodded slowly. "Tag team it is."

"Out, Michael. Go through to the kitchen and tell the girls to get the food out. Bring Autumn back a plate."

Chapter Twenty-Three

I barely ate, then with the help of more eufori, I slept like I never remember doing before. When I woke up to Paisley sitting on the chair halfway across the room. I moved slowly, assessing how my body felt. It wasn't top form, but I didn't need to groan with each muscle movement. I was about the ask what time it was when I noticed her bobbing her head. She had earbuds in. I sat up slowly.

"Hey." She pulled out the earbuds and got up.

I managed to get my feet over the side of the bed. "Your turn to babysit?"

She came over. "They're all down in the cells trying to find out where that guard is."

I sat there for a minute, deciding if I wanted to see how standing went. "Are they having any luck?"

"I haven't heard anything yet." She sighed. "How are you feeling?"

I shifted to the edge of the bed and stood up slowly. "Better, not ready to move fast though."

"It sounded awful when the doctor gave you that stuff."

I snorted. "Yeah, he won't get any product endorsements from me." I tried stretching one way, and then the other carefully. I definitely had a way to go. I stopped and looked at her. "Did I meet your great-grandfather last night?"

She grinned. "Yes, you did." Tucking her phone into her jacket, she smiled. "It's kind of why I'm here and not at the cells glaring through the glass."

"Oh? The lab did the test?" My heart skipped a few beats as I stood there. Did I want it to be a positive match or whatever it was called?

She nodded. "Yes." She grinned, "and they're ninety-eight percent sure we're sisters." She bit her lip and looked at me.

Eyes wide, I stared back at her. "That's..." I closed my mouth, then opened it again. "I don't even know what to say."

She nodded. "I know you think you're it. Totally alone in this life, then..." she blew out a breath, "I'm really hoping my theory about our father is true." She inhaled sharply, "and that he's somewhere out there, because I have some serious questions for him."

I nodded my head slowly. "Like, why they hell I was on my own at six."

"I know." She hugged her waist, then dropped her arms again and motioned up and down me, "but look at you. You beat the odds..." she hugged her waist again, "I'm dying to hug you, but I think we'll let you recover before I scream and jump up and down."

I laughed. "Yeah, jumping isn't happening today." I felt numb, completely blown away. I had a sister. "So, so they—or can they tell if we're twins, or who is older?"

"I think so. The tech was saying something about more tests, but I ran out all giddy to tell Arius, then come here and wait to tell you."

I stood there and looked at her, then waved my hand beside my head. "It hasn't sunk it yet...I just..." I puffed up my cheeks, then blew out as my eyes teared up.

She smiled, with teary eyes and leaned forward, resting her forehead on mine.

We stood there looking at each others' blurry eyes.

"Sisters." I whispered. "I have a sister."

"A pretty cool one." She said quietly.

I grinned. "Definitely, a cool one."

"My sister kicks ass like no other." She said lifting her head away.

"She tries." I answered, then blew out another breath. "This is pretty epic."

She nodded her head quickly. "That we met in another realm and are mated to brothers?"

I blinked. "I was referring to the fact we're sisters, but when you put it that way, it's crazy."

Mitz came rushing in the door, then stopped on the spot. "Well, you're on your feet, that's an improvement."

I gave her a wide-eyed look. "Standing works, I haven't tried anything else yet."

She shook her head. "You shouldn't just yet." Going past us, she hurried into the closet. "I've got Emil taking you and introducing you to Rena." She came back out carrying clothes. "A few track suits should be enough. You're only over there for two days." With a soft smile, she turned and went back in the closet.

Paisley looked at me. "You're staying at Alona's apartment for a few days?"

Before I could speak Mitz came back out. "She's going there to recover and heal." She smiled at Paisley, "and to make someone miss her."

I looked back to Paisley, she grinned and nodded.

"Might make him think." She glanced at Mitz. "Does he know you're leaving?"

Mitz shook her head and started putting the clothes into a bag. "No. He went out early to check around the palace."

Paisley's gave me a sideways look. "This could get interesting."

I was going to like having a sister, I decided. "Paisley and I are sisters." I blurted out.

Mitz paused and looked from me to Paisley. "The results are back so soon?"

She nodded. "Yes. I came here and waited for her to wake up so I could tell her."

Mitz looked so happy, she rushed over and touched Paisley's cheek then mine. "I'm so pleased." She took a deep breath and nodded. "Family can be your whole heart and soul." She gave us a look, one eyebrow raised, "when they're not annoying you to no end." With a chuckle she went back over and picked up the bag and motioned to the clothes on the bed. "Emil will be here shortly if you'd like to freshen up and change, Autumn."

Paisley leaned over and kissed my cheek. "Get some rest, sister, we have evil forces to beat in a few days." With a smile she turned and walked out of the room.

My stomach clenched. I closed my eyes and took a few slow breaths.

"It does get better." Emil said quietly.

I nodded and then looked at him. "I'm just sore from throwing up so much last night. You really do use every muscle in your body I think."

"Mmm, I don't think the body is designed for what goes in to come back that way." He stepped away from the door and glanced down the hallway. "Rena?"

I stood there holding my bag and looked around. This place was nice. Like, *nice* nice, like I'd never seen with my own eyes before. It did fit Alona though, the sparse but eloquent décor.

"I'm here, dad." A tall woman came out. Her hair was so blonde, it was almost white. "I've been standing in the bathroom waiting to see if breakfast wanted to stay or not.

Emil went over and kissed her forehead. "You look less transparent today."

She rolled her eyes at him. "Wait a few hours, that will change." She gave me a polite smile.

"Autumn is going to stay for a few days while she recuperates."

I lifted my hand to say hi.

"Oh, are you hurt?" Her brows were drawn together.

Emil looked briefly at me. "It seems to be her natural way of being." He motioned to the stool by the kitchen island, then held Rena's elbow as she went to it. "I told you about Autumn."

Rena's dark brown eyes went huge as she looked at me. "You're the one that got that red-headed demon?"

I grinned. "That's what they tell me. I couldn't see at the time."

"It was a thing of beauty, you sent her flying to the pavement, face first." Emil nodded.

"I'm so glad she's out of the picture. There was something really off with her." Rena said quietly.

I snorted. "That's putting it politely." I rubbed my hands over my ribs. "As soon as these heal, I'm hoping to find her friends and end this once and for all."

She gave me a hopeful look. "I won't feel safe again until it's over."

I gave her an abrupt nod. "We'll get them. Every last one of them."

Emil pulled his phone out of his pocket and looked at it. "I have to get back. They know where the guard is."

"In a good way?" I leaned against the island.

He glanced up from typing. "He was ambushed on his way to his post. As far as they know he's still alive, but there's always a chance of an ambush."

I sighed. "Wished I could be in on that."

He shook his head. "You need to recover to get us into the palace."

"Palace? A real palace?" Rena looked at me. "And you have to get them in?"

Emil smiled, "Autumn will have to explain. I'll call you later." He stepped back and pushed the button on his device, vanishing.

She shook her head. "Sends a shiver down my spine every time one of them just disappears."

I sat on the other stool, still feeling weaker then I'd like. "Yeah it's, uh, not that fun to be the one disappearing either."

"I've done it once when my father found me on the island and brought me back here. I was a complete mess, so I'm not sure I even realized what had happened."

I smirked. "Lucky you. My guts try to come out my throat every time I do it."

She sighed, "my stomach acting up is a daily thing right now."

I'd almost forgotten her situation. "How are you doing?"

"Managing." She motioned to the counter. "The doctor told my father to get me vitamins, he came back with that."

I turned to look. There had to fifteen bottles on the counter. "Guess he didn't specify prenatal?"

"Oh, he got those too." She grinned. "I'll have enough vitamins for the next two years. Those are just the ones I don't require at the moment, the rest are in the bedroom."

I shrugged, "I guess he's trying to be helpful."

"Smothering more like, both him and my brothers. I love them, but…" She waved her hand. "So, the palace?"

I got up, took my shoes off and set them by the door. Stepped down into the sitting area, I looked at the white furniture and decided I'd sit in the chair. When I sat down, I noticed she'd followed. "I don't even know where to begin to explain that." I studied her. "You probably know more about this magic and stuff then I do."

"Magic? I don't know anything about magic, I've just recently discovered I'm related to the royal family in another realm." Rena smiled. "I always knew there was a reason I was almost two hundred and fifty years old and still alive, but I never thought any of that would be part of it."

I decided her story was probably going to be more interesting then mine.

Chapter Twenty-Four

"I think I slept for eight hours. Totally knocked-out kind of sleep." I told the girls.

"I guess your body needed it after that elixir." Beth said in a quiet tone.

"After hearing how that *miracle* sounded first-hand, I'm surprised she's been awake at all." Daxx sounded tired.

I looked out the window to see it was almost dawn. On a normal day I'd been going for my jog now. Normal days weren't what I was living now, I reminded myself. "How's that guard doing?"

"He's recovering." Alona answered.

From the tone of her voice, she was probably still waking up.

"I can't believe they just left him locked up there, starving." Paisley sighed. "Arius said another day and he may not have survived."

Bethany hissed in annoyance.

I smiled, realizing I recognized it was her. For the first time in my life, I could honestly say I had close friends.

"Having seen what happens when they go too long without feeding, I can't believe they did that to one of their own kind." Beth finished.

I hadn't thought of that, what happened when they didn't feed. I knew they ate food—mountains of food, but had no idea what the difference was. "I have so much to learn about Alterealm…people." I mumbled.

Crissy laughed. "They have a whole library of information."

I grimaced, "that's way too much reading for me. I'd rather ask questions."

"You can ask me." She said. "I might know the answers."

"I don't think she meant right now, Crissy." Alona told her.

"Oh. Okay."

I could hear the ball bouncing and wondered what she was trying to figure out. Hopefully it was the lightning thing she'd been seeing. I didn't know much about lightning, only enough that I knew I didn't want to find out what being struck by it was like.

"Have Clairee and Romulus been over?" Daxx yawned.

"For a bit. They had to rethink the plan." I stared at the floor. "Both required taking something in that wouldn't have worked because of the herb or that ward."

"I hope they get it figured out. The guys are going stir crazy." Beth said.

Daxx snorted. "Serves them right. Now they know how we feel."

I debated asking about Michael, but decided not to. Rena came wandering into the room. She looked like she had just woken up. She went over to the counter and put the kettle on.

"Hey, is there a way to put this on speaker? Rena's up."

"If you look in the bottom left corner on the call screen." Paisley informed me.

"Ok, hang on." I looked for the button and pushed it. "Did it work?"

"Yes." Paisley's voice came out of the speaker on the phone.

"Okay, now Rena can hear too." I set the phone on the counter between us.

"Hi, Rena." Alona said softly.

"Hi." She replied.

I watched her face, and even though she smiled I could still see the hesitation.

"Hi, Rena, it's Daxx. Later on—when we can sneak away, we'll come over and have a girl's night."

Rena's eyebrows went up. "Don't get in trouble…"

"Trouble? We understand being under house arrest, you must be losing your mind over there." I could picture Daxx rolling her eyes as she said that.

"I'm not really feeling like going out, so it's okay now." Rena stared at her hands, clasped on the counter as she spoke.

"Hi, it's Bethany. Do you have to stay there until after the baby is born?" Bethany asked. "I mean, I figured you'd decided to have it…"

Rena took a deep breath before speaking. "I have. I-I don't know what I'm doing beyond that, but I can't bring myself to end it."

We'd spent some time talking about that the day before. I felt for her, I really did. I don't know what I'd do if I were in her situation. Given the fact that I could never have children, I'd never had to think about things like that before.

"If you need anything we're here." Alona's calm voice came through the speaker.

"Thank you. And I don't understand about this porting thing—Dad asked Uncle Chase about it and the explanation was complicated."

"How do you mean?" Daxx asked.

Rena looked at me and then to the phone.

I stared at the little counter of the call time increasing. "Isn't that something we should find out? Once she's feeling better?"

"Apparently, I can't cross over?" she looked at me, I nodded, "and take a chance that the baby can't."

"Oh. I didn't even think of that." Paisley said quickly.

"I can ask the man who is not one, but all, at the library and see if there is a book about it." Crissy said.

Rena's eyebrows went up.

I shrugged, if she didn't know Crissy, there was no way I could explain her. "Can you do that, Crissy? I mean what happens if she has one of those stabilizer watch things on, does that protect the baby too? No offense, Alona, your digs are sweet, but I've been here a day and I'm losing my mind, I can't imagine being stuck in here for months."

"I'll go now." Crissy said quickly.

"No offense taken, Autumn. I agree, Emil can't expect her to stay in that apartment indefinitely." Alona sighed.

"We'll have to come over and visit often." Bethany added. "Try to break up the monotony."

"I appreciate your sentiment." Rena said, a brief smile on her face. "I'm still," she sighed loudly, "coming to terms with everything."

I snorted. "You're not the only one. This other realm stuff is..."

She nodded, "that too. After two hundred and forty-eight years to find out I have family, in another realm and I'm not some mutation from a gene gone wrong..."

Alona chuckled, "I feel like an infant."

Rena grinned, a real smile, "that's how I'm feeling right now. I thought I was ancient then to find out I'm not..."

I cocked my head to the side. "You look amazing for an old doll."

She smiled again, the pain in her eyes fading for a moment. "Pregnant at almost two hundred and fifty years old, it is something."

"What about your half-siblings," Paisley asked in a quiet way, "did you know them? Their children?"

Rena shook her head. "Only Abraham. Dad keeps track of the family line and checks up on the descendants of Milton and Eliza—I guess to see if they're like us." She offered me a small smile. "So far, all of them have been completely normal humans." She shrugged, "Uncle Michael and Victor think Ellis and my mother, Anexis, as well as Abraham's mother, Emma, must have had Alterealm genes in there somewhere for us to be as we are."

"So, you only need one of the surviving descendants' mate with someone with genes from here, the children will live longer?" Bethany asked.

Rena came around the island and sat on a stool. "It's a lot to grasp. Dad is half Alterealm, I guess you'd call it. If my mother had some trace of it in her, that makes me about three quarters... Alterealm." She took a deep breath and exhaled slowly. "This baby will be almost one hundred percent Alterealm."

"So, there's a good chance it will be able to live on the other side?" I looked from her to the phone, hoping someone had an answer.

"I would think so." Alona said, "however I don't blame them for being cautious, if there's even a one percent chance that child will be more human than not..."

Rena touched her stomach. "That's why I'm staying here. I'd much rather be hidden in the chambers Abraham described, safe from ever being taken again, but I can't condemn an innocent life to death just so I can feel safe."

There was a long painful pause.

"Michael is having another shouting match, with Troy and Arius this time." Paisley whispered. "I'm going to go and see if I can break it up."

I frowned at the phone. "Shouting match?"

"Yeah," Daxx sounded bored, "they're running interference all the time to stop him from coming to you, per Mitz's orders."

Rena gave me a wide-eyed look.

I shrugged. "I'm feeling pretty good for someone who broke their ribs two days ago. Although I wouldn't suggest that elixir mix, or whatever it is, to anyone."

"Seeing how it affected you was enough for me." Bethany said quickly.

"Crap." Daxx whispered. "Troy and Michael are in each other's face. I know that look, you might have…"

Michael appeared on the other side of the counter. "Is there something wrong with your phone?"

"And never mind." Daxx said quickly. "We'll let you go. Talk later."

Michael scowled at my phone.

"Later, girls." Alona said.

"Bye." Bethany said with a chuckle.

I pushed the button to turn off the phone, then looked at Michael. "Phone works great."

Rena stood up. "I'm going to drink my tea in the bedroom." She inclined her head to Michael and quickly walked down the hallway.

"I have been trying to reach you for hours."

He stood there with his hands on his hips looking like he was ten feet tall.

I shrugged, "not much to do here, so the girls call to check up on me."

Michael dropped his head forward and closed his eyes. Taking a deep breath, he exhaled slowly before looking back at me. "I was concerned."

I motioned to the space around me. "This place is very secure. We never open the door, so unless someone can walk through walls, I think I'm safe."

His blue eyes moved over me slowly, assessing. "How are you feeling?"

"I won't be taking body shots for a few more days, but considering how I was, I'm doing good." I stood up and lifted the arm on the side of my injury. "Movement is slow, but I don't want to scream through it."

Clairee appeared by the door. "Oh." She looked at Michael. "I didn't know you'd be here." She lifted a cloth bag in her hand. "I want to go over a few things with Autumn, my part, before Romulus arrives."

Michael crossed his arms over his chest. "Who is bringing Romulus?"

"I believe our night king is." She gave me a quick look. "I can't teach her how to get through the ward."

His jaw clenched a few times. "I'm aware." He motioned to me. "I'll just observe." He leaned back against the counter and crossed his arms.

I looked at him for a moment, then gave Clairee a wide-eyed look.

Giving me the universal female look that said 'tread lightly grumpy man present' look, Clairee went around the counter and set the bag down. "This is going to be a strange request, but please put your hand in the bag."

I looked at the bag, then back to her. "What's in it?"

"Ground up herbs." She nodded. "As you know the plan involved a magical talisman, which you couldn't use." She looked quickly to Michael. "Too many days without sleep caught up to me." She gave me a smile. "I've gotten some sleep now." She motioned to the bag. "I need to know if you have any sort of reactions to this herb, as you're going to have to use it to negate the witch's curse powder in the room."

"Oh." I pulled up my sleeve and held out my hand as she opened the bag. I put my hand into the prickly powder inside.

"You'll need to wear a mask or scarf to cover your mouth and nose when you do this. The reaction can be quite toxic."

"How toxic?" Michael asked, leaning on the island and looking down at us.

"It's very brief, the reaction. Autumn will be able to see when it's finished and it's safe to remove the mask." She paused. "We'll get you protective eyewear as well."

I glanced to Michael, he didn't look reassured.

Clairee motioned to the bag. "Any burning sensations on your hand?"

I shook my head.

"Okay, you can take your hand out now."

I pulled it out and looked at it. "Should I wash this off?"

"If you like. It's harmless on it's own."

I wasn't taking any chances and got up. I went to the sink. Michael turned the water on when I reached it.

"Is she to spread this herb around the room?"

I turned to see her nod. "More or less."

Turning the water off, Michael handed me a towel. "And that's it? Spread herbs around, wait for the reaction to be over and it won't hurt anyone entering?"

She nodded. "There may be a bit of residue left, but unless they lick it, they shouldn't do harm."

"Okay." I felt there was a catch, but didn't want to say it.

"You're going to have to take quite a bit of it. We're depleting our supply making enough."

"I could lower it down to her…"

Clairee's expression changed. "We're not certain if you'll be able to be on the roof with her."

"Why?" His harsh tone was back.

"Oh, I thought perhaps your brother would have filled you in." Clairee bit her lip.

Michael raised an eyebrow. "Which brother? About what?"

"Quinton. He's been taking us and the mages to check our progress and theories. We've hit a few snags."

Michael rubbed the back of his neck. "Like?"

"We can't, we, as in the magical folk or your brothers—we can't seem to get close to the palace now."

"What do you mean? They were on the roof when we were there?" I went back around and sat down, trying not to get hyped up, which was hard.

"Yes, and the first few times we were able to as well. Now he can not port to the roof and the closest he's been able to get to any entrance is, at best, five feet." She gave Michael a look. "They're changing their wards."

"Why wasn't I told any of this?" Michael scowled at her.

"I was just going to do that, brother."

We all jolted and turned to see Troy and Romulus standing by the door.

"Romulus has just come back from confirming." Troy said calmly, in a way that left no room for questions.

Romulus nodded and looked to Clairee. "You were correct. Royal blood and magic holders can't get close, but humans with no abilities, or royal blood in their system and nothing magical on them can."

"So, I still can?" I asked looking to Troy for the answer.

He nodded. "Yes."

"What about this dual key?" Michael asked. "Isn't it magical?"

Romulus shook his head. "No. While I don't understand all of the science tech's rambling, as near as I can tell it's a sort of polymer that can hide the royal blood inside it from detection."

"You tested this?" Michael asked.

"Yes. Our normal human—" He paused and looked at me. "I apologize for the term."

I smirked. "I've been called worse."

He gave me a relieved look. "The human was able to walk up and touch the palace walls."

"Okay, so that's good." I looked at Michael who did not look happy. Turning my head slowly I glanced to Clairee. "So, I go down, spread the herb stuff around, wait until it does its thing, then what? Use that blood key thing?"

"More or less." Clairee glanced to Romulus then gave Michael a hesitant look. "We discovered something else on those guards that held those keys—and previous hostiles that have been captured."

Romulus nodded, "we believe it's part of the puzzle."

"Puzzle?" Michael crossed his arms over his chest.

Maybe it was just the angle from sitting on the stool, but he looked larger now and very unimpressed.

"What is it?" His tone was low.

"A tattoo." Troy said plainly. He glanced to me and then to his brother. "We actually confirmed it was on many of the others and missed."

"And how was that missed?" Michael turned to his brother and king.

Troy shrugged. "We weren't looking for something in plain sight."

I held my hand up. "Wait. Are you saying I'm going to have to get a tattoo?" I looked at each person standing there. "A tattoo that is part of the lunatic cult that took me? That are still taking people?"

"I'm afraid so." Clairee said softly.

I blew out a breath and got up. Ignoring all of them, I went and looked out the huge window and stared down at the street. There were people down there, all starting their day. Innocent people—okay, maybe not innocent. I'm sure a lot were jerks, but even those were innocent to the fact that another realm existed. And lunatics trying to bring down barriers and rule the realms, or whatever it was the sickos were actually doing. "Has Crissy seen it?" I turned around and looked at them. "The tattoo? Has she *seen* it?"

Troy nodded.

Michael glared at him. "Why haven't I been informed of *any* of this?"

Troy gave him a bored look. "You've been a little distracted lately. When we discovered it, Autumn was going through the effects of the **hyper-nostrum elixir process.**"

Michael heaved a loud sigh. "What do you know about it?" He looked at Romulus and Clairee.

"We're analyzing what it's comprised of. Checking if it is ink or has other matter."

"Other matter?" Michael became iceman in a single breath.

Clairee gave Troy a nervous look. "We're not certain if it's the mark, or what was used, that's the key to surviving the wards."

I just stood there, trying to process everything they were saying. "What's the tattoo of?"

Everyone turned to look at me, except Michael, who stared at them waiting.

"Symbols." Clairee said.

"Of?" Michael put his hands on his hips.

"The Hubert crest." Troy answered without fear.

Michael threw his hands up in the air, then motioned to me. "You want Autumn to get a tattoo, *on her body* of the Hubert family crest with some sort of *substance*?" He growled. "Unfuckingbelievable!" He paced away from them until he was in front of the wall. Where he just stood hands on his hips, and head down.

Part of me was with him on this—then I noticed Rena standing in the hallway. Her brown eyes reflecting every reason why they had to be stopped. I blew out a breath, then went over to Michael. I stood almost in front of him, but where I could still see the others. I looked up at him. "They have to be stopped. We have to find *every* place they're using Michael. I need to get us in the palace." I whispered.

He just stood there looking down at me.

"When I do, you can have an army of soldiers, witches and mage people—"

"We actually—"

I looked over at Romulus, hoping my face portrayed that he should not speak right now. "*When* I get us in, they can make it so no one can ever go in there again—without the secret handshake or whatever else they use." I glanced to Clairee, "right?"

She nodded quickly.

Moving my gaze back to him, his blue eyes were searching my face. I saw his chest rise as he took a deep breath. Then fall as he exhaled with his eyes closed.

He turned and pointed to Romulus. "You figure out the tattoo and test it."

Romulus frowned. "You-you want us to tattoo someone else?"

"Yes!" Michael and troy answered in unison.

"Oh-okay." Romulus answered hesitantly.

"You have twenty-four hours to perfect your plans for Autumn to go in." He clenched his jaw for a moment. "*If* they're not—then any life harmed because you can't get her in there is on you."

Romulus gave a small non-committal nod.

Troy cleared his throat. "You may not be aware, but Autumn is Princess Paisley's blood sister…"

Michael's gazed snapped to me. I nodded.

"And," Troy continued, "therefore, *very* important to our Warden of Justice—not to mention our *Law's* mate. So, it is in the best interest of your health that nothing happens to Autumn."

Romulus's eyes went huge. "Yes. Yes, of course." He looked at me and bowed his head.

Troy sighed. "Go. Your twenty-four hours starts now."

"Oh." Clairee opened the device on her wrist as Romulus put his hand on her shoulder.

They vanished.

Troy turned and looked at Michael. "Coming brother?"

Michael frowned. "I—"

"You need to come back with me, so you don't do something we'll all regret." Troy gave him a patient look.

"What are you implying?" Michael put his hands on his hips and glared at Troy.

Troy smiled. "Exactly what you think."

Michael glared at him. "You do know I'm the older brother, right?"

"King." Troy said trying to keep a straight face while pointing at his own chest.

"Am I allowed to call her later to check on her?"

Troy nodded. "Only if you're in different realms."

Michael shook his head, gave me a quick look then was gone.

Troy inclined his head to me, then looked at Rena. "Niece."

She smiled. "Uncle."

Then he was gone.

She gave me an amused look. "That was interesting."

I laughed carefully, so I wouldn't hurt my ribs. "It always seems to be that way with all of them."

Chapter Twenty-Five

I looked down at the eight-hour old tattoo on my forearm. They'd figured out what was in the ink and it hadn't been complicated, or thankfully, toxic in any way. It could be worse, I thought. At least it was simple, not an ugly design, even though it symbolized everything wrong with this situation. I held my arm in the air and looked at it again, it was always the same, no matter which way you looked at it.

I felt when Michael walked into the armory. It was odd I always knew without looking. When I wasn't getting ready to break spells and wards, I'd have to think about that. I glanced at him. Of course, he looked hot dressed in his warrior gear. That's just what I didn't need, hormones interfering when I needed to focus on my instructions.

Paisley came over and stood with me. "I wish we could come with you."

"Me too." I motioned to her arm, "but with your bond, or whatever, it's too risky."

She grimaced, "yeah, and feeling what that witch's curse did once was enough for me." She appraised me with a look. "Are you going to be okay climbing to get up there?"

I pointed to the rope in the corner. "Michael had them bring knotted rope, so I don't have to work too hard to get up there."

"Better you then me."

I grinned. "Heights don't bother me." I glanced at Crissy. "Lightning on the other hand…"

"Did she figure out what it meant?" She gnawed on her lip looking worried.

I shook my head. "No, and if she's worried, then I'm scared."

She glanced at my arm. "Can they remove it after?"

"I hope so." I looked at it again. "I feel dirty just having it on me."

Michael headed in our direction. Paisley gave me a hesitant look, full of concern. "I'll be over with the girls if you need us."

I nodded, but was watching Michael walk toward me. His posture meant he was iceman right now, which I was okay with. Icy cold meant he was focused and had my back.

He stopped in front of me, with a thorough once-over. "Your ribs are healed enough for this?"

I nodded. "Yeah, adrenalin will kick in and I'll be solid."

His gaze moved to the tattoo. I pulled my sleeve down. "Looking forward to getting it removed as soon as possible." I bit my lip, "Romulus said the fact it's healing won't change its purpose."

"Romulus better hope his theories are all correct." He held out a wrist device. "It's made of the same polymer as the blood key, so it shouldn't interfere or be detected." He continued to stand there with it, so I held out my arm.

I watched him do it up. "So, just push the button and I'm outta there?"

"Yes." Michael turned to look at the others coming in. There were a lot of people going with us. "We've added Clairee and Romulus to the group call, temporarily, so they can talk you through it."

"That-that actually makes me feel better. I've been wondering what I'd do if some of their instructions didn't pan out."

He inhaled deeply. "They'd better pan out."

Troy came over. "You and I will be on the west side, if you want to go over now."

Michael nodded, glancing at me. "It's the best location to get up on that roof."

Troy gave me a serious look. "Last chance to change your mind."

I shrugged, then lifted my left arm. "And waste this lovely ink, nah, I'm good to go."

"If it gets rough, get out of there." He ordered, then an abrupt nod before he headed to stand near Michael.

"No worries there, I know when I'm beat."

Rafael came over and held out a back pack. "Your herb powder."

I took it and swung the pack over my shoulder.

"We'll be right behind you, sister." He gave me a small smile.

I nodded, the nerves were starting to buzz inside me. "Let's get over there."

Michael motioned to Woods and two other guards. Woods picked up the big pile of rope and came over. The three put their hand on Michael's shoulder as he pulled me closer and held me against his chest.

My stomach bottomed out. I took a few breaths, blowing them out before I opened my eyes. I was looking down a road that led down the side of a mountain. Turning, I stared at the stone wall of the palace. Lifting my chin, I looked up to see how far I was going to have to climb. It looked pretty far from my vantage point.

Michael dropped a bag I hadn't even noticed him holding. Kneeling down, he opened it and reached in. He held out some glasses, that looked almost like goggles, minus the rubber strap.

Pushing my hood back, I tightened the elastic holding my hair in a ponytail, then rested the glasses on top of my head.

He pulled out his phone. "Connect to the call."

I nodded and took the earpiece out of my pocket, putting it in I unzipped the pocket with my phone and tapped the screen over the icon. I put the phone back in my pocket and closed the zipper. I wasn't dropping it this time.

"We're here." It was Daxx. "Jeeze guys, front doors big enough?"

"It's a *palace* not a supermarket." Chase said.

"My group are below the back balcony. I'll port us up as soon as the ward is down." Quinton said.

"I just talk?" Clairee asked.

"We can hear you." Bethany said.

"Okay. We're at the cave entrance. Leone will bring us up as soon as possible." She explained.

It was comforting to hear them.

Michael stood up and stepped behind me, he put some sort of cloth around my neck and did it up.

I pulled it up, it covered my nose and mouth. I turned to look at him. "Do I look like a ninja?"

The side of his mouth moved like he wanted to smirk, but wasn't allowed to. He pulled up my hood and tucked the ends of the scarf into the front of my jacket. He glanced behind me.

I turned to see Woods had put the rope on the roof. He was holding what looked like a crossbow. I went over, pulled the scarf off my face. "It will hold?"

He nodded.

"Okay. I'm going to start the climb." I reached for the rope again then looked over my shoulder to where Michael stood. His expression relayed how worried he was. I walked back to him and stretched up as I pulled his head down. I kissed his mouth softly, then walked away before I could change my mind. If this didn't go as planned, I wanted to go out on a good note.

"You've got this, sis." Paisley said.

"Did she go?" Crissy sounded frantic.

"Not yet, Criss. She's just starting the climb." Daxx informed her.

"Okay. Good. Autumn are the souls of your shoes rubber?" Crissy asked, talking very fast.

I looked down at my feet and lifted one up. "Yeah. I'm wearing my runners for traction and flexibility."

"Okay. Okay. I couldn't figure out the lightning, so I researched lightning. You're not wearing any metal, right?"

I held my arms out and looked down my body. "No." I frowned. "Wait, wearing or have?"

"None." She said quickly. "None at all."

"I have my kama with the blade inside…"

"Take it off." She made a blowing sound. "No metal. It's a conductor."

Michael came over as I slipped one of the backpack's straps off, he pulled it out of the case on my back.

"Okay, Michael has it now."

"Okay. I'm sorry I couldn't see more." She whispered.

I put the backpack on and adjusted my gloves. "Don't sweat it. I have, hundreds of years of knowledge in my ear on this group call, I'll get it done."

Michael put his hand on my chin and tipped my face up. He kissed my mouth softly, lingering for a moment before releasing me and stepping back. His expression told me to be careful.

I gave him a brief nod. "Going up now." I grabbed the highest knot I could reach. I don't know why, but I tugged on the rope, like you always see anyone do before they climb one.

The silence in my ear was unnerving. I realized they probably didn't want to break my concentration with chatter, but I needed it. "So, I'm going to need directions once I get out of that room. Hope someone has floor plans." Tightening my grasp, I hopped up then caught the next knot between my feet.   Straightening slowly, I kept one hand on the old knot and reached for the next.

"We'll guide you once you're out of that room." Victor said.

I went up two more knots, then glanced down to see Troy was standing with Michael now. They couldn't come any closer to the building or I knew Michael would be climbing right behind me. "This is a great ab workout."

I continued to climb, too nervous and hyped at the same time—completely ignoring the muscles pulling against my ribs. "Clairee?" I went up another knot, pausing to catch my breath. "Would it be better if," I adjusted my footing, "I tossed this herb around while," I paused to get my feet better situated. "half way down the ladder?" I went up a few more.

"That would cover more area. Good idea Autumn." She answered.

I nodded to the wall a few inches from my face. "Just thinking it through." I didn't look down again, I knew I was up quite a bit further. I could feel a breeze now. I looked up, I was no where near the top. "How tall is this thing?" I mumbled.

"The side you're climbing is the shortest distance because of the incline and build up of the mountain." Crissy answered.

I did four jumps in a row, not pausing. I smiled, that she answered. I was okay with her not giving me the exact height, it would have psyched me out. I paused again to catch my breath. "Did some reading, huh?"

"I like reading." She said quietly. "It gets me out of my head."

My arms were starting to complain. "I get that." I told her. I looked up again. "I'm getting closer to the top." My footing slipped, I gripped the rope tight and adjusted them. "Five, maybe six knots to go." I grabbed the next one. "Does the trap door just pull open?"

"There's a small sliding bolt on one side, you'll feel it easily, just push it over and the door will be unlocked." Quinton said calmly.

"Okay." I reached for the next knot and noticed the air was warmer. "Temperature is changing the closer I get." Clairee had asked me to be alert to all sensations and or things that seemed off.

"Hot or cold?" Romulus asked.

"Warmer." I hopped up to the next one.

"Warmer is better than cold." He informed me.

I looked up at the last knot. "Okay. Last knot." I straightened my legs and reached for it. "The ladder. How do I put it down?" I pulled and held tight while I brought my feet up. I could see the surface of the roof now.

"Small lever to the left of the hatch." Victor said. "Push it and the ladder will descend."

"Okay." I pulled myself over the top and crawled a few feet from the edge. "I'm up. The air is pretty warm up here." I looked up at the sky, it wasn't a bright day at all.

"Be careful." Bethany said in a hushed tone.

"I plan on it." I told her. I pulled the scarf up, just in case and made sure it was in place. One less thing to remember when I was balancing on the ladder.

I stood up and looked for the door. "I see the door." I paused and looked at the roof surface in all directions. "I don't see anything unusual, or anything that would prevent you guys from getting up here." I took one step, then another, testing my footing. The surface beneath my shoe seemed fine. I took a few more steps. "So far so—" Sparks and arcs of light shot up in the air. "Holy!"

"What is it?" Troy asked.

"They've done something to the roof." I lifted my foot and looked at my shoe. There was no mark.

"Describe it and what you see, Autumn." Clairee said calmly.

"Okay." I blew out a breath, reaching for some courage. "Let me try again." I stepped forward again. The sparks arced up and hit my shoe. I felt it all the way up my shin. "It's like lightning coming off the surface. If I didn't have these shoes on or was carrying metal, I'm pretty sure I'd be getting quite the jolt."

"Can you walk on it?" Romulus asked.

"As soon as my shoe is close, they come shooting up."

"Try a few fast steps." Clairee suggested.

I nodded. "Okay." I backed up and shook my arms, preparing to run for the hatch. I got three steps and the arcs were strong enough to knock me back a few feet. I caught my balance. "It's getting stronger and knocking me back."

"Test carefully to see where the boundary is." Romulus told me.

I turned my body to the right, then tapped the roof with my toe. Nothing happened. I moved it inward and did it again. My shoe was zapped. I did this over and over all around the edge of the—whatever the hell it was, until I was back to where I started. "It's all around the door."

"Does it respond to your hand? Use your left hand." Clairee told me.

I remembered the tattoo, hoping it proved its usefulness. "Let me check." Squatting down, I pulled up my sleeve and held my hand out where the sparks had gotten my foot. They jumped up and zapped my hand. I sucked in a breath. "Nope. Likes my hand even less then my shoes." I paused, I could hear some kind of humming noise. "Hang on." I pulled out the ear piece, wondering if it was from that, and could clearly hear something whirring in the air. I put it back in. "There's some kind of faint humming sound."

Someone swore.

"They've placed a seeker spell on the roof." Clairee sounded exasperated.

"I'm going to pluck their eyelashes out when we find out who—"

"Romulus, focus." Michael barked.

"What do I do?" I stood up again, looking all around me like something was going to jump out of thin air and grab me.

"It could be the space between." Romulus murmured like he was talking to himself.

"The what where?" I frowned.

"Try sliding your feet, Autumn, don't lift them at all." Romulus said quickly.

I nodded. "Okay." Turning back toward the hatch, I slid one foot across the roof. Nothing happened. I moved the other one the same way. "It's working so far. Going to be slow, but no more electricity."

"When you go to go down the ladder, you're going to have to move quickly. Lifting both feet at once." Clairee said.

"Yes." Romulus added. "It will most likely be the strongest near the door."

"Awesome." I murmured. "Lightning, poison herbs, blood wards—they're just trying it all, aren't they?" It was slower then I'd preferred, but I was getting closer.

"It means they're desperate." Arius said.

"And running out of options." Chase's voice was the most serious I'd ever heard it.

"At the door." I said as I squatted down slowly, making sure my feet stayed flat against the roof. I ran my hand across the edge, trying to ignore the sparks hitting them. I felt a small lip. "Slide left or right?"

"Right" Quinton answered.

I did it quickly, then pulled the door up. Taking my hands away from the roof, I checked my balance and leaned over and saw the lever. I pushed it. A ladder came out of nowhere, extending one section at a time until it reached the floor. "Ladder is down."

I looked at the ladder and where I could place my hands without getting zapped, trying to figure how I was going to do this all at once without landing on the floor—on my face.

"Remember—"

"Let her concentrate." Michael cut off whatever Romulus was going to say.

I put the glasses on and made sure my mouth and nose were covered. I wasn't normally the type to hesitate, but I did pause for a few breaths. Putting my hands on either side of the hole, I clenched my teeth when I felt the jolts going through them. My plan was to hit the first, or second, rung. "Going down."

Tensing, I popped up and dropped my feet down the hole. Arcs of light flashed all around me. My feet hit the rung. I pulled my hands clear quickly, ducking down and grabbing the bar one second too late. My slowest hand was hit with a painful snap.

I blew out a breath. "That was fun. It just tried to fry my fingers."

"Are you all right?" Michael didn't sound pleased.

I looked at one hand. "The gloves took the brunt of it. I'm good." I glanced back up. The light was flashing without pause now. "I think I made it mad though. Light show up there."

"We can see it." Troy told me.

I climbed down a few rungs and gauged the distance to the floor. I wanted to hit as much as I could with the herb. Hooking my arm through the bar, I pulled the backpack off one arm and tucked it between my body and the ladder. "Spreading the herb now." I opened the pack and reaching in…I was touching plastic? I pulled it out to see a small scoop Clairee must have put in. Filling it, I flicked my arm out and watched dust flow toward the floor. I did it again, then circled my way around the ladder, repeating the process until I was back where I started. "May not have reached the whole room." I said more to myself then the others.

"We'll vacuum later." Alona replied.

I could hear crackling, I looked down to see a thick mist rising from the floor. I glanced up, trying to decide if I want to deal with the sparks above or the mist below. "It's like an eerie horror show up here. Sparks and mist." The quiet was getting to me. "You guys have your mics muted?"

"We thought it best, so not to distract you." Victor informed me.

"Trust me, it's a good thing." Daxx said. "They're rambling away driving me crazy."

"Appreciate the concern, but the quiet it is killing me. I'm way out of my comfort zone doing all of this. I usually just beat it up and move on."

Daxx snorted.

"How's the reaction?" Clairee asked.

I looked down. "It seems to be clearing. I'm going down." I went down a few rungs, then realized the floor looked charred now. "Might need a mop with that vacuum, Alona." I stepped on the floor, half expecting something to happen. "Tell me how this key works."

"You will need to use your left hand with the tattoo visible." Clairee said.

I pulled up my sleeve.

"I've marked one end of the key, use that first." Romulus told me.

I took the key out of my pocket. "Just," I turned it over, "how do I use it? It doesn't look like a key."

"You just have to touch the door or the handle."

I waited for more instruction, but he didn't say any more. I looked at the door. "And then what?" I didn't believe it was that simple. The roof was practically electrified, so this blood ward thing couldn't be that simple.

"After all they've done to deter anyone making it *in* that room and surviving, there may be something more for show, but I highly doubt it will amount to much." Romulus continued, "they're forgetting who taught them everything *they* know—not what I know. Imbeciles."

"Let's hope you're right." I cut him off, not wanting to stand here while he ranted. I walked over to the door and stopped. Holding up my hand, I made sure the marked end of the plastic *key* was pointing out. I widened my stance, in case I had to move fast. "Here we go." I whispered.

I touched the door handle and held it there for a moment. Nothing happened. "Nothing happened."

"Can you open the door?" Clairee asked, "use your left hand." She added quickly.

I put the key in my other hand and reached for the door knob. Touching it with one finger, testing to see if I would get electrified, I glared at it when nothing happened. It was cool to the touch. I grasped it and turned. It moved. Pushing the door open and inch, I peaked out. "It opened." I whispered. "Where do I go from here?"

Michael said. "Remove the ward on the balcony so Quinton and Raf can get up there with you."

I nodded. "Okay. Let me see if anyone is out here." I pushed the glasses back to the top of my head and pulled the mask down. I tucked my right hand in my pocket with the key, but kept my left one and the tattoo visible, just in case anyone was there.

Pushing the door slowly, I checked all areas I could see. It was empty. I opened it more and stepped out to look the other way. "I can't see anyone." I said under my breath so I was quiet. "Coming to you, Quinton."

"We're ready." He answered in a serious tone.

Chapter Twenty-Six

I moved down the hall as fast and quietly as I could. My nerves were zinging with energy, a feeling of warning moved over my skin. I knew this wasn't going to be free and clear the whole way, I just hoped I got some of the guys in here before my guts turned out to be right. Because my guts were always right.

I reached the door and grasped the handle with my left hand. It opened without issue. The room was large and empty of furniture and people. "I'm in the room." I darted across it to the glass doors. "How do I bring this ward down?"

"Use the key if it doesn't open," Clairee said, "if the marked end and left hand doesn't work, use your right and the other end of the key."

I looked at the key, checking which end was up. I touched the door with my other hand, trying the handle. It didn't budge, so I touched it with the key. Grasping the doorknob, it turned this time.

I stepped out onto the balcony, which was a good fifteen feet to the railing. I had no idea what I was doing, so I tapped the key against the railing, then waved my hand past it. It met no resistance. I leaned over and looked down to see Quinton, Rafael and four big guys standing there. "Can you get up here now?"

"Hang on." Quinton said, then they were gone.

"We're up."

I jumped and turned to see them behind me. I grinned as he gave me a nod.

"I think Autumn should do the entire upper balcony first. So more can come up." Quinton said for the others to hear.

"She'll have to lead." Clairee told him.

"You watch her back." Michael said firmly.

"We will." Quinton looked at two of the guards. "You two stay here with Rafael. Shout if anyone shows up, brother."

Rafael saluted him, then he winked at me.

Quinton motioned for me to go. I nodded and turned back. "Just touch the railing and all the doors?"

"To be certain, yes." Victor answered. "We don't want to hit a barrier once we're all in there."

"I think a few more of us should go up, Troy." Daxx said, "drive any they encounter down to those waiting at the entrances."

"I agree, brother." Chase said.

I touched the railing again, it was weird running along touching things.

"Beth, you and Paisley go around to the front with Daxx and your guards." Troy said with a voice of authority.

"On our way." Bethany said quickly.

"Leone, you and Victor go up with some men, the more porters up there the better." Chase added.

"We'll be at the south side before she reaches it." Leone answered.

I tapped the railing again.

"Beloved, you and cutie stay ready if we find any women in there." Chase added quickly, "Romulus, I'm coming to get you and some of your mages, you can start taking down the light show on the roof."

"Of course, my king."

I touched the railing for the third time as they shifted people around. I slowed down when we came to another glass door. Stopping, I looked around to see inside the room. Shaking my head to Quinton, I touched it with the key, then turned the handle and pushed it open.

With a nod to him, I kept going along the balcony.

"We're at the front." Paisley reported. "Ready to tag-team anyone that comes out."

As I turned the corner of the balcony, Quinton tapped my shoulder so I'd stop. I touched the railing once again then looked over it to see Leone, Victor and four guards below. "You're clear to come up, Victor."

"Our pleasure." He replied.

Then they were standing beside me.

"Two porters escorting Autumn now." Leone stated.

"Cameras picked up three men with two women in jumpsuits coming to the lower cavern entrance."

I didn't recognize the voice.

"Okay, Ellis. Let them pass, Emil. We want them inside." Michael told them calmly.

"We're out of sight." Emil replied.

"We need to find out where they're landing that is near the entrance." Rafael stated, sounding bored.

"We're working on it, brother." Troy told him. "Clairee's temple has been setting traps with the help of Elder Arian."

I kept going around the balcony, it seemed to go on forever.

"Now I feel bad for them." Chase said sounding more like himself.

"You can visit them often in the cells." Arius' tone was flat.

"I shall." Chase quipped.

"We're almost to the courtyard, Arius, I'll port Autumn down to open the gate, then back up." Quinton said as I opened another door.

"Can't wait." Arius said, again with no emotion in his voice at all.

I darted around a corner and touched the rail. Glancing down, there was a huge yard with a fountain and elaborate stone patio.

"Ready?" Quinton was beside me.

I nodded. "Let's do it." I stepped closer and closed my eyes. Quinton put his hand on my shoulder.

My stomach lurched. I didn't pause long to let it settle. Opening my eyes, I turned to see a huge gate. Running over, I held my hand out and touched the key against it.

Quinton was beside me, pushing the large latch aside and shoving the gate open.

Arius stood with the five guards and whom I could only guess was a mage. His eyes were purple.

He briefly assessed me, then nodded to the other end of the yard. I turned to see another gate and took off running toward it.

"I'm in the courtyard." Arius said quietly. "Do we want Autumn to open the patio entrance inside?"

"Leave it sealed for now." Victor said. "The more we contain, the less chasing for us."

I touched the other gate, then slid the latch and pushed. It was much heavier then Quinton had made it look. A man with long white hair and pale eyes stood there. I would have freaked out if I hadn't recognized him from the armory. He smiled at me. Behind him stood five guards.

"Autumn, lets get you back up there. Time to head down the stairs and see who we find." Quinton said coming toward me.

"I'll be coming from the roof shortly," Michael said, "Romulus almost has the ward down."

Quinton gave no warning, just touched my shoulder and I was back on the balcony. I made a face that made him smirk. Inhaling, I breathed through the nausea, then nodded and we were moving once again.

We quickly connected back to the call. Zipping the pocket I took off jogging around the balcony again.

As I went around the next corner, I saw Rafael standing there looking around.

"We're back to Raf," Quinton said jogging beside me, "we'll head down to the next level."

Next level? "How many levels are there?" I stopped in front of Rafael.

"Three." Quinton answered.

"Okay, lets get moving then. I want to reach the first floor." At least I was assuming that's where the throne room would be, that they wanted to get inside. Apparently, it had been warded to block them before the rest of the palace was.

I let Quinton lead us down the stairs, staying close behind in case he hit any invisible barriers. The stairs weren't fancy like I'd expected to see in a palace, then again, what did I know about things like that. I knew what was real and what was movie real—or at least I used to.

Quinton stopped at the bottom and looked around.

There were no signs of life.

"Going to open doors, but it looks like they're not on this level either." He said into the mic softly.

I went to the first door and opened it with my right hand. I looked in. Empty. I turned to see Rafael open another door. "No wards on this floor." I whispered. As Quinton and the guards moved to check the other rooms.

"Second floor clear." Rafael told them through the mic.

"We know that first floor isn't, so wait for Woods, Troy and I to get there." Michael told them, sounding like he was out of breath.

"On my way down." Chase said quickly.

I felt better with those odds. We would be hitting the bottom level with a sizeable team. I went back to the stairs and waited, not even sure where the next flight of stairs was. Looking up I saw Chase coming down them and right behind him was a few more guards and Michael.

When they reached the bottom, they gave me a brief nod. Michael's icy gaze moved over me for a moment, then he turned and headed down the hall to the left.

I followed. The stairs were here. He paused at the top and let me catch up.

"Going to the first floor. Watch those exits now." He said, hushed.

"Those men are going all the way up." Emil reported.

"We'll grab them when they reach the back entrance." Troy glanced to me and gave me a nod to continue down the stairs.

"Welsley has that entrance covered." Arius said.

I moved down the stairs carefully, knowing that feeling in the pit of my stomach was about to be proven right again. I stopped when I could see the lobby below and squatted down. I could see people down there. I held up my hand and five fingers, then looked over my shoulder back to the men.

"Five visible in the lobby." Rafael whispered.

"Send them our way," Paisley said, "we're ready."

Michael touched my shoulder, so I'd continue. I went down several more steps quickly, then slowed just before they'd see me. Before I could reach the bottom, Troy and Rafael jumped over the handrail and landed at the bottom. So much for stealth.

I hit the floor fast. The men I'd seen charged at Troy and Rafael. The guards moved quickly past me to engage them. One turned and ran the other way, Rafael right on his heels. Michael was beside me, he pointed to a door on the other side of the lobby. I nodded and headed that way. He and Woods were right behind me. I needed to take down the wards before I'd be able to engage in any fighting. I reached the door and touched it with the key, not taking the time to see if that was needed. Woods opened the door and stepped in. There were men in there. Michael gave me a gentle push out of the way. "Take down the rest." He said quickly and went in the room.

I could hear grunts through the earpiece now and realized most had unmuted their mics for fast communication.

"More coming into the courtyard." Arius said, sounding a little too happy.

"Get the rest of the wards down, Autumn," Troy said, "so the others can get in if needed."

"On it." I reached the next door and used the key. I didn't know if I should open it and look or just keep going. I decided to keep going. "Going clockwise around the maze of doors." I said, hoping the men would know what I was saying.

"We're right behind you." Victor said.

I nodded and kept going. I'd done three more when I came to what looked like an elaborate entrance. "At the front door."

"Knock, knock." Daxx said with an impatient tone.

I touched it, then opened it quickly to see her standing there grinning. "Come on in." I didn't pause to see if they did.

"Cristy. We need you and Alona in here. There are women being held in the first room to the left of the entrance." Victor reported.

"I'll go port them in." Quinton said breathlessly.

"We're ready." Alona said. "Perhaps our tag team can clear the way to the nearest exit."

"We've got it." Paisley said.

"Felix and Mac won't let anyone get too close." Beth grunted.

I didn't pause to see why, I still had more doors and halls to cover. "Going right, down this hallway." I said, hoping if that was a bad direction someone would tell me.

"Right behind you." Leone said.

I hit the next door, barely pausing.

"Sitting room open." Leone said.

He must have been looking in rooms.

"Heading to the throne room." He huffed out a breath.

"Hold on that until more of us are with you." Quinton said quickly.

I paused and looked behind to Leone, he nodded. There was only one door left and it looked pretty fancy, with scrolls carved into it and what I was pretty sure was gold trim. "Chop, chop guys, I have more halls to clear."

Leone smirked at me.

"On our way." Michael said.

"Warding the outer perimeters." Romulus said. "No one will get in if they're not on the short list we've allowed."

"Thinking of that a century ago, would have saved us the stress of today." Clairee said.

"Bicker later." Alona said abruptly. "I need a porter box in here."

"Sorry, had to take out a dirtbag." Daxx said. "Can't let my blocker have *all* the fun."

Michael, Troy and Chase came running down the hall. They stopped beside Leone and I. Troy gave me a quick nod and pulled the second sword off his back. His brothers did the same.

"Opening the throne room." Leone whispered.

My stomach knotted, and I knew this was the part I'd been dreading. I touch the door quickly with the key, then stuffed it in my pocket and prepared for what might be on the other side.

Chase touched the door and turned the handle. He shoved it open.

All I could see were the backs of two men going through another door.

"Willis and Nelson just went through to the staff kitchens." Victor said and bolted into the room, turning to see if there were more. He pointed to a desk in the corner then looked at Leone. "Stand there until guards arrive. I need two guards to the throne room. *Now.*" He followed Troy and Chase out the door the men had used.

I glanced to Michael, "Follow or go to the next hall?"

"Go and open the back hallway, so Arius can get in here." He looked at Leone, then headed after his kings. "Woods, you stay with Autumn."

"I'm waiting by the hall." He reported. I hadn't even realized he was connected to the call.

I turned and ran back down the hall. As I entered the lobby I was met with mayhem. Bodies fighting all over, it was hard to make out our men from Hubert's. I quickly checked that the key was safely in my pocket.

Woods was trying to block two men from going down the hall.

"Hubert got past us." Troy said.

I skirted around Woods' large frame to take on one of his problems.

"He can only go," Michael grunted, "two places from there."

I ducked the man's swing and turned, quickly landing a scissor kick on his jaw.

"He's not in the back hall." Quinton said, sounding out of breath.

"Two more women to get out." Daxx slid behind me, aiming her port box in the air.

I tried unsuccessfully to trip up the goon I was fighting. He had really good balance. "Lending a hand," he swung, I evaded, "here, then I'll," I tried for a back kick, he jumped out of reach. I slid down and popped up behind him. "Open more wards." My second attempt connected with his kidneys.

"I'll help the girls get clear." Leone charged past us, heading to Crissy and Alona.

I chanced a quick glance to see how Woods was making out and was almost caught in the face with what looked like a club. Turning I kicked my attacker and blocked his second swing with my arms crossed, clenching my teeth as it connected. "Would love my kama." I sang into the mic.

"We're following Hubert." Michael answered.

"Think he's doubled back to the lobby." Troy grunted.

Daxx vanished the guy Woods was fighting. He turned and got the attention of the one I was trying to take down.

"Get their seer." Someone behind me said.

I turned to see an older rounded man standing on the bottom step, beside him was a tall man with black hair slicked back. His whole aura was ice cold, like Victor.

"Think they're here." I reported as I watched the tall man draw a large blade with serrated edges. He was looking behind me. I turned to see Crissy ushering a woman out the entrance.

"Crissy." I yelled as I dove toward her. I connected, and she went flying just as pain pierced my right side. I hit the floor, grunting as I landed on my not quite healed ribs. Blowing out a breath, I lifted my head to see a blade sticking out of my front. My jacket was turning red.

"Autumn." Michael roared through my ear piece.

I looked up and saw Victor and Leone standing over me blocking anyone from coming too near.

Michael slid into view, horror etched on his face.

I tried for a smile around the pain coursing through me. "I didn't block with my face." I tried to reassure him. Reaching for the key, I hit the edge of the blade and bit back a groan. "Key." I said under my breath.

"Get her out of here, brother." Troy ordered.

Michael was holding my side. Crissy was holding my head. Michael leaned over me and we were no longer at the palace. We were in my room.

"I'll get the doctor." Crissy said and vanished.

Victor knelt on the other side of me. He shook his head and reached across me. "We can't pull it out yet."

I glanced up to see Michael had tears running down his face, his blue eyes were drowning.

"That bad?" I whispered, too numb to lift my head and look. I didn't see the handle in the front of me, so I knew the blade was sticking out both sides.

"Hurry." I heard Crissy say.

The doctor came into view. Victor moved out of the way. I was having a hard time focusing.

"Arius, we're going to need Paisley here." Victor's voice echoed in my ear.

Michael reached and pulled the earpiece out.

The doctor was checking my pulse.

I heard other voices in the room, but was having trouble figuring out who was talking.

"Blood healing won't work this soon after the elixir." The doctor said, at least I think it was him.

"Brother, release him."

Troy was here? I opened my eyes to see Troy prying Michael's hand off the doctor's throat.

"The mating mark."

Bethany?

"It worked for me."

"Michael can't…"

I closed my eyes again.

"Autumn." Someone was touching my face.

I forced my eyes open to see Michael all up in my face.

"I need your consent." He said, is blue eyes were so sad. "No. Look at me."

I focused hard.

"I need your consent for the mating mark."

I tried to keep my eyes open and figure out what he was saying. "I don't think," I drifted for a second, "I'm up for sex." I tried for a smile. "Iceman." I mumbled, or maybe I just said that in my head.

"Autumn. Little warrior. Look at me…"

"Michael hurry."

The panic in Daxx's voice brought me back.

I looked to see Michael hovering over my face.

"Tell me to mark you, little warrior. Say yes." He pleaded.

I knew something was bad for Michael to be begging. "Yes, iceman." I whispered.

He was kissing my face now, whispering something to me.

Someone was holding my hand, which I thought was nice.

I felt fangs bite me and tried to tell Michael I wasn't in pain, but coughed, choking on something they were giving me to drink.

There were soul-piercing screams. They were coming from me. Pain tore through my side, my chest, ribs and arms. I was paralyzed with it.

Everything faded slowly.

Chapter Twenty-Seven

"She's coming around." Mitz said.

I opened my eyes to see everyone I knew in Alterealm standing around the bed. It's a good thing the bed, and the room were large. I frowned, remembering things. "Crissy. They were going after her—is she all right?"

Crissy bounced across the bed and flopped down, hugging me.

"Guess so." I looked to Daxx and gave her a 'help me' look.

Victor moved over and peeled his crying woman off me. "I am eternally grateful to you." He inclined his head to me as he straightened up with Crissy held close in his arms.

I turned to look at Troy. "Did we do it? Did we get them all?"

He nodded. "We did it. But Willis Hubert and Nelson Bosworth got away." He inhaled deeply, then gave me a look, I wasn't sure what it meant. "We captured many and freed several more women."

"They won't be able to use the palace again." Bethany added.

I dropped my head back on the pillow. "We'll find him."

"Let's give them some privacy." Mitz pushed between Quinton and Rafael. She gave me one of her sweet motherly smiles. "I'm going to stay for a few moments if that's all right?"

I smiled back at her. "Sure." I had no idea what was going on. I touched my ribs, they felt good. Then recalling that blade, I touched my other side. Must not have been as serious as I'd thought. I pushed up until I was sitting. I actually felt great.

Everyone was backing away and leaving. I couldn't figure out why they had such odd looks on their faces.

Michael stood at the end of the bed. His arms crossed over his chest.

"I'll turn some lights on." Mitz said softly.

"How much do you remember?" Michael asked, hesitant.

I puffed up my cheeks and blew out a breath. "It's still mostly fog." I closed my eyes. "The fat guy told the other one to get their seer, so I dove for Crissy and shoved her out of the way." I touched my side again, "then he tossed that scary-ass blade and got me." I shook my head and opened my eyes. Michael stood there with his hands behind his back like he was standing guard or something. "You brought me back here and I'm guessing some super blood healing took place because I feel five by five right now." I smirked. "Like I could go ten rounds with an ogre or three, kind of good."

Mitz sat on the end of the bed. "You almost died, love, you were taking your last breaths despite Paisley's blood pouring into your veins."

I gave her a wide-eyed look. "It was—I can't piece it together."

She nodded, understanding on her face. "Do you remember Michael talking to you?"

I nodded slowly, remembering, but not fully. "He was asking me something." I glanced to him, his facial expression was so guarded I wasn't going to get any clues from him. "What did I do?"

He gave his head a slight shake. "You didn't do anything. I asked your permission to mark you, to save your life."

I couldn't grasp what they were getting to. "I take it I said yes." I grinned and lifted my arms, "because I'm still here and breathing." I froze and looked at my arm. My left arm, the one I'd had the horrible tattoo on to trick the wards. That tattoo was gone. Now, my entire arm had intricate woven lines and designs on it. I turned it over and looked at the other side. I jumped up and stood on the bed. "Holy—my—*that* mark." I looked to see him standing with his arms at his side now. He had the matching ink covering his arm too. "But-but—" I frowned and looked at the bed, then to Mitz. "I-I thought that mark," I held up my left arm, "*this* mark could only happen if-if…" I couldn't say it to her. Not when she was giving me that understanding, caring, kind of motherly look.

Finally, she shook her head slowly. "The mating mark doesn't just happen during sex, Autumn, yes it's a nice way to receive it, but all that is needed are true mates and a commitment to complete it."

I opened my mouth, then snapped it closed. Scowling, I walked off the bed onto the floor and paced toward the closet. I lifted my arm and looked at it. Then turned and looked at Michael for a moment. Putting my hands on my hips I took a deep breath and let it out slowly as I tried to figure out what to say. "So, you, bound yourself to me—to save my life?"

"I did."

That was it. No emotions showing on his face or any sign of caring what he'd done. The man that wanted nothing to do with me was now stuck with me. "There was no other way?" I snorted and shook my head, "never mind, I know the answer to that." I felt like I was dreaming all of this. "Okay," I turned back to Michael, "first, thank you." He didn't move or speak, I'm not even sure he was breathing. I looked away from him to Mitz, who was no better sitting there looking all patient and serene. "And, now, wh-what does this mean?" I lifted my tattooed arm like they needed a visual reminder of what we were talking about.

Mitz looked to Michael expecting him to say something. He didn't move, his blue eyes locked on me. She gave a soft sigh and then looked back to me. "You'll have a bond, share emotions, feelings—"

I smirked and looked to Michael again. "Yeah because emotions just pour off him." Touching my arm, I could feel the lines in my skin. "So, there's no catch or anything I need to know about this?"

"No catches, dear." Mitz answered.

"Right. Okay, so just go on like any other day?"

Turning her head slowly, she looked to Michael once more. She didn't look away from him this time.

His gaze moved over my face for a very long, awkward silent minute. "If that is what you wish."

I shrugged, not sure what to say to any of this.

Inclining his head, Michael finally looked away from me. "I'd like to get down to the cells now to see if Troy has been able to find out where Hubert may be now."

I nodded. "Give me a shout if he does. I want the guy that was with him."

With an abrupt nod, he spun on his heel and left.

"I'm sure you'd like some quiet time to process all of this." Mitz said softly.

I gave her a 'ya think' look and didn't even feel bad for doing it.

She stood up. "I'm going to get some food ready."

My stomach growled on cue. "I could eat." Hunger was right behind confused, as I took stock of how I was feeling.

"Okay, love. Come find me in the kitchen when you're ready." She gave me one more of those understanding looks and left.

I stared at my arm for I don't know how long. Snapping out of it, I looked down my body to see I was dressed in clean, undamaged clothes. I moved over to the bed and sat down. Putting my shoes on, I paused and stared off into the air. Shaking my head, I spotted my phone on the table. I got up to get it. As days went, this was way up on the top of my crazy shit list. I tapped the screen to unlock it. Crazy…from an electrified roof to… I paused and wondered how they fixed that, the roof. Not that I planned to be on it ever again.

My mind was like left-over stew. A little of everything swirling in a pot. I couldn't focus on one thing. Closing my eyes, I took a deep breath and blew it out slowly. Focus Autumn, the roof is the last thing you need to know about right now—even if you'll have lightning chasing you in your sleep.

My stomach bottomed out. I opened my eyes. "Food is…" I froze. I was on that roof again. I looked at my phone like it was responsible somehow. It rang in my hand, startling me like a scared cat. It was Michael. I answered it in slow motion, afraid to move.

"Autumn?" He sounded concerned.

I swallowed and looked to my left to see how far I was from the edge of the roof. "Yeah?"

"Are you all right? I sense…"

"Fear?" I checked the other way.

"Yes."

I shook my head quickly. "Not all right. So far from all right at this moment," I blew out a breath trying to control my frantically beating heart, "Michael?"

"I'm here."

"I'm on the roof." I looked over at the hatch I'd jumped through earlier, wondering if I could just go climb down.

I heard a door close. "The roof?"

I nodded. "Yeah, you know the one that tried to fry me? That one."

"How…"

"If I knew that, I wouldn't be on the roof."

"Do you have your device on?" His tone was softer now.

I looked at my wrist. "Negative."

"I'll be there shortly." He hung up.

I stared at the phone, then held it tight in my hand. If I hadn't picked it up before this happened, I'd be stuck here.

Michael appeared ten feet away.

"I was afraid to move, after the last time up here."

He came over quickly and held out my device.

I took it with a shaking hand. "Thanks. I'm never taking this off again." I put it on, then looked to see he was watching me with a strange look on his face. "What?" I couldn't take much more today.

Michael shook his head. "I'm trying to figure out how you got here."

"I don't know. One second I'm in my room and the next, I'm here."

He pulled out his phone and tapped the screen, then put it to his ear. "Clairee, have you been checking for spells and traps in the chambers?" He nodded. "No, just curious. Thank you." He hung up and crossed his arms over his chest. "You must have done it on your own." Shrugging, he frowned, "No one has this quickly…"

I held up my hand. "Wait. I did what?" I looked around. "I brought myself here?" I smirked, "last I checked I didn't have that power."

"You do now." He lifted his arm. "Any mate with royal blood can port unassisted."

I opened my mouth and paused for a second. "Is there an instruction book for this?" I frowned. "What else is there? Mitz said sharing emotions but didn't say teleporting at whim."

"Normally it takes a great deal of practice and focus." His harsh expression softened. "What were you thinking about directly before you were here?"

That question was easy. "How this day has made the top of my crazy shit list. I… I was thinking about… the roof." I brushed the hair back from my eyes. "How do I *not* do this again?"

"Practice." Michael held out his hand.

I blew out a breath and took it. The touch somehow made me feel more at ease, immediately. I had to talk to the girls and find out how this mate connection worked.

"Think of somewhere—in *this* realm, picture it and close your eyes." His tone was soft and soothing.

I nodded. "That's it?" I looked up at him.

His gaze moved from my eyes to my mouth, then back. "That's it."

"Okay." I took a deep breath and closed my eyes, focusing and picturing the practice room. My stomach clenched. I opened my eyes to see we were in the practice room.

Daxx stood less than a foot from us. "Scared the hell out of me." She glared at us. "Teaching her to port already?"

Michael smirked. "No. I had to go rescue her from the palace roof."

Her eyes went wide. "You ported to the roof? On purpose?"

I shook my head. "No, I was going to get something to eat and thought of that electrified roof... then I was *standing* on it."

"Oh. Well," she looked at my arm checking for a device, "better leave that on."

I nodded. "Yeah. Might put one on the other wrist for backup."

Michael gave me a gentle, appraising look. "If you're all right now, I have to get back."

"I'm good. Thanks, iceman. That was..." I didn't have words to describe it, "well, I'm really looking forward to tomorrow being boring."

He smirked, his gaze holding mine for a moment. "I don't think boredom will ever plague us again." He inclined his head to Daxx and turned, walking with long strides out the double doors.

Daxx sighed loud. "I was just heading to the girl cave, if you want to grab something to eat and come help."

"Definitely." I bobbed my head. "Alone isn't working out for me today."

Chapter Twenty-Eight

I glanced over the screen to Paisley. "What do you mean longer life?"

She grinned. "Your life expectancy is longer, like theirs after your mated."

Bethany nodded when I looked to her for clarification.

I straightened up, "how much longer?"

Daxx shrugged. "No one asks."

I frowned.

"You don't want to live longer? Do more?" Alona asked, leaning against the table with papers in her hand.

I shrugged. "I guess." I sat back in the chair. "I just always thought maybe in my next life I could be a mom and wife—" I rolled my eyes. "Shit like that. Survive the odds in this one and then have a smooth sailing one."

Alona smiled. "I don't think you'll be or have been a complacent housewife going to PTA meetings in any life."

I grinned. "You know what I mean."

Paisley laughed. "I'm pretty sure you've been on the kick-ass side of history in every life."

"I think Michael is being an ass, the way he's acting." Daxx said. "And trust me as far as the mating process goes, I had the biggest one in the bunch."

"Yeah," Beth gave me a sympathetic look, "I thought after the mark and all he'd be more…" she glanced to the other, "warm toward you."

I blew out a breath, still not ready to face the new reality that was my life. We'd talked about it when I'd first followed Daxx to avoid being alone with my thoughts. Mating usually meant happily-ever-after, well, various versions of it. I was mated to a man that didn't want to be mated to me, or anyone—ever. I couldn't find fault in what he'd done because I was still here breathing. The fact that now that he'd bound us together meant neither of us would ever be intimate with anyone else, was a huge sacrifice on his part, in my opinion. Me though, I wanted the man on the other end of my new tattoo, so it was going to be all moony eyes and cravings for something I couldn't have.

"She's lost again." Bethany said.

I blinked and gave her a startled look. "Yeah." I touched my head. "Left-over stew up here."

Beth grinned.

Crissy jumped up and jogged to the table and set papers on it. "Sorting helps, reading, will take you out of your head." She nodded, then gave me a sappy teary-eyed look.

I held up my hand. "Do not thank me again."

She clamped her mouth together and nodded, then quickly sat back down.

I sighed and looked at the screen in front of me. This was so far out of my comfort zone. I looked at Paisley. "Show me this again." I motioned to the screen and papers, determined to be helpful.

She got up to come over and lean on the desk. "Most of these files are garbled-guck to all of us too, so don't let it get to you." She pointed to the words on the screen. "Mixed in the long lines of mashed up code," she gave me an exasperated look, "when we grabbed this, there was no time to just download relevant files, so we got the whole shebang of old deleted files and *everything*." Shaking her head, she motioned to the screen. "We go through, highlight the important information, names, addresses and so on, then print them." She pointed to the pages sitting beside the laptop. "That top page was right," she scrolled back on the screen, "here." With skill she highlighted the part that was now printed.

I picked up the page and looked at it, then to the screen, comparing it, hoping it would become clearer to me. "So, what are these numbers?" I pointed to them on the paper in my hand. "Do we add that, or does the printer?"

"Numbers?" Beth looked at the paper, then to the screen. She glanced around at the others and then looked again.

Crissy jumped up and came over quickly. I pointed to the numbers on the page a few lines above names. Her eyes squinted together as she picked up the page and looked at it. She almost shoved me back on the wheeled chair to look at the screen. Clutching the page, she went over to the table with the piles all over it. She flipped through a few. "I didn't see it. How could I not see it? I should have seen it." She said something I couldn't make out. "They're hidden, on the screen, not the print out. Some kind of hidden system..."

"See what?" Alona asked.

"The numbers." She mumbled and slid down to the end pile of pages. Almost frantically she flipped through them, pausing and looking at the board.

"We've all seen the numbers, Crissy." Bethany said.

"Random numbers…"

"They're not." She shook her head, then turned to Daxx, "random. They're not." She waved the page in her hand so fast it was a white blur. "It's their system that shows which are found and which are not. I don't know how it's hidden on the screen though." She looked back at the page. "If I take these and compare them, I should see a pattern to tell us which were found that we haven't gotten yet." She nodded and grabbed a stack, then ran over to the other end of the room and started spreading them out on the floor. "You are so smart, Autumn."

I looked at Paisley, having no clue what she was talking about, she shook her head, not having any idea either, which made me feel less uneducated.

"I think we should call the men." Alona suggested.

Daxx was frowning and watching Crissy carefully. She nodded her head and pulled an earpiece out of her pocket.

I sat at the desk with a front row seat, watching Crissy run back and forth from the map on the wall, the pages all over the floor and whatever it was she was doing at her desk. All of the brothers were in the room, a few guards now as well. Leone and Rafael were on the floor moving pages around.

"I feel like I missed the instructional portion of what we're doing here." Chase said giving Troy an odd look.

"That's because there wasn't any." Troy motioned to the papers on the floor. "She can't explain it, if she doesn't know yet."

"Leave it up to Cutie to find some secret code." Chase smiled.

Crissy stopped moving. "I didn't find it. Autumn did." She was on the move again. "It was right in front of my face and I didn't see it." She frowned and then knelt down checking what Rafael and Leone had done.

Quinton pushed away from the wall and went over, looking to see what his brothers were doing. "When did you two get good at math?"

Leone smirked. "Its not math. It's a cypher."

Quinton crossed his arms over his chest. "A cypher?"

Leone nodded. "Yeah. Remember that movie about during the war when they'd use a cypher to pass messages in case they fell into enemy hands?"

"And you guys think Willis is smart enough to do this?" Arius gave Michael a quick look.

Crissy got up and went back to the map. "No. Well," she waved her hand to the map, "I don't know if they are." She shrugged. "It wasn't to hide from us, it was for them to keep information straight." She nodded. "They tracked down so many, they had to use some sort of system to know which were located or not."

"Have you figured out that system, heart?" Victor crossed his arms over his chest, but gave her a patient look.

Crissy puffed out her cheeks, then exhaled quickly. "I'm not sure. I mean I can't check most of the ones already found… or not found, by them," she gave him a wide-eyed look, "but if I can confirm one or two and check the pattern…"

"Criss, yes or no?" Daxx got up and went over to look at the map, probably trying to figure out what she'd been doing. I couldn't follow any of it, so I was staying where I sat.

"I…" Crissy paused then pointed to the map, "think the first four numbers are the grid reference from the map." She nodded and looked around at everyone. No one moved. "I don't have enough of the pages of those we found to confirm what I think the last four numbers mean."

Victor looked over her shoulder at the map, then to the page in her hand. "Zero nine would be h on the map?" He leaned closer, "and zero six, so," he stepped to her side and touched the line on the top of the map, "six and h," he followed the two points until they met, "here."

Everyone moved closer to see what he was doing. I stood up, so I could at least pretend I knew what they were talking about.

"Yes." Crissy looked excited. "We found her there too, but I don't know what the end numbers mean."

"The fact that you figure out the first four is phenomenal." Alona hugged her arms around her waist. "So, we know map coordinates, now what to we do?"

"Get help." Michael pulled out his phone. "We have scholars and mathematicians, surely they can be of some assistance with all this." He tapped the screen, then put the phone to his ear and walked out of the crowd of bodies.

"We need to start marking the map with those we haven't found." Daxx said.

Troy was typing on his phone. "I'm getting a larger map brought in here."

"We'll need a new color system." Paisley went over and looked at the pages on the floor. "Green for those we've found. Yellow for the ones we've confirmed, but haven't moved yet. Red for an unchecked site."

Alona went over and got her phone. "I need to get in touch with Liza, we may need more space soon."

I looked away from the map to her, "have you thought of finding an old apartment building or empty school or something and have it converted into apartments? There's so many empty buildings just crumbling to the ground."

Troy pointed at me and nodded. "We'll help with that."

Alona took a deep breath and then exhaled and smiled. "It would save looking for new houses." She bit her lip. "It might take some time…" she looked at Chase, her mouth dropping, "I saw a listing for something like that…" She spun around and dashed over to her desk.

Chase turned and looked at me, then to his twin, "we may have to buy a construction company, brother."

Troy grinned, "it would save us time and issues."

Rafael nodded. "I'm going to go through the teams and see if we need to adjust patrols to come up with a few more around the clock teams for the houses."

Arius kissed the top of Paisley's head, "I'm going to go through the lists of those we've found with women again… someone has to have something useful in their head."

"I'll help with that." Troy gave Daxx a quick glance.

I watched Crissy sticking pins in the map. Now that some of the bodies had dispersed, I was able to see the whole map. I went over. "So, the red means it's a place we suspect a woman might be held?"

Crissy nodded. "We can check, then change it to yellow before we send teams in."

I pointed to a red pin. "So, there's a woman there?"

Crissy checked which one I was pointing to. "I'm going to mark the map when it gets here so the numbers that correspond with the letters are easier to see." She moved a few pages. "Yes. There's a woman there, here's her name." She handed me the paper. "Only some have addresses with them, that's why there are so many not found…by us." She frowned, "I have to check the numbers with the ones that have addresses," her eyes went huge, "maybe it's the location they're moved to."

I took it and looked down at it. There was a name, no address. "Maybe get a street view map on the computer so we can see where that is?" I motioned the map. "That means nothing to me."

She nodded. "Good idea." I had meant later, but she ran over and unplugged the closest laptop and brought it back. She opened a window and typed something. A street view map came up. "Right there."

I leaned down and looked at it. "I know that area. It's not the best, but could be worse."

Bethany came over, "I think that describes most of the city."

I turned to see Michael come back in the room and go over to talk to Chase. The feeling of wanting to go and hug Michael hit me. I frowned, it was going to be a long day-night, whatever it was, working with him.

Woods stood by the door with Felix, both looking bored.

"So," I glanced at the map again, or more precisely the red pin in the map, "we confirm they're there, change the pin to yellow and a team is sent?"

Beth shrugged, Crissy nodded.

"The teams take a female guard, so they don't scare the women. The other guards go to deal with any problems." Beth said.

I gnawed on my lip for a second. "You send a recon team to check?"

"We were just showing up, ready for a fight, but now that we know the system…"

I nodded and cut of Beth. "Sounds good." I looked at the building on the laptop screen, then turned to watch Michael for a second. "I think I'll be good for the recon." I turned and went over to Woods. "Up for an adventure?" I glanced at his wrist to make sure he had a device on.

He nodded.

"Excellent." I inhaled deep as I put my hand on his arm. Closing my eyes, I blew it out and pictured the diner near the building. I was just about to open my eyes and see why it wasn't working when my stomach tightened.

I opened my eyes to see it had worked. Mostly. We were in the alley behind the diner, not at the front as I had pictured. I'd have to fine tune that part later.

Woods shook his head. "That's new. When did you learn that?"

I checked which way the alley went. "Earlier. Come on." We walked down the litter strewn alley, both of us alert to everything around us. I was really liking how the guards from Alterealm were quiet, focused people.

As we reached the street, my phone buzzed in my pocket, I pulled it out and answered it without looking.

"Autumn." It was Daxx.

"Yeah. I'll have an answer for you in a minute—hopefully."

"You ported to that address?"

She sounded stressed, which was odd for Daxx, she was usually sarcastic or blunt. I motioned to Woods to cross the street. "Yeah. Figured I'd get the recon started while everyone gets things set up there."

"Uh, well we don't just pop somewhere without planning and—"

"Is Michael glaring at you right now?" That would explain her behavior. "I'm getting this weird feeling of being annoyed, but I'm not feeling that myself."

"Yes, and I'm jealous that you can pick up on that when the rest of us can't." She whispered.

We reached the address the code had given us. I stared at the buzzer list. There were twelve apartments in the building. "Daxx, can you do me a favor and see what the other numbers were, that go with this address."

"Ah, yeah, hang on." I could hear voices in the background. Some of the clearer then others. From the sounds of it Victor was taking control there. "Okay, after the coordinates its one, one, zero, zero."

I stared at the list of apartments. "What was her last name?"

"Hall. Autumn you need—"

"Apartment eleven *or* one, one is listed with Hall." I told her.

"What? Really? Wait, I'm putting you on speaker. Everyone shut up."

I tried the door, it wasn't locked. With a shrug to Woods we went in.

"Autumn is at the building that Criss marked on the map. The numbers after the coordinates are one, one, zero, zero. A tenant with the last name Hall lives in apartment eleven."

There was a lot of talking, I couldn't make out what anyone was saying. "We're going up there now."

"You shouldn't be there with only one guard." Michael sounded very angry.

I looked over my shoulder at Woods following me up the stairs. "Easier to blend in with only one, than a pack of large dudes."

"They know you, Autumn…Hubert and his crew." Paisley said quietly.

"I'm not running down the street saying here I am. I just want to see if she's here and all right, then we'll be back." I touched the device on my wrist. "If we run into any problems, we'll use the watch things and pop back."

"How are you going to ascertain if she's all right?" That was Victor.

I stopped and looked back at Woods. "Okay, I hadn't gotten that far."

"Oh."

I'd recognize Crissy's *oh* anywhere.

"You can say you are canvassing about your self-defence classes." She said sounding excited.

I nodded. "That's good. That'll work." I continued up the stairs.

"Stay on the call and mute your speaker." Michael all but barked, sounding like he was inside the phone.

"Got it." I looked at the phone for the button. "Okay you're muted," I grinned, "but you'll hear everything." I waited for a reply, then realized if they did, I wouldn't hear it.

We reached the fourth floor and headed to the end of the hallway. "Maybe start figuring out the zero, zero while you're listening." I shrugged. I stopped at apartment eleven and glanced to Woods, "try to look smaller and less scary." I smiled at him when he stepped back and stood there. I knocked on the door, humming. I don't know what I was humming, with Paisley there was always music playing, so it must have been something she had on.

There was the sound of locks opening, then the door opened a crack, a chain preventing it from opening further. A scared woman looked out at me.

"Hey there. My name is Autumn." I smiled. "We're just going around to tell people about a free self defense class I hold at parks around the city."

She looked at me, then to Woods, warily.

"I'm sorry, what's your name?" I shrugged. "I tend to talk to fast and not give people a chance to answer.

"Melanie." She whispered.

That was the name on the page Crissy had handed me. I smiled again. "Hi, Melanie. So," I frowned, "hey, are you all right?"

She gave me a hesitant glance, the kind people give you when they don't want to lie to your face and then she nodded.

"Okay. Well, the class at the park just around the corner will be tomorrow if you'd like to attend." I pointed to Woods, "I'll show you how to take down guys as big as him." I smiled again and held up my phone. "Can I put you down?" I shrugged. "I'll just add your name in my phone, then I'll remember the face that goes with it."

She gave a half non-committal nod.

"Awesome. Okay, so Melanie…" I opened the bottom of the screen and brought up Daxx's name so I could message her. *Something not right here.*

"Hall." Melanie whispered.

I smiled at her. "Melanie is a pretty name." I typed, *need someone here asap I think.* "Okay, you're on the list." I nodded. "Oh, hey if someone else shows up here for the same thing, they're part of my crew, so don't be alarmed. We're all over the place today."

"Oh, okay." She said in a quiet voice.

"Nice to meet you, Melanie, hope to see you soon." I wanted to stay and *do* something, but I'd all but promised I'd behave and go back as soon as I'd done this. I gave her another smile and backed away from the door. It closed, and locks clicked into place.

Woods and I turned and headed down the stairs. I hit the speaker on the phone and put it to my ear. "You guys get that?"

"Yes. The guys are getting the team. Get back here. Rafael knows that area and will take them over." Daxx said sounding like a queen for once.

I nodded. "Okay. Tell them to hurry, something has really scared her." We hit the landing and I reached over and touched Woods arm. Closing my eyes, I pictured the woman cave.

My stomach hit my pelvis. I opened my eyes to see a very unhappy looking Michael a foot away. I blew out a breath to settle my stomach. "Guess I've got the knack for this porting thing, huh?" I looked away from his glare to Paisley, she gave me a half grin, then grimaced and looked at Michael.

"I'd like to speak to you." He said in a quiet tone.

"Yeah, I gathered that." I answered.

He motioned to the door, then inclined his head.

Yeah, he was pissed. I gave Daxx a quick look, she was smirking, then turned and went out into the hallway.

Michael came out and turned, walking toward the corner.

I followed. When he stopped, I stood there. "So, what's up?" Maybe if I played dumb, he'd settle down. I could feel anger, or something worse, bouncing off me and it took a bit to stay calm and not react. He still didn't speak. "Okay, so this link between us," I motioned back and forth among us, "it's feeling pretty heavy right now, like almost choking me."

His brows drew together as he looked down at me.

Then the feeling was gone, like he'd shut it off.

I nodded. "Better. Now spill before you explode and blow the veins out in your forehead."

Michael lifted his hand and pointed to me, then dropped it. "You *can not* just port somewhere without thinking it through."

"I just wanted to do something helpful, while you guys set everything up here." I pointed to the door of the cave, "there's a lot of information in there. If each one turns out to be a woman in trouble, then—" I stopped, the expression on his face told me regardless of how I reasoned this out, he wasn't buying it. "I'm drowning here, iceman." I held up my tattooed arm, "this, another realm, women being taken…"

He moved so fast I didn't see it coming. Grasping my chin in a firm hold, he kissed me so hard and fast I didn't have time to do a thing. Releasing me, his red eyes locked on mine. "If you port into unknown circumstances again, I *will* lock you in a cell." He stepped back. "For your own good." Turning on his heel, he strode back down the hall.

I stood there, my chin was probably on the floor, offended he'd even think such a thing, but completely turned on by the alpha pouring off him. I blew out a breath and looked to see Daxx and Paisley standing in the woman cave doorway. "He said he'd lock me in a cell." I frowned, "I can't port out of one can I?"

Daxx shook her head, a smirk on her face. She looked in the direction he'd walked. "Who knew Michael was all he-man."

Paisley gave me a wide-eyed look. "Please don't get locked in a cell."

I put my hands on my hips and inhaled deeply, not sure what I was, or wasn't, willing to do yet.

Chapter Twenty-Nine

I sat at the table waiting for everyone to arrive. I'd been here and hour now. Mitz had made me breakfast, somehow knowing I didn't want happy, cheery and left me alone with my thoughts.

It had been three days since I'd gone to that apartment. The teams were finding more women that the other side had tracked down. For the most part the women knew something was off, and were willing to move to a safe house. I needed to ask how they were feeding that many—and about a hundred other questions and details, like what were these women supposed to do with their lives now. That question plagued at me as well, so maybe I just wondered for myself more than them. Either way, I could probably help with something as they adjusted. Something. Anything.

For three days I'd been doing nothing, no that was a lie. I did get to change pin colors on the map. While I knew the significance of changing a red or yellow to green, I wasn't feeling like I was actually *doing* anything important.

"Pretty serious thoughts for so early in the day, dynamo." Chase stood leaning in the kitchen door, a coffee mug in his hand.

I grinned. "Thinking is the only thing I'm allowed to do right now."

Alona came out of the kitchen. "You'll get used to house arrest."

I rolled my eyes at her. "Speaking of that, I went to see Rena yesterday," I shrugged, "she's okay with never leaving the apartment."

They went and sat in their chairs, giving each other side glances and heated looks.

"I can't blame her for not wanting to leave." Alona sent me a sympathetic look, "we're known to Hubert's team, but we didn't suffer at their hands the way she did."

I nodded and poked with my fork at the food on my plate. "She's decided to keep it." I glanced up at Alona, "she just doesn't know how she's going to feel, after—" I stopped when Alona covered her mouth with her hand and her eyes teared up.

"None of that, beloved." Chase hugged her.

"None of what?" Leone and Bethany came in carrying their plates.

"Emotional moments." Chase said as he kissed Alona's hand.

"I'm all for that." Daxx said as her and Troy came in. She gave Alona a hard look. "No crying and stuff."

Alona cleared her throat. "Right. Sorry." She grinned.

"Today is going to be a good day." Rafael entered from the hall door.

Quinton was right behind him. "Guard trials today."

"What's that?" I looked at Daxx.

She yawned. "The day the second-year guards show us if they're ready to join the royal guard." She smiled. "I'm looking forward to it. Even had a nap so I could stay up."

"Oh." I nodded. "That will be cool to see." I glanced to Rafael. "Is it tournament style?"

Rafael sat down. "More or less, but we do watch for certain styles and execution skill. A few are usually selected that don't make the top grades—if we think they can improve with further training."

I sipped my water. "And the rest? What happens to them?"

Quinton watched Mitz come in carrying a few plates. When neither of them were his, he looked at me. "They're all guards by this point, but we only select the top fifteen or twenty to become part of the royal guards. The others will fill various posts."

I nodded and watched as Arius and Paisley came in, all smiles and secrets mirrored in their expressions. I couldn't begrudge their being happy.

Michael came in carrying his own plate. He looked at me sitting at the end of the table, then went and sat in his usual chair.

I had to work hard to not sigh out loud.

Victor and Crissy came in, holding hands.

I looked back at Rafael. "Maybe pick a few more at the top this year."

His eyebrows when up. "For?"

I pushed my plate away and sat back. Crossing my arms over my chest, I glanced at my left arm. "I've accepted I'm living here," I motioned around me, "in this realm." Everyone looked at me. Michael sat there like he was a statue. "Am I wrong?"

Troy gave me a look that said I wasn't.

"I mean between this," I held up my tattooed arm, like they all didn't know about it, "and now Hubert's ogres know me, so I'm a new resident of Alterealm." I shrugged.

"So why do you need more guards?" Daxx smirked at me, "thinking of starting a new team of your own?"

I looked at her. "That's not a bad idea, but no." I glanced at Michael and held his look as I spoke. "Because I'm not living here. Underground." Michael's jaw clenched. I looked at Troy. "Don't get me wrong. These chambers are pretty cool, but I can't do it. I need air, sunlight and—" I sighed. "Windows." I shrugged. "I grew up, living on a ledge, in the air, I need the outside to be right there." I looked at Paisley.

"I can't live underground, it makes me restless and I feel trapped." She gave me a sympathetic look and a slight nod.

A feeling of warmth and comfort moved over me. I glared at Michael, "don't do that." I pushed back from the table. "You can't avoid me, bark orders, and then try to comfort me." I shook my head and stood up, glancing around the table. "I'm going to live at the palace, so find me some guards to help me watch a place that size." I took a deep breath. "I'm going to the practice room." I didn't wait for any comments, just turned and left quickly. I could have been dramatic and ported, but that just wasn't me. I was trying to stay who I was in all of this, despite overwhelming odds.

I looked at the bag. I wasn't into it today. You could only hit a defenseless bag and pole so much before you just didn't feel like exerting energy to do it. I'd been beating on these two inanimate objects for the last three days—a lot.

Paisley came over. "Are you willing it to participate?"

I smirked, "something like that." I rolled my shoulders. "I just, need a real body on the other end of my frustration I think."

She looked over her shoulder. "I could think of one."

I glanced over to see Michael, standing off to the side of the mat talking on his phone. "Yeah, I can't decide if I want to beat him or…" I shrugged.

She laughed. "I understand that. Completely." She sighed. "So, the palace huh?" Paisley grimaced. "I'll come visit, just don't ask me to go on the roof or balcony. Actually, inside would be great away from windows."

I'd forgotten she didn't like heights. "It's a whole palace, I didn't get to see much but I'm sure there will probably be somewhere away from windows."

"I've seen a bit of it too." She motioned to the others, "Quinton said he wouldn't mind living there again, Rafael, Leone and Beth as well."

I was surprised. "Really? Even better I won't be alone up there."

"They moved to the underground chambers when Troy and Chase were born, because people knew they were the prophesised twin kings and wanted them dead."

My eyebrows shot up.

"Right," she nodded, "so our kings, Arius, Leone and Raf have only ever lived in the chambers."

I started to pull the wrap off my hand. "I had no idea."

"I don't see the kings or Victor moving there though, and they shouldn't as they're the tops in Alterealm." She shrugged, "at least until all of team bad is stopped."

I glanced over to where everyone else was. "I didn't even think about ranks among them."

Paisley smirked, "not that it stops them most of the time, but when it comes down to it there is an order to things."

"Yeah, where does Arius rank?" I watched Arius spar with Quinton, they were really trying to get the other one.

"Fifth. After the kings, Victor, Michael and Leone."

I looked back at her. "Michael is third around here?"

She nodded.

I shrugged, "explains why he's so cold sometimes, I guess. Running a realm can't be an easy gig."

The rest of the women started coming toward us.

"None of them have an easy position. They don't rule while sitting on a throne or gilded chairs. They're the first ones up and last ones to sleep each day, or night."

"I've noticed. They have my respect there. I wouldn't have known any of them were royalty if I hadn't been told."

She grinned at me. "You're royalty now, sis."

My neck almost snapped when I looked back at her quickly. "I totally forgot that princess stuff."

"Yep, you are Princess Autumn mated to The Law of Alterealm, Prince Michael Whitham."

Several thoughts when through my head at once, I couldn't speak a single one.

"What did you just do?" Daxx asked Paisley.

She grinned. "I just told her she's a princess and her rank here."

"Oh," Daxx rolled her eyes, "at least you don't have to be addressed that way."

I huffed out a breath. "I guess. But really, in my whole life of wishing for things, being a princess was not one of them."

"Says the woman that demanded to live in the palace earlier." Alona said with a smirk.

I laughed, "I thought of asking for a house outside of here but thought that would just open up all sorts of new arguments and issues. The palace is theirs, and is sitting there empty."

"It's a good point." Beth smiled. "Leone and I want to move there too." She shrugged, "I know these halls here are endless, but once babies start being born, the rooms and renovations underground…" she shook her head, "Some of us moving to the palace will help with all of that."

"I hadn't thought of that." Daxx mumbled. "Then again I still don't want to think that either Alona or I, hopefully Alona, will be having the next twin kings."

"Really? You know this?" I looked from one to the other.

"Prophecy says new twin rulers every five hundred years." Crissy stated.

I didn't know which part interested me the most, the twin rulers or that they'd be alive in five hundred years. I'd be alive then? "Wait, how long are we going to live?"

Daxx shrugged. "I'm guessing a long time if we're having twins in two hundred and forty years."

"Maybe they'll be queen rulers, not kings." Paisley smirked then motioned to the men. "That would change things around here."

"I think the math is wrong." Crissy said.

We all looked at her, she shrugged. "If there are new twin rulers in five hundred years, and they're always coronated at one hundred years old, the twins will be born in one hundred and forty years, not two hundred and forty years."

Daxx looked at her for a long moment. "Okay, but I can't freak out about it for at least another seventy-five years." She shook her head, "but yeah, queens would balance the testosterone around here."

All of us turned to look at the men. Arius and Chase noticed immediately and stopped mid-action.

"Right now, I'd just like to fix Michael." Daxx mumbled. "He's being ridiculous."

I snorted. "I overheard a conversation with Mitz after I busted my ribs. He doesn't want a mate because he can't live through the loss if anything happens to them," I frowned, "me."

Alona's mouth dropped. "You're joking, right?"

I shook my head. "No."

"Men." Daxx muttered. "They don't even know when they're being stupid."

We all looked at her.

"They do," Beth looked all around the space above her head, "okay, most do. They just don't know how to stop being stupid."

I watched Michael sparing with Troy. His moves were fluid, without thought. I could watch him fight all day, I thought to myself. Saying it out loud would have sounded lame.

"What can we do?" Alona asked with a mischievous tone.

"There has to be something." Daxx looked from Beth to Paisley, "to get through to him, or just to make a point so he'll rethink things correctly." She turned back to me, "guess you don't want to beat on him yet."

I looked over at Michael and bit my lip.

"That's a no." Alona said softly.

"Maybe not beat him, what about shove him around a bit?" Paisley looked at Beth.

Bethany grinned.

"Can I help?" Crissy asked. "Autumn saved my life, I don't know how else to help her."

"You don't need to do anything, Crissy." I assured her.

She looked disappointed. "Okay, but I'm telling Victor to get your guards. I understand needing space to breathe."

"Thank you." My gaze, without my permission, went back to Michael. Part of me was hoping he would keep looking at me. I sighed, "So what's the plan?"

"A little tag-team action. Get the men out of the way first." Paisley said quietly.

"I don't think the men will interfere." Daxx motioned toward them. "They're on Autumn's side, even if they don't say it out loud."

"I can't physically contribute, but I can block his path if he tries to evade." Alona smiled at me.

"Go grab a bo, Autumn." Daxx started walking to the mat.

"A bo?" I looked at Alona.

"I think she means for you to challenge Michael." Alona went toward the single door near the targets.

"A bo won't do me any good, he's got a sword, wooden or not a bo becomes a stick."

"Grab whatever works then." Paisley smirked and walked away with Beth.

"Going up." Crissy whispered and ran for the ropes.

Exhaling, I went toward the weapons wall. I wasn't skilled enough with a sword to fight Michael. I stopped and looked at my options. Shaking my head, I grabbed two batons. Sticking with what I knew was better. I still didn't want to fight him, but I wasn't going to bail on the girls. Spinning them from offensive to defensive, I walked toward the mat. Victor was standing with Troy off to the side, he kept glancing up to where Crissy was perched. Beth and Paisley were side by side, watching the men still sparring.

Quinton stumbled and fell back. He glared in the direction of Paisley and Beth. With a shake of his head, he got up and walked off the mat.

Rafael was the next to stumble back. He scowled at Beth, but didn't say anything as he moved out of the way.

I turned to see both women's hands up, arcs of light hovering over Beth's and Paisley with a look of intense focus. Beth flicked her hand. I looked quickly to see Arius sitting on the mat giving his mate a curious look, before lifting his hands as he stood up and backed off the mat.

Leone watched Arius move and turned toward Beth. She shrugged at him. With a smirk on his face he followed his brother to the sideline.

That left Michael and Chase sparring.

Daxx gave me a look. I stepped onto the mat and watched for a moment to step in on Chase. I didn't want to get smacked with a wooden sword. They were only practicing, but from the sound of their weapons colliding, it would still do damage.

Chase ducked the next swing, I took that opening and went under his weapon as he raised it—hoping Paisley would have my back and stop it before it came down on me.

I met a very surprised Michael's swing, and blocked it with both batons raised against my forearms.

Michael lifted his sword away and frowned. He looked around to see his brothers off the mat. A serious blue-eyed stare came back to me. I stood in ready stance. He gave his head a brief shake and turned to go. He stopped suddenly, his head snapping to Arius. "Arius, ask your mate to release me."

Arius stood there with his arms crossed over his chest. He turned his head slowly to look at his mate then shook his head. "Sorry, brother, can't do it."

Michael lifted his hands in surrender, then spun on his heel to head the other way. Daxx blocked his path. Michael turned to look at Troy, who shook his head denying the silent request to step in.

I watched his chest expand as he took a deep breath and looked to where Alona stood with her chucks spinning nonchalantly at her side.

"Chase," Michael growled.

Chase grinned. "If you think I'm taking on our women to save your pride, brother, you'd be mistaken."

Michael lifted his hand and dropped the wooden sword to the mat, then turned back to me. He held my look, his facial expressions giving nothing away.

In that moment I wished I could get a sense of how he was feeling, but there was nothing there but impenetrable ice. I lowered my arms, letting the batons hang loosely. I didn't want this man's surrender. Not like this. I wanted the warrior I knew him to be. If I was to have a mate, which I did now, for life it seemed, I wanted a man that could be an equal and understood my values. A man that understood who I had to be. My gaze moved over his face, noting the scar that had forever changed him. I inhaled slowly and turned to look at Daxx, I gave a slight shake of my head letting her know that this wasn't going to go anywhere. Disappointment was evident in her expression. I dropped the batons, "I have furniture to choose." I stepped back slowly, holding his look, hoping the delay would give him the time to say something. He didn't. He turned on his heel and walked past Daxx to the single door.

Nodding to myself. I glanced over to Paisley and Beth, hoping the look on my face said thanks for trying.

"I'm an expert shopper." Alona said, handing Chase her chucks. "I think we should furnish a palace today."

Crissy dropped down from the ceiling on her cable. "Mitz will help." She undid her cable, then turned to Victor. "Pick good guards for the palace, I'll be visiting there often."

He gave her a soft look. "As you wish, heart." He said softly.

Troy came over to me. "Tell Mitz to give you the key for the storage. There's more than enough furniture in there to furnish a few palaces." Daxx came over, she gave him a look that I'm sure had some internal mate communication with it. He inclined his head. "I'll see if we can get through to my brother."

I shook my head. "It's his own mind he has to accept, Troy, don't waste your time." I turned to go, then spotted the apologetic look Rafael was giving me. "What time do the guard trials start?"

"About three hours." He answered, still with the look on his face.

"I'll be there to check out the action." I started for the door, then paused when I moved by Quinton. "I was thinking of starting a self defense class, for some of the women that we've rescued." I shrugged. "Give them a boost in confidence and help them feel like they have some control in their lives."

Quinton grinned. "I'll talk to Liza and see how many women want that. It's a great idea. I'll help with them."

I gave him an abrupt nod. "Thanks."

Alona met me at the door. "Did I hear Troy say there was a whole storage room of furnishings?"

I nodded.

She looked elated. "Then we are re-decorating these chambers and a palace." She laughed, excited. "And the best part is it's free."

I realized then, I wasn't going to get away with a bed and table with a few chairs. I went out into the hall.

Daxx met my look, she rolled her eyes. "Shopping, oh goodie."

"I had another idea." Paisley said as she caught up to us. "I think we should give Autumn a makeover too."

I frowned at her. "For what?"

She shrugged, "nothing drastic, just a different outfit, maybe some lipstick. For the buffet before we go to the training yard."

I looked down at my leggings and tank top. She was right, maybe I could change it up a bit. "Okay. No frills, flowers, or poofy anything."

Daxx laughed. "I really like you."

Paisley nodded. "Got it nothing girly."

We started down the hall. "And I'm putting my workout clothes back on before we go to the yard for the trials."

"Of course." She said with a smile.

Chapter Thirty

I looked down at my outfit. They had kept their word and it wasn't girly, but I still felt like I was trying to be someone else.

"He's not going to recognize you." Alona said with a grin.

"I don't recognize me." I ran my hand over the *turquoise* blouse I was wearing. It looked blue to me, but they told me is wasn't *only* blue, whatever that meant. I could honestly say I'd never worn a blouse in my life. It wasn't fluffy or frilly, it just felt strange to my touch. Silk wasn't something I was familiar with. It didn't really have sleeves, or complete sleeves, it had a strap on my shoulder like a shirt should be, then there were these other straps hanging down my arm.

The only part I was comfortable with was what I had on my feet. They were cute, not that I'd admit it out loud and thrill Alona, but the boots were like hiking boots, only shiny. The skirt had shorts built in, I think they called it a skort. It was black, I was good with that, and stopped right above my knees. It wasn't tight or fluffy either, it was loose and *flowed* as Alona had put it. I sighed loudly.

"Go look in the mirror. You look great." Paisley gave me a gentle shove toward the mirror.

I went over to the closet and looked in the mirror and it took a moment for recognition to set in. That was my reflection. They'd pulled my hair up and it was honestly the first time I'd seen my hair neatly sitting on my head and not hanging wherever it fell. Bethany added liner to my eyes and mascara, which almost blinded me at first when my eyes watered. She'd sighed and fixed that mess. My lips were pink and shiny now. I had a nice mouth when it wasn't swollen from a punch or elbow, at least.

"It's not what I expected. I was thinking, you know pants and nice t-shirt…"

"But?" Crissy asked.

I nodded slowly, "but I do look nice." I glanced at Paisley's reflection in the mirror, "I've never dressed like this in my life."

She smiled, wide. "You look amazing."

I turned around. "I'm not getting how this is supposed to change anything with Michael."

Bethany grinned. "It's kind of a tease, you know, look, don't touch."

Paisley nodded. "Or a see what you're missing thing."

"The right boots and skirt can help a male overcome many walls inside his head." Alona's cheeks flushed.

"T.M.I." Bethany sang.

Alona laughed, "it's true though. Michael sees you as a warrior, he even calls you little warrior, which is sweet, but I think he needs reminding that you are so much more."

I blew out a nervous breath and looked down the front of my body again. "I'm so much more dressed in so much less?"

Daxx snorted. "The leggings and tank tops you wear show *more* then this outfit." She shrugged. "I'd even wear that outfit."

Alona's eyebrow went up.

"No. Not today." Daxx said quickly.

I took a quick breath and went over, grabbing my phone. I looked down at the skort. "I have no pockets."

"Oh," Bethany ran over. "Yes, you do." She lifted the edge of my skirt up and pointed to the pocket on the shorts.

"Huh." I tucked the phone in. "I can work with this." I grinned at Daxx. "If I have to do a roundhouse, the shorts keep everything down there covered."

Daxx laughed. Alona just covered her mouth.

We walked into the dinning room and all the men were already there. I gave Paisley a look, she shrugged and smirked at me. They'd purposely made us arrive late.

All the men stood. which wasn't unusual, the fact they all looked like we'd smacked them in the head wasn't normal. I frowned and looked around at them. "Close your gobs and sit down." I hesitantly glanced at Michael, he was definitely surprised to see me look like this. I sat down quickly.

Daxx chuckled and went to her chair.

Chase waited for Alona, then sat down. "How was the furniture hunt?"

Alona smiled at him. "Fabulous. Not only did we find adequate furnishings for the palace rooms, our new bedroom and sitting area furniture will be delivered to our room tomorrow."

Chase frowned, "we're redecorating?"

She gave him a soft look. "Yes. I want our space to feel homier."

"Homier?" Chase looked from his mate to Troy. Troy shrugged.

"All of us found some new pieces." Daxx said looking amused.

Troy looked quickly back to her but didn't say a word.

Beth looked at Leone, "I found some nice pieces for our new rooms at the palace."

"Oh, we're not taking what's in our room now?" He glanced to Chase, then back to her.

She shook her head. "Some of it."

"I was thinking of offering Emil a room there." Quinton said, not taking his eyes off the trays Mitz carried out.

Chase nodded. "He is spending more time over here."

Quinton straightened in his chair to see what was on the tray she set down. "Might make him feel more settled being over here, if he has somewhere of his own."

"He spends a lot of time with Rena though." Alona said quietly.

I shrugged. "As soon as the doctor clears it, she's coming over here—he's going to run some tests and make sure she can port here safely, for her and the baby. She doesn't want to stay over there alone." I smiled at the tray of fruit and vegetables Mitz set close to my end of the table. "She's going to stay at the palace with me, well, in her own room, but then she'll have all of us to help her." I paused and looked around at the others, "that's okay, right? I thought maybe if she's not comfortable with motherhood," I motioned around the table, "we could help. That whole it takes a village thing?" I sat there as the surprised looks appeared on all the faces. "I mean," I lifted my left arm, "the mark didn't fix that part of me, right? I still can't have kids, so I thought, her baby— which I think would be kind of related to me anyway…" I sent Alona a help me look, "I thought I could raise it if she can't, or-or you know help her."

The room was complete utter silence. Mitz even stood frozen in the doorway.

"I talked to her about it." I said as an afterthought, just in case they thought I was making this up as I went. "I was going to wait until we knew she could come over…"

"I think that's a wonderful idea." Alona said, with her eyes glistening. "And yes, I would most certainly help her and you, before and after."

Paisley was nodding her hand over her mouth.

"Oh my goodness. We get to decorate a nursery!" Bethany squealed.

I swallowed the lump in my throat. "So, it's okay, right? That I did that, told her she could, that I would?" I looked at Troy, hoping I hadn't overstepped boundaries. "I mean," I waved my hand around, "I-I've seen so many children without homes." I huffed out a breath, "I *was* one of them, with no parents. I just didn't want that. This baby is your family, right?"

Crissy was up off her chair running at me. I shoved the chair back just in time for her to hurl herself at me and grip my neck in a death grip. I gave her an awkward hug back.

Victor must have recognized my comfort zone being crushed because he stood up and moved down the table. He pulled his overwhelmed mate off me and hugged her. "I can't think of a better role model than you." He gave me a genuine smile and carried her back to their chairs.

Mitz sniffled and then moved down the table with her never flagging energy. She grabbed my face in her hands and then kissed my forehead. With teary-eyes she smiled and released me, then walked back down the table. As she passed Michael, she cuffed him in the back of the head, then reached around him to take his plate away and continued into the kitchen.

Michael looked at the door she'd gone out and then sat back in his chair. He inhaled a deep breath and looked down at me. "Of course, we'll do anything to help." He gave Victor a nervous look.

Quinton smiled "Its been a long time since this family had children running around." He glared at Rafael.

Rafael nodded, "about a hundred and ninety years ago." He smiled at me. "I look forward to it."

Relief washed through me. I still didn't know why I felt so strongly about this baby, but I couldn't walk away. Something inside me made me *have* to ensure it had a good life. A loving home, education. Everything I didn't get.

Emil came running in from the hallway. "Where is Autumn?"

Everyone looked at me.

Emil turned and did a physical double take. "My god." He gasped. "You're—" he waved his hand up and down, "not bruised or swollen and-and quite breath taking." I felt my cheeks heat. Giving his head a shake, "I'm sorry. I wanted to thank you. Sincerely." He smiled at me. "I've just left Rena and she is actually smiling and vibrant, not washed out and barely… her." He took a deep breath. "So, thank you."

I nodded. "You don't need to thank me." I motioned to the table. "We were just talking about her and the baby."

Emil sat down in the chair at the side of the table. "Are you really going to live in the palace, and Rena?" He shook his head, "she's completely elated that she's going to live in a palace."

"Yeah, we are. A few of us are going to move there." I glanced to Quinton, he gave a slight nod. "We were wondering if you'd like a room there as well, you know somewhere over here to call home."

His eyes brows went up. "I, actually yes, I'd like that." Emil turned and grinned at Chase, "to have a room in the palace."

Chase shrugged. "If Ellis is staying over here, we can give him one of the rooms here in the chambers." He looked to Rafael and Quinton, "Seems we're going to have vacancies."

"Have the mages, or whomever, secured the palace?" Emil looked from Chase to Troy. "No one can get in it again?"

Michael glanced to me briefly before answering. "They gained access through the underground caverns, so we're closing them off, and adding more surveillance to the entrances."

"There will also be guards posted around the premises, going forward." Victor said with his gaze still on Crissy.

"I will feel better if Rena is over here, since they found Alona's apartment once, I've been half out of my mind with worry."

Alona gave Emil an understanding look. "No one can get in if I'm not there to open it."

Beth met her look for a moment.

Emil stood up and picked up a few of the vegetables from the tray. "I'm looking forward to the guard trials today." He sat down. "Should we get Rena a personal one when she comes over?" He looked at me, then around at the other women.

"It's a thought." Daxx nodded, "although maybe one of the female guards would be better for her, for now."

I hadn't thought of things like that, I was still coming to terms with having Woods shadow me. "Maybe we can let her decide? You know, adjust a bit at a time." I smirked at Daxx, "this is a bit much to take on at once."

She laughed. "You don't have to tell me."

"Warden."

We turned to see a guard in the door.

"What is it?" Arius stood up.

"We're having some issues with one of the prisoners, sir." He gave Arius a nervous look.

"Which one?" He walked to the end of the table and took the tablet the guard held out.

Arius raised and eyebrow. "Eunice seems unhappy." He said quietly.

I looked to Michael, our eyes met briefly. "She can't possibly know we got in the palace, can she?"

He shook his head and got up. "No. No one goes near her. Arius or one of us take her meals, no one else."

Troy got up. "Shall we go see what the problem is?" He leaned down and kissed Daxx quickly. "Grab me some food and I'll eat while I watch the trials."

She nodded.

Chase and Victor stood up as well.

"I'll have Mitz toss some food together for all of you and meet you at the yard." Alona said.

I pushed back from the table and got up as well. "Hey, let me know if my presence will help with her." I was talking to Troy, but Michael turned. His checked me out from my cute boots to the top of my head, then nodded and followed his brothers out.

Quinton grabbed his plate and heaped more on it, then quickly went out the door.

Bethany looked at Leone. "Go, or you'll sit here fidgeting waiting to hear something."

He grinned and kissed her quickly. "I'll see you at the yard, love."

Emil looked to Rafael, who jumped up. Both went to go see what was going on.

I looked at the trays of food on the table. "Do they ever sit down and eat a whole meal?"

Daxx shook her head. "Rarely."

Alona stood up. "I'm going to have Mitz send all this over so they can snack while watching the trials from the guard house."

"Good idea." Bethany stood up and picked up one of the trays and followed her into the kitchen.

Chapter Thirty-One

I'd changed and watched part of the trials. Normally that sort of exhibition would have been a blast for me to see. I was so far from normal right now. I was restless, antsy and completely unfocused, none of which were familiar to me. I didn't know what was going on but decided a good run might clear it right out of my system.

I ran at an easy pace, watching my step on the trail. This wasn't level pavement I was on.

I still couldn't believe I'd managed to get out of the yard without being stopped, although with the commotion of trials going on, no one was watching me.

I looked around, nothing but field and fresh air. This was nothing like jogging at home.

Home. That was here now. I couldn't go back. I definitely couldn't do much of anything until that Hubert jerk and his crew were found. That was just something I couldn't walk away from. Now with Eunice acting strangely, that just added more reasons to stay. She said she didn't know how she got in the cells, which was really pushing it as far as all of us were concerned—but on the off chance that she really didn't remember, it added to the element of intrigue and I had to find out the answers. Not that they'd change how I felt about her.

I slowed for a few steps. Then there was Michael. I wasn't sure I could walk away from him either. Mates or not, I'd never felt the kind of pull to a man in the way I did him. The fact he was stuck in his own personal hell with ghosts from the past and unable to find his way out just made me think he needed me to stay. Even if he didn't know it.

Then there was Rena and her baby. I wasn't going to let either of them down.

My phone ringing brought me out of my head. I pulled it from my pocket and jogged on the spot while I answered it. It was a group call. "Do we have someone to beat down?"

"Ha. I wish." Daxx answered. "I was calling—"

"Where are you?" Michael demanded.

"Yeah that." Daxx mumbled.

"I went for a run. I've been feeling really confined the last few days." Not to mention was stuck in my head more than out of it.

"You left your guard here." Troy said in an unemotional way.

"Yeah, didn't think Woods had to run with me." I stopped and paced to keep the adrenalin pumping.

"Where are you?" Michael asked again, even louder than the first time.

I looked around. "In the middle of a field with a path going through it." There were no landmarks. "I went out the gate and turned right."

"May want to head back now, Autumn." Paisley said in a hushed tone.

I turned around. "Oh?" I started walking back in the direction I'd come, maybe they had a new lead. I hadn't gone ten feet before I heard it. The sound of hooves hitting the ground. I wasn't a psychic or anything, but I knew who it would be. Hachi and the man that wanted nothing to do with me, but couldn't leave me alone, rode into view. "I'll talk to you soon." I hung up the phone and continued to stand here and watch him ride toward me like a demon was chasing him.

Michael was off the horse before it completely stopped and stomped the remaining few feet until he was right up in my face. "What part of *for your own safety* is confusing you?"

He was standing so close I could feel his breath on my face as he barked at me. I lifted my arms. "I'm in the middle of a huge open field. If anyone were here, I'd see them and port out."

"And if they're cloaked and you couldn't *see* them?" His voice was so quiet I almost didn't hear him.

I held up my arm with the device on my wrist in front of his face. "I'd use this."

"And if they drug you again?" He hissed out a breath. "All of those scenarios have happened. No one goes anywhere without guards."

I looked behind him, looking for *his* guard. "Your guard fall behind?" I watched the nerve in his jaw twitch. "I just needed to move, standing around was driving me crazy." He didn't move or say a word, so I kept going. "The past few days I'm restless, unfocused," I lifted my arms and dropped them for emphasis, "my brain is all over the place. I thought once I decided I was staying here it would get better, but it's not." His blue eyes were locked on mine. "I'm losing my mind Michael, and I don't know why." I waved my hand at the field, "so I thought a good run might burn some of that off and help me settle down."

Michael took a deep breath, and straightened. "It's not your—frustration."

I cocked my head to the side. "Oh? And you know this how? Are you in my head?"

"No, well, not entirely. I can't get *in* your head."

I glared at him. "What are you talking about?"

He held up his left arm. "It's this."

I looked at his tattoo, then lifted my own arm and looked at it. "The tattoo is making me crazy?"

"Yes—no."

I huffed out a breath. "Well, thanks for clearing that up." I gave him my best 'are we done' look.

He scowled at me in return.

I didn't know if I wanted to kiss him or hit him, my head was that messed up.

"It's the mate's bond." He blurted out.

I lifted my arm again, "a tattoo is making me lose my mind?"

"No. The bond—" Michael looked up at the sky and took a deep breath. His blue eyes came back to me. "Because we are marked and bound, but spend no time together—it knows."

Both eyebrows raised as I looked up at him. Then what he was trying, and failing, to explain sunk in. "Well, that's a bit of a problem isn't it?"

He just looked at me, showing no signs that he was intending to reply.

Shaking my head, I turned and pace a few feet away, the spun back around. I lifted my arm one more time. "I've examined this *a lot* and I'm pretty sure it's not something that can be undone."

"It can't."

I nodded. "Right, so what then? We hang out together and make *it* happy?"

"I can't."

"Of course not, so that brings us right back to the *now what?*" I glared at him, hoping he had answers because my level of annoyance was rising.

"I don't know."

"You don't know. This is your thing, your-your culture. I just got here, so I don't have the answers." He didn't move a muscle. "I can't change what happened to you several hundred years before I existed, but I can't function with my head like this." I was close to growling now. "I stayed to fight. To help you, your family," I waved my hand in the air, "your realm and all those women…"

"You shouldn't have had to."

I gave him a blank look.

"Fight." A look of defeat appeared on his face. "You shouldn't have been dragged into this." Pain and regret were clear in his eyes. "It was my family's failing that led to this…"

I chuffed at that. "I'm pretty sure this started long before you or your brothers were in charge." I put my hand on my hips. "The planning and backup plans and many contingency plans that Eunice and her brother have… this started, I can't believe I'm saying this, many *centuries* ago." I flipped my hand in the air, "you guys are just stuck cleaning up your ancestor's failings."

Michael watched me for a moment. "I should have put you in a safe house. You shouldn't have been injured as many times as you have."

My head was starting to spin when he changed directions again so suddenly. "I wouldn't have stayed in a safe house, not when I was needed to help end this."

He looked angry again. "You've suffered too much in your life, no home, then living off garbage *is* a result of our failings. I can't watch you get hurt again. I've almost lost you several times and I can't do it again." His voice cracked with emotion.

"I'm sorry, but this is who I am. I don't know anything but fighting and after years of doing it to live, I am sure as hell not stopping when I can do it so others can live freely, without fear." I shook my head, "I can't walk away until every single person involved with these sick lunatics are stopped, Michael. I just can't. You, the warrior that you are, without your unfailing sense of justice should understand that more than anyone."

Michael closed his eyes and inhaled deeply. I couldn't tell what he was thinking with his eyes closed. His emotions were, as always, blocked off.

He opened his eyes suddenly. "You're staying in Alterealm for good?"

I nodded. "I have family here." I'd never imagined I would be able to say that.

"You were serious, about Rena's child? You want to raise it?"

"Yeah. You have a problem with children?"

Michael shook his head. "I adore children." He said softly.

"Well-good." I was running out of steam. Completely unable to feel angry now that his tone and demeanor had changed. "We have to figure this out, iceman, I can't fight when my head is a baggage carousel. I'm miserable when I can't fight."

He was doing his statue impression again.

I walked right over to him and if I wasn't as short as I was, would have been all up in his face. "What are we going to do?"

The look in his eyes made my heart accelerate. With lightning speed, he grasped the back of my head and pulled me closer. "This." He whispered just as his mouth crushed mine.

I didn't object at all, I'd craved this, even when I didn't want to. Either he picked me up or I'd climbed him, I wasn't sure, but I was wrapped around him and he held me tight.

When he tore his mouth from mine, neither of us could breathe. His eyes were red and they were caressing my face. Just seeing his eyes like that again had me shaking. I titled my head to the side in an obvious invitation, Michael didn't hesitate, biting into my neck faster than a heartbeat. I moaned and held a fistful of his hair so he couldn't move away.

Licking over his bite, he nipped at my jaw with his fangs. "What room in the palace?"

It took a moment to focus on his words instead of the desire tearing me apart. "I haven't picked one."

He growled in the back of his throat. Turning his head, he looked at his horse. "Hachi. Home." The horse took off back toward the yard. Turning, he lightly bit my bottom lip. "My room it is." His mouth assaulted mine at the same moment my stomach tensed. He'd ported us to his bedroom. Kissing me hard again, he set me on the floor and pulled his shirt over his head.

My heart paused as I took in his form, appreciating every indent and bulge of his finely tuned muscles. Snapping out of it, I pushed on the back of my runners to get them off my feet. My jacket hit the floor, then I pulled the tank top off quickly and tossed it aside. "You're not going to vanish again right after, are you?" I was trying to decide if that was a deal-breaker, but couldn't think through the moment.

Michael undid his jeans and then pulled a knife out of the back of them. My heart skipped.

He grasped the back of my head and held it as his scored his chest. "I want to feel everything you do, and share with you all I feel."

The thick rasp in his voice sent shivers over my skin. I leaned in and licked the trail of blood off his skin, then closed my mouth around the wound and sucked, not so gently. As the cut healed closed, he titled my head and bit into my neck again. My knees went weak when he sucked on it, before sealing it. Out of breath, dizzy with lust, I clung to him and looked up at him. "Doesn't the bond do that?"

He made a noise in the back of his throat. "I want no doubts between us." I heard the material tearing and looked down to see he'd cut through my sports bra. Before I could get out of it, he dropped the knife and picked me up by the waist. I hugged his head as his mouth moved across my skin, his unshaven jaw branding me as he did.

Wrapping my legs around his waist, I locked them, not wanting this closeness to end. He carried us to the bed and lowered both of us down. I couldn't stop my hands from moving over any part of him I could touch. I knew I'd been hungry for him, I hadn't realized I was starving for this man.

He got to his knees and grasped the waist of my legging and started to peel them off. As they cleared my feet, I was on my knees on the bed shoving his jeans over his hips. I wasn't shy, and I definitely wasn't going to waste time waiting for him to do everything.

Michael made fast work of his boots and getting his jeans off the rest of the way. With a look that almost consumed me in flames, he pushed me back on the bed and crawled up. Sliding me so I was laying under him, he rested his weight on his arm and grasped my left hand and held it over my head. Changing hands, he held it with his left and leaned down to kiss me slowly.

I almost bit him. I didn't want slow.

"Our bond should have been more pleasant then it was." He spoke softly, close to my ear.

I tugged his head, so he'd bring his mouth back to mine. "I'm alive, that's all that matters."

He growled in the back of his throat, and finally kissed me again. This kiss wasn't gentle or slow.

How could I ever have questioned if I should walk away? I was completely swamped with need and lust, I thought I was going to ignite into flames. He shifted and aligned our bodies and the moment we were joined I was flooded with his feelings too. I could feel his need for me, joy and his hunger for me, both for essence and to be close to me. When he bit into me again my whole body exploded without warning. It was the most erotic and sensual thing I'd ever felt.

Michael didn't slow his movements, just kept taking me higher as I clung to him and tried to stay with him. He released my neck and then began kissing me again. I didn't care if I couldn't breathe, I just needed this man in ways I could never have imagined.

He growled and lifted his head, his body stiffening as he finally joined me while I floated around like I was having some sort of outer body experience.

Both of us were covered in sweat, gasping, trying to catch our breath, but couldn't stop touching each other at the same time. I tucked my face against his shoulder and closed my eyes, thinking I could stay like this forever.

Michael shifted his weight, but didn't move off me. "Don't fall asleep on me." He hot breath was against my ear.

"I'm not done with you yet." He chuckled. "Figure if I keep you exhausted you can't fight and put yourself at risk."

I grinned and opened my eyes. "I'm up for that challenge."

"What is that awful noise?" Michael growled against the back of my neck.

I lifted my head, pausing, then remembered we'd fallen off the bed. "It's my phone." I looked around. "My jacket is behind you."

He shifted and then flung my jacket in front of me, curling up against my back again.

Sitting up, I found the pocket and pulled out the phone. I hit the answer button. "We're here." I smiled at Michael, he did not look impressed.

He leaned on his elbow, so I held the phone between us.

"Who initiated this call?" Arius didn't sound happy.

"I did." Crissy answered.

"Criss, where are you?" Daxx's voice was groggy with sleep.

"I'm on my roof."

"You have a roof?" Alona asked.

"Yes, on my side." She said in a quiet way.

"Does Victor..."

"He does," Victor cut off Rafael's question. "What's going on, heart?"

"I'm using those little binocular things you got me, Vic—"

"Focus." Michael lay back down and gave me a heated look.

"Oh. You guys need to get here. Now." She paused. "Not on my roof, on the ground."

"What's wrong?" Victor's tone wasn't gentle now.

Michael sat up, watching the phone with an icy stare.

"There's—I counted eight, but I don't know if I can see them all—"

"Criss." Daxx interrupted, "eight what?"

"Devices." She made a strange noise, "well, not devices,

but people wearing devices." She inhaled quickly. "There are girls down there. I think they're going to take the girls. You need to hurry."

KEEP READING FOR AN EXCERPT OF

The Telepath

Alterealm Series

Book 7

By J. Risk

Prologue

I held my breath and went back around the corner, there were too many of them. *He* was here and there were others with him. I couldn't use myself as bait against eight men of that size. I also couldn't be that close and not have all their thoughts churning inside my brain. I looked around and spotted the fire escape, it had a few missing sections, but as long as I stayed below that missing section, I should be okay. I'd watch from above and see how this played out.

Climbing was scary, it wasn't in the best condition even on the way up to the parts that were hanging off the building. To distract myself from thinking about plummeting to the ground, I ran through the past months in my head. What was going on? Had there been some sort of solar flare or meteorological event that had caused so many strange things to take place? I didn't know, but things were getting really whack and I was ready to find some off the grid cave to live in. I hadn't survived the epic bull crap I'd had the misfortune to live through only to be stuck in some insane place where weird things were happening, and women kept going missing, and no one—NO one noticed.

By the time I reached the halfway point, I decided this was a far enough. Perching on a hidden corner of the fire escape platform, I looked out between the bars. There were four women, near my age, hanging out behind the old supermarket building. Were they intellectually challenged? It was the only reason I could think of why someone would be that stupid to hang out in this neighborhood, without large friends to keep them company and safe.

Safe. Why didn't anyone think about safe anymore?

I looked back to where the guys had been, I couldn't see them. I looked to the other end of the alley. Where did they go? I studied the darker areas trying to see if they were sneaking up on them. Eight men against four women. It was disgusting. I could say that without a doubt, because their thoughts had almost made me scream when they'd popped into my head.

Standing up, I leaned over and looked further down into the forgotten space. I still didn't see them. I was just about to climb down and go tell those girls to get their butts home and stay there until they grew a brain, when a guy came running out of the back of a building and headed toward them.

Big and blond was all I could think. Where were his buddies though? They had to be somewhere. Maybe they sent the pretty face in to distract the women. I'd seen that happen way too often. He was heading straight for them, holding his hand over his ear. Ugh. Just ugh. They were coordinating this abduction. What a slag.

Shaking my head, I'd had enough. I was *so* done with this city. Pulling my bag off my shoulders, I set it by my feet. As soon as I saved these clueless females, I was out of here. I'd rather live in a forest and take my chances with the wild creatures then with human beings. They were disgusting.

Opening my bag, I pulled out the two pieces of my bow. Quickly, while keeping an eye on the blond slag below, I locked the socket together and secured the string onto the string nocks. I tightened the riser, so I had good tension, and flipped the sight slide out. Opening the quiver, I debated over which arrow to choose. Did I want to slow him down or stop him? I looked at him again as he moved closer, trying to appear like he wasn't rushing toward them, he was looking all around, probably making sure no one was around. I was glad he couldn't see me.

I decided I wanted to stop him. I pulled out one of my bodkin point arrows. It wasn't a blunt point, but more of a nasty metal spike that stopped any target it hit very thoroughly. It also wasn't one of my cheap arrows, but stopping yet another woman from being taken was worth it.

I nocked the arrow and stood up, making sure my arms and bow were clear of obstacles. Drawing back, I got him in the sight and then moved it down, I didn't want to kill anyone, that I couldn't live with, but leaving a mark on his backside I could do. Too bad it was a nice-looking backside, was my last thought before I released.

He went down, then mayhem followed. Four other guys came out of nowhere, and a few women as well. These were not the pieces of dross I'd inadvertently heard in my head. The women went rushing toward those clueless females just 'hanging out', and a couple of the men went to my target.

Two dropped down beside where he lay—with my arrow sticking up in the air. One male with brown hair was looking at the arrow sticking out of that nice butt and shaking his head. I think he was smiling.

Then I noticed the other two men, looking quite unhappy, as they looked all around them. I squatted back down. Probably a good time to get gone. I quickly disassembled my bow and put it back in my bag. I was just about to get up and climb to the top of the building when a tiny woman jumped down onto the landing with me.

She pulled the cable from her waist and turned to glare at me. "You shot my Rafael."

At least twenty voices flooded into my head out of nowhere. I grimaced, I'd thought the building was abandoned. I focused to block them, then turned my attention back to her.

I was just about to defend my actions when a very large, very scary redheaded man dropped down behind her. His icy pale eyes moved over me, scorn and loathing clear in his expression. He reached for me. I put my arm up to block his hand and then my head felt like it exploded into a thousand pieces.

I dropped to my knees and threw up. That's when I noticed I was no longer on the fire escape.

Chapter One

Where the frack was I?

I pushed up to my knees, wiping my mouth while trying to figure out how I'd gotten from a fire escape into a tiny clear cubicle. I looked behind me, no, make that a box. Looking up, I blew out a breath, wrong again, a cube.

I looked all around me. My gear was gone. Getting to my feet, I paused and looked down, and see my boots were gone too. Still shaking from the nausea and strange container, I stepped around the puddle of spew and went over to a wall. I ran my hand along it, feeling for a door or seam.

A noise startled me, I froze and watched a red bar of light go down the side of the wall. It went to the floor, then moved back up slowly. I wasn't sure, but I think I was just scanned. For what, I didn't know, but I was at an eight on my freak out scale—or FOS as I liked to refer to it. If I reached a ten, it wasn't going to be pretty.

I went over closer to the wall and cupped my hands around my eyes, pressing my face against it. I was hoping it was a two-way mirror or—something. I couldn't see anything. Okay, I could do this. I huffed out a few breaths, the 'room' was clear, no bars, no cement walls, I may not be able to see out, but it gave the illusion of more space.

My heart started beating out of rhythm. Maybe that big scary guy was one of the abductors. If so, why did he have a girl with him, and why did the girl get so mad because I shot her Rafael? Rafael, really? Who named their kid that? A few hundred years ago, maybe. Didn't his mother like him?

I realized I was breathing like I had just run a mile, and knew I had to slow it down or my behavior would change without notice. I took a deep breath and closed my eyes. Don't freak out until you know the facts. You are not locked up. You are not there again. You will never be there again. Opening my eyes, I turned to put my back against the wall and slide down it. I'd just sit here and focus on my breathing for a few minutes.

Grabbing my shins, I pulled my legs tight into me, then froze. I ran my hands down my legs to my ankles. Pish! My knives were gone. How? Did I pass out? Is that how I got here?

The light's reflection on the far wall changed, then there was someone standing on the other side. He had long black hair and didn't look friendly. From my vantage point on the floor, he looked like a giant.

I stood up slowly, then realized he was just as big from this angle. His eyes were grey, not green or blue, but grey, and right now they were assessing me thoroughly. Crossing his arms over his large chest, he turned his head and spoke to someone. I couldn't see anyone else. I also couldn't hear him.

Turning, I looked all around me. Actually, I couldn't hear any thoughts either. I put my hands against the sides of my head. Complete silence. That was rare. I wonder what these walls were made of, and if I could get some of it and make my own bigger cube—if I ever got out of here that was.

Taking a deep breath, I dropped my hands and blew out slowly. When I turned around, the man looked concerned about something. I stepped over opposite him. Did I want to try reasoning with him? Other than abnormally large and scary looking, he appeared fairly intelligent.

"Hello?" I said quietly.

His grey eyes connected with mine.

"Good. You can hear me." I motioned around me. "I'm not sure where I am, but I believe there has been some sort of error, on my part mostly." He didn't move a muscle. "I *may* have shot the wrong man by mistake." I rolled my eyes, "okay, I meant to hit him, I never miss my target—" I realized that wasn't going to buy me favor. "I-I thought he was someone else that intended to harm," I waved my hand around, "or abduct, these clueless twits that probably don't have a whole brain cell among them."

I took a deep breath and tried to tone down the hostility. I smiled, not sure what else to say. "So-so if I could have my gear," I looked down, "and my boots back, I'll get gone." I nodded. "I was on my way out of this insane city before I spotted those disgusting men scoping out the aforementioned idiots." I took a quick breath, "I was just trying to stop more women from vanishing." I shrugged, not sure what else I could add to plead my case. He hadn't moved, his expression hadn't changed. "You should play poker," I blurted out before I could stop my mouth, "you have the face for it."

He turned to look at something, then shook his head. A woman, the same size as me, came into view. She had short black hair and there was something familiar about her. The giant looked unhappy as she walked by him to the wall and did something there.

"What's your name?" She asked.

I looked all around for the speaker but didn't see anything. "Kara." I gave her a weak smile.

"Cara…"

I shook my head. "Kar-a, like a car."

She gave me a patient look. "Kara, where are you from?"

I frowned, that was not a question I expected. "Planet earth?" I huffed out a breath. "The same city I was trying to leave. Okay, I'm not originally from there—actually I don't know where I'm from, originally, but I've been in that decaying city for the last few years." I needed to shut up. I didn't spend a lot of time around people, for obvious reasons, and tended to ramble when I was. That and I was really trying not to freak out from being contained in a clear cube.

She nodded, then turned to the man and said something. I couldn't hear them again. They both turned to look at something.

Another man came into view. He had pale blonde hair and a goatee. He was also as large as the other one. The one with the black hair moved out of view, then that red bar of light was moving down the wall again.

I watched it for a second, then turned to see him come back in. The three of them were looking at a tablet.

"Did I pass?" I asked sarcastically, then regretted it. My mouth and brain needed to work together if I was ever going to get out of here.

The woman moved to the corner again. "We're just making sure it's safe to move you out of there, Kara."

I frowned. "Why wouldn't it be safe?" I moved up to a nine on my FOS. "What's wrong? What did your scan say?" Had all the experimental drugs and therapy they'd tried done permanent damage? My heart moved into my throat.

Reaching for the button, she nodded to the men. "Nothing bad. You're fine. You're completely human though, so that's a concern."

I stood there for a second, not even sure if I heard her correctly. I looked from her to the men, then back. "Whew," I pretended to wipe my brow, "and here I was worried I wasn't completely *human.*"

The blond smirked and looked at the dark haired one for a moment before moving over to the button. "How many men?" He asked.

"How many men what?" I looked to the others like they could tell me. "How many men does it take to screw in a light bulb?" No one moved. "I don't know what you're asking." I reached into my pocket and they all gave me a hard look. "Relax." I pulled out a hair tie with two fingers and held it up for them to see, "just pulling my hair back." I motioned to the floor behind me where I had thrown up. "Feeling a little soiled at the moment." I made fast work of a loose bun and then crossed my arms over my chest.

"How many *disgusting* men did you see stalking those women?" The blond asked calmly.

"Oh." I glared at him, why hadn't he just said that? "Eight."

"How did you know they were after those women?" He raised one eyebrow at me.

"Because I…" I almost said heard their thoughts, which never ended well when you told people *that*. "I overheard them." I had to play it cool. If I could fool doctors that stared at me for hours on end for years, I could fool some complete strangers into thinking I was perfectly normal.

"So why didn't you yell or call the police?" He crossed his arms over his chest.

I moved just my eyes from him to the other two and then back again. "Clearly you're not from the city. Call the cops and say what?" I snorted, "you think they give a pish? Nothing would have happened." I motioned up and down my body, "Do I look big to you? Yelling would have just added me to their to-do list."

The woman gave me an understanding look. I still couldn't figure out why she looked familiar.

I lifted my hands. "Look, I'm sorry I shot Rafael. He just appeared at the wrong time and was running right for those girls."

"How do you know my brother's name?"

Ugh. His brother. Just great.

He looked almost as scary as the dark haired one now.

"Uh, the girl that dropped down onto the fire escape with the big scary dude said *you shot my Rafael*." I tried to look concerned, but honestly, I was at a nine point eight right now and it wasn't looking like I was going to go back down on my FOS anytime soon. "I'm sorry. Is he all right? I aimed for his tush, lots of meaty tissue, nothing important to worry about—"

He looked like he wanted to grin but cocked his head to the side instead. He turned and started talking to the other two, waving a hand around. The woman was nodding, so I really hoped this talk was in favor of releasing me. She turned and walked out of my view.

I sighed and crossed my arms over my stomach, tying to think calm thoughts, which was never going to happen, but I didn't want to start ranting like a lunatic. I turned to pace and saw the spew in the middle of the very tiny space. "Um, I really hate to put you out, but could I at least get housekeeping in here?" I looked behind me to see the blond was paying attention. "Or, bring me a mop and pail, maybe some air freshener?"

The woman came back and handed the blond something. He went back to the corner. There was a noise and his hand appeared through a small window. "Put this on."

I looked at it. It looked like a Fitbit monitor. I glanced to the woman to see she raised her arm and was wearing one that looked similar. Hesitantly, I stepped over and took it out of his hand. If it got me out of here, I'd dance, however pretty that wouldn't be.

He pulled his hand back and the small window was gone. I couldn't even tell where it had been on the wall. Looking at the device, I turned it over, then put it around my wrist. Why I needed to wear a Fitbit, I didn't know. Maybe they wanted to monitor my vitals. Vitals that would sound like a heavy metal band right now. I did it up, then wanted to undo it when the thought it could be some sort of lie detector. I didn't normally lie, I just didn't always include all the facts. I held up my arm to show it was on.

"Step out the door and through the door across from it." The blond said.

There was a whooshing noise and a door opened in the wall I'd been leaning on. I went over and stepped out. Two large men were on either side. So, running was out of the question. I did as instructed as it whooshed closed behind me. I was now in a slightly larger, by that I mean maybe a foot larger, cube. This one had a bed and in a little cubby hole in the corner was a toilet. "Oh, this is *much* better." I said, not even attempting to hide the sarcasm in my voice.

I turned to see them looking through a wall at me. "So, I guess leaving has been taken off the table?"

The blond gave me a quick look. "That's up to Rafael and Victor."

Oh good. The man I'd shot in the butt had some say in whether I got out. "Victor?" I was hoping he was a reasonable person.

He nodded. "I believe you met him on the fire escape."

I was going to be living in a cube for the rest of my life.

SCENT

Animal Senses Book 2

Jacqueline Paige

Chapter One

Gage watched the eyes of the man he passed to climb into his truck. His expression was hollow, his eyes were void. He had to be close to his own six foot five, but this man held himself close, small and inward.

Turning, he glanced at Jesse. "What the hell happened Jesse? He looks like he's been broken like a god damned horse."

Jesse sighed and rubbed his jaw, the exhaustion clear on his face. "The sad thing is, he's in better shape than the others." Flicking his eyes back to the passenger in the truck, he met Gage's stare. "Devin said it would do him good to be around other shifters of his kind," he shook his head, "I don't know if he'll ever fully recover though."

"What about the others?"

A haunted look flashed in Jesse's pale eyes. "They're at the camp. I doubt any of them will ever be able to integrate back into society."

"What the hell did Tomas do to them?" Gage struggled to keep his anger from showing.

Slamming the door on the car, Jesse spun around shaking his head. "The two women we managed to get out were used as breeders, as near as we can figure. They shrink away from any male like they've…" He stopped, clearly not wanting to continue.

Gage fought the bile that rose in his stomach, swallowing it down with an audible sound.

"The three men, including him," he motioned to the other vehicle, "were used worse than slaves. They're not very forthcoming with details." Shoving his hands in his pockets, he looked up and Gage's muscles tensed when he saw the depth of the anger in the otherwise mild-mannered man. "They've been beaten into complacency and carry the scars to prove it."

"Aren't they all pure bloods?"

"Yeah."

Something in Jesse's tone made Gage's cat want to growl. "Then why are they scarred? Shifting heals fresh…"

"Not if they're prevented from shifting until after the wounds have healed."

"Holy hell." Shuddering at the thought of the torture the man now hunched in his truck had survived, Gage took a deep breath and nodded to Jesse. "I'll see what I can do for him."

Jesse stepped back toward his car. "Devin said to give him a call."

"Will do." Gage watched him get in his car and then slowly walked around to the driver's side of his truck. He had hundreds of questions but didn't want to bombard the damaged man with them.

Forcing an easy smile, he looked at the man beside him. "I suppose Jesse should have introduced us." He held out his hand, "I'm Gage Lockman. You'll be staying with some of my clan."

With hesitation, the man extended his hand and grasped his briefly. "Noah Reyes."

"They're getting in touch with your family, Noah. If later on you decide to go be with them, then we'll get you there." He watched as emotions flickered through Noah's amber tinted eyes.

"No," his voice was heartrending, "I-I don't want to go there." Apprehensively his eyes met Gage's again. "I'll stay with your clan, if that's all right?"

Nodding, Gage put the key in the ignition and tried to appear relaxed, even though he wasn't. "That's fine by me, we can always use a hand at the shop."

"Shop?"

Starting the truck, he put it into gear and pulled out of the empty parking lot. Watching the dust kick up behind them in his mirror, he kept his eyes from going back to the injured soul beside him. "Yeah, my family owns a heavy equipment business. We lease all the big rigs and do the repairs and upkeep ourselves."

"I don't know anything about shop work."

Ignoring the fear in his voice, Gage shrugged. "We'll find something for you to do that leans to your strengths."

"I doubt it."

Glancing at the empty man beside him, he gave him an easy smile. "Why's that?"

Noah turned and looked out the window. "I've only been a guard."

"Like a bodyguard?"

The silence was tense as he waited for an answer.

"No. Like a guard that keeps others against their will."

Shit. "Well, we'll find a place for you." Every muscle in Gage's body was taut, he had to strain to keep his animal under control. He breathed it away for a few seconds. "I don't want to pry, and for the most part I won't, but I'm bringing you into my family and need to know some of the facts." He paused for objections then continued when none were voiced. "How long did Tomas have you?"

"Fifteen years."

It was said with venom that Gage was almost happy to hear, that brief expression of hatred meant there was some fight left in the younger man. He was going to ask more when Noah's tortured voice silenced him.

"Since I was six. They got my sister and I."

He glanced at Noah for a moment to let him know he was listening.

"I don't know what happened to her. I tried to find out when I got older, but..." His voice cracked, "I wouldn't even know her now."

Swallowing, Gage kept his eyes on the road. "Your cat would know family. If she ever crosses your path, you'll know."

"I didn't know that." Noah sighed softly. "I don't know a lot about what I am, or how to function in a group. The things I do know are only from what others that worked..." he cleared his throat, "were held by Tomas told me."

Gage glanced at him and tried to give him a look of encouragement. "We'll work it out, Noah." He took a moment to look at him. Biologically this man was only twenty-one, but he appeared much older, and Gage suspected was aged beyond anything he would ever understand.

"So, are you the clan alpha?"

Gage grinned. "No. The second. My father's the alpha, but he's away right now."

Noah nodded and then sat there for a moment, Gage could see the questions going through his mind.

"Do you have a mate?"

Snorting, Gage nodded, "Yeah, only she doesn't know she is." He grinned, not even knowing how to explain his own personal torment. "I'm sure the boys will love filling in the details for you."

"I found mine...at least that's what the others told me."

The silence that followed his admission stabbed pain right through Gage. "And?"

"When," Noah closed his eyes and inhaled deep for a moment, "when I recovered enough to remember, she was gone."

Holy hell. Is Devin aware of any of this? What the hell do I say to that? "You may still find her someday. Fate is a tricky bitch."

"Yeah."

The word meant he agreed, but the heavy overlay of emotion inside the cab told Gage the man beside him didn't believe it would happen. He tried to keep his tone from revealing anything that could be considered close to sympathy. "You'll be bunking in with four others while you're here. Jake, Gary and Blair are close to your age. Then there's old Cooper, no one can even guess his age, but he's fairly easy to be around." He continued to ramble out the stories of things the men closest to him did in hopes to give Noah a sense of what he could expect. Not once did he offer comment or ask for more.

Dropping him off at the large house his men lived in just off the shop site, Gage backed out, heading for his own home just along the roughly paved road. He needed to talk to Devin and find out just what he was supposed to do to help Noah.

He didn't even get both boots on the ground when his phone started vibrating in his shirt pocket. Glancing at the screen, he shook his head and answered it.

"I just dropped him off."

Devin's whispered on the other end. "I figured you'd be there by now. Jesse called when he left you."

"Why are you whispering?" Slamming the door, he walked up the path and stomped up the porch. Deciding he needed the air, he dropped into one of his mother's favorite white wicker chairs and swung his boots up to rest on the railing.

"Rayne is exhausted and just went to try and rest."

He heard a door close quietly.

"She's been helping the two women that were brought back and is emotionally fragile, to say the least."

Gage's shoulders tensed. "Jesse mentioned a bit." Running a hand through his hair, he sighed. "Don't tell me any details right now; I'm still digesting the shit I learned from Noah on our trip back."

"Then you probably know more than I do. I'm sorry I had to send him your way, but the women were terrified of him."

Gage closed his eyes, feeling the pain he'd heard in Noah's voice. "With good reason, he was probably forced to be the guard used to make them stay put."

"Listen, if he gets out of hand…"

"My instincts say he won't." He kicked his feet back to the porch and leaned forward on his knee. "The boys will keep an eye on him." Rubbing a hand over the back of his neck, he sat up again. "Where the hell is the Alliance in bringing that bastard Tomas down for good?"

"They've gotten a lot of the captives out. We have close to a dozen here at the camp, healing as much as they'll be able to. Some were born into Tomas's organization, Gage, I don't know if we'll be able to get through to them, they've never been associated with their own kind, or understand the dynamics of a clan and family."

"Yeah, Noah said something to that effect."

He could hear the exhaustion in Devin's tone.

"Look, Gage, I really didn't want to send Noah there, not with everything you have going on." He heard another door close and could then make out the sounds of nature at the camp as Devin must have gone outside. "Is Kelsey back?"

Not able to sit any longer, Gage got up and paced to the other end of the large porch. "She was supposed to be back this week, but decided to stop and see my folks on the way home."

"I thought your parents left so you'd have some alone time with Kelsey."

"They did. I'm one hair from going insane, Dev."

He heard the soft chuckle on the other end. "I don't know how you've held out this long, my friend. I didn't last a day when I was near Rayne."

Jamming his hand into his pocket, he leaned back against the wall of the house. "Well, she was only sixteen when I realized what she was to me. That worked like fucking ice water in my pants for a few years. Then she bailed and took off to school, and you know that's been three years of hell for me." Pushing away from the wall, he stepped over to the railing and looked out into the thick trees surrounding the house. "I can't hold on much longer." He closed his eyes and swallowed. "I just hope…"

"You'll do the right thing, Gage, the animal inside you won't let you do anything but."

"I hope you're right because it will kill me to wait this long and then screw it up."

Devin chuckled again. "I can relate."

"Speaking of…how is our Queen now?"

"Surprisingly forgiving. Thank God for that."

Not wanting to dwell on his mate, Gage opened his eyes and stared out into the bush again. "Calum reach you before he left?"

"Yeah. He said he knew the region where his missing clan members had been seen last. He's supposed to contact you if I'm out of touch once he knows more."

"I'll be here if he needs me. Is the Alliance up to speed?" Turning, he went inside to see if there were any messages on the house phone.

"For the most part, they have their hands full right now trying to bring Aiden Tomas down."

"They don't think the clan members Calum is tracking down are part of Tomas's ring?"

The silence stretched out for a few moments before Devin answered. "It's nowhere near the regions he operates in, but who knows?"

Gage could hear voices in the background and knew Devin would be ending the call soon.

"Listen, Gage, keep Kelsey close to home. We've been calling all the clans and warning them. Tomas isn't going to take all of this without striking back."

"Will do."

"Good luck with your mate, my friend, you're going to need it."

Gage sighed loudly and grinned at the phone. "Yeah, thanks for the vote of confidence."

"Oh, I have every faith in you, but I also know the fucking hell you're walking into when nothing you know is as it was."

Gage's stomach tightened. "Something to look forward to."

"I'll talk to you later."

"Will do." He hung up the phone and stared at it for a moment. *Good news all round today.* Glancing at the phone as he walked into the office, he stopped when there were no messages. The tension in his neck was multiplying as it had been for the past month. *Kelsey, whatever games you're playing, you better end them soon.* He felt like a time bomb just waiting to go off.

The cat inside him moved over his skin, wanting out. He'd spent more time in animal form the last seven years as he waited for his mate to be old enough to claim. Of course, there was no law stating the age, but his own morals wouldn't allow him to do anything until she was old enough to understand.

Snorting out loud, he turned on his heal and headed for the door. Kelsey knew nothing of her own heritage. She didn't know what her parents had been before they were killed, or that her family were part of the clan and not just good friends they'd known for years. Many times, after she had come to live with his parents he'd wanted to tell her. She was only fifteen at the time and completely devastated her parents were gone. His jaw clenched knowing it had been Aiden Tomas's father that was responsible for their death. After that, the more time that passed the harder it got to tell her she was part of a world she didn't even know existed.

Gage didn't know why his folks hadn't told her when she got older, and as the son of the Alpha, it wasn't his place to overstep his position and fill her in. In hindsight, he wished he'd disobeyed and told her. Maybe then he wouldn't be walking out his back door stripping off his clothes so he could go run off his frustration.

By the time he reached the bottom step he was in his animal form. Large paws padded across the grass, as he scented the air to choose a direction. Jumping across the creek in one motion, he landed his eight foot, four-hundred-pound body with fluid grace and then turned to look at his reflection. A pale, almost white, Bengal tiger stared at him through his deep blue eyes.

The scent of prey filled his nostrils as he lifted his head. With a low sound from the back of his throat he turned to start the chase.

Come home soon, Kelsey.

About the Author

J. Risk is a pseudonym used by Jacqueline Paige

I wanted to write a story that would fit into new adult levels as well as adult. Something that was serious with fun elements--paranormal / fantasy that everyone could read and enjoy.

I've decided to use J. Risk as the pen name for this to separate this series from my other writing which is definitely adult reading material.

Jacqueline Paige lives in Ontario in a small town that's part of the popular Georgian Triangle area.

She began her writing career in 2006 and since her first published works in 2009 she hasn't stopped. Jacqueline describes her writing as *all things paranormal*, which she has proven is her niche with stories of witches, ghosts, psychics and shifters now on the shelves.

When Jacqueline isn't lost in her writing, she spends time with her five children, most of whom are finally able to look after her instead of the other way around. Together they do random road trips, that usually end up with them lost, shopping trips where they push every button in the toy aisle, hiking when there's enough time to escape and bizarre things like creating new daring recipes in the kitchen. She's a grandmother to eight (so far) and looks forward to corrupting many more in the years to come.

Jacqueline loves to hear from her readers, you can find her at

http://jacquelinepaige.com

Author note:

Did you enjoy reading one of my books?

If so, PLEASE help spread the word on social media. You can help by sharing on Facebook, tweet about it, post something on Instagram, Pinterest. Posting a review on your favorite book sites go a long way to help authors. With your help in keeping my books "out there", I can continue writing to keep those stories coming.

Writing and promoting can be very time consuming. I love talking to readers, but the hours spent on keeping so many social media outlets current can become overwhelming and time for writing pays the price. If you can take a few minutes to help, that would be awesome. Thank you!